DAVID LINDS

FAR POINT

© 2016/18 David Lindsley

ISBN-13: 978-1540769862
ISBN-10: 1540769860

Book One of the Dan Foster Trilogy

Book Two: The Darkfall Switch
Book Three: Blind to Danger

Also by David Lindsley
Ribbons of Steel
Frame by Frame

Cover painting by Nina Avins

FAR POINT

AUTHOR'S FOREWORD

On the first of July 1997 Hong Kong reverted to Chinese sovereignty, ending 156 years of British rule. This story is set in the months and weeks around that pivotal moment when, quite simply, everything changed in the territory.

This story is a yarn with a fanciful technical basis. It revolves around the premise that Britain would be contracted to build a nuclear power station in China. Sadly, this is now beyond the bounds of possibility. The country that once led the way in nuclear power-plant technology lost the plot a long time ago. Nevertheless, the technical details behind my story are based on reality. The type of nuclear reactor that I describe is real and the concept of the computer-control systems are realistic.

You don't have to have a technical background to understand this story, any more than you need medical knowledge to appreciate a forensic science thriller.

In telling this story I have tried to throw some light on the personal lives of professional engineers working in a field of operations that drives all aspects of modern society—the generation of electricity. These are real people, who spend long periods away from their homes and families—and who often pay a high price for that separation.

David Lindsley, July 2018.

Chapter 1

The vast building braced itself to face the storm; wet concrete and steel glistening in the pale, yellow-tinged light that filtered weakly through the heavy banks of scudding, squally clouds overhead. Steel shutters had been installed to protect the doors and windows of the building's administration block, steel flood-barriers had been slotted into place at the thresholds of doors, steel grids covered the windscreens of the ambulances and fire trucks that stood stationed at strategic points, ready to deal with any emergency.

The vehicles had appeared overnight, and their drivers had then dispersed, leaving them parked around the many roads on the site, unsettling evidence of an approaching storm. But if the eighty or so men working on the plant felt their pulses quicken, or if their breathing became slower and deeper in response to these passive reminders of the approaching storm, they showed no sign of it; they carried on with their tasks as though nothing untoward was about to happen.

They trusted the massive structure surrounding them to provide protection. It was clad in steel. Armoured to face any enemy, and prepared to withstand it.

There was no way they could have been aware that the protection was fatally flawed. They could not be aware that the machinery around them itself carried an insidious threat—because a deadly cancer had already started to destroy it from within.

The men worked on, more concerned about the visible, identified enemy that was sweeping remorselessly nearer. They were unaware that it was just a decoy, distracting their attention.

Born in the hot Western Pacific, Tropical Storm Vincent had started as a gathering of raw power: a steadily accelerating exchange of energy between the warm ocean and the sky, whipped like a spinning top by the rotation of the earth itself. Watched warily by weather satellites high in space, it had fed on itself and grown and developed steadily over a period of days until it was now just short of a full-scale typhoon: a huge, howling, whirling mass of heavy, hot, humid air: a gigantic spiral of destructive force.

Bursting from its cradle in the Pacific, Vincent had come spiralling West and South, gathering power as it swirled over the heaving waves it had itself created, to hurl itself along the line of the Ryukyu Islands before vectoring towards mainland China, speeding like a lethal dart aimed at a target somewhere between Shanghai and Hong Kong.

The forecast from the Peoples' Observatory in Shanghai provided a crumb of comfort; once it was overland, and hence denied the succour of the ocean, the storm would die out quite quickly. But at this time Vincent was big, very big. The weather-satellite photographs, taken from the calm emptiness of space high above the region, showed a deceptively beautiful, blinding white spiral of cloud lying seemingly motionless across a huge sector of the cobalt Pacific, stretching from Taiwan to Japan.

But from that site on Kung Tau Island the clouds were anything but white or peaceful. They hunched threateningly overhead like huge dark-grey pot-bellied dragons; crowding the sky, waiting to swoop in furious assault on the buildings and machinery that man had dared to construct on the island. The heavy rain of the first front of the storm had dissipated almost an hour earlier, but any appearance of calm was utterly misleading. As a reminder of the nearing threat, shrapnel-like pellets of warm rain would be hurled through the heavy air every now and then by sudden, violent gusts of wind.

The building facing the weather was a power station, a critical supplier of modern society's life-blood–electricity. Its machines had to be kept running through any weather, and the work-shift of staff who had been unlucky enough to be on duty when the storm warning was raised had been forced to stay on site. It was a known hazard, expected at any time during the summer typhoon season, but never welcome. If you were off duty when a typhoon or a tropical storm arrived you were lucky; you won an unexpected holiday, because it was too hazardous to travel on open roads. You made the most of the break, even if the weather did imprison you in your hotel or apartment.

But if you were on duty, you were trapped.

That day, Tony Crabtree and Paul Lee had been among the unlucky ones. Imprisoned on the site by the sudden approach of the storm, they had diverted their apprehension by looking into an engineering puzzle that had been tantalising them for a few days, but which had not been important enough to come to the top of their list of priorities. Now, their unexpected confinement at site by the storm had given them time to deal with it.

Lee was a Hong Kong Chinese, drafted up here from his regular employment with New Age Energy Projects, a specialized Kowloon-based design and construction enterprise that was providing advice and assistance to Gold Win Energy, the plant's operators. Like many of his countrymen, Lee was clever and quick-witted, a well-educated and experienced engineer with a bright future stretching ahead of him in the soon to be enlarged People's Republic of China.

Crabtree was a British engineer, assigned to the site by his employers, EuroPower plc, a giant pan-European power-plant constructor that had provided much of the machinery and supporting expertise for the plant at Kung Tau.

Now, as they approached the gaunt grey structure of the massive plant, the two men could hear a spine-tingling chorus of power, nature's might playing with man's construction to produce an anthem of fury—the generating machines' continuous deep hum forming a drone to the fluctuating whistle and shriek of the wind sawing at the towering structure around them.

As they neared the plant the men automatically lowered the ear-defenders of their safety-helmets and clamped them against their ears to deaden all sound. But despite this precaution the din grew to a deep roar as they entered the building, a noise that was sensed by vibration through the floor as much as by the ears.

In spite of the noise, and in spite of the fact that massive amounts of energy were being generated and used around the machines, everything here looked immobile. It was only as a handrail was touched that the vibration became apparent. Everything was gently shaking: the massive steel girders, the stairways, the very ground on which it all stood.

Crabtree was used to all this. But today some deep instinct nagged at him.

Something was wrong. It was difficult to pin down the cause of his concern. With the instinct of years of experience working with power plant like this, his senses told him that the machines around him were running sweetly. There had been plenty of occasions when an odd smell, a subtle change of tone or a strangeness in a noise had made him aware that something was wrong. And on more than one occasion in the past, that knowledge had saved his life. There was no such warning now; everything was apparently all right.

Yet still he was worried.

He shouldered aside his doubts, touched Lee's elbow and mouthed his question over the noise, 'Are you going up?'

Lee nodded.

They had decided to look at an electronic sensor that had been producing strange readings on the plant's computers. Earlier in the day, in the quiet of the control room, the two men had puzzled over data being printed out from the system, and they had decided that something very odd was happening. It could have been something intermittent, like a badly-made connection or a frayed wire, but when they had gone to the spot and inspected the cables from the ground they had seen no obvious damage to them, so now they needed to take a closer look, climbing a vertical ladder to reach the sensor itself.

The device, fixed into a large pipe carrying superheated steam produced by a massive boiler, was reached from a small gallery high up the side of the plant. The two men began the climb.

Although the Kung Tau plant had a great sloping roof to protect it from the worst of any rain, it was open to the elements on three sides and as Crabtree climbed the steel rungs he was constantly buffeted by hot eddies of the wind that howled relentlessly through the plant's complex three-dimensional labyrinth of girders, galleries and pipes. The warm rain it carried swept almost horizontally across the plant and stung his face under his safety helmet. He licked his lips and found they were salty, but he couldn't tell if it was the sweat of the effort of the climb or from the sea-spray being driven through the maze of hot steel around him.

Even after years of working in tropic and sub-tropical areas he could still be caught off-guard by the heat. Whenever he looked out of the window of a cool, air-conditioned office and saw dark grey skies and rain outside, his temperate-climate background still lulled him into believing it would be cold out there as well. Instead, if he wiped at the mist on the glass he would be reminded that it was deposited on the outside surface. If he were to step outside, it would be as if someone had wrapped him in a warm, damp blanket.

Today was no different. The humidity level was almost one hundred percent, and here, inside the boiler-house, he was facing the additional discomfort of a wall of heat mercilessly radiating through the insulation lining the metal surfaces of the plant. Under that thick blanket of insulation, the steel itself would have been glowing dull red, and although the insulation was efficient the remains of heat that escaped from the metal underneath was like the breath of Hell.

After a long hard climb the men reached the gallery and looked at the steam pipe. The sensor formed part of a thermometer, a steel rod buried in a pocket in the pipe, its terminals contained in a cylindrical box with a sloping aluminium cover. Lee used the sleeve of his white boiler-suit to mop the sweat and rain dripping off the tip of his nose as he looked at the instrument, then he shook his head. 'I see nothing wrong,' he shouted. 'I take the cover off.'

He unscrewed the cover, inspected the terminals underneath and shook his head again.

'Nothing?' Crabtree asked. Another sudden gust of wind swayed him and he gripped the steel handrail to steady himself.

'No,' Lee replied. 'Nothing to see.'

'OK,' Crabtree said. 'That's as far as we can go right now.'

They had told the control-room staff that they were going to inspect the instrument and, as a result, the relevant part of the plant's automatic control system had been switched off, for safety. The plant itself continued to operate; it would run safely for a while with this part of the automatic system shut off, with only occasional adjustment required from the operator. But looking at the wiring inside the thermometer was a job that could be done only in a workshop. That would require the instrument to be disconnected and another inserted in its place, and that would be a long job.

Crabtree bent to look at a metal box clamped to a strut nearby. The armoured cable from the thermometer that ran to this box was, like the two other cables emerging from it, coloured bright blue. This pair of cables split as it emerged from the box; one ran sideways across the back of the boiler, the other disappeared down the side of the plant. Both were clipped to perforated steel channels bolted to the steel structure.

'You see something?' Lee asked. He had bent his head near Crabtree's to look.

Crabtree shook his head. 'I'm not about to take that cover off,' he shouted against the din.

The blue box and its connections were part of the power station's sophisticated computer control system. It was one of several such boxes that were scattered at strategic locations all over the plant. Small, inexpensive units, they were linked to each other and to the other computers, to collect information and send it to the control room by means of flashes of light that continually twinkled millions of messages over the vast web of the plant's fibre-optic data highway.

Now, at least to the men's visual inspection, it seemed there was nothing wrong. Disappointed at having achieved nothing, they climbed carefully down to ground level and picked their way past the roaring machinery.

At the side of the building a door led to a flight of stairs to an office near the top of the central control block, a four-storey structure containing the control room, plus various offices and workshops.

There was a lift available, but it was almost always busy, ferrying men and machines between the floors, so it was usually quicker to walk up the stairs. As the stairwell was efficiently air-conditioned it wasn't a difficult task, and soon they were at the commissioning-office level, two floors above the control room.

As the heavy door closed behind them, cutting off the din of the machinery, they lifted their ear defenders and parked them at the sides of their helmets. But the sensation of power was here as well; even here a deep musical hum pervaded the building—although up here it wasn't a loud or unpleasant noise.

At the top of the stairs, Crabtree opened a door to reveal a room simply furnished with a long plastic-topped table surrounded by eight chairs. In contrast with the stark utilitarian look of the table, the chairs with their ornate carved teak frames had a distinctly Chinese look. The room had been used as an office during the construction phase of the plant and was now retained as a conference room. On the side opposite the door was a large aluminium flask containing green tea for the Chinese workers, and a machine nearby for dispensing instant tea or coffee for Westerners. The supplies were continually replenished by a crew of women who flitted unobtrusively through all areas of the building throughout the working day.

As the two men entered the room, they took off their helmets and put them on a filing cabinet near the door. Lee headed towards the machine, poured a cup of coffee for himself and one for Crabtree and added processed milk from a tin nearby.

The two men placed their cups on the table, pushing aside the drawings that were strewn over it.

'There's something weird about those readings, Paul,' Crabtree said as they sat down. 'What worries me most is this: it's the third or fourth time it's happened; always in different areas of the plant. And we've no clue as to what's causing it. Each time we try to find out what's going on, the problem seems to disappear.'

'Interference?'

'I don't think so. If it was, I'd expect it to be more or less continuous. But it isn't, and as I said, it seems to disappear as soon as we look at it.'

From under the heap of drawings, Lee extracted a sheaf of printout paper on which the computer had spun out strings of time-stamped numbers. They started to look at the figures again but whatever ideas they considered, none seemed to fit. After a few minutes Crabtree stood up and walked over to the window.

A pair of fluorescent tubes lit the room brightly, and in contrast the storm-swept world outside seemed very dark and grey. The glass of the window was spattered with brightly-shining raindrops, and beneath him puddles on the flat roof of the administration building were rippling with a pale ochre light reflected from the stormy sky as the wind brushed the water. In the distance a cable looping to a communications antenna was dancing a crazy tango against the lurid sky.

They sipped their coffees and thought about the fault. It wasn't really a significant problem. Everything seemed to work all right, though the computers flashed up minor alarm messages if they detected the fault at a critical time. It was just an irritation which would be recorded in the fault logs. They were looking into it now simply because they felt there was nothing better to do while they were trapped here by the storm.

It was Lee who made the first move, and in doing so he set in motion a fatal chain of events. He put his cup down, picked up his hard-hat, clapped it to his head, and said, 'I go down and walk around. See if I find something to explain it. Many plant item to see.'

Crabtree smiled inwardly. In spite of the high standard of education Lee had received in a quintessentially British school in Hong Kong, he spoke with a strong American accent, though his grammar was tinged with the slightly odd sentence constructions that were common to many Hong Kong Chinese. In particular, he had always struggled with plurals, inserting the stray 's' when it wasn't needed and leaving it out when it was.

'Good idea,' Crabtree said, looking at his watch. 'I'd come with you, but I have to be at a meeting with Brian Ward in half an hour.'

Ward was New Age's project manager. In touch with every aspect of the complex undertaking under his control, from trivial minutiae to the broad financial overview, he maintained his knowledge by keeping in constant close contact with the key project staff.

'Tell you what, though,' Crabtree added, stopping Lee as he was about to leave the room. 'How about coming over to the apartment this evening, with Pauline? They say the worst of the storm will have passed by then.'

Paul and Pauline! How often they had joked about the coincidence of the Lee names, and the confusion it must often have caused in their household.

Lee's wife was a petite, pretty and very outward-going woman. Unlike many of the other Chinese wives, she was keen to socialize with Western families in the apartment block that was provided by Gold Win, and close to the Kung Tau site. Now that the accommodation had been completed in the administration block, Lee had moved up here from his office in Hong Kong and Crabtree had also moved in, on a 12-month contract.

Initially, Anne Crabtree had been very unhappy about it. At the start of this project two years earlier, when EuroPower had first won the Kung Tau contract, she had been reluctant enough to move from their home in the familiar surroundings of the green and hilly Cotswolds to a hot and crowded Hong Kong, but in the end she had made the move. Eventually she had settled in very well. It made a change for her to be with her husband in a foreign country. Normally, as his assignments usually lasted for no more than a few weeks, he travelled alone; but this time he was scheduled to be in China for over a year, and under those circumstances Corporate rules allowed wives to accompany their spouses.

Quickly fascinated by the thousands of shops and the cosmopolitan bustle of Hong Kong, Anne had built up a circle of friends in the British colony. Then, just as she was getting thoroughly used to it all, her husband had announced that they would be moving to Kung Tau. She had been very disappointed. She had become used to Hong Kong and a life of luxury, and she viewed the proposal of a new posting with disdain. 'A plain grey apartment in a boring apartment block, built in the middle of nowhere', was how she had described it after her first visit.

Still, she had come.

Two English-speaking castaways in a sparsely populated land, mostly surrounded by Chinese, she and Pauline Lee had soon become inseparable companions. The three Lee children—two boys and a girl—had also benefited from their English-language conversations with Anne Crabtree. Meanwhile, the excitement of settling into a Chinese school had occupied them fully and they had found no difficulty in making friends.

Although the Crabtrees were not averse to the idea of children themselves, they had deferred raising a family - and now it was too late. Tony's job often took him away and there was always a risk that an extended assignment, like this one, would necessitate them both going to remote areas where medical and educational facilities could be very basic. In the beginning they had felt there was plenty of time. But time had silently slipped by, and now they had missed the opportunity.

Anne enjoyed her times with the Lee children. They were really delightful—intelligent and well-behaved—and she had virtually adopted them as surrogate children of her own.

In response to Crabtree's invitation now, Lee accepted with pleasure. A baby-sitter wouldn't be needed since their apartments were adjacent to each other, and Pauline could pop over during the evening and check that the children were safely asleep.

Having accepted the invitation, Lee went off on his visit of inspection to see if he could trace the trouble, while Crabtree picked up the telephone to call Anne and tell her about the arrangement he'd just made. He didn't feel guilty about the short notice; Anne had herself suggested they should have the Lees over to dinner this week.

He heard her voice answer. 'That's fine Tony,' she said when he told her about it. 'I bought some provisions in the market this morning, in case the storm lasted. Actually, it's a good thing we'll have company; I got a bit flustered in the place—it was so packed and so noisy—and I ended up buying far too much for just the two of us. We've got some Chianti left in the fridge too.'

'Go easy on the wine,' her husband said. 'You know how little it takes to poleaxe Paul.'

She giggled. 'I'll do spaghetti. That should lay down a good stodgy base for the alcohol.'

'Great! We don't want to have to carry him back once again, even if it's not far. It's getting to be a habit.'

Although Paul Lee knew he couldn't handle alcohol, he kept trying to keep pace with the Crabtrees. It was a source of some embarrassment to Pauline.

'Anyway,' Crabtree continued. 'It should be a pleasant evening to look forward to. I'll see if ...'

But he never finished the sentence.

A brutal, violent jolt interrupted him. His mind, until then relaxed in talking to his wife, suddenly snapped back to the reality of his being at the plant. He grabbed at the table as the door behind him crashed open and the empty coffee-cups vanished off the table. Drawings and papers were whirled up and around by the hot maelstrom of wind that had violently invaded the room. The window exploded out of its frame and the fluorescent light winked out.

In the gloom, Crabtree realized that he hadn't been aware of any noise as such. But he knew there must have been an explosion, and it must have deafened him temporarily, even before he realized it had happened. His whole being tensed in fear and primeval readiness. An explosion was always the nightmare at the feast; forever threatening, rarely happening. Adrenaline surged through him.

Over the rush of the storm that now raged into the room through the suddenly-empty window, the voice in the earpiece was shrill. Worried.

'Tony? Tony? What's happened?'

Crabtree's dazed mind sluggishly focussed on the instrument—at least the 'phone was still working!

He stammered a response: 'I... I don't know. But I don't think... It's not good....'

He sneered at his own understatement.

'Are you all right?' Her voice was alarmed.

He started to reassure her when, suddenly, he remembered Lee.

'Christ!' he exclaimed. 'Paul! He just went out there.'

'Where? Oh God, Tony! Is he all right?'

'Don't know,' he said. 'I'll find out and ring you back. Got to see what happened.'

He had almost hung up when a thought struck him and he brought the handset back to his mouth. 'Wait!' he shouted. 'Don't talk to Pauline. Don't say anything to her. Not until you hear from me.' Then he thought about it again and changed his mind. If it was bad news it would be better if to give it to her face to face rather than impersonally over the telephone. 'No! Better go over to the flat. Just *be* with her. Don't say anything's happened here, though. I'll call you there. Just make sure you answer the phone if it rings. Got that? *You* answer it.'

He slammed the 'phone down finally, picked up his hard-hat and scrambled for the door.

Apart from being fairly dark—the emergency lights had come on automatically and were the only illumination now - the stairwell was almost normal. The blast must have come straight up the space, blowing away the heavy fire-doors as though they were made of paper.

The stairs were concrete and the handrails very solid steel. They were untouched. Lying on the stairs though, were fragments of wood.

Slamming his hat on his head, Crabtree bounced off the wall at the top of the stairwell opposite him and reached across to grasp both handrails so that he could slide down them, his feet in his stout safety-shoes hardly touching the stairs.

At the base of the stairs, the door leading to the plant had disappeared, and Crabtree realized then that the splinters of wood he had seen lying on the stairs were all that remained of the solid blast door. He raced through the void and stopped, his eyes widening in horror. Through the space once occupied by the door the area he had walked through a few minutes ago was now a wasteland filled with twisted, scorched metal. Billowing smoke and dust were everywhere.

Christ! he thought. *Jesus Christ! It's gone! The whole fucking place ... It's gone! What's happened?*

Somehow his mind accepted the smoke, but he was surprised by the dust. It was everywhere. Being picked up by the eddying winds of the storm and flung in every direction.

Then he understood. It was the insulation that had once covered all the pipes and ducts, shattered and blown to powder by whatever had happened here. Luckily for them all, the use of asbestos insulation had long since been discontinued. Foster had lost many friends and colleagues to the horrible ravages of asbestosis and he didn't wan to lose any more.

It was difficult to see a path through the smoke and wreckage. From somewhere high above, steam was bellowing and hissing from ruptured pipes, the condensation cloud enveloping everything, even this far below the fracture. In the distance, its source hidden from his direct view, something was burning fiercely. A pale, blue-white glow flickered there, illuminating the scene with a ghastly radiance.

Strangely, other than the howl of the storm, there was very little noise at first, just the steam and occasional metallic clangs of a few metal fragments still falling.

Then he heard a deep-throated rumble, and something moved into his view.

From behind a piece of twisted steel ducting an amazing sight appeared, a tall, grey and dull-yellow metal cylinder, gleaming in the fireglow, standing absurdly vertical on its narrow tip, swaying and bobbing like a drunken man looking for a brawl, sparring with his own shadow. But this was like a giant steel top.

Crabtree stared at it uncomprehendingly for a moment. Then he realized that he was looking at the rotor of a pump that must have burst from its casing while still spinning. Tons of metal standing on end, held vertical by its own rotational momentum, gradually precessing across the floor... and heading straight for him. Drunkenly, but very definitely coming at him.

He watched, almost hypnotized, as it surged forward, swaying nearer and nearer.

Christ! What am I thinking of? Barely in time, he flung himself sideways as the thing ploughed into the doorway where he had been standing a moment before. He crashed into a pool of dirty rainwater. The rotor scythed away the door-frame and the wall alongside him, the concrete crumpling in an explosion of grey dust.

The action was like a brake on the spinning column and, its energy dissipated, the huge mass of metal swayed to a stop and toppled and crashed against what was left of the wall, the tired old drunk, his aggression spent, falling down in a dead sleep in the doorway. It lay propped against the stairs and was safe for a while.

Crabtree felt his heart pounding as he picked himself up and looked at the destruction around him. He shook his head. In all this devastation, where could Paul be?

He looked up. Everything twisted. Massive steel beams tilting crazily downwards. Leaning at strange angles.

The wall at the far side of the boiler-house had been seriously damaged, leaving the beams running across the width of the building largely unsupported.

He checked that his safety-helmet was on, thinking even as he did so how foolishly inadequate it would be. The hard-hat wouldn't do him much good if any of that mass of wreckage above him came down.

In the gloom, he started to pick his way across the débris, warily watching out for hot, sharp metal and tangled cables waiting to entrap him.

Above the hellish chorus of the wind, steam and fire—over the occasional metallic crash in the distance as an unseen arm-wrestling of forces was resolved and something finally collapsed—he heard the first faint sounds of approaching voices. Shouting. Calling. Pleading in Mandarin and English if anybody was there. Asking if they were hurt.

Where the Hell are the rescue trucks? Although he knew it was far too soon for help to arrive, somehow it seemed to help, to ask the redundant question.

At last, shadowy shapes appeared through the swirling mist of dust, smoke and steam. Several boiler-suited figures came towards him. As he saw them, Crabtree became absurdly aware that in contrast with the pristine whiteness of their overalls his own were covered in wet filth as a result of his leap away from the path of the pump rotor.

He brushed away their anxious, fearful questions.

'Paul Lee came out here,' he yelled urgently. 'Help me find him.'

They stared at him for perhaps two seconds, and then understood. They turned away, going as fast as they could, fanning out to cover the area of their search without losing sight of each other, stepping carefully over fallen steel while at the same time warily looking above them for signs of heavy, hot and unstable masses about to fall. The glow of the emergency lights above them was dimmed by swirling steam and dust, and it was hard to see anything up there. Evidently the roof was still largely intact, because it was dark beyond the yellow gleam of the overhead lights. The steam was beginning to dissipate in the wind, but it could have concealed anything.

As they came past the far side of what remained of the boiler-house, in the distance Crabtree caught sight of the massive gas pipeline that brought the fuel to the plant, and he now had confirmation of the seat of the fire he has seen earlier. The pipe was totally fractured, and from its obscenely gawping end an intense sheet of blue flame was blasting across the ground. Even at this range he could feel the heat on his face. He was surprised that there were not more fires around. But most of the structure was metal and although the paintwork was badly blistered and scorched, there had been little to feed the flame.

The entire area, though, was festooned with charred, smouldering, stinking black cables, like so many incinerated snakes. The blowtorch that had swept through that space had done a thorough job.

It was too dangerous to go towards the flame, and in any case Crabtree knew Lee would not have been interested in anything out there, even if he'd had time to reach it. The problem they'd been investigating had not been on the gas supply-line.

Now a new sound appeared. At last! The two-tone siren chorus of approaching emergency vehicles. And as they circled back towards the turbine hall, a fire truck came racing round the rear access road. It screeched to a stop and men leaped out and sped towards the foam-jets that stood at each corner of the valve compound where the pipe was fractured. Fortunately for them, the roaring flame was directed away from the foam nozzles.

At that moment, a sudden shift in the wind fanned a smell at Crabtree, and he gagged at it.

Melding into the acrid stench of scorched paint and melted plastic there was something else. Something unfamiliar. Yet something horribly recognisable. He signalled the others to be quiet and they all stopped to listen carefully, trying to filter away the other sounds of Bedlam. Then he saw the two Chinese wrinkle their noses, and knew they had smelt it too.

Barbecuing meat!

Then he heard something. It was a low moan of agony. He moved cautiously towards the pile of wreckage from where the sound had seemed to come, waving for the others to come with him.

He peered into the gloom and pulled his torch out of his pocket. As the intense white beam swept over the twisted steel and fragmented concrete, he saw something.

The beam settled on what at first had looked like a pile of dirty wet rags, half-buried under the débris. Then Crabtree recoiled as he realized what he was looking at.

It was a charred and blackened body, barely recognisable as what had once been a human being.

It was Paul Lee. His skin had almost all gone, exposing a sticky wet, suppurating mass of red and black flesh.

Superheated steam was a cruel destroyer.

A girder had removed most of one of Paul's legs, and blood was pumping from a severed artery near the smashed and blackened region of his thigh. Crabtree knelt and braced himself to press down at what he hoped was a pressure point, in an attempt to stop the bleeding. One of the other men lifted Lee's head, gently easing the helmet away from the bloody pulp of his face. One of Lee's arms twitched in response.

'All right pal,' Crabtree said, in case any life remained in the body. 'Help's coming.' He wished to hell it would hurry. He jerked his head at one of the others. Go! Get help! he mouthed and the man got to his feet and sprinted off as quickly as he could over the wreckage.

'Help me! Get all this off him,' Crabtree said, and the remaining man stood up and began to heave as much as he could of the metal away from the body on the ground. Crabtree felt the bile rising in his throat at what was then exposed. The cockroaches that were ever-present in the network of cable ducts that criss-crossed the site had not been slow to seize on the sudden bounty which had fallen to them. Normally they survived on the scraps of food dropped or discarded by the labourers working on the plant; now they had a better option, and they had not been slow to take advantage of it. Crabtree swore at them and angrily struck out at them to drive them away. He tried to ignore the pieces of charred flesh adhering to the girder as he thrust it to one side.

Then he thought about the crazy stupidity of it all and a quiet rage welled up inside him. Throughout his life he had been able to accept that accidents sometimes happened. But somehow he knew that this was beyond a simple accident. Right from the beginning, he had known something was wrong—and the scale of what had happened, all this destruction, confirmed his thought. Devastation on this scale had to have been caused by something other than an accident.

It wasn't bad luck. Somebody had screwed up, badly. It was blatant irresponsibility—it was *somebody's* fault.

'I'll get them, pal,' he whispered towards Lee. 'Whoever's to blame for this, I'll get them. I promise you.'

As if Lee had heard his words, and been satisfied by them, he took a slow, shuddering, deep breath. Then, with a final violent twitching, the life was gone from the charred and shattered mess that had so recently been that vibrant young man.

Chapter 2

Fiona Wilson stood outside the tiny shop for a minute or more, looking through the window and wondering about the man she planned to meet inside. The window was cluttered with vacuum cleaners, torches, lamps and the other hardware that small electrical shops like this could still continue to sell in the face of intense competition from the large supermarkets and on-line retailers. Stickers in the window offered services that were simply unavailable in the big stores: 'Microwaves repaired', 'Cleaners refurbished', and so on.

Behind her, an incessant stream of traffic crawled towards the town nearby. This was a small village, almost a hamlet, close to a big commercial centre and struggling for survival in a world where big retail centres sucked the trading life from nearby communities.

She felt mildly ill at ease. Having fought her way through the traffic and found a parking space only after a desperate search, she had momentarily lost her usual composure. Now, catching sight of her reflection in the window, she took the opportunity to tidy the collar of her smart grey business suit and to smooth her auburn hair until she looked calm and in control once again. Then she pushed open the door.

A chime alerted the man standing behind the counter, who stopped studying the sheaf of papers in his hand and peered over the top of his glasses at her. 'Can I help you?' he asked. His voice was deep, his accent a mixture of cultured English and something else: an American mid-West twang, she thought.

'Dr Dan Foster?' she asked as she closed the door behind her, the chime jingling again as the noise of the traffic was shut out. Inside, the shop was somehow cosy, with rows of shelves and display stands bearing a wide assortment of electrical tools and accessories. The air smelt mildly dusty.

She saw a frown flicker briefly across the man's face before he nodded. He was obviously unused to having strangers visit him in his shop and ask for him by name.

With his deep tan, his thatch of black hair greying at the sides and his silver-flecked beard, he had the air of a rugged wanderer. It was an appearance that seemed strangely out of place in this little shop, tucked away in a cold wet street in what—in spite of being a suburb—was essentially a small village. She already knew that he was in his early fifties, but his hard-muscled and well-preserved body belied the fact. He caught at the corner of his spectacles and removed them to study her with flinty grey eyes that had deep laughter-lines angling from their corners.

'Who's asking?' His tone was quiet, wary.

She responded by opening her briefcase and withdrawing a business card. He took it from her, put his glasses on again, and studied the print. It was a classy card, on heavy stock and deeply embossed. The company logo was an eagle with outspread wings, etched in red, black and gold. The card spoke of a big, expensive company: a powerful operation.

'Fiona Wilson,' she said. 'I'm with Arnold Coward and Partners.'

'*Researcher*,' he read out aloud from the card. He took off his glasses and put them on the counter to study her again.

'Yes.' Her reply was brief and hardly informative.

'You want something fixed?' he asked. 'You don't need to show me a business card for that, you know!'

She grinned. 'No. I'm here on other business.'

He dropped his chin and looked hard at her for a moment, then turned and picked up a small box from the counter. It was full of odds and ends: pencil stubs, ball-pen caps, drawing pins and clips. He shook the box and slowly took out a paper clip, which he proceeded to apply to a small collection of papers.

'People come here to buy things,' he said after he had finished, 'from somebody who understands these things. Or they want to get something mended. Either that or they're sales people trying to get me to stock some useless product. Mostly, these days, it's to give to a charity—but you're not one of those. Oh, and then there are the others, from the Council, trying to tell me how some pettifogging new regulations are going to 'help' me. You're none of those things.'

'No. It's much more important than that.'

Behind her the chime sounded again as the door opened. She turned to see an elderly woman come in.

'Deal with your customer,' she said quietly. 'I'll wait.'

The other woman smiled gratefully at her and asked for replacement bags for an obscure make of vacuum cleaner. She seemed to be an old friend, because the two of them chatted happily about small-town events while Foster found a bag that would fit her machine. After she had paid, he escorted her to the door and let her out. He stood at the doorway and watched as she wobbled away, clutching happily at her purchase.

'She seemed pleased,' Fiona said when he returned to the counter.

'That's what keeps me afloat. They come here when the big stores can't help, or won't help. In fact, a couple of the big outfits even keep my name on a list and send people to me when they want spare parts, or if they want something repaired. The big boys aren't in business for that sort of thing; the margins aren't big enough, or the volume's too small to make it worthwhile. But if they can keep their customers happy by pointing them at me, that's what they'll do.'

'Good for you, then.' Her smile seemed forced. She had been discomfited at the interruption; she had wanted a clear run to discuss her business with Foster. 'Look, what I want to talk about isn't something I can do quickly or easily,' she said. 'I'd appreciate it if we could talk quietly. Have you got somewhere we can go? Where there won't be any interruptions?'

He stared at her, the puzzled frown forming again. 'Nope,' he said simply, gesturing round the tiny premises. 'What you see is what you get. I don't have staff. There's only me, so I can't leave the shop. Anyway, I don't see what a 'researcher' could want to talk to me about.' A thought seemed to hit him, and he added: 'A law firm! You're not going to tell me that somebody's died and left me a fortune, are you?'

She gave a small, brittle laugh. 'No. Not this time at least. But what I have to say is still important. Very, very important.'

'Can't be that important.' He shrugged and picked up his glasses again. 'Look, it may not seem like it to you, but I'm very busy right now. My VAT returns are due and I've got to sort out these receipts.' He nodded towards the papers he had been holding when she came in.

He started towards the door to show her out.

She took a deep breath, squared her shoulders and looked him in the eye. 'If I mentioned Universal Digital,' she said. 'Would that make you interested?'

He stopped in his tracks, looking ahead and not at her. She saw his head lift and his jaw stiffen. He stood still for a long moment, staring through the glass door. Eventually he turned to face her.

When his response eventually came, it was very brief and quiet: 'Ah!'

'You worked for them once.'

'Once. A long time ago.'

'I know. It's about that.'

'Can't be,' he said. 'Everything between me and them is long since over.'

'It was. But there's something else now. Something new.'

'No!' The answer was suddenly very firm. Not angry, but definite. 'I don't know what it is, and I don't want to know either. I've left that world a long way behind me and I'm not touching it again.' Then he continued his walk towards the door.

She looked at him as he opened the door for her.

'We need your help …' she began.

'I said: no doing, Miss Wilson. I mean it. So I'd appreciate it if you left now.'

'You haven't given me a chance to explain,' she said, her tone desperate.

'You don't need to. I'm not interested.'

She paused by the door, unwilling to give up. She had little choice but to play the one trump card she held: 'Not even to know why Paul Lee was killed?'

She saw his grip tighten on the door handle. His knuckles whitened, and she took advantage of the hesitation.

'You knew him, I believe,' she said.

'Paul? *Dead*?' he said sharply.

'Yes.' Then, seeing his blank expression, she asked, 'You haven't heard about the accident?'

The answer came through gritted teeth, 'What accident?'

'That's what I wanted to discuss.' She looked at him earnestly. 'Please. It won't take long. And it could be worth a lot to you.'

He took a deep breath, stared at her for a long moment, and then looked resignedly at his watch. 'OK,' he said. 'I close for lunch in twenty minutes. I'll see you in the pub across the road then.' He nodded in the direction. 'I'll give you an hour.'

She looked across the road and saw the pub he indicated. It was a small white building with a false Dutch gable. It looked pleasant enough, and a sign chalked on an easel outside announced that a range of hot cooked meals was available all day.

'I'll be there,' she said.

'And you'll be buying.'

She smiled, but there was no humour in his expression.

'All right,' she concurred and walked out at last.

He watched her as she crossed the road, and there was a thoughtful expression on his face as he closed the door.

Inside, the pub was wood-panelled and cosy. It was not one of those re-created from a mock-Victorian mould so lovingly favoured by the big brewers' architects, but the genuine thing, lovingly preserved over the years by a succession of caring owners. It was obviously popular with local business people, because it was crowded and the air was smoky. When he pushed his way into the throng, Foster eventually spotted her sitting at one end of the bar and made his way through the crowd to join her. She was sipping at a white-wine spritzer.

She looked up as he arrived and asked him what he was having, but the question was academic, because the barmaid was already pumping honey-coloured bitter into a straight-sided glass.

'Thanks Catherine,' he said and the girl smiled flirtatiously at him.

'I see you're known here,' Fiona said and held her glass up. 'Cheers!'

'Cheers!' he said, tipping his glass in her direction. 'Now, you wanted to talk.'

'You don't hang about, do you?'

'I said: you've got just an hour. If you want to waste it, that's up to you.' His tone was neither unfriendly nor insulting, just firm.

'All right. But we should order the food first. Then… can we find a quiet table to sit down?'

'Sure. There's one free in that corner.' He nodded towards a couple that had stood up. She felt vaguely annoyed that she hadn't spotted them about to leave. It put him in the driving seat, and she hadn't wanted that. 'Mine's a Stilton ploughman's,' he said. 'I'll grab the table.'

He headed off, leaving her to order their meals and when she joined him he was looking pensively across his glass at the people crowding the room. But it was the look of somebody who wasn't seeing them at all, someone whose mind was thousands of miles away.

As she sat down he shook his mind clear of the hidden thoughts and looked at her. 'It brought back a lot of memories,' he said. 'You know… Your mention of Universal.'

'Good or bad memories?'

He grimaced. 'Mostly good. A few bad.'

'I've only seen an outline,' she said. 'A report. On what happened between you and Universal.'

He stared at her, puzzled. 'Somebody's written down what happened?'

She nodded. 'People have been asking a lot of questions about it.'

He shook his head in amazement. 'Why? Why now? It's been… what? Five years?'

She took a deep breath, reached for her briefcase and took out some papers. She was just about to put them on the table when the barmaid arrived with their food, so she selected one page from the pile and handed it to Foster.

It was a photocopy of a newspaper article and as he read it his expression became increasingly stern. Under a photograph of enormous wreckage—a mass of tangled steel and concrete, the text told a bleak story:

Photographs have just been released of the damaged Kung Tau power station in the Peoples' Republic of China. A gas leak was thought to be responsible for the explosion two weeks ago that destroyed the newly-constructed plant. Three men were killed and twenty injured, some seriously, in the blast. Gold Win Energy, owners of the plant on Kung Tau island, about 160 miles from Hong Kong, have claimed that the low level of casualties was largely due to this being the most highly automated power station in the world, and claimed that sophisticated computer protection systems prevented a more major loss of life.

'Kung Tau!' he breathed. 'Now I see!'

'You hadn't heard?'

He shook his head. 'I can't understand how I missed it.'

'It was a one-day thing over here: there was very little press coverage, and nothing on TV at all, so it's not all that surprising. Anyway, your old company—Universal Digital Systems—they supplied the computer control systems that operated the plant, didn't they?'

'That's right. But you can't possibly think the computers did all that!' He put the paper down beside his plate and jabbed his forefinger at the picture.

'I don't know anything about it,' she said. 'I'm a trainee lawyer—with no knowledge of engineering.'

He scowled at her for a moment and then picked up a knife and fork wrapped in a green paper napkin. 'But somebody must be thinking that,' he said as he unwrapped the cutlery. 'Because you've tracked me down and, as you said, somebody's been asking questions.'

'OK. Yes, a preliminary investigation has been carried out; it blamed the computer system. There are no other suspects.'

'Christ!' he said quietly, as he started on the ploughman's.

She had ordered the same for herself, and as she ate she said, 'As I understand it, the power station was under the control of a very sophisticated computer system …'

'Not one,' he corrected her. 'Dozens. Each of them working independently.'

'All right. But all supplied by the company you used to work for.'

'The company I left five years ago.' His tone was defensive.

'OK. But you were involved with the early development of those systems.'

'Yes. I was their Director of Engineering. We had a team of about a hundred people working on the systems, one way or another.'

'A hundred!'

'Yes. Half of them designing the electronic bits and bobs and the basic software, the rest *using* the designs: applications engineers, they call them.'

'And you were in charge of them all.'

'Yes. But, as I said already, I find it incredible that anybody could have blamed the systems for that ...' He pointed at the photograph. 'There are all sorts of checks and balances to prevent accidents like that. And on top of it all, there are operators: the human beings, who supervise the plant, day and night.'

'That's precisely the mystery,' she said. 'All sorts of experts have been over it in minute detail, but none of them can find any fault or weakness in the design of the systems. But *something* happened all right. And there's no doubt the computers caused it.'

He shook his head slowly, picked up his beer and looked thoughtfully at her over the rim of the glass as he drank.

'So why bring me in at all? If an expert says it's the computers, then it's the computers. End of story.'

'No. We need to know *exactly* what happened. The precise reason. Down to the last detail.'

'Why?'

'Isn't it enough that we want to know?'

'No,' he replied. 'Something stinks about this. Why's a firm like your's involved? Why throw good money after bad? If somebody's fingered the computers, then that's it.' He shrugged. 'They'll either scrap the design or put in more and better safety-nets. Unless ...' his eyes widened and he paused.

'Unless what?' she asked.

'Unless there's something else.'

'Like?'

'Like I don't know. You tell me.'

'No,' she said. 'There's nothing else. We just need to know what happened.'

He looked seriously at her, trying to judge if she was lying, or perhaps just hiding something. Then he changed the subject.

'You know... that guy Paul Lee... the one who died. You were right, I did know him,' he said.

'I know.'

He looked past her towards the crowded room, but again it was apparent that his thoughts were far, far away. 'He was a good guy,' he said, finally. 'I worked with him. It was about ten years ago, I think. I seem to remember that he was married.'

'That's right. They had three children.'

'Oh fuck!'

'Yes,' she said simply. 'It's a real mess.'

'That's putting it mildly.' They were silent for a while as they ate and drank. Then he asked, 'But I still don't know what it's got to do with me. Apart from the obvious link of my job at Universal.'

Then he tensed as a sudden thought hit him. 'You're not going to tell me that somebody's trying to blame me for what happened, are you?' he asked.

'No. Absolutely not. But let me explain.

'The firm I work for has been retained by somebody to look into what happened...'

'Somebody?' he interrupted.

'Yes.' She shook her head as she saw his question coming. 'No, don't ask. That's one thing I'm not allowed to tell you. I can't say who it is. Not at this stage; at least, not yet. But let's say that they have a strong interest in knowing the facts. And, since all the experts who have looked at it are foxed, it's been suggested that you'd be the best person to find out.'

'You have to tell me,' he said, with a slow shake of his head. 'Who's hired you? Not Universal. Because if it's them you can forget it.'

'No. Not Universal. I can assure you of that. But ... I'm sorry, I just can't divulge our client's name.'

He stared at her for a while and then shrugged his reluctant acceptance. 'OK.'

'You'll do it, then?'

'Christ no!' he exclaimed. 'I haven't said anything like that. There are other people who do this sort of thing. What about the Health and Safety Executive?'

'It happened out of the country: outside their jurisdiction.'

'OK,' he agreed. 'But I'm sure they could be hired to go and take a look. As independent experts. They've got a special outfit that does that sort of work.'

'Yes, and they *have* been involved! But all they can say is that it definitely was the computers.'

'So? Case over!'

'No,' she said. 'Not over. The problem is, they can't tell exactly *what* went wrong. It needs somebody with very, very detailed knowledge of those particular computer system to do that.'

'And that's me?'

'Yes.'

He stared at her. 'I see how somebody could think that I could help,' he said. 'I know the design of the system. But I've been out of the business for five years. For Christ's sake! I run a shop now: a little repair outfit. It's a quiet life. No huge responsibilities.' He looked thoughtful before continuing quietly, 'Not like before. I like it here. I like my life. It's fine. There's no reason for me to change.'

'What about money?'

He scowled and looked at what was left of his beer. 'I manage OK. Not great, but OK.'

'I don't think that's true,' she said, very quietly, and something in her tone made him look up at her. 'Because, as I understand it, your business is insolvent.'

He stared at her angrily. 'You've been snooping into my affairs,' he snapped, his voice quiet, angry. He leaned forward as though he didn't want anybody nearby to hear his words. 'You've no right to do that.'

'Hardly snooping,' she said with a shrug. 'You run a Limited Company. Your accounts are filed with Companies House, for anybody to inspect. Anybody's got the right.'

'OK,' he growled. 'But Joe Public doesn't run about looking at Companies House records. Not without good cause—like they're owed money, or they're thinking about investing.'

'We're hardly Joe Public.'

'Perhaps not. But anyway, so the company's insolvent. What of it? I hold it up on my own. I don't owe anybody any money—apart from the Bank, and that's an agreed overdraft, secured by a lien on the shop—which I own outright by the way. I pay my suppliers in full each month, and I pay all my taxes.'

'I know. And you can continue to do that, as long as you carry the responsibility for paying off the debts. But that's not the point—face it, your business is struggling.'

'That's up to me.' His tone was angry, aggressive.

'Of course. But what if the Bank called in the overdraft?'

He stared at her. 'They wouldn't.' Then he frowned as another thought hit him. 'You wouldn't do that ...' he started to say, but she cut him short.

'No, of course we wouldn't,' she said. 'But the bank can call in an overdraft any time they like. And in the current financial situation, lots of them are feeling a bit exposed and trying to cut that exposure.

'I could handle it,' he said. 'Sell off the shop, and the stock. There'd be enough to pay the bank off, and that would be the end of it.'

'And how would you live?'

'I'd manage. A twentieth-Century tinker with engineering knowledge will always get work.'

She changed tack. 'You live on a houseboat,' she observed.

He scowled at her. He didn't like knowing that somebody had been looking into the minutiae of his life, without him being aware of it. 'Yes. And I own it outright.'

'Yes, but there are expenses. Mooring fees, power, services ...'

He pushed his chair back and started to rise. 'Look,' he said, with irritation in his voice. 'I've heard enough.'

She reached out and held his arm lightly. 'Please,' she said. 'Help me. And in return I can help you.'

He looked down at her hand with its long, elegant fingers and then at her face. She seemed genuinely disturbed.

'We're desperate,' she said earnestly. 'And we *have* to know what happened.'

'And I've said, *I can't help you.*'

'But what about Tony Crabtree?'

He scowled at her.

'Yes,' she said. 'Another old friend.'

'How's he get into this? You're not going to tell me he's dead too?'

'No, but he *is* in trouble. Bad trouble. The Chinese are holding him.'

He recoiled, staring at her.

'Not in prison,' she continued. 'But they won't let him out of the country until this business has been settled. Meanwhile, they let him carry on working.'

He took a deep breath and sat down again.

'He's another old mate,' he said.

'I know. And you're in a position to help him. And in doing that, we can help you.'

'Go on.'

'Give us a few days of your time,' she said. 'Or rather, sell us your time.'

'How many days?'

'Ten. Twenty at the most.'

'And?'

'When you've found out what happened, you can go back to your shop. Or you can do anything else you want to do: sell up, do something different ... I don't know, retire even. Whatever you want. Because, either way, your money problems will be over.'

His eyes narrowed. 'Over?' he asked sharply.

'Yes.'

He finished drinking his beer and held the empty glass for a while, pensively.

'Another one?' she asked, breaking into his thoughts.

He shook his head. 'No. I have to get back to work, and I need a clear head.'

'OK. Mind if I get one for myself?'

He shook himself free of his thoughts. 'Oh no ... I mean, I'll buy. White-wine spritzer, wasn't it?'

The walk to the bar gave him more time to think.

When he returned with her glass he asked, 'So what happens ... If I do what you want. What happens if I mess up?'

'What do you mean?'

'What if I *can't* find out? After all, you said other people had looked at it—no doubt good people, probably the best—and even they've found nothing, you say.'

'Well, for a start, nobody who's looked at it so far has anything like your detailed knowledge of the computer system. So you stand the best chance of finding out.'

'But, looking at the picture you showed me back there, everything seems to have been blown to pieces. It'll be bloody difficult to put together what happened. There's a fair chance I won't be able to pin down the cause.'

'We understand. And if that happens that's the end of it. The Chinese have agreed that, once you've put in your report, Tony Crabtree will be free to come home with his wife ...'

'And you believe them?' he interrupted.

'We don't have any choice. Anyway, you'll be able to come home, open up the shop, and start again; but, this time, solvent.'

'Yes.' He looked at her for a moment before continuing: 'You said earlier on that my money problems would be over.'

'Certainly!' She hesitated and watched his face as she continued, 'Seventy-five thousand pounds should be enough, shouldn't it?'

He leant back in his chair and stared at her in amazement.

'*How* much?' he asked, the words barely above a whisper.

She repeated the sum, and added, 'Fifty percent when you start, the rest when you hand in your report. And all expenses paid.'

'I don't believe you.'

She looked at him wordlessly for a while, then drew out an envelope from her briefcase and put it down on the table in front of him.

'Go on,' she said, nodding towards the envelope. 'Open it.'

He stared at it warily for a while. Then he picked it up, opened it and studied the cheque it contained.

'Christ Almighty!' he breathed. 'You're serious.'

'Deadly!' she agreed. 'That's half the payment. As I said, you get the rest when you submit the report.'

He looked down at the cheque again, almost as if he expected it to dematerialise in front of his eyes. 'Somebody's desperate.'

'That's right.'

He took a deep breath and looked out of the window at his shop. After a while, he returned his attention to her. 'I'd need to finish off a few jobs,' he said. 'People have left me things …'

'Of course. How long do you want?'

'A few days. There's not much to do really.'

'OK. Though we were hoping you'd be on board by the end of next week, and it's Saturday now.'

'Doesn't seem impossible to me.'

'I guess not, though we'll need you to sign a contract.' She reached into the case again and handed him a thin set of papers. 'It's here. I'll give you time to read it. Though I can assure you that there's nothing to worry about in it. I'll come back and collect it.' She thought for a moment and then checked herself, 'Though if I wait 'til Monday it'll be another delay. Can I pick it up tomorrow?'

'Sunday?'

'Yes.'

'All right, but where?'

'Your place, if you like.'

'The houseboat?'

'Yes, where is it?'

'On the river, close to here.' Giving her the information, he felt sure she knew anyway.

'OK. I'll be there. About twelve?'

After giving her directions to his boat, he said, 'You're very trusting.'

'Trusting?'

'Sure. What's to stop me paying in this cheque and disappearing?'

'Simple!' she said coldly. 'We'd stop payment. Anyway, as it's the weekend you won't be able to pay it in until Monday. But I don't think it'll come to that. From what I know about you, I don't think you'd renege on an agreement.'

'We don't have an agreement.'

'Shake my hand,' she said. 'That'll be enough.'

He stared at her seriously, and then a trace of a smile came to his eyes. He held out his hand and they shook on the deal.

When Foster returned to his shop he left the 'Closed' sign up while he turned on his computer, selected an option and clicked the mouse. In no time, a world time clock had appeared on the screen. He selected Beijing and saw that it was late in the evening there now.

'I wonder if they'll be up?' he mused to himself. He clicked over to the computer's address book and set the machine to ring Crabtree's number. He was connected within seconds.

Crabtree's wife, Anne, answered. Her voice was so clear it was hard to believe they were geographically separated by six thousand miles, even harder to credit that their conversation was travelling very much farther than that, bouncing off a tiny man-made star hanging high in space: a communications satellite.

She was surprised and delighted to hear from Foster. He had been a good friend to her husband over many years. She quickly told him that Tony was all right, though he was away from home, still at a meeting, even at this hour.

Then, as she started to talk about the shattering accident, her voice changed. Even over the distance that separated them, Foster could sense her helpless fear. She and Tony were alone, thousands of miles from their friends: far from any sort of legal framework that they could hope to understand and trust.

'It's been awful out here, Dan' she said. Her voice was small, child-like. 'Since ... since the explosion, I mean. I hardly see Tony—it's typical of them to keep him at work as late as this—and when I do see him he looks so tired. He's so withdrawn. It wasn't his fault, you know... the accident, I mean. We don't know exactly what happened, but somehow ... well, I sense that he feels responsible. It's got to him. He needs a break, but he won't take one. *Can't* take one, in fact.

'And we've been almost completely imprisoned by the company. They've held onto our passports and won't let us leave the country.

'Then, the Press has been trying to get hold of anybody who may know something, and the Company's made us all swear not to speak to anybody. They're even going to change our telephone numbers. Then we'll be ex-directory. In fact, it's lucky you called when you did...'

'Anne,' Foster interrupted, his tone urgent. 'If they do that—if they change your 'phone number—make sure you get the new one to me as soon as possible.'

''Course, Dan. I will.'

'So what's happening now?' he asked.

'Well, there's an internal inquiry going on, and there may even be some sort of public court case ...

'That's the worst part—we really don't know what's happening, or what's going to happen. I'm worried that they'll make Tony a scapegoat.

And it won't be fair. Back home, at least we'd know there was going to be an inquiry or an inquest. Impartial. But out here ...'

The words poured out as she told him as much about it as she knew.

Foster expressed his sorrow at Paul Lee's death. He had worked alongside the man once, for quite an extended time, on a power station in Hong Kong, and had come to respect his abilities—and to like him personally. Anne explained that, after the accident, a lot of her time had been spent in comforting his widow and the children. Comforting them and trying to take their minds off what had happened—at least as much as that was possible.

'Dan,' she asked eventually. 'Are you going to get involved in this one?' Her husband had once told her a little about Foster, and now she clutched at the straw.

'I don't know, Anne, but I've been asked to consider it. I don't know who's involved, and I don't know an awful lot about what's going on. But ... Look, just tell Tony that something's happening over here. And tell him I'll do whatever I can to help. I mean that.

'And make sure you ring and tell me if they change your number.'

She promised again to do that and he hung up, feeling that in some small way he had brought her a crumb of comfort. The thought that she was not all alone and isolated in that foreign place, so far from her home and her friends.

That must have helped.

Chapter 3

Fiona looked up from her notes and identified Lake Goddess moored alongside a line of chestnut trees. The vessel was a fifty-foot steel narrowboat, lying amongst several others just beyond the graceful white arches of the bridge she had just crossed. The craft formed a pretty sight, with lines of hanging baskets alongside the moorings trailing profusions of bright fuchsia and impatiens.

She walked along the towpath, feeling the warmth of the sunlight on her face. When she reached the chestnuts the shadows dappled her skin. She reached the boat, mounted its gangplank and called out, 'Dr Foster?'

His response came from below, and she looked around for somewhere to enter. Just then his head emerged from a door at the stern and he waved at her.

She had never been on any kind of houseboat before and what she saw inside came as a total surprise. The cabin was cosy: a comfortable haven. A stereo system in one corner was playing some classical music quietly.

Foster showed her into the main saloon and then excused himself. 'Just finishing off something,' he said. 'I won't be long. Make yourself at home.'

She walked over to a glass-fronted book-case that lined one bulkhead and tilted her head to read the titles. They ranged from classics, old and new, to literary reference books.

She moved along to the adjoining bulkhead, where a separate case housed a complete set of *Groves' Dictionary of Music*. Diagonally across the cabin from these cases was a deep-buttoned leather armchair, and at the desk was a swivelling captain's chair, also leather-covered.

There was a silver photograph frame on the bookcase. The frame held a picture of two teenagers, smiling in bright sunshine against a backdrop of rhododendrons.

She looked at them thoughtfully for a while, then continued her tour of the cabin until he reappeared.

'I'm impressed,' she said. 'I never thought a boat could be so comfortable.'

'Glad you like it. I'm just doing lunch. Join me?'

'Well, I'd only planned on collecting the contract.'

'It's nothing special,' he said. 'Just bread and cheese. And wine.'

'Oh, all right then,' she said. She realized that she was hungry, and this sounded too good to pass up.

He put plates, glasses and cutlery on the table and then brought in a nutty farmhouse loaf. This he followed with a board bearing an imposing array of cheeses and a bottle of Australian Merlot.

Fiona sniffed. The bread, fresh and warm, smelled wonderful. With the music in the background it seemed a civilised way to spend a peaceful Sunday afternoon.

She sat down as he poured the wine for them.

'Did you read the contract?' she asked as she took a sip of the wine.

'Yep!'

'All OK?'

'I couldn't see any problem. In fact, I've signed it already.' He reached over to a nearby shelf and passed the document to her.

'Good!' she said as she scanned it. 'Then it's rolling.'

'I suppose so,' he replied as she put the contract into her briefcase.

'Do you always carry that?' he asked, nodding towards the case.

'Yes–at least, when I'm working.'

'It's Sunday!'

'Maybe. But I'm still working.'

'Suppose so,' he said.

'Anyway, I'm not quite in my city-girl gear, am I?'

She was wearing jeans and a crisp white blouse. Foster looked at her and gave a faint smile of approval.

'Look,' she said. 'Before we start. There are a few things I'd like to get clear. Just to fill in the background.'

'Like what?'

'Well …' she hesitated before saying, 'About you and Universal Digital, actually.'

'I thought you'd read all about that,' he said. 'In the reports.' His tone was suddenly sour, the earlier relaxed, almost jocular spirit gone.

'I did. But the reports give just the bare bones. I'd like to know a bit more.'

'Why?'

'No reason really,' she answered. She took another sip of wine and looked at him. 'Curiosity, if you like. Anyway, it's up to you. You don't have to tell me any more. I'd respect your privacy. But it seems an interesting story.'

There was a long silence while he considered her request, then he sighed as if he had reached some sort of conclusion. He looked at her and said, 'There wasn't a lot to it, actually.' He sipped thoughtfully at his wine before continuing, as though he was taking the opportunity to rake through old memories and put them in order.

'I worked with the company for twenty years. We made control systems for power stations, refineries, and so on. And for ships ...' He paused there, and a pensive look crossed his face. Then he shook his head clear of whatever thought had cross his mind and continued: 'Mostly, it was good. Fun even. But, somewhere along the line I made an enemy—a guy called Andy Johns.'

'Yes, I saw a mention of his name in the report.'

Foster looked at her and she saw a muscle at the side of his face twitch slightly. 'Well, we rose through the ranks together until, after a while, we were both appointed to the Board of Directors. It worked for a bit. Then, after a few years, he was made M.D. —and became my boss.

'It was a very unstable set-up. Andy was completely ruthless. For as long as I'd known him he'd driven out people who didn't go along with his ideas. And when he became my boss I could see I'd be next in his sights. I tried to paper over the cracks; but it was like trying to hold the San Andreas Fault together with Sellotape. We were two bloody great tectonic plates pushing against each other.'

'So he got rid of you.'

'Eventually. But I wasn't such an easy mark as the other poor sods. I was different from the others he'd got rid of: I was a bigger obstacle. Too powerful, too well known.'

'How did he do it, then?'

'He made sure I couldn't do anything right. Like setting me impossible targets and loading me with pettifogging form-filling. Eventually he worked me into a corner. But even then he couldn't get enough to fire me—or he didn't have the faith in what his acolytes said. So he set it up so that, though I could stay on... same title, same salary..., it was only as a figurehead. All my staff would report to somebody new. He knew I wouldn't wear that.'

He paused and looked at her. 'I had other problems then, too.'

'Other problems?'

There was a long silence before he answered. 'Yes. My marriage. We broke up.'

'Oh.' It was a simple statement, neither critical nor questioning.

'It'd been coming for a long time, I guess,' he said. 'At first it was all the travelling. I was never home. I used to write home, to try and keep in touch but ...' He looked thoughtfully at her and after a moment asked, 'Do you know any Auden?'

'The poet?'

When he nodded she said, 'Wasn't one of his poems used in that film, *Four Weddings and a Funeral* ?'

'Yes - *Funeral Blues*. But in another poem, *A Penny Life*, he wrote about a man travelling the world. It ends:

> '..... *answered some*
> *Of his long marvellous letters but kept none.*'

'That's how she was; though I don't think she actually kept any of my letters.' As an afterthought, he added, 'Not that I think they were marvellous, mind!'

'That's very sad. Her not keeping the letters, I mean.'

He shrugged. 'It didn't worry me too much. Anyway, to get back to what happened: the battle with Andy started to get to me. I guess I hadn't been good company for my wife... not for a long time.'

'She left you?'

'No.' He took a deep breath and looked thoughtfully at her before continuing, as though he was wondering how much to say. 'It's the corny old story. Husband comes home early. Finds neglected wife in bed with another guy.'

'Oh no! I'm sorry.'

'Not your fault!' he said. 'Anyway, I never thought it would happen to me, but it did. I'd suspected it was going on, but ... anyway, when I found them... Well, I threw him out. Literally. Out in the street. And him bollock naked. I always wondered what he did—wandering the streets in broad daylight and arriving home wearing just his pasty skin. But I couldn't care less.'

She giggled.

'And then I grabbed whatever I could and walked out of her life,' he concluded.

'You don't do things by halves, do you?'

'No.' He smiled.

'How did she react?'

'At first?' he asked, and when she nodded he said, 'She broke down and cried. Said it wasn't anything serious, that she'd been lonely. Then she tried to shift the blame onto me: said that I'd left her alone too much. Travelling all the time.'

'Couldn't you have forgiven her?' she asked. 'After all, you had a long marriage. And ... that bit about travelling and leaving her lonely. There must have been a bit of truth in it.'

'Probably a lot of truth,' he said. 'But the reality was that we'd drifted apart. She didn't appreciate any of the things I liked.'

'And you probably didn't appreciate the things she liked.'

He stared at her, then shrugged. 'Perhaps, though I did try. But anyway, for whatever reason, I walked out. We got divorced a year or so later.'

'Anybody in your life now?' she asked.

He looked at her, his expression serious.

'They come and go,' he said eventually.

They looked at each other for a while, and then she broke the eye contact and nodded towards the silver-framed photograph. 'Are those your children?'

He looked at the picture and said simply, 'Yes, Cindy and Mark. They're both grown up now; working.'

'Do you see them?'

'From time to time.'

From his tone she guessed the subject of the children was painful, so she changed tack: 'You didn't marry again?'

'No. Good God! It was only five years ago.'

They were quiet for a moment, each deep in their own thoughts.

'Anyway,' he squared his shoulders and continued eventually. 'When I walked out of the job I was more sensible over the situation at work than I was with my personal life. I'd got everything well documented there, and I had a good lawyer. Andy thought he'd boxed me in. He thought a court would see that I hadn't actually been fired, so he thought they'd feel I had no claim against the company. He'd arranged it so that I had the same job, the same money—so what was I complaining about? But my lawyer raked up something called 'Repudiatory Breach of Contract'.'

'What's that?'

'Some legal term.' He gave her a grin and asked, 'You're a lawyer—surely you must know?'

'I'm a researcher. Anyway, we don't do employment law.'

'OK. Basically, it meant that they'd acted in such a way that I could breach my contract of employment. Anyway, it really didn't matter what we hit them with. I knew they wouldn't want to go to court—they hated publicity—so I worked it round, to get as much money out of them as I could.'

'Sounds like blackmail to me!'

'Perhaps! But I needed a fair amount of money, you see. The economy was in recession then and, at my age, out-of-work executives were finding it difficult to get work. Some had to take really menial jobs, just to survive. I wasn't about to do that, so we hit them with a massive claim.'

'Could they pay?' she asked.

'You bet!' He laughed. 'I wasn't too worried about them. They were big and they were fat. I'd made a lot of money for them in my time and I was going out, cold, into a very uncertain world.

'They wriggled a bit—for the form of it, I guess—and then they made me an out-of-court settlement. It wasn't all we'd asked for. We knew that'd never happen, so we'd pitched the ante high. But what we settled for was enough to buy all this,' he waved his arm to indicate the boat. 'And the shop. Even after I'd paid the lawyer! Your lot are expensive!'

'But you'd been in a high-flying job. Wasn't running a shop a huge come-down?'

He looked at her angrily. 'It's not a come down.'

'I didn't mean…'

'What didn't you mean?'

'I didn't intend to put you down… To denigrate running a shop, I suppose.'

He relaxed a little. 'OK. Yes, it was a hell of a change,' he admitted. 'No more executive power. No more jetting around the world in Business Class. No more fancy hotels and expense accounts.'

Then his mood changed, and a pensive look came to his face. 'You take your choice in life,' he said. 'I didn't realise that, but one day— a long time ago, while I was still with Universal—I went to Mark's school. They were putting on a concert for the Head Teacher's retirement. It was a super thing: the kids had a ball, and everybody was smiling and clapping the old man. At the end, he came onto on the stage for the presentation, and you know what? He was in tears.'

'Nice!'

'Yes. I don't think there was a dry eye in the house. He'd been a popular and effective Head. Then, suddenly I saw that I'd never have that.'

'What do you mean?'

'Well, he'd been in the same job for decades. Always going in to the same place at the same time. Nine to five, Monday to Friday. Year after year.

'Boring? Perhaps, but at the end of it he fitted the place. And the place fitted him. And when the time came to go, it was OK. He'd had a full and happy life, and now all those kids, and the staff, and the parents, they were applauding him; celebrating his life—*with* him.

'I could never have that. I was never in the same place for long, and my friends and work-mates were scattered all round the planet.'

She looked at him in silence, but he was looking out of the window, lost in his own thoughts …

Eventually he continued, 'So that was what I meant. I'd made my choice and, by and large, it was a good one. But I couldn't have that … that place in a community.'

'We all make choices,' she said.

'Yes, and I made mine when I went to university, determined to be an engineer! And that's what was so wrong with what Andy did. If I had done what he wanted, I was going to be just a paper-pusher. It wasn't what I joined Universal to do. I joined them to be an *engineer*, because I loved engineering. I mean it!'

He saw a smile come to the corners of her mouth, and countered her clear disbelief: 'No, really! I did. With a passion! I loved the job because it was a continual challenge: a tough mental and physical challenge.

'I'd always thought how lucky I was to be paid for doing something I really enjoyed doing: a stimulating job that needed brains … and one that took me round the world, to places I'd never have seen otherwise; wild, remote places that most people never get to see. Well, not then … at that time mass tourism hadn't turned the world into an endless repetition of the same old things—what with Western hotels, flush toilets, Body Shops and Macdonald's. Travel was an adventure then. A real adventure.

'I was good at the job too, I think. And while I was with them I'd been promoted. Again and again.

'But under Andy I was just going to end up a pen-pusher, while he made all the decisions.'

'Could he?' she asked. 'Make the decisions, I mean. Did he have the technical knowledge.'

'Not really! He always reckoned on getting his minions to work it out and put it all down in front of him, so he would just rubber-stamp what they said. But you could bet that if anything went wrong he'd make sure that he'd never get the blame. It was all he wanted. Then, when he had me in that situation he really *could* fire me.

'So I didn't really mind getting out. And—do you know?—what I do now is engineering too. Real engineering. That little old lady who came in when you were here yesterday, she comes in quite often. I help her out and I know she's very grateful. There are others like her too. OK, I don't have the power I had before—the influence—but I'm not pushing paper either.'

He paused as a thought came to him. 'Well, there's the VAT stuff. But the point is that there was a hell of a lot of paperwork in Universal. Far too much.'

He turned to look out of the window. 'In fact,' he said. 'When I think about it, what I'm doing now is a very direct, focussed thing. Someone brings me a vacuum cleaner: I look at it; take it apart; fix it. It's only a few minutes, an hour at the most, from beginning to end. Before, I was heading up a big team, doing engineering on a grand scale. But things took months and years to reach any sort of conclusion. And the job was broken into lots of parts.'

He paused again for a while, still staring out of the window. 'Then there's another thing,' he said, so quietly she could hardly hear his words. 'Running a shop is a lot less risky.'

'Risky?'

'Yes. We were pushing technology in huge plants where, if anything went wrong, the results could be lethal.'

'I don't really understand,' she said. 'It seems that your company was involved with much more than I would have expected.'

'Yes, it must seem odd. But you see, the control systems—computers, these days—govern everything that happens in the power station ... or ship, or refinery, or whatever else the plant may be. To design those systems, you need to know exactly how the main machinery of the plant works. Every bit of it.'

'I see!'

'And if the design is wrong the plant won't work properly. At best, its performance may not meet the client's expectations. At worst, it could jeopardize the safety of the whole thing, if it goes badly wrong. As it may have done at Kung Tau.'

'But if safety's so critical, how is the risk minimized?'

'By designing everything very carefully. In areas of extreme risk, things are triplicated so that no decision is made unless there is agreement by at least two separate systems.'

'But even then, things can go wrong?'

'Yes...'

In the silence that followed she willed him to finish.

'I have to admit it,' he continued eventually. 'At times it was scary.'

'Scary?' It didn't fit the image she had built up of him. 'Was there physical risk?'

He laughed. 'Only if you count clinging to a handhold a hundred feet above the ground!'

'But that's not the sort of risk you meant, was it?'

'No. You see, although Andy never liked it, I made sure I was out there, 'at the coal face', whenever we got to the commissioning stage. I felt it was important that I should be there. But every time I got out there I'd find myself worrying whenever something big, noisy and dangerous was about to start up. Wondering if it'd be OK.'

She shook her head. 'I see,' she said, but felt unconvincing. Suddenly she was seeing a different side of him: a vulnerable side. He was a thinker. She cleared her throat before continuing: 'I don't know anything about engineering... but the impression I have is that it's very complicated. Lots of maths and stuff.'

He smiled. 'It's complicated all right. But generally, engineering problems are logical. It's a long—sometimes *very* long—chain of cause-and-effect things. You keep cool, and if you work at it for long enough, if you think it through clearly and logically, then you'll eventually disentangle it.'

She remembered the photograph in her file. 'What if you can't?' she asked. 'I'm thinking about the wreckage of that plant.'

'Things can go wrong,' he admitted. 'I guess badly wrong, sometimes.'

Once again, he turned his attention to the view from the window. He'd suddenly had a premonition, a shapeless dread that had come to him when she had shown him the article in the newspaper about the Kung Tau explosion. And memories too: many phantoms had been stirred in his mind. He didn't understand why his heart was beating so urgently, or why he was breathing so slowly.

But he was.

He filled his wine-glass again and when he offered the bottle to her she nodded and held out her glass.

'I shouldn't,' she said. 'I'm feeling quite happy enough.'

He grinned at her and saw her blush. It was a surprise. He'd seen her as very self-possessed.

'What's that music?' she asked, as if to break the silence that had fallen on them.

'Gounod. The end of 'Faust'. It's a neglected piece these days.'

'It's beautiful.'

As he replenished her glass, he found himself looking at her mouth. It was a very pretty mouth with soft, full lips framing tiny, perfect white teeth. Suddenly it was very quiet. He looked up into her eyes and saw that she was smiling a challenge at him.

Then he made a decision and leaned back in his chair, as if putting a little more distance between them.

Suddenly she realized that she had wanted him to lean forward and kiss her. And if he had she knew she wouldn't have tried to stop him. He was a strangely attractive man.

There was a long silence as they looked at each other.

'You're a very beautiful woman,' he said finally. 'Dangerously so.'

'Is that a compliment?'

He grinned. 'Close as you'll get from me,' he said.

She looked down at her glass and ran a fingertip lightly round its rim. 'And you're a strange man,' she said. Her voice was husky and quiet, but the spell was broken. She turned to look out of the window at the river flowing slowly past.

Then she decided to change tack. 'Tell me, what about your title?'

'Title?'

'Yes. All the papers they gave me said you were a Ph.D—a doctor. But you don't seem to use the title.'

He grimaced. 'Titles don't come to much when their owner's running a small shop. *Doctor Foster*? Doesn't sound right—not here. Makes me think of the nursery rhyme, 'Doctor Foster went to Gloucester …'—and then there are the people who think it means you're a medic. You know, the in-flight announcement: 'Is there a doctor on board?' I feel bad when it happens. Feel I should put my hand up, but I wouldn't be any good dealing with somebody having a heart attack or, worse still, about to give birth.'

She gave an amused smile and an easy silence fell on them.

After a long while he said, 'I've told you about me. What about yourself?'

'Not much to tell,' she said.

'Well, start with the men in your life.'

'There's nobody special at the moment.'

'That surprises me,' he said.

'Thanks. But the lack of a steady boyfriend—that's just how it is at the moment.'

'OK then. What about your job?' he asked. 'What brought you into the legal world?'

She was thoughtful for a while, and then she continued: 'After I left school I drifted about a bit. Didn't really know what I wanted to do. Got jobs temping with all sorts of firms. Then I got sent to a solicitors'…' She paused for a while before continuing. It was as if she was wondering how much to tell. Finally, she finished: 'And I fell in love.'

He grinned. 'With somebody, or the job?'

She sniffed. 'Both, actually. But he was married. I found out later—much later—that he was the office roué. He had slept with most of the girls in the office. But I only found out when one of the others told me.' She smiled at the bitter-sweet memory. 'I suppose I was very young and innocent.'

'He took advantage.'

'No! Not really.' There was a defensive tone in her voice, making Foster think she was still fond of the man. 'He led a pretty sad existence, actually,' she continued. 'His wife had lost all interest in sex after the children grew up.'

'*That* old one!'

'No!' she said indignantly. 'It wasn't like that. She never actually denied him sex. But she made it very plain that it did nothing for her.'

'A common enough story.'

'Yes. But I genuinely don't think he was putting it on so that he could get me into bed. I think he really was very lonely. He told me how his wife's rejection made him feel pretty useless. For her, he could never do anything right. Well ... she never praised him when he did something right, though she was always quick to point out when something was wrong.'

'Was he much older than you?'

'Oh, yes!' And then she stopped suddenly. She frowned and asked, 'Hang on! Why am I telling you all this?'

'Because I'm a good listener.' He grinned at her, and she relaxed.

'Carry on,' he said. 'Tell me.'

'I was 25,' she continued. 'And he was well over 50. But I've never felt that age should make any difference. It often works, you know—an older man with a younger woman. I never saw age as being a problem between two people.'

For a while their eyes met, and he wondered if her words were intended as a signal.

'That's the popular image,' he said eventually, moving away from the danger area. 'But people don't think about what happens twenty or thirty years on. When he's getting doddery and she's still in her prime.'

'No,' she said quietly. 'I suppose not.'

'How old are you now, Fiona?' His question came naturally in the silence.

'Twenty-eight,' she replied.

He grinned. 'I wish I was that age again. Almost thirty years younger than I am now.'

'You don't look it,' she said.

'I keep myself fit. Run every morning, work out in the gym once a week.'

'Well done, you!' There was genuine admiration in her exclamation.

He broke off the track of the conversation. 'Anyway,' he said. 'What happened to him? The office roué?'

'I felt we were getting too close,' she said. Her expression was sad as she watched a pair of swans drift by. 'There was nothing in it. I knew he'd never leave his wife. I didn't really want him to do that, I suppose. So I left the firm.'

'Where did you go?'

'Oh, by then I was hooked on law, so I signed up with another practice. Now I'm even thinking about taking articles. And that's where I am now. Just a dogsbody, really.'

'So finding me, and getting me involved with the accident in China ... it's work for a dogsbody, is it?' He was smiling a challenge at her as he asked the question.

'No,' she replied sharply. Then she frowned as a thought crossed her mind. 'Actually,' she said quietly. 'I've been wondering about that. Why me?'

'Why you?'

'Yes. This is very high profile case for the firm, so why am *I* here—a mere researcher? I can understand them giving me the basic work, but after I located you I expected them to hand the case over to somebody higher up the ladder.'

'Perhaps they felt I was a sucker for a pretty face,' he ventured, grinning impishly at her.

She glanced up at him and blushed. 'Whatever the reason,' she continued. 'I saw this as a challenge. I felt that if I did well, it would be very good for my career.'

'And it will be?'

'Yes, which is why I think they let me take it a bit further than they'd originally planned. But I'm under no illusion: when the time comes, somebody else will step in. A partner. Somebody suitably qualified, and mature enough to confront the client.'

'Ah, the mysterious client!'

She didn't rise to the bait. 'Anyway,' she said, reaching for her briefcase. 'I've got your instructions here.'

'Instructions?'

She took an envelope from the case and handed it to him. He opened it to find a British Airways ticket to Hong Kong, and an itinerary. He raised his eyebrows as he read the ticket. 'Your lot move quickly,' he said. 'According to this, I leave on Wednesday.'

'You knew we were in a hurry. And you said you needed a couple of days to tidy things up here.'

He nodded and returned to examine the ticket. 'First Class, too,' he said.

'We were told to do that,' she said. 'But anyway, it helped us get you on a flight. They're pretty full.'

'Hong Kong,' he said. 'Kung Tau's north of the border: in the PRC.'

'That's right. But the Chinese have made special arrangements for people to fly between the site and Hong Kong. Originally it was because everybody involved with it was based in Hong Kong but, after the accident …'

Foster shrugged. He could understand that nobody would want to be seen to be putting barriers in the way of an investigation. And hotels and other facilities in the Hong Kong territory were bound to be considerably better than those in an isolated and rural part of Mainland China.

Then he read the itinerary and looked up at her again. He'd been booked into the Mandarin Oriental. 'Somebody's certainly been doing some research,' he said. 'They've even picked my favourite hotel.'

Her expression was innocent as she said, 'Oh? I didn't know about that.'

'Didn't you now?' he said acidly. Somehow he doubted that there was much she didn't know. 'What about my jabs?'

'Immunization? We've assumed that whatever you once had has long since expired, so you're booked into a private clinic tomorrow afternoon. Here's the address.' She passed him a card.

'You're right,' he said as he read the card. 'I was permanently jabbed-up once. Still got the ICOV somewhere. Will I need to take it?'

'ICOV?'

'International Certificate of Vaccination.'

'Oh, yes, take it along if you can find it. But don't worry if you can't. I'm sure it'll be OK.'

There was a small packet of business cards in the envelope. He picked up the top one and saw that, according to it, he now worked for Arnold Coward and Partners, Fiona's firm. He was identified as 'Dr Foster, PhD, Senior Engineering Consultant'. He liked the sound of that: it brought back memories of the glory days gone by.

'You had these printed before I came on board?'

'Yes.'

'You must have been pretty confident.'

'We were. We knew you wouldn't let down Tony Crabtree.'

He took a deep breath and looked slowly around him at the boat before looking back at her. 'And what if I change my mind?' he asked.

'You wouldn't, would you? Not now?' Her tone was slightly panicky.

'It's a possibility.'

'But why? The money …'

'I've not paid the cheque in yet. Money isn't everything, you know.'

'I know,' she said, now slightly annoyed. It had seemed to be in the bag earlier; now he was casting doubts. 'But you're in a financial hole and the money gets you out of it. No problems. A week or two in Hong Kong, a report to our client, and it's all over.'

'Sounds easy.'

'No it isn't. Not for most people, but it's something you can do.'
'You've got a lot of faith in me.'
'I have.'

She stared at him until he was forced to continue.

'Don't worry,' he said, with a sudden grin. 'I won't back out. Not now. It's for the reason you said. I know the people involved. I want to help them.'

She let out a long pent-up breath. 'You'll be back in a week—two at most,' she said.

Chapter 4

As Foster stepped out of the lift and onto the gleaming black marble floor of the Mandarin's entrance hall, the red-coated doorman waiting at the glass door recognised him and saluted.

'Your car, Dr Foster?' he asked and when Foster nodded he went outside to summon the hotel car that Foster had ordered the night before.

While he waited, Foster looked through the huge windows at the busy stream of traffic outside. From within the hotel the noise was subdued, and the building's efficient air-conditioning system kept at bay the warm syrupy stench outside. Inside, the air was faintly scented with traces of furniture polish and expensive perfume, masking Hong Kong's atmosphere of damp, warm sea air, the all-pervasive odour of stir-fries, the stink of countless diesel exhausts and the faint stench of stagnant water and seeping sewage.

It was cool, fresh and civilised inside the hotel ... but very definitely Hong Kong outside of it.

1997 was approaching and when it arrived British rule would come to an end. But for now there was little sign of change. In fact, the seemingly endless changes continued: changes that had constantly swept to and fro across the place, from its inception as a busy harbour and throughout its precarious existence as a British Crown Colony, far away from its rulers' base, perched impudently on the hem of Red China's enormous territory.

The sweep of elevated highways, the sudden dive of major roads into tunnels, the steady encroachment of the land into the harbour, the endless thrusting, skyward soaring of tall steel-and-glass towers; all of this tumbled heedlessly on as it had done for decades.

He had often wondered how the place would change when the Chinese took over. Now everybody knew; would their rule change even the mailboxes in the streets? He had noticed one as he strolled through the covered walkways and tunnels the evening before and had walked closer to take a look. Cast into the sturdy metal door was the Royal coat of arms and the entwined initials of Britain's Queen. The Communists would no doubt quickly paint over it to make it less obvious.

The previous evening, he had roamed around, finding his bearings again in the confusion of streets, alleys and shops, he wondered what would happen to the cripples and hungry-looking crones who still begged for alms in the various tunnels and walkways. Surely their poverty was incompatible with Communism's universal levelling? There were fewer of them now and he felt sure those that hung on would soon be removed.

Meanwhile, it was all still familiar to him, and memories came flooding back as he turned each corner. It was like seeing an old friend again, recognising once-familiar features and mannerisms. But this time the friend was subtly altered; no longer quite the same Hong Kong he had known. The place was indeed changing, as it had always changed; but soon China's red flag would be flying over the Mandarin in place of the red, white and blue of the Union flag.

But perhaps he was reading too much into it. After all, he had changed too. When he had first come here he had been a young man, hardly more than a boy; a brash youngster who thought he knew it all. In Hong Kong it had been the end of an era, when the Wanchai district was—if only just!—still a heaving mass of ragged humanity, the packed, jostling crowds filling the narrow streets and alleys, the dark canyons in the permanent shadow of the filthy grey tenements above. High above, at each level of those tenements, washing hung from stacked tiers of balconies that almost touched each other across the chasms, crowding out all but the tiniest glimpses of sky.

But, in spite of the noise, stench, squalor and human degradation of the place at that time, he had found it exciting. Its dubious shops and roadside stalls, its night-clubs, dingy bars and brothels; all of it had been vibrant and exciting to his young Western eyes then.

He remembered that the U.S. Sixth Fleet had been here on his first visit. The American soldiers and sailors had been on leave from the horrors of war in Vietnam, and he had seen unconscious young men being carried out of bars by Shore Patrols. These were generally foolish, naïve young greenhorns who had failed to buy enough of the things on offer: drink, or the girls who waited in tiny rooms upstairs. These failings would not satisfy the financial needs of the hard-eyed *mama-sans*, the crones who ran the establishments, and who therefore slipped them doctored drinks to quickly poleaxe them ... to make way for the next client.

There had seemed to be some hidden communication between the *mama-sans* and the Navy Shore Patrols waiting in the streets outside, because the limp bodies were very quickly removed by the smartly-uniformed marines almost as soon as they tumbled to the floor.

The establishments were too small to accommodate time-wasters—and unconscious bodies were a deterrent to other punters.

It had been very different then from the busy commercial centre that it had since become. Foster had been back to Hong Kong time and time again, over almost four decades, and each time he had seen the influence of civilisation encroaching relentlessly into the sprawl and squalor. It surged onwards as quickly as the various reclamation projects stole away the sea; as relentlessly as maturity changed him from a carefree young blood to a mature, urbane man.

He had had his moments here. He remembered the drunken pub-crawls where he and his colleagues, young men all, had teased the *mama-sans* in various bars and night-clubs, feigning interest in the girls on offer and then making a quick exit before the deal was consummated, until they were finally pursued, panting and laughing, by angry bouncers along labyrinths of narrow, winding alleys glistening wetly in pale lamplight.

Yes, Hong Kong was a place of memories for him. Memories of a changing metropolis; mirroring his own changing and maturing life.

In those days he had stayed in hotels less classy then the Mandarin, though still very large and good by European standards. He had saved money by smuggling his dirty clothes out to a tiny hole-in-the-wall laundry down a narrow alley nearby, to save money out of the fixed allowance the company made to cover out-of-pocket expenses. The official hotel laundry was fast and efficient, and if you used it the clothes were hung up in your wardrobe by the time you returned from work each evening, but it was a comparatively expensive service. The unofficial alternative outside saved valuable funds, which would be much better used to pay for drinks.

Again, to save money he had eaten in small cafés that abounded in the alleys outside.

Once, he had taken a visiting British engineer with him to one of these places. The man had been a rather prissy type who usually avoided becoming involved in anything even mildly adventurous, and clearly he had been pleased to walk away afterwards from what he had later described as "a rather *ethnic* experience", his lip curling at the adjective.

True, one was never completely sure of what would arrive on the plate, or how it had been prepared. On one occasion Foster had seen one of the café staff washing the evening's vegetables in the gutter outside. But the food always tasted good, and he had not suffered too many serious stomach upsets. What was more, the proprietor had been trained to present a receipt that concealed the cost of numerous beers under the general title of "food" (the company had been going through one of its petty "we don't cover alcohol in expense claims" phases at the time).

Now he looked at his watch and saw that it was time he went to his appointment.

Foster's thoughts were interrupted by the doorman returning to tell him that the car was waiting. A white Mercedes had drawn up at the service road in front of the hotel and the doorman opened the rear passenger door to let Foster in.

'Pacific Place One,' he said to the driver as he sank back into the seat and they pulled out past the red taxis picking up other guests from the queue at the hotel entrance. The address was the headquarters of New Age Energy Projects, the company that had been responsible for the engineering design of the doomed plant.

Young Paul Lee had been one of their employees.

As the car jockeyed for position with the other traffic piling into Ice House Street, Foster opened his case and checked that he had brought his map of mainland China. Then he picked up the briefing pack that Fiona had couriered to him.

The pack's arrival had interrupted his efforts to contact an old friend: someone he had hoped would be able to give him some background information on the Kung Tau incident. But the friend had proved to be elusive and Foster had wasted valuable time in his fruitless search. Consequently, he had not had enough time for anything more than a cursory scan of the briefing pack's contents. But he had read the accompanying letter, which gave a provisional itinerary for his visits to site and told him to present himself at New Age Energy's offices at 9 am. It added that he would not need an overnight bag on the first day, since this was expected to be little more than a quick tour of the site, in preparation for a more extended visit over the succeeding few days. However, the letter reminded him to take his passport, which would be needed for identification at several points during the day.

As usual, Fiona's company had been extremely efficient. They'd thought of everything.

On reading the itinerary, Foster had consulted his map and wondered how he was going to manage to reach Kung Tau, look over the damage and return within a single day. He reckoned it was a distance of a couple of hundred kilometres each way.

The note provided a brief summary of what was known about the incident. It included a résumé of what had been arranged for his visit. It told him that the New Age representative who would be accompanying him would be Chau Ki-On, a senior projects engineer with the company. Once on site, they would be meeting Tony Crabtree, who would accompany Foster during the initial survey.

The information on the Kung Tau incident was sparse, but it filled in some of the detail that had been missing from the newspaper reports. The notes summarised the preliminary assessment by New Age themselves, though the conclusions were very vague.

The damage to the plant had been so extensive that finding clues had been difficult. Only one thing was clear: a massive gas leak had been ignited by *something*. The difficulty was in knowing what that something could have been.

The New Age people had been hampered by being instructed to leave everything exactly as they found it, until an independent engineer arrived: Foster. And both Gold Win, the owner and operators of the plant, and New China Energy had themselves been told to keep away from the site.

Reading the report, Foster wondered once again who could be behind his assignment to the inquiry. Somebody very influential must be driving the show—to have held off those powerful organisations. Not to mention the insurance-company engineers and the Chinese Government itself. Whoever it was, they were applying pressure that seemed out of proportion to the scale of the incident.

And they had very deep pockets.

It went without saying that what had happened had indeed been a human tragedy and a loss of capital plant worth a lot of money. But large operational sites were hazardous places, and such things happened. An accident was usually a source of interest in the local papers for a few days, and then it would disappear from the front pages. True, this one had been big but, in spite of the fatalities, no members of the general public had been hurt. If they had, then the media would have shown more interest.

But as it was, it should have been a small deal: a nine-day wonder. Even if, to the intensely proud Chinese, the embarrassment may have been more serious than any other factor.

Given all that, the level of interest seemed excessive. It was clear that somebody had weighed it all up and been prepared to spend a great deal of money to find out what had happened.

But who? And why?

Foster was deep into his study of the documents and didn't notice that the car had pulled up at the kerbside until the driver opened the door. He looked up and packed the papers away when he realized where they were.

'I'll walk back,' he said in answer to the driver's question. The journey hadn't been too long; in fact, he had toyed with the idea of walking both ways. In the end, though, he had decided to take the hotel car—because he wanted to make a statement: he needed his arrival to be noticed.

That was another reason why he was glad that Fiona's firm had booked him into the Mandarin rather than the J W Marriott or Conrad, which were, after all, more conveniently adjacent to Pacific Place. They were each stylish in their own right but the Mandarin had a subtle class and authority that the others simply couldn't equal. In Hong Kong, appearance was everything, and the method of his arrival would have been efficiently signalled by unseen watchers.

The owner of the devastated power station, Gold Win Energy, was a sprawling conglomerate ruled by a true tycoon, Albert Leung. New Age was independent of his empire, but it was certain that his spies would be everywhere.

Foster knew that the Mandarin was totally independent of New Age or their partners and business associates. Even if the nearer hotels were equally autonomous—and he didn't know enough about their ownership to be sure—their proximity to the New Age offices meant that careless talk, or a casual encounter, could easily result in the leaking of information to interested parties.

On one occasion, many years previously, before computers and e-mails brought the means of instant electronic communication to everybody, he had asked his hotel's telex operator to send some confidential information to his headquarters, only to find a copy of his message—and the reply—waiting on the meeting-room table in front of his client the next morning. Wrong-footed and embarrassed, he had sworn never to repeat that mistake.

Now, as he arrived at the enquiry desk in the glitzy entrance hall of Pacific Place One, the uniformed porter checked his name carefully against the list of expected visitors before issuing him with an identity label on a blue ribbon that Foster put round his neck.

The New Age offices were on the tenth floor of the tower, and when he stepped out of the lift there a smartly-dressed female receptionist was waiting for him. The man at the enquiry desk must have rung through when he arrived.

'Dr Foster?' the receptionist asked, smiling up at him. She was a diminutive but pretty Chinese girl with her gleaming, sleek black hair expensively coiffeured. 'Come with me please.'

With her absurdly slender high heels clicking away on the tiled floor, she led him along the corridor, through a busy open-plan office, to an empty glass-walled conference room. There, in response to the receptionist's offer of a drink, Foster asked for a black coffee.

While he waited, he looked out of the window. He could just see where the old barracks and naval dockyard he had once known had been replaced by an extensive area of landscaped reclamation, with expressways threading through the widely spaced towers.

The door opened and a man came across the room, offering Foster his hand. He was tall for a Chinese, and his manner spoke of somebody who had travelled extensively. 'Dr Foster,' he said. 'I am pleased to meet you. My name is Chau Ki-On.' He took a business card from a smart black leather holder and offered it to Foster, bowing and holding it with both hands, Japanese-fashion. 'Please call me Chau,' he concluded.

Foster bowed in response and exchanged the card for one that Fiona had given him. He watched as Chau read it with an expressionless face.

'You have nice offices here,' Foster said. 'I was just admiring the view.'

Chau gestured to the window and the two of them stood for a moment, looking at the soundless bustle far below them. 'Ah, yes!' Chau said finally. 'We can still see the Harbour, but with the new development here we never know if that pleasure will last. We have moved here one year ago. With all the work in the north, we are growing fast.'

As they turned away from the window, Foster decided to wade right in to the purpose of his visit. He needed to know everything, up to and including the financial effects on all the participants, since the information they would give him could have in consequence been partial, and slanted in their favour. 'This Kung Tau incident: it must have been a severe blow to you,' he said. 'Will it affect your business much?'

There was a momentary pause before Chau replied. When it came, the response was guarded, hesitant, carefully phrased. 'We do not know yet. We are certain we were not responsible, but the investigation—*your* investigation, Dr Foster—will confirm that, I am sure.'

Foster wondered if it was a veiled prompt.

The receptionist arrived with two cups of coffee on a small silver tray. Chau offered one to Foster and held out the cream-jug, but it was declined. Foster was still jet-lagged, and he badly needed the stimulus of undiluted caffeine.

In response to Chau's questions, Foster explained his involvement. Then he asked how New Age were intending to proceed and what the authorities and the insurers would require. Kung Tau was an island off mainland China, and very much a part of the Peoples' Republic, but it seemed that the Chinese Government was taking a secondary role at the moment. Chau himself was clearly taking instructions from Fiona's company, and this seemed to carry considerable weight. The insurers, also, seemed to be content to wait for the results of his investigation.

There were still no clues regarding the identity of the ultimate mover behind Foster's presence here.

'We will arrange for you to go to the site as soon as you are ready,' Chau continued. 'This day will be a preliminary one: for you to form picture and make plans. You will come back tonight.'

'Good idea!' Foster looked at his watch and decided to probe the matter of their means of travel. 'But how long before we can get on site?' It was already 9.30 am.

'We have helicopter,' Chau said. 'It waiting at Wanchai Stadium. It will take you to airfield at Shantou. Kung Tau not far from there.'

At last Foster had the answer to how he would get there and back in a day, and he was impressed. High-level political involvement in the affair was becoming ever more clearly apparent. The fact that the stadium had been made available for this journey indicated the involvement of a powerful agency, perhaps the Government.

They finished their coffees and went out to the lift lobby.

At the basement car park a limousine was waiting to take them the short distance to the stadium.

To Foster's mind, helicopters were vaguely unnerving means of transportation. When a fixed-wing aircraft banks, centrifugal force presses the occupants into their seats, so that they are largely unaware of course changes unless the view from their window shows the earth rising or falling beneath the wing. In contrast, helicopter manoeuvres are stomach-churning lurches that threaten to tip you out of your seat if you are not firmly belted in.

Foster felt the familiar tightening of the belt against his midriff as their course curved out over the Harbour.

The sea below them was a glistening sheet of translucent jade, criss-crossed by the myriad ferries, cruise ships, freighters and dirty little working boats that ploughed their way busily through the choppy waters below, their wakes startlingly white against the green sea. The helicopter climbed over the gleaming silver and gold towers of Kowloon and for a moment Foster found himself looking down on the grey finger of the Pacific Club jetty pointing out across the waterway from Harbour City. Then they were away, across the yellow-grey sprawl of the city, punctuated by the deep green of its parks, up and up, over the colossal winding curve of the new airport highway, and soon they were sweeping across the towers of Sha Tin, looking like a toy town below them.

The waters of Tolo Harbour and the Plover Cove Reservoir were shining sheets of dimpled metal below them as they headed northeast along the coast. At one point the pilot took a broad loop to the north. No doubt the air space around the Daya Bay nuclear power-plant was a prohibited area, kept free of flights to avoid any risk of a terrorist attack or an aircraft crashing into the reactor buildings.

Foster was getting a chance to see one of the few parts of China that he hadn't yet visited. In the distance, a line of blue-grey mountains to the north of their track paralleled the coast. He took the map out of his case to identify them. They were the Lianhua Shan range: Lotus Mountain. Foster remembered reading somewhere that it had served as a line of defence against the British in the Opium Wars and was known locally as the 'Great Wall of Guangzhou'.

Before long they were at their destination. They circled the airfield once and hovered briefly over the helipad before descending to land precisely on the cross-bar of the letter 'H' painted in yellow in the centre of the circle.

A car bearing New Age livery was waiting for them, and within half an hour they were driving over the narrow causeway to the island.

Until that moment, Foster had seen only the one newspaper photograph that Fiona had shown him in the pub. It had been inadequate preparation for the appalling scene that confronted him now.

It was awesome. Chillingly frightening.

One whole flank of the power station had been torn away. Jagged steel bars protruded from the rubble, like the ribs of the huge, half-buried skeleton of some monstrous pre-historic beast. A strange, uncanny silence hung over the scene, broken only by the occasional flapping of scraps of cloth and paper impaled on the sharp splinters of steel; the wind that, at the height of its fury had witnessed the destruction of the plant, was now gently playing with the wreckage. Even after all this time, the air still bore an acrid stench of burnt plastic and scorched concrete.

Foster understood then how lucky the survivors had been. The sturdy control block had shielded the administration building from the blast, and Albert Leung's imposing headquarters had been largely unscathed.

They alighted from the car and stood looking at the wreckage in silence. During the journey Chau had told Foster that he had already seen the devastation but, in spite of this, he still seemed to be shocked to confront it again.

Foster shook his head slowly in stunned amazement and took a camera from his case. 'Let's start, shall we?' he asked grimly. This was not going to be pleasant. He had seen damaged plant before, possibly the worst being when he had been flown in to Kuwait after the First Gulf War.

But in the Middle East then the damage had been deliberate: the vengeful, calculated destruction of an enemy's infrastructure by a thwarted army in retreat. Strangely enough, for all the power of its modern weaponry, the Iraqi Army's impact on the Kuwaiti power stations had somehow seemed limited, contained to small areas of severe damage.

Walls had been knocked down; pipework bore the impression of rampaging tanks; control rooms had been torn apart by explosives.

But in contrast with the damage there—which had been mindless and deliberate but in the end largely repairable—the destruction here, although accidental, was total. Incredibly complete.

The wreckage had been sealed off by a hastily-erected wire-mesh fence, and an armed Chinese PLA soldier guarded the single entry gate. He stared hard at Foster as he checked their papers. Then he opened the gate and let them pass.

Starting from a point just inside the gate, Foster worked methodically from one end of the shattered building to the other, photographing major items and carefully writing notes on a small notepad as they progressed. With Chau's help he took careful measurements and wrote down the location, angle and height of each picture as he took it. At each move, he checked carefully to ensure that they were well away from unsafe masses hanging above them.

At one point he reached out and held Chau's arm, pointing upwards. The New Age man had been about to walk over to examine the wreckage of a pump that had caught his interest. He had apparently not seen the threat of a huge steel beam that was hanging high over his head. It was bent and tilted downwards now, but it still supported a mass of dangerous brickwork: part of a wall that was still, incredibly, balanced there. The whole unstable mass was crazily cantilevered from the remaining wall, ready to come crashing down at the merest vibration or puff of wind.

As they progressed, Foster began to develop an idea of where the blast had originated and its height from the ground. He did this by looking at the direction in which debris had been ejected and by noticing the impact damage on parts of the structure that were still standing.

After almost an hour of this painstaking work, he stopped in front of three large metal objects: they were massive valves that had once controlled the flow of gas to the plant. He stared at them in amazement.

Amongst all the wreckage, and although they had been torn from their mountings and their actuating mechanisms ripped off, the valves themselves were almost unscathed. He examined each of them minutely and then photographed them from all possible angles. Then he moved on.

'Mr Chau,' he said eventually. 'I'll need to see the plant logs.'

Chau's normally impassive face showed a brief flicker of concern. 'The logs?' he asked.

'Yes.'

The logs were the routine hard-copy records—on paper—of events that had occurred in the plant. Some of the logs were generated automatically by the computers, the others were journal entries, hand-written by the plant operators.

'Ah yes,' Chau said, looking relieved. 'I think all logs were put in room in administration block. For safe keeping. Block damaged very little. But some records still in control room.'

'OK,' Foster said. 'We'll start there.'

They went up to what remained of the control-room and Foster sifted through the computer print-outs and the operator's journals. The latter were in Mandarin, and Foster had to ask Chau to itemise the key points and expand on areas which could be of special interest.

'That's fine for the moment,' Foster said after he had scanned through much of the data. 'Now, can I see the Interlock Defeat Log?'

This was a record of any actions that may have been taken to temporarily by-pass the plant's safety interlocks: the vital safety-net that protected it against failure and mal-operation.

During the construction and even during the routine operation of a power-plant, it was occasionally necessary to override some of the safety precautions, to avoid a delay or to test something. But because of the importance of the interlocks, any action taken to bypass them has to be authorised by a competent and responsible engineer, and the act of disabling them had to be recorded in a logbook: the Interlock Defeat Log that Foster had now requested.

It would be crucial to discover if somebody had overridden a protective interlock prior to the explosion.

Once again, Chau looked uncomfortable at Foster's request. 'So sorry,' he said, in a voice that was scarcely above a whisper. 'Not possible.'

Foster frowned at him. 'I was promised full co-operation,' he said. 'Are you saying you're not willing …?'

'No, not unwilling.' Chau blurted out the interruption. 'Not possible. Interlock Defeat Log … it is lost.'

'Lost?'

'Yes,' Chau said. 'We not sure if log under debris, or thrown somewhere. By blast.'

'But it's very important!' Foster protested, frowning his concern.

'I know, Dr Foster. We have searched. Very thoroughly. It is not found.'

Foster gave him a long look and sighed. 'Very well. But you will continue to search?'

'The instant it found, then we bring to you.' Chau's tone sounded evident relief that Foster was not pressing harder for the log.

'Thanks,' Foster said. It was unfortunate, but he had to continue. He'd have to manage as well as he could without the log. 'Well,' he continued. 'Then, can I see the detailed layout drawings of the plant, please?' By relating the photographs to the drawings he would be able to pinpoint the source of the explosion more exactly.

Chau was ready for that. He nodded and said that the drawings were already waiting in the administration block. He suggested they could look at them after lunch.

The pair left the wreckage and headed towards the administration block.

A light buffet lunch had been laid on in one of the offices, for just the two of them. Evidently Gold Win did not want them to be delayed by having to queue in the site canteen … or was it that they didn't want Foster to talk to anybody working in the place?

Foster was poor company while they ate. He was deep in thought. By then, he had begun to form a rough idea of the situation and, although it was far too soon to be sure, if what he was beginning to suspect had in fact happened, something very strange indeed had been responsible for the explosion.

After they had finished eating, Chau telephoned somebody and the buffet was wheeled away by two uniformed waitresses. Chau picked up a stack of drawings from a chair and put them on the cleared table.

Then, just as they were getting ready to study the drawings, the office door opened and Tony Crabtree came in.

'Dan! It's good to see you,' he said, striding forward and offering his hand.

Foster grinned in pleasure at meeting his old friend. But he was shocked by the change in Crabtree's appearance. He remained a handsome, well-built man and there was still something of the old devilish twinkle in his eye. The neatly-trimmed moustache and the thin gold chain visible at the open neck of his crisp white shirt spoke of a somewhat raffish character, but he now looked ten years older than his true age. Deep lines of tiredness edged his eyes and his cheeks were drawn.

'Tony!' Foster clasped the hand. 'It's been too long. And I'm sorry that it had to be under these circumstances.'

'I know, Dan. It's been … what, five years, I guess?'

'About that. Perhaps more.'

'What have you been up to since we met?'

Foster smiled. 'A lot, Tony, and life's just great—never been better in fact! But it's a lot to tell. Perhaps one night, over a beer?'

Crabtree nodded and said, 'Good idea! I could do with the break.' There was a wistful look on his face, showing the strain of being virtually imprisoned in China.

Crabtree said that he had heard about what had happened to Foster at Universal Digital and, to his way of thinking, Foster hadn't deserved the treatment he'd been given. He looked forward to hearing what had happened afterwards.

'Still, that's for later,' Foster said. He pointed to chairs round the table. 'Come and sit down, Tony. I want to talk to you about what happened here. I've heard you were on site at the time.'

They sat facing each other across the table while Crabtree told him about the storm and about his and Paul Lee's attempt, just before the explosion, to trace the cause of the strange disturbances in the readings.

Foster's ears pricked up at the reference to the intermittent fault. 'Oh?' he said.

'Yes, it was weird. Do you think there's any relation between the two things? The computer readings and the explosion, I mean.'

Foster shook his head thoughtfully. 'It's too early to say. I hadn't heard about the odd readings 'til you told me just now. But at the moment I can't see it. It hardly seems credible that there could be a link.

'Anyway, tell me… you said Paul went to look at something. Do you think he could have done something while he was down on the plant? Something he shouldn't have?'

It was Crabtree's turn to shake his head. 'No,' he replied vehemently. 'Paul was too experienced to do anything stupid, Dan. You know that.'

'Yes, of course. But anybody can make a mistake, and it's a question that has to be asked; if not now, by me, then later, by somebody else. After all, the events do coincide in time, roughly.'

'Yes, but so does the storm.' Crabtree said. 'Like a hundred other things.' His tone was irritated.

'Sure. And believe me; I'll be looking at them all.'

They went on, discussing what had been happening immediately before the explosion. And as he detailed the events, Crabtree re-ran the scene in his memory…

Chapter 5

Under the blaze of the tropical sun, the island was a gaunt outcrop of craggy rock jutting out of the surging, glistening, jade-green waters of the South China Sea. Against the heat-hazed, washed-out sky, shrieking gulls wheeled and dived at it. Diamond-bright patches of noise and movement, the birds seemed to be screaming in frenzied protest at the rock, almost as though it was an intruder; a massive fist of sinew and bone, suddenly bursting through the surface of the sea in a spray of white sparking spume, thrust from below the waves by some violent submerged giant.

From a vantage-point on the cliff overlooking the site, Crabtree and Lee stood and watched the huge yellow machines roaring and clanking in a thin haze of blue diesel exhaust, levelling the rock-strewn ground to form a platform. They were extending the massive base for the steel-and-concrete structures that was already taking shape where once there had been a mountain.

A few months before, construction engineers had detonated a series of controlled explosions that had brought part of the mountain crashing into the sea, roughly shaping the rocky platform where the machines now laboured. Afterwards, towering above the bulldozers and the confusion of activity, the newly-exposed face of rock stared stolidly at the frenzied comings and goings at its feet. Its sharp features shone wetly as streams trickled down the scarred surface; like tears of pain being shed at the injuries it was suffering.

To the northern side of the construction site, a slab of putty-coloured concrete had already risen, an imposing administration building and, alongside that, the vast shell housing the giant machines that formed the first part—Phase 1—of the new power plant being constructed by the Gold Win Energy Company.

The island was now linked to the mainland to the North, beyond the administration block, by a causeway carrying a four-lane highway, now almost lost in the dust raised by the continuous stream of trucks bringing construction materials to the site and taking away the spoil.

Crabtree could feel the sun burning the back of his shirt as he lifted his safety-helmet briefly by its peak, allowing the welcome draught of air sweeping up the rock face to cool his head a little. He pulled a handkerchief from his trouser pocket and mopped his brow.

He had been living and breathing the Kung Tau project for many months but, although he had been working on such dramatically large undertakings for many years, he could still feel exhilarated when months of careful planning and engineering began to bear tangible fruit such as the giant sprawl of bustling activity that stretched before him now.

From a distance, a power station looks like a factory: a stark, bulky structure beneath towering chimneys. Indeed, it *is* a factory, though the commodity it produces can't be seen.

Its product is *energy*, transmitted to the consumers along cables that straddle the landscape in giant leaps, swaying from tall lattice-work towers, or hidden from view, deep underground. Nothing moves in the cables, yet the energy they deliver can move mountains. It serves the needs of entire cities and isolated houses alike, factories and hotels, hospitals shops and night-clubs.

As they looked down at the site, Lee's voice broke into Crabtree's thoughts, 'It's looking good, Tony?' It was a statement of fact more than a question.

Crabtree nodded. 'Yes. It certainly is. And it's on time.'

That alone should have given Crabtree cause for rejoicing. After ten years of working on projects that had run hopelessly late, at last he was involved with one that was actually well within target, on schedule and under budget, against all the odds.

At one time, meeting the stringent Kung Tau programme had looked impossible. Nobody had expected that a plant as big and as complex as this one could have been built in such an incredibly short timescale. But already the first of the huge machines was complete, well ahead of schedule; already providing power for the engineering and administrative staff that had started to arrive on this previously deserted spot, to drive the remainder of the project onward. The original schedule had been defined in a mood of enthusiasm, almost a challenge hurled down by a team of consultants and contractors who had been desperate to show what could be done with the emerging resources and skills of the People's Republic of China.

Inevitably, however, it had to be an international effort. Although skilled engineers had been made available from Beijing and Hong Kong, and although the construction workforce was almost entirely Chinese, the design and supervision teams comprised many Europeans, North Americans and Australians.

'This'll be something to tell your grandchildren, eh, Paul?' Crabtree said.

'Yes, Tony. You know my family come here to see this constructions, once?'

'No! When?' Crabtree asked in response to the question. He had long ago developed a blind spot for Lee's linguistic vagaries; after all, Lee's grasp of English was streets ahead of Crabtree's abilities in Cantonese or Mandarin.

'The company have big Open Day when first generator set started. Everybody asked to come, with family. They stop construction for two day; one to get ready, one for the visitors.'

'They must have been confident of the programme!' Crabtree laughed. It was so rare to be on target with big construction projects that any advance on the planned programme was grasped eagerly, carefully gathered up and saved for a rainy day that everybody half-expected to come sometime. Either saved, or used to claw back a financial reward for generating electricity early; the millions of watt-hours sold starting to repay the huge cost of the investment, ahead of the financial backers' expectations.

To have given up that opportunity ... now *that* showed real confidence. But start-up of the first set, the huge generator with its driving gas turbine and all the auxiliary plant... that was a key date on the programme, and here it had happened ahead of time.

'They had six week, Tony,' Lee grinned in return. 'Six week ahead of target. Easy to spare one day, or two. It good luck to celebrate!'

Crabtree smiled. In spite of their rapid development over the past century, it was sometimes hard for the Chinese to abandon old and deep-seated superstitions. Even when it came to the construction of a huge modern plant like Kung Tau, in nearby Hong Kong—with all its sophistications—it was usually considered wise to hold a preliminary consultation with a Feng Shui man, a sort of Oriental witch-doctor, before embarking on any construction project, from a small outhouse to a complete factory. Here in the PRC such superstitions were officially deprecated, but everybody knew that the basic fears lay hidden deep within the workers' psyche. Everybody knew the importance of ensuring that the building aligned with all the good influences and allowed no scope for bad spirits to enter. This time, however, the Chinese authorities had decreed that the designers should turn their backs on the old ways. The decision had caused some concern among many of the local Chinese, and the celebration had doubtless been an opportunity to propitiate any spirits that may have been offended by this slight on the part of the administrators.

'How did it go?' Crabtree asked. 'The open day.'

'Great! They lay on many coach for us ...'

'I suppose the usual rules applied and you had to split off from the other engineers?' Crabtree asked mischievously. 'Diversifying the risk!'

It was a standing order in Gold Win Energy that no large group of key staff should ever share the same train, bus or aircraft, so that no single accident could take out too many of the company's important people at a stroke.

Lee smiled broadly. 'Yes, but Pauline and the kids … they travel with me.' Then he added a little joke, conspiratorially. It was a demonstration of his Western thinking. 'Diversifying risk apply only to company,' he said. 'Not to family!'

Crabtree laughed. 'But did they enjoy their visit?'

'Oh yes! You know, they have never seen a power plant in construction? Pauline has seen one when it was finished, but the kids? Never!'

Large power-plant construction sites are dangerous places. In spite of stringent safety precautions, close observation of safety procedures and strict enforcement of rules, accidents did happen—and when they did, at a plant full of massive metal structures spinning at colossal speeds, pipes carrying superheated steam, and cables bearing very high voltages, accidents could be spectacularly severe. Superheated steam is instantly lethal. More than five times the temperature of the visible steam escaping from a boiling kettle, an emerging jet of superheated steam forms no condensation cloud for some distance from its source, so it is totally invisible.

Invisible, but instantly lethal to anybody who walks into it. They will be sliced in two.

And steam was only one of the hazards; there are many more.

Construction workers and staff did occasionally get injured or killed on these sites. For this reason, families or casual visitors were never shown round until construction activities were completely ended. And even then unforeseen incidents sometimes happened.

'Did they lay on a good show for the kids?' Crabtree asked.

'Very good! They even set up mini-train ride through turbine hall, and full-scale space simulator. Even Pauline impressed!'

'Right! Now she'll understand what keeps you working so late every day.' Crabtree smiled and then looked at his watch. 'Whoops!' he exclaimed. 'We're nearly out of time, Paul.' They were scheduled to attend a progress meeting in the administration building's conference facility at 10 am.

'OK. Fine!' Lee responded. 'We be in good time if we go down now.'

Crabtree had arrived early for the meeting that day. Desk-bound for too long by the heavy involvement with the details of the engineering design, he had been interested in seeing how the reality was going; how it compared with the designs he had seen evolving on the computer screens every day. His old friend Lee had taken him on a tour of the site, culminating with the visit to the cliff-top to get an overall view.

They began the steep climb down to the construction grade, picking their way carefully over the rough ground, their steel-capped safety boots scattering the loose scree and sending it clattering down the slope in a amall dusty avalanche.

As Lee and Crabtree neared the administration building a long black car came into view, bouncing and swaying slowly along the rough approach road. It was a stretched Lincoln with smoked windows, and its suspension gave it a lolloping motion as it traversed the roughly made-up road, leaving a cloud of ochre dust hanging in its wake.

'The brass is here then,' Crabtree said softly. The car was well known in this part of China; it belonged to Albert Leung, President of Gold Win Energy.

Leung was a millionaire property-owner whose fortunes had blossomed with the emergence of China into the new age of freedom. He epitomized the new breed of young, ambitious and determined Chinese entrepreneurs. Starting from humble beginnings in importing and exporting consumer goods, he had built up his personal fortune and quickly diversified into property; initially building and selling apartments in the new Special Economic Zones, and afterwards entering the lucrative hotel trade. He had built a massive tourist hotel in Guangzhou, and then others in Shanghai and Beijing; just in time to benefit from the boom in the local economy and the explosive growth of tourist traffic to those areas.

But, although it had developed rapidly, the Chinese infrastructure of the time was still a fragile thing, and all too often it broke down under the strain of coping with a burgeoning population. Power cuts were frequent, and Leung's hotel guests were often subjected to power blackouts that plagued the area at the time. Left stranded in stalled lifts, sweating without air conditioning and with no hot food in the restaurants, the tourists became understandably fractious and difficult to placate. Soon a trickle of compensation claims built up to a flood, and as the stories began to circulate the cancellations mounted.

Leung swore to rectify the situation. Targeting the root cause of the blackouts, he formed his own power-generating company, Gold Win Energy, and embarked on a visionary programme of building power stations on a joint-venture basis with state-owned Greater China Power Collaborative, the central power-generation authority of the People's Republic. The plants were designed to augment those already built many years previously by other entrepreneurs, and they were very effective. Real stability of electricity supply at last started to arrive as the commissioning of the first of the Gold Win plants began. Then, slowly, Leung began to encircle his competitors. Power-generation had restored the fortunes of his hotel empire; now he saw an opportunity to extend his influence. The more he controlled electricity, the life-blood of modern commerce and industry, the more his competitors would be dependent on him. And then they would be at his mercy.

Kung Tau had been planned to seal the knot and, for the first time, to apply real competitive pressure on the rival power suppliers.

And it was Albert Leung's baby: his, and his alone.

All the same, as proud as he was of the project, it was virtually certain that he would not actually be in the car that was on site now. He had once been quoted to have said: 'Great leaders do not get too near the coalface'.

However, to his friends and allies he was remarkably generous; a powerful tycoon who liked to flaunt his material possessions and, on this basis, he often made his personal limousine available for the use of carefully selected visitors.

Crabtree had wondering who had earned this high honour today, and how he had done it; so he had watched closely as the Lincoln rocked to a standstill and the driver stepped out to open the passenger door.

'Good God!' Crabtree said quietly when he identified the man emerging from the car. 'What's he doing here?' It was Andy Johns, the Managing Director of Universal Digital Systems. Dan Foster's nemesis.

After months of work, developing their proposals for Kung Tau's powerful computer control systems, putting prices together and then engaging in a great deal of hard bargaining with the client, Universal had triumphantly won the contract to supply the plant's critical and all-powerful automation systems.

Although Andy Johns had, as was his habit, been very active and highly visible while the contract was being negotiated, it was also his practice to disappear from the scene after the accolades had died down. As soon as the order was safely in the bag he would move on, to start the process all over again in another country, on another project. He never involved himself in the day-to-day running of any project.

And that was what was so strange about his appearance at a routine progress meeting today. It indicated that something unusual was brewing.

'You think Mr Johns try to re-negotiate contract?' Lee asked with a frown. Johns was known as a commercial wheeler-dealer who left the complex engineering aspects of his company's operations to his minions, but who quickly became involved again if anything looked like presenting an opportunity to increase profits—or if it risked diminishing them.

'Good Lord, no!' Crabtree laughed. 'He'd never risk annoying his pal Albert Leung by doing that. It's all sewn up, and *nobody* changes the terms of a deal on our Albert; not even a shrewd cookie like Andy Johns; *'Specially* a shrewd cookie like him. Pals they may seem to be, but Albert trusts him as much as he'd trust a rattlesnake. But something's up, you can be sure of that, and I suspect it won't be long before we find out what it is.'

By then Crabtree and Lee had moved to a point that permitted them a view of the other side of the Lincoln as the chauffeur opened the door on the opposite side of the vehicle. 'Wow! Who's that?' Crabtree exclaimed as, to his delighted approval, an elegant female leg appeared through the door.

Lee shook his head. 'I don't know. Mr John's wife, you think?'

It was an honest, innocent question, and Crabtree suppressed a smile. 'Oh no!' he said. 'Definitely not!' He had met Enid Johns once, at a reception thrown by Universal when Universal was angling for the Kung Tau project. Because of Andy Johns' showiness Crabtree had imagined him to be married to a model, or an elegant, sophisticated society beauty. It had been a shock to find that Enid Johns was a timid little thing, a pale, slender woman with fine mousy-coloured hair. Although not quite plain, she wasn't the vivacious beauty one somehow expected to be on the arm of someone as flamboyant as Andy Johns. She had seemed a little ill at ease at the reception, as though it was not really her scene. From her occasional giggles and swaying, Crabtree had guessed that she had quietened her nerves with a cocktail or two before arriving.

In contrast with Mrs Johns, the woman who had emerged from the Lincoln now was strikingly beautiful and composed. She was tall and well dressed, with a light tan and glistening dark hair that gave her something of a Spanish look. Even though the move from the cool air-conditioned comfort of the car to the heat and dust outside must have hit her like a hammer, she showed no sign of being discomfited. She still managed to look cool and self-possessed.

'Perhaps mistress?' Lee ventured seriously, guessing at the woman's role as he ogled her lasciviously. In his mind, he could see the two of them entwined on black silk sheets.

Crabtree laughed. 'I doubt it! Oh, I don't doubt he's got a woman in tow here somewhere—I know he's a bit of a lad with the girls. But he'd hardly bring a mistress to a meeting, would he?'

The party made its way from the limo to the building. They walked along a rough gravel path, and Crabtree had to admire how the woman maintained her balance on her high heels.

Johns and the woman entered the administration block, and within a few moments Crabtree and Lee followed them in.

The building was spectacular, an immense open area of grey and silver; its glistening marble floor reflecting a cascading fountain that was its centrepiece. Near the fountain, giant pot-plants flanked a gleaming stainless-steel reception desk that encircled a tall tree. The tree was a ginkgo, the so-called 'living fossil' that Leung had adopted as the main emblem of his elaborate company logo. It had been moved here at enormous expense shortly after the building had been completed.

From the tall, crystal-domed atrium at the centre of the reception area, arched corridors led away to the various offices that for the past few weeks had begun to be occupied by the administrators and staff of Leung's vast empire.

The time and money spent in creating this showpiece had drawn some criticism from the hard-pressed construction companies who had worked on the project. But when it had been completed there was no doubt that it was a powerful statement of Kung Tau's position as the jewel in Albert Leung's crown. It underscored how all of those involved should be proud to be part of a grand enterprise.

In contrast with the oppressive heat and humidity outside, the crisp, cool, air-conditioned environment inside the building hit like a physical shock and Crabtree shivered momentarily as he and Lee entered and signed in.

Crabtree won a smile from the pretty receptionist as he signed the visitors' book, and he grinned his appreciation at her.

Many years ago, he had developed what he had called the 'Crabtree Scale' for evaluating women in foreign lands. Like the Richter Scale for classifying earthquakes, the Crabtree Scale judged a woman's explosive impact on men with a scale of numbers. But this time the numbers were based on how many days he had to be alone in the country before he would come round to finding the local women appealing. On this basis, the higher numbers were accorded to the less attractive women. In some of the remote tribal areas in which he had worked Crabtree would have had to have had to be desperate for sex before he became involved with the women. Even if they were young and bare-breasted, ritual scars on their cheeks and columns of brass rings stretching their necks were off-putting to his Western eyes. After a few weeks of monastic living, however, repulsion inevitably gave way to lust.

In recognition of the basic nature of the human male, the Crabtree scale had three component numbers that related to three areas, started at ground level and working upwards. The first number defined the legs, the second the torso, the third the face. The tribal woman would have been something like a 3-2-9 on his scale; what one colleague had once crudely described as 'a paper-bag-over-her-head job'. With such a woman, the legs would have seemed quite shapely after just three days, and her breasts looked good from day two, but it would take nine days before the face seemed appealing.

Top of the scale was a 1-1-1, and the Kung Tau receptionist was definitely in this class. Any part of her would look good on day 1.

Apparently ignoring Crabtree's frank admiration, but aware of it and flattered by it, the receptionist directed the two men towards the main conference room, down the building's central corridor.

Crabtree's eyebrows arched in surprise. The choice of this room indicated a high-level attendance at the meeting. Lesser events were always accommodated in smaller rooms near the sides of the building.

Crabtree and Lee had arrived ahead of the meeting's scheduled starting time, but when they entered the room several people were already standing around the long mahogany table that ran down its centre. At the far end, their images reflected in the highly-polished surface of the table, Andy Johns and his attractive companion were talking to Brian Ward, the Project Manager.

Ward was a short, stocky Texan with bright red hair. Not a desk man, he was always happier clambering precariously on some high structural steelwork, sorting out the truth behind a foul-up, rather than chairing a meeting. But, a veteran of half a dozen massive projects in as many continents, he fully understood the need for strict control and discussion and he knew that these meetings were crucial and needed firm control.

And he controlled them firmly.

As he saw the two men enter, he smilingly beckoned them over.

'Tony, Paul,' he said. 'Come and meet Andy Johns and Carol Lopez, of Universal Digital.'

As they shook hands, Crabtree found the woman gazing levelly at him. Her grip was cool and firm, and he sensed that she was something rather special in this game; a combination of looks and brains. She gave her name again and added, 'Hello Tony, I'm Universal's Technical Director.'

Crabtree was impressed.

'I'm pleased to meet you,' she continued. 'I've heard a lot about you.' Spanish-looking she may have been, but her accent was pure Oxbridge.

'Good things, I hope,' Crabtree replied.

She tilted her head and smiled briefly, saying nothing before turning to greet Lee.

Andy Johns took the opportunity to come round and speak to Crabtree. 'Hi, Tony,' he said, expansive and affable as ever. Then, true to his usual form, with no idle preamble, he launched himself straight at the point. 'I suppose you're wondering why Universal's sent two Directors to a routine project meeting,' he asked, and then his tone dropped and he looked around to make sure nobody was in earshot before he concluded conspiratorially: 'Well, something very special's come up. We'll tell you about it in a moment.'

And he was right about Crabtree's un-asked question. Ordinarily, technical meetings such as this would have been attended by the Project Manager and engineers from the major participants: in this case, Gold Win, Greater China Power, New Age, Universal Digital and perhaps some of the main subcontractors. Apart from the project manager, senior administrators would rarely become involved in the many routine meetings about equipment and systems that were held through the months while the project grew and evolved.

As Johns had surmised, Crabtree was indeed wondering about what was happening.

Because something was definitely up! His mind was racing ahead, exploring every possibility so that he would be prepared to deal with the unexpected.

He knew Johns of old, and had a deep-seated distrust of him; though if he stopped to think about it he would have wondered exactly *why* he was so wary of him, since they had never actually crossed swords seriously.

He knew that shortly after Johns' appointment as Universal's Managing Director, Dan Foster had abruptly left the company. For many years previously, Foster had been a friend, but in spite of that Crabtree's had never discovered the reason behind the feud. Foster had been unwilling to talk about it in any depth. Crabtree had known that the two men had been long-time rivals and when Foster resigned he assumed it had been the result of a boardroom battle. Putting aside his friendship with Foster, Crabtree had a strong interest in knowing that no personal conflict would endanger his own livelihood. He had been concerned at the time that something about the feud would jeopardize progress on the Kung Tau project, but—so far at least—there had been no evidence to justify his fears. So far, the project had run to time and without any hint of trouble.

So far.

As the meeting room began to fill, Crabtree was further alarmed to see that an unusually wide cross-section of Gold Win people were present, and he even spotted a couple of faces from Greater China Power. Although

GCP were Gold Win's joint-venture partners on Kung Tau, it was unusual for them to play any significant part in what should have been a routine meeting, so the presence of two of their senior executives was ominous.

Ward's voice rang out over the hubbub: 'Folks, let's get started.' Every head turned to him as he waved expansively towards the table, and then everybody started to move along to find seats. Andy Johns and Carol Lopez sat at Ward's left, at the head of the table, while Crabtree and Lee sat nearest to them, opposite each other. On the wall behind behind the Universal people, a large video screen had been set up.

The quiet murmur from the Europeans, Americans and Australians took a few moments to die down; the Chinese, as usual at the opening of formal meetings, had quietly taken their seats and were now sitting impassively, saying nothing.

'You're probably wonderin' what's goin' on,' Ward said, and looked around at the nodding heads. 'Well, somethin' special's come up,' he continued. 'And the GCP and Gold Win managements have decided that this project should look at takin' a new direction. A *whole* new direction.'

The room was hushed, every eye on him. 'Watch my lips, people: I said we should *look at* the thing for the present. I don't want anybody rushin' to conclusions. Nothin'—but nothin's, cast in concrete yet.

'I won't say anythin' more for a while—I'll hand you over to Andy Johns. You all know him, I think.'

There were puzzled looks all round as Ward sat down. His statements at meetings were always brief, but even by his standards this one had been unusually short.

Johns stood up and scanned the faces round the table for a few moments before he spoke. The effect of that long silence was dramatic.

'Gentlemen,' he said finally, his cultured English accent contrasting with Ward's American drawl. 'A few months ago, we at Universal Digital Systems completed a major project that has been occupying our best brains for more than two years. That project represents a truly revolutionary advance in control technology, and we have decided to give certain key clients the opportunity of taking advantage of it. So we have approached the senior management of each of those client companies and put the idea before them.

'We know the concern everybody in the industry has over using new, untried technology, but we had reason to be unusually confident that this would be the exception, allowing the client to win considerable operational benefits ... with no risk to himself at all.' He paused and looked round the room again. 'I am pleased to say that the senior management of Greater

China Power and Gold Win Energy immediately grasped the true significance of what we could offer, and have agreed to let us put it forward to this meeting for your consideration and approval. At this stage it is no more than that: a proposal of course, purely for discussion.'

For a moment his eyes met Crabtree's and there was a brief hesitation before he continued. 'I must stress that point. At this stage this is purely an idea, for discussion by all of you here. Because no decision will be made without the full approval of all the important people in this room.'

Crabtree snorted bitterly. *Fat chance!* he thought cynically. *You've virtually told them that Albert Leung has okayed the idea—whatever it may be—and you know that nobody here would dare to second-guess him: it's more than their jobs are worth. In any case, it would be a severe loss of face to back away from something when it's put over like that... and these guys don't like losing face.*

Johns' last phrase–'all the important people in this room'–had left just enough doubt. Was the room filled with only important people, who would jointly give the nod to the proposal, or would only a handful of those present here make the decision?

Crabtree shifted his gaze to look at Lee. It seemed incredible that New Age management would have not involved *him* in the secret, long before allowing matters to reach this point. Its presentation at a full-scale meeting of all the main contractors virtually guaranteed that the participants would be expected to rubber-stamp the decision: a decision that had, to all intents and purposes, already been made. Yet Lee had not even hinted of such developments to Crabtree. The two men were good friends, with a comradeship that went back over several years and many power projects, so it was odd that he had said nothing of something as significant as this. Also, Johns and Ward had talked only about the joint-venture operators, Greater China and Gold Win. They hadn't mentioned New Age.

And when Lee returned Crabtree's look he looked serious and gave a slow, small shake of his head, so that Crabtree understood.

So it was new to Lee too!

Crabtree wondered if anybody else at New Age had been in on the secret and if not, how the company would accept being cut out of the action.

'But, gentlemen,' Johns continued. 'I won't be able to tell you the virtues of the new concept as effectively as a true engineer, so I'll ask my Technical Director, Carol Lopez, to explain the concept to you in detail, and when she's finished I'll round up with a detailed summary of the financial and operational implications.

But for now, I'll summarise the development by saying that the new concept, which we have called Galaxy 2000, will be a revolutionary step into the systems of this Millennium.'

Crabtree's dark thoughts about this flowery introduction were interrupted by Carol Lopez. 'Good morning gentlemen,' she said, sweeping her gaze coolly and confidently around the table. 'Thank you for sparing the time to come here today. I hope you'll find it instructive and interesting, because I want to tell you about Galaxy 2000. It's a really amazing advance in technology, and we're very proud of it. I want to show how it came about, how we developed it, what it is, what it achieves and how it will benefit your project here—that is, if you decide to take it on board.'

She picked up a small remote-control unit and pressed a button on it. The video screen behind her came alive with the single title 'GALAXY 2000' written in gold on a blue background. In the bottom right-hand corner of the screen was the Universal Digital Systems logo, a golden globe held within a large golden 'U'.

Crabtree listened as she explained the concept. In spite of his concern, and his resentment at having all of this sprung on him at such a late stage in the programme, he admired the way Lopez put it over. After running quickly over Universal's background and experience in the field of power-plant control she explained, with the help of pie-charts and photographs projected on the screen, how they had decided to address the obstacles that all contracts such as Kung Tau faced once they had been running for a few years.

'Gentlemen,' she said as she pressed the button again. 'We all know the fundamental problems.' Another click at the button and the picture on the screen slipped upwards. Three lines of text appeared:

TECHNOLOGICAL OBSOLESCENCE
PROBLEMS OF RE-TRAINING STAFF
ESCALATING OPERATIONAL COSTS

'Here's the reality,' she said, and then spun the remote's trackball in her hand so that the arrow on the screen pointed to the first line. 'Item one refers to the very different lifespans of capital plant and the electronic systems that control them. A plant like Kung Tau is designed to last—what? —twenty years or more; but electronic systems, no matter how state-of-the-art they may be at first, are quickly out-dated.

'Some may say that the big control companies such as Universal are contributing to creating the problems by bringing out new systems every two or three years.' She turned from the screen to confront the nodding heads in the audience. 'But it's not like that,' she said, smiling. 'Manufacturers of advanced systems, such as ourselves, are always being driven by the advances in basic computer technology. If we were to stand back and say, 'Hey! What we've got here is pretty good, let's freeze it there,' we'd be driven out of business within five to ten years by competitors who had taken advantage of later developments in computer technology. Their systems would beat ours on price and would offer speed and power we couldn't match.'

She looked round at the sagely-nodding heads in the audience. Looking around him, Crabtree could see she had won her point.

'But we *do* know that the ones who have to bear the burden are you,' she said. 'You, the end users. Having made a massive investment in the latest and best technology, your company then finds itself having to cope with equipment that inevitably and inexorably becomes outdated. Systems become more and more difficult to maintain as spare parts become harder to find, and as the pool of engineers with knowledge of the older systems gradually shrinks.' She spun the trackball again to highlight the middle line on the screen.

'And that leads to item two: problems of re-training staff. When you do eventually buy a new system, you have to re-train all your maintenance staff to look after it, and your operators to use it. That's a high cost, gentlemen, and one that's often ignored.'

She pointed to the third and final line on the screen: ESCALATING OPERATIONAL COSTS.

'Re-training is a significant cost. But the term 'Operational Costs'—here—refers to the fact that, as your computer systems get older, maintenance costs grow out of all proportion to anything else, until you are eventually forced to start all over again. And then you get drawn into making yet another massive investment, and have to pay for yet more training that you hadn't anticipated.

'It all contributes to rising operational costs,' she continued.

There was a pregnant pause before she spoke again: 'And here's the truth, gentlemen ... It's something we all know, but few will admit. A plant's computer control system may not be the most expensive thing on it, but it's certainly very critical, and it's still a huge expense! Although computer prices may fall, the cost of ownership of the systems always climbs. And it soars whenever a refurbishment is forced on you.'

Lopez had touched a nerve there, one that was very raw to many in her audience. She spoke the next sentence slowly, stressing each and every word carefully: 'We all know it: computers control our plants absolutely, but the support costs never stop rising—until they threaten to outstrip every other operational cost on your plant.'

Then she paused and asked, 'So—and now here's a thought—what if someone were to offer you a system that would *always* be state-of-the-art; and yet one that would always remain truly cost-effective?'

In the ensuing hubbub, Crabtree smiled. *That'll get 'em! Right in the pocket!*

Plant people were always cost-conscious, but the Chinese as a race were truly canny, and the Chinese engineers working for Albert Leung were the canniest of them all.

The woman seemed to lean upward and backward, as though taking in a deep breath to say something extra important. 'Well, gentlemen,' she said. 'Two years ago, Universal Digital grasped that particular nettle; and here's the result.'

The video display flicked from screen to screen and as she spoke Crabtree began to see the idea.

The control systems of a modern power station are made up of many computers. They all work together; talk together. That's why they are called a DCS: a Distributed Computer System. The adjective 'Distributed' means that the computing functions are not centralized. The tasks they perform are shared between several computers, but all of these are housed in one place. The electronics systems in their suites of cabinets read information on the plant's operation, relay it to the operators' screens, and control everything that happens.

With the new system that Lopez was describing, the computing functions would be broken down and *really* distributed around the whole site. Every item of equipment that made up the complexity of the plant, each pump, fan and valve on it, would be provided with its own small computer, mounted close to the machine itself. And all of these would be linked together, to work as a cohesive whole. Given its own local intelligence, each machine would be aware of what it was supposed to be doing, and what other related equipment was doing at the time, that should cause it to change what it itself had to do.

The beauty of the Galaxy 2000 concept was that, because the computing power had been broken down into many, very small, inexpensive packages, any part of the system could be replaced at any time—at minimal cost.

'The system provides each plant item with its own computer,' Lopez said at the conclusion of her description. 'A bespoke controller, fitting its partner like a glove. They are all linked together and to the central computer.'

Around the table every eye was wide open, all attention on the woman as she continued. 'And now, the real beauty of it is this: when any change in technology comes along, all you need to do is replace a small part of the whole system, to take advantage of what the new technology offers. Improvements will be achieved incrementally, and this avoids disruption of your operations.'

The audience was still. Stunned into silence. Totally mesmerized.

Then Crabtree broke the silence. 'But what about the cost?' he asked. 'Surely you sacrifice the economies of scale when you break the system up into so many parts?'

'Good point!' Lopez replied. 'It was a factor that worried us at first. And then we saw that since there would be so many of the satellite computers, all identical, we'd actually *benefit* from economies of scale. Sure, we lose the cost-savings of putting everything together in one place, but we *gain* benefits by having so many identical small computers. Since they are small, they are very inexpensive. *They are small, tough and intelligent plant attendants.*'

Crabtree had to admire it all. As the talk continued he began to appreciate more and more of the whole idea. The thing was planned from the bottom up to be easy to install, simple to use and very easy to upgrade when something better came along.

The last feature was achieved by having standardised plug-in assemblies at the heart of the system. When something new came along you simply unplugged the old and plugged in the new. Advancing gradually. Step by step.

The one consistent thing—the thread that linked it all together—was the way the computers were communicated with each other. The component parts of the system talked amongst themselves in a well-established, industry-standard language. And by doing this, Universal Digital had made the system truly 'future-proof'.

Just as modern man is able to read and understand Shakespeare because of the common thread of the English language used by both ages of Elizabethans, each new development of the Galaxy system, no matter how novel or advanced it was, would always be able to work together with the older machines.

As each new development arrived the users could simply phase it into the system without altering the operation of the whole.

Lopez shut off the video projector at that point and addressed the audience. 'Now, gentlemen,' she said. 'The significant point is this: you already have the bones of the new system here—now.'

There was a muted buzz round the table. Lee caught Crabtree's eye and looked heavenward as if to say: *They're coming thick and fast! God knows what's in store for us next.*

Lopez continued, 'You see, with your agreement, we can supply the new system on Phase 1.'

With that an uproar broke out and she held up her hands to quell it, 'Yes, I know,' she said. 'I appreciate your concerns. But I'll ask you to listen to my colleague, Andy Johns, now. He'll explain.'

She sat down and, against the quiet buzz of whispers going round the room, Johns took over.

'Gentlemen,' he said. 'You've seen what we have to offer technically. Now, I want you to understand our commitment.'

Again he paused for dramatic effect before continuing, 'Last week, we made an offer to your management which is quite unique; and which I believe will prove our faith in the new system.

'At no cost to yourselves, and with a comprehensive guarantee to compensate you in full, should there be any failure to meet your present production targets, we at Universal Digital Systems will undertake to replace the present systems on Phase 1 with a full working set of Galaxy 2000 equipment. We will also provide you with comprehensive training in its use and we will undertake to ship the old systems off your site when you are quite satisfied with the new ones. And we'll do it without any escalation of the existing contract value or extension of its timescale.'

It was too much. Kung Tau was already in operation. Such major changes as those that Universal were proposing would represent a serious hazard to the important matter of generating electricity, and thereby jeopardise the vital aim of earning money.

Uproar broke out again, with everybody in the room shouting questions. Crabtree sat still for a moment, shocked by the possible consequences of what he had heard, and by his understanding of the implications behind them. It was a while before he spoke, but when he did he caught a brief lull in the hubbub, and all the others listened.

'But what if it *doesn't* do what you say?' he asked. 'OK, maybe the stuff we've got here now is soon going to be old-fashioned, *but at least we know it works*. It's here, and it's got a long, proven and good track record. The new system has none.'

There was a murmur of agreement from the audience.

'I know you're very confident,' he continued. 'But just for a moment let's imagine that the new system *doesn't* work out like you say. What then? Even if you reinstate the older system, what about the loss of production?'

With potential profits of over three quarters of a million US dollars for every day that they were running at full capacity, plants like Kung Tau threatened very expensive liabilities if they were out of action for even a moment.

Johns stared at him. He was smiling, but there was a small hard glitter in his eye. 'Of course,' he said confidently. 'Our offer is absolutely unconditional in that respect. I've indicated this already, but I'll repeat the details: *we will compensate you for any proven operational losses during the evaluation period.*'

Crabtree stared at him in amazement. The devil would be in the detail, and he felt sure Johns' use of the word 'proven' would be pivotal, but for Universal Digital to make such an offer, he must have put forward a pretty convincing argument to Albert Leung. The cost of delays would be astronomical; far, far beyond Universal's own resources, and probably beyond the cover of any insurance indemnity they could afford.

He must have persuaded GAI to cover it, Crabtree thought. Universal's parent company was a huge industrial conglomerate, Global Associated Industries. GAI was *very* cash-rich, and its massive resources, coupled with its reputation as a shrewd investor gave GAI the financial clout to provide the sort of protection that Johns was now promising. Although it was a prospective rival to his own company, GAI in fact maintained a healthy working relationship with EuroPower.

There was another outburst of speaking.

'Folks, listen,' Ward cried, rapping the table with his knuckles to restore order. 'We're not yet committed to this... But you must understand that the company has to consider Universal's generous offer very carefully. We all know that time is pressing. If we are going to do this thing at all, we have a very short window of opportunity to do it in.

'Therefore, we've drawn up a programme. The target is to reach a decision in time for a limited sub-set of the new systems to be incorporated into Phase 1 of this project. If that works out OK, the full scope will be installed on Phase 2.'

He paused and looked around at the open-mouthed engineers staring at him. 'That is,' he added, 'that is, *if* you agree to proceed. Because—like we said at the beginning—the ultimate decision will be yours.'

Then he announced a programme of meetings, and listed the names of the people who would attend. There was a frantic scratching of pens as everybody wrote down the schedule.

Crabtree and Lee figured high on the list for each meeting.

Ward closed the proceedings, adding that the routine progress meeting they had planned would be held in that conference room at the same time on the next day. By then, the engineers were expected to have made up their minds, and to say whether or not they wanted to take up the challenge. Any previous appointment that any of the delegates may have had was automatically cancelled...

This was big.

The press of people leaving the room was such that Crabtree didn't meet up with Lee until they had both emerged in the main entrance hall, where the delegates were milling around, discussing the morning's extraordinary proceedings.

Lee held up his hands and shook his head. 'I just didn't know, Tony,' he said. 'Believe me.'

Crabtree smiled grimly. 'Oh, I believe you, Paul. But what gets me is that they've manoeuvred us all into rubber-stamping the decision. A decision they've made already, and got Albert signed up to.'

Leung wouldn't have the faintest idea of the technical implications. He would merely have looked at the bottom line and seen something that pleased him very much indeed: greatly improved profitability for the project, no risk to the timetable—and a chance to show the world a brand new and revolutionary technological concept. The profits were the ultimate draw, but the chance to preen himself in front of his rivals—*that* would be the icing on the cake indeed. Because, after money, Albert Leung liked nothing more than the chance to show off, whether it was by entering a glitzy hotel with a stunningly beautiful Western woman on his arm, or by flaunting a spectacular new project to an admiring world.

The two men stood in silence for a while, trying to take it all in.

'Look,' Crabtree said eventually. 'When all the ballyhoo's died down, Paul, it's you and I who have to make the damn thing work.'

'And on time.' Lee shook his head, contemplating all the extra activities that would have to be crammed into a schedule that was already cripplingly packed.

Just then, Johns arrived with Carol Lopez. 'Ah, Tony,' he called. 'I think we need to talk. Brian's made a room available for us. Can you spare a moment?'

He knew very well that the progress meeting had been scheduled to last the whole morning, and since the performance they'd just attended had lasted less than an hour there certainly *was* time available—plenty of it.

The four of them went off to a small room, this time on the outer side of the block, with a splendid view out over the shimmering sea.

'I was sorry to drop that on you,' Johns opened as they sat down. 'But we had no choice. I'm sure you'll realise that this is commercially very sensitive. Our competitors would love to know what we're up to. That's why the development had to be kept under wraps until the last moment, and why we had to get the nod from Albert before we went any further.'

Crabtree could see that this much was true, and to some extent he understood Universal's dilemma. Industrial competitors were always trying to find out about their rivals' new developments, and word of something as revolutionary as this would spread like wildfire through the efficient bush-telegraph of the world's power-generation communities.

Crabtree shrugged. 'I guess you're right. All the same, you've given us quite a headache, you know.'

Carol Lopez smiled to reassure him. 'Probably a smaller one than you think,' she said quietly, and as Crabtree looked questioningly at her she continued, 'We really do think that the way we've structured the thing makes it very easy to change. But, because we know it means extra work for you, we intend to do more than our usual share of the engineering: to assist your people with meeting all the targets.'

'Oh?' Crabtree asked, with some bitterness. 'And how will that help? For Christ's sake, *everything* will have to be changed. Changing the control systems now just has to involve extra work, and we're snowed under as it is already. It would need a miracle to get us back on the programme again.'

She smiled. 'Of course,' she said. 'I do realize that there must be a lot of extra work. We understand that fully. But because we'll be drafting in extra engineering help—informed and experienced help—we'll make up the time.

'And remember this, what we're proposing for Phase 1 is a *limited subset* of Galaxy. OK, you won't be able to take the maximum advantage of the new concept. But the equipment will be fully compatible with Phase 2. And, of course, you'll gain some significant benefits.

'There's simply *no* down-side. You won't lose *anything*. We simply unplug the old and plug in the new.'

'You'll bring in people to handle the extra work?' Crabtree asked.

'Yes. For Phase 1 we will do all the engineering for the new system: from design to installation and commissioning. There's no extra work for you to do at all... unless you want to, of course. For Phase 2, on the other hand, we still do a lot, so that your programme doesn't slip, though you can still get involved if you want, so that your people learn about the technology.'

As she spoke, Crabtree's initial doubts began to evaporate, in spite of his instincts and fears. By the end of it, he could see that perhaps—just perhaps—it *could* all come together well. And if it did, it really would be a huge step forward for everybody.

He was forced to give Carol Lopez his grudging admiration. She knew her subject very well and was articulate in putting it over. She had the ability to quickly grasp the tangles of a complex idea, shake it loose and iron it out into something simple. He liked her direct and forthright approach; it was certainly very different from Johns' glib assurances. He felt he could trust her to meet her promises and he judged that she had enough power and influence in Universal to marshal the resources to make it all happen.

'So, can we assume that you're willing to proceed with the change?' Johns interrupted. He had sensed Lee and Crabtree were teetering on the brink; that they were more confident now.

He was closing in for the kill.

Crabtree wouldn't have been surprised to see him produce a pre-printed agreement from his pocket, there and then, for them to sign.

'No, wait a minute, Andy,' he laughed. 'Not so fast. We aren't the only ones you have to convince, you know.'

'Of course! You have your various departments to convince.'

'And our bosses,' Lee added.

'Yes, but you two... you're the *real* dealers here, aren't you.' Johns' smile and conspiratorial tone showed that he believed he had already won them over, that they were now all in the same exclusive club.

'The others will do what you say,' he concluded.

Crabtree looked at Lee and shrugged his shoulders. Johns was probably right. Over the years, the two men had built up solid reputations in their respective companies and it would be unusual for their departments to come up with something that they hadn't anticipated. No doubt that was why the project-management meeting had been hi-jacked: to ensure their attendance. Also, the lead provided by a man as powerful and as hard to please as Brian Ward, plus the presence of so many other departmental heads at the meeting, virtually guaranteed that the organisations as a whole would be keen for the concepts to be accepted; if they were not actually slavering for it.

No, it was tightly sewn up all right.

Johns sighed, as though it was all over. 'Good!' he said. 'Now to more pleasant things.

'Look, I'd like you two to come to dinner with us this evening. How about it?'

'Thanks, Andy,' Crabtree said, with a wry smile. 'But you know, we're a long way away from civilisation here.' He considered the prospect of a dinner in the only local restaurant, a sort of Chinese transport cafe that was usually full of people working on Kung Tau. It didn't appeal to him at all.

'Oh?' Johns asked, his features creased into a puzzled frown. 'Aren't you two going back to Hong Kong?'

'Yes,' Lee said, looking at his friend. 'But not until tomorrow morning.'

They hadn't really discussed their plans. Both of their normal office bases were in Hong Kong. The small air-strip at Shantou, a few kilometres from the site, was now busy with the comings and goings of people involved with Kung Tau. Gold Win's own aircraft made just two shuttle flights in and out each day, ferrying their own staff and New Age's to and from their offices in Hong Kong. Lee knew that the afternoon shuttle was already full, which was why he had been expecting to stay the night in one of the apartments provided by Gold Win, and to take the shuttle back to his office the next day.

'Why wait 'til tomorrow?' Johns asked. 'Come with us! We're flying back this afternoon.'

'Flying?' Crabtree asked. He knew the day's shuttle schedules were full.

'Of course! I thought this meeting was important enough to warrant chartering a plane. There's plenty of room.'

Crabtree stared at him. He wondered what the landing fees at Hong Kong's Kai Tak airport would have been for a chartered plane.

Pending the completion of the new International Terminal at Chek Lap Kok, the old airport at Kai Tak was still very busy, and in Hong Kong if there was an excess of demand over supply anything could be done, but it would get expensive. Facilities for executive jets would command high prices indeed.

'Well, I don't know ...' he began.

'Look,' Johns said. 'The seats will be wasted unless you two come along. We'll be in Hong Kong by the end of the afternoon. And I'd be delighted if you and Paul would be our guests at dinner tonight. How about La Ronda at the Furama? Come on, Tony, be sensible.'

Crabtree looked at Lee and saw from his starry-eyed look that he was hooked. A flight back on a private aircraft ... *and* dinner in the revolving restaurant at the top of the Furama tower ... it was too good an offer to refuse.

Both engineers had to complete some small but urgent tasks, and the Universal people said that Brian Ward had offered to take them to have a look over the site, so they arranged to go their separate ways and meet again at the airfield at 2 o'clock.

As it turned out, Crabtree's path didn't cross Lee's again for a while, and the next time they met was at the airfield, where Johns and Lopez were waiting.

The humidity and heat at the shimmering apron was almost unbearable as they walked across to the sleek aircraft parked on the concrete. It was a small seven-seat Jetstream, and after it had hoisted them effortlessly and quickly skyward Crabtree noticed that the 'plane turned to the east, whereas the route taken by the regular shuttle was broadly westward and southward. Then he understood.

This way, they would pass almost directly over the Kung Tau site.

He was sitting at the starboard window and as the wing-tip dropped at their turn he saw the island from the air for the first time. Even from this height, where the big machines crawling over the earth looked like so many tiny yellow beetles, it still looked impressive. The rock was lapped by breakers that were startlingly white against the blue-green sea, and the scarred brown of newly-exposed rock contrasted strongly with the dark green of the dense vegetation inshore. The cables that would carry the plant's energy back to the cities of the mainland area glistened in the sun like silver threads.

Johns was sitting on Crabtree's left and he leant forward to see the view. 'Looks good, Tony! Looks good!' he said.

And suddenly Crabtree knew that it had all been planned in advance: the offer of the flight, and this routing, with its turning point exactly here, right over the site, so that they could get a good view.

The Johns showmanship again.

Chapter 6

It had all seemed so easy at the time. But now, long after the event, as he sat answering Foster's questions Crabtree's regret was bitter. He should have fought harder. He remembered the uneasy, trapped feeling that he'd experienced at the time that the decision had been made. Instinctively, even then, he had known it was all wrong. It had been foolhardy to rush into accepting the proposal from Universal without proper consideration, and dangerous to play into Andy Johns' hands by accepting the offer of this flight. If anything went wrong it could be used to hint that they had been persuaded—bribed him, even—to suspend their engineering judgement.

It was as irrational as the superstition, overt or concealed, of the Chinese engineers; their fear that, without proper consultation with the Feng Shui man at its inception, Kung Tau had been doomed from the outset. But he hadn't been able to shake it off.

And sure enough, with a dreadful inevitability, all those fears had been realised.

Even though the cause of the accident had not yet been determined, he was certain that the change in the control system was somehow implicated. If it was, then the resulting devastation—and the death of his friend—had stemmed from that pivotal moment of weakness, when he had decided not to oppose the change that Universal's team had proposed.

Foster's voice cut across his thoughts. 'And they did that?' he asked. 'They took out the old equipment and replaced it with a brand new system?' His tone was incredulous. His briefing hadn't mentioned any of this. 'After you'd just finished commissioning the first part of the plant? After they'd got it all working? They started over?'

Crabtree nodded . 'I know. And I was worried about it as well. But they convinced me, Dan. They convinced us all, even hard-nosed old Albert Leung. What chance do you think we would've had to override what was effectively *his* decision. He's the boss. The head honcho out here, almost an emperor. Anyway, you said it yourself: it's hard to believe that the computer could have done all that damage by itself. Though I'm damn sure it did. It was the one new thing. Everything else was tried and proven.'

'Well,' Foster said. He was looking worried. 'Before I got here I believed the computer system was tried and proven too. But what you've just told me puts a whole new dimension to the thing.' He thought deeply for a while before continuing. 'And that makes me wonder whether I should back out of this thing; now, before I get in any deeper.'

'Why, Dan? It's your line of business, after all. Or it used to be.'

'Yes, but I've left it behind. Or at least I thought I had. Anyway, when I started ... when I was asked to get involved, I didn't think for a moment that Universal's system would actually come under suspicion. The very idea seemed quite incredible. The damage was too widespread, too severe. OK, the other people who had looked at it thought it had been responsible, but I suppose I hoped to find something to show that they were wrong.'

'But you haven't.'

Foster shook his head. 'Seems pretty bloody obvious,' he said. ''Specially now. So now it's back to square one. To accept they were right and pin down the exact cause.

'But I don't like it. I'm a bit too close for comfort.'

He stared at Crabtree, his expression sad as he said, 'You see, before I left Universal I was heading up the project to develop the new system. The one they installed here.'

'Oh shit!' Crabtree said. He thought about it in silence for a while and then said, 'But that's the normal thing, isn't it? You design something new, based on the previous generation, only better. It's called progress.'

'I wish that was all.'

Crabtree frowned. 'What do you mean?'

'Well, there were a couple of things in the new system that were ... well, quite revolutionary.'

'They told us. At the presentation.'

'Yes. But I'd been worried about them. I was seriously beginning to think about pulling the plug on the concept.'

'Why?'

'Because it was too far ahead of everything else we'd done,' Foster replied. 'I couldn't be sure it'd work out. I needed more time. Large-scale prototype trials.'

'But?'

'But Andy wouldn't hear of it. He said that trials would be too expensive and they'd hold up the project.'

He stood up and walked slowly towards the window. When he spoke, the words came slowly, quietly. 'Then I left.'

'Because Andy wouldn't let you pull the plug?'

'No. Not that alone. That was only part of the thing. But quitting left me with a bad taste in my mouth. And now, people could say I had every reason to bear the company a grudge.'

'Now that I know that it *had* to be the control system, I realize that I shouldn't carry on. I'm too personally involved. People could say my findings were biassed. To get some sort of revenge. You must see that.

'Christ, man! Can you imagine what would happen if I said it was Andy Johns' company that did all that damage? Killed those people? They'd say it was just me getting revenge on him. Everybody knows how much I disliked the bastard.'

Inside, he felt bleak. The dream of getting his finances into some sort of order had suddenly turned into a nightmare. Any prospect of receiving the second half of his fee was rapidly disappearing. He almost shuddered at a sudden thought: perhaps he would have to repay the first tranche.

Crabtree shook his head slowly. 'You can't back away from this now, Dan,' he said quietly. 'I need your help. It's personal. And it's not just the fact that I'm in a bind here—virtually a prisoner of the state. I *need* to know what happened. And I know you *can* get to the bottom of it.

'It's not just for me, Dan. It's for Paul too, and Pauline, and the kids. What happened to Paul was bloody awful. You should have seen him ...' His voice tailed off as he remembered. 'The poor sod. He didn't deserve it, Dan. Nobody does. He was a great guy. And as for his wife and kids ... Nothing that you find out can bring him back, but that's not the point.

'The company's being pretty generous to Pauline and the family. If you pin the blame on Universal it won't make a difference to her—not financially. But at the moment there's a strong undertow that Paul somehow caused the explosion. It's convenient. He's dead and can't defend himself, and blaming him means they can wrap it all up, all neat and tidy!

'You can stop that happening, Dan. You can lift any question of blame from Paul.

'And there's something even more important. If there *is* something dangerously wrong with the system, there's a chance that the same thing could happen at another plant. Don't you see? Somebody has to stop that happening.'

Foster turned and stared at Crabtree for a long time.

'You're right,' he said eventually; quietly, almost as if thinking aloud. He took a deep breath and continued, 'OK. I'll do my best. And if it *was* Universal's fault. *If* it was ... then I have to find out.'

Alex Cooper was in his late forties. A short, stocky man with thinning greyish-brown hair, he had the physique of somebody who had once been quite fit, before age and good living had taken their toll. But now, age was indeed beginning to tell. An elaborately-tooled leather belt strained against the bulk of the vast belly that overhung it.

He grinned with genuine pleasure at meeting his old friend again, and shook Foster's hand warmly. 'Wot-cher, Mate,' he said in the broad Cockney accent he had maintained in spite of his years of living in Hong Kong. 'What brings you here this time?' he paused and then winked and smiled knowingly. 'Nope! Don't tell me: it's gotta be Kung Tau.'

It was the day after the initial site visit, and after a long wearisome day at New Age's offices, poring over drawings and asking questions, Foster had telephoned Cooper and suggested they meet at the Mandarin. It was possible that Cooper could give him some background information. But in any case he needed to talk to somebody—somebody who would understand the technicalities—who could act as a sort of sounding board.

He had been relieved to find Cooper at work. After having spent some time during the previous evening in fruitless attempts to find him at home, Foster had begun to fear that he was out of town. But eventually he had succeeded in making contact.

Foster had taken care to be guarded on the 'phone, but it was apparent now that Cooper had already made the link between his visit and the Kung Tau incident.

Foster wasn't really surprised. A long time ago, the two had worked together on another power plant. It had been back in the 70s, when Cooper had already been working in Hong Kong for several years, and the pair had soon become firm friends. Over six months or so Foster had discovered that in his taciturn, almost reclusive way, Cooper was a solid, trustworthy and extremely competent engineer; a man firmly on top of his job. He was deeply involved with the power-generation business in the territory and, without doubt, he would have heard about the accident. Knowing Foster's history, he would have immediately connected his arrival here with the investigation, so his statement was not altogether unexpected.

'Right on the nose, Alex,' Foster chuckled. 'As usual. Anyway, let's talk over a drink.'

They headed towards the hotel bar beside the lobby, *The Captain's Bar*. It was relatively quiet at this hour, since the hotel's excellent Filipino band had not yet arrived for their regular evening gig. The two men sat at the bar and Foster asked, '*Black Label*, still, Alex? On the rocks?' Cooper nodded.

Foster's own choice was taken for granted; in the Mandarin it was already understood that he would have *Balvenie Double Wood*, served straight, with a small measure of water in a separate jug, and no ice. It was also understood that the glass should be filled as soon as he entered the bar, and that it should be refilled at his slightest nod to the barman.

Foster had slipped easily back into the saddle. It was good to have the trappings of power once again.

While they waited for Cooper's drink to arrive, Foster asked, 'So, how's Tina?'

Cooper's wife was a hard-bitten Canadian who had married him for the wealth and status that accompanied his job. A woman with few charms and no artistic leanings, she was a social chameleon, instantly developing those attributes that she felt enabled her to fit in better with any high-flying acquaintances.

Many years earlier, long before Foster's divorce, she and Alex had visited his home in the UK, and evidently she had been impressed by what she had seen, particularly Foster's collection of books. Soon after her return to Hong Kong, extensive shelving appeared in the Cooper apartment and this soon began to fill up with lines of impressively-bound books that she had trawled from the many local antique shops.

Once, thinking she possessed interests that he had hitherto not noticed, Foster had tried to open up a dialogue with her on one book that he had spotted among the collection. It was a particular favourite of his: Saint Exupery's *'Wind Sand and Stars'*, and he hoped this would form some sort of a bridge that could span the chasm between himself and his friend's wife. However, it quickly became very apparent that she had never read it. Soon he came to suspect that she had not read even one page of any of the other books on those shelves. It saddened him to think of all those volumes stacked up in that clinical apartment, all bought by the yard, to impress people; all of them unread.

Soon after that, a cottage grand piano had been delivered to the Coopers' apartment. She had evidently noticed Foster's own piano. The one she bought had had to be hauled painfully up the outside of the tower block, with the workers' usual disregard to the safety of people in the street below. It had been installed in their seventh-floor flat. Its arrival was much to the chagrin of her husband, who found it obstructing the view of the harbour that he had previously enjoyed while sitting in his favourite armchair, sipping his *Black Label*. To Foster's knowledge, nobody ever played the instrument, though it was always kept meticulously polished and tuned.

In contrast with his wife, Alex Cooper had no pretensions at all. An intelligent, pragmatic and quick-thinking man, he saw himself as a practical engineer who had too much on his plate to enjoy the arts. He had no interest in either adopting the arty lifestyle that his wife so much admired, or in dealing with her own façade of culture. Instead, he immersed himself in his work. Even his hobbies and pastimes were wrapped up with engineering.

His wife's airs vaguely amused him and, if the truth was to be known, he was probably somewhat embarrassed by them. His defence was to retreat behind the shield afforded by his work and his hobbies. He stayed long hours at the power station, and spent every possible evening and weekend with his cronies.

As a result, he had become a mine of information on the industry, with extensive connections in the region, on both sides of the harbour as well as in Mainland China. His lack of 'side' and his bluff Cockney charm could ease him past any defences, so that he could always be relied upon to obtain information on a wide variety of engineering topics.

Now, Foster needed to tap into that knowledge.

'OK Alex,' he said as the drinks arrived. 'What's the scuttlebutt?'

'Difficult to know where to start, Mate,' Cooper said as he took his first pensive sip of whisky. 'There was a fair amount of the old chat goin' on about Kung Tau before the accident, but … once it blew, well, everythin' went wild. Problem now is separatin' fact from fantasy.'

'I know,' Foster endorsed it from his personal experience. 'But what was being said before the explosion?'

'I suppose you know they swapped the control systems? Universal, I mean. Put in brand new kit.'

'Yes. though I've only just found that out. Up to then I'd been hoping that I'd find that the systems weren't responsible. Now I'm not so sure.'

Cooper looked up at him. He too knew the background to Foster's departure from Universal Digital. In fact, as a staunch friend he probably knew more about it than anybody else. And he could understand the bitterness; why Foster afterwards wanted nothing to do with anything involving the company, why he had distanced himself so completely from power plant and big business.

'It seems amazin', Dan,' he said thoughtfully. 'The explosion was so fuckin' big. How could the computers make a balls-up like that? They were ultra-safe. And what about the operators? They should have seen what was happenin'. Were they all asleep?'

'I don't know, Alex. I just don't know…'

'You're sure it was the computers? You don't think you're …?' Cooper hesitated. He was avoiding making eye contact with his friend, and he stared thoughtfully into his glass. His tone was embarrassed. 'You don't think you could be … well, actually *lookin'* to blame 'em?'

He knew it was a stupid question. Foster was too big a man to harbour grudges, or to try to wreak revenge on old enemies.

It was a question that Foster had wondered about himself. But he had set out with the background thought of exonerating the computer system.

And when he had discovered that his hope was a fantasy, he had immediately tried to extricate himself from any further involvement with it all.

In spite of his earlier resolution to keep hold of the investigation, whatever the implications of his involvement with Universal, he had telephoned Fiona for reassurance and confirmation, but she had been quite adamant that he was to proceed. She was grateful for Foster's honesty but insisted that he was *definitely* the best man to deal with it, the only man who *could* deal with it, in fact. If any question of a conflict of interests did arise then well... maybe they might have to do something about it. But for now ...

But Foster still wasn't sure that he wanted to have anything more to do with it. He had parted with Universal. The company and Andy Johns, they were all in his past. Finished. History. He had a new life, and he didn't need this complication.

'No,' Foster said, to counter Cooper's suggestion that he may have had a subconscious desire to point the finger at his old enemy. 'OK, I did wonder whether a part of me *wants* to blame them,' he admitted. 'I suppose I can't really know for sure. But the coincidence is there.

'A brand new, untried system, in control of a plant that just happens to explode ... Anyway, they've had someone else out here. And they had no doubt; they just didn't know *why*.'

Cooper shook his head. 'Doesn't bear thinkin' about!' was all he could say.

'What I've been asked to do is to answer the question they couldn't answer, to pinpoint what happened,' Foster said eventually. 'But so far I'm baffled. I've only just started looking into things, but it seems weird...'

'Weird?'

Foster took a deep breath. 'Yes,' he said. 'You see, the way the explosion happened, it was really strange. Almost as if there had been several explosions, all more or less at the same time. It certainly wasn't a simple gas leak, as I'd hoped before I came here. The gas-detection system was working perfectly and the records show no sign of a leak—at least not until *after* the explosion.'

Gas can be dangerous and, as with all gas-burning industrial plants, Kung Tau had been plastered with sensitive electronic detectors to pick up any trace of gas escapes. Any leakage would have been quickly found, no matter how small the quantity; the control-room operators would have been alerted, and the time and location of the leak automatically recorded by the plant's electronic data-logger. Foster had found no record to show that any such leakage alarm had operated before the accident, and the operators on duty on that fateful day had confirmed it. In fact, they were adamant that no alarm had occurred.

After the explosion though, the few monitors that had been left undamaged had detected gas just about everywhere; small traces here, huge clouds elsewhere. It was conclusive proof, if anybody needed it, that the leak-detection system had indeed been fully functional up to the moment of the explosion, and for a short time after it.

'No,' Foster continued. 'It was a huge blast; it split the machines right along their length. And all the ducting. Everything.'

'Could gas have collected in it? And been ignited?' Cooper asked, and then flung the fingers of his right hand apart in an expressive gesture. 'Boom!'

'I suspect it had, though I don't see how. The machine was shut down. Surprisingly, the double-block-and-bleeds were more or less undamaged. They'd been thrown quite a distance, but they were almost intact. I had a good look at them. They were as they should have been.'

The gas supply to each of the power-plant engines was obtained via a set of two giant valves, one placed after the other, each designed to shut off tightly when closed. Two of them to make sure; and between them a third valve, a smaller 'bleed', opening to the atmosphere when the two blocking valves were shut, and closing when they were open. If, against all the odds, any gas should ever have seeped through the tightly closed upstream valve, it would have been safely vented to the air through the bleed valve. There, sensitive electronic sensors were always monitoring the atmosphere, 'sniffers' that would detect any leakage and instantly raise an alarm.

Because of this open 'bleed' valve, when the engines were shut down there could simply never be enough gas present in the space between the two block valves to pass through and enter the plant.

'Did you check the openin'?' Cooper asked.

Foster nodded. 'Yup! The block valves were both tight shut, the bleed wide open. I've got the pictures to prove it.'

'You don't think anybody could have fixed them? Tampered with the evidence?'

It was a fair question. If the valves had somehow been wrongly set it would have indicated that somebody—or something—had deliberately admitted gas to the plant at the wrong time, and against all the rules. It would not have been easy; every safety interlock would have had to be disabled. But it *could* have been done, and that would have been the first step in the chain of events leading to the explosion. If somebody had thought that they might be blamed, they would have known that re-setting the valves after the accident would remove any pointer to their involvement.

Foster shook his head. 'Nope. The one thing I *can* be sure of is that those valves didn't move after the explosion.'

His examination had shown that the actuators that had once been used to open and shut the valves had been damaged beyond repair by the explosion, brutally wrenched and twisted aside by the blast. And at that cataclysmic instant—in those brief milliseconds of unimaginable ferocity—any hope of being able to operate the valves again had been destroyed.

At the instant of the explosion they had been locked permanently in a sort of mechanical *rigor mortis*, frozen in the condition he had seen. There was no doubt of that. The block valves were tightly closed, the bleed wide open.

There was no doubt that the explosion had been caused by the presence of gas in the plant, beyond this complex of valves. *Ergo*, somebody—or something—must have opened them, let gas flood into the plant, *and then shut them again*.

And then, by a mechanism Foster didn't understand, something had ignited the explosive mixture of gas and air that had developed.

Cooper thought for a while, taking several sips of his whisky as he did. Eventually he said, 'You know, mate... ' His words came hesitantly. 'Well... you know where this's goin'?'

Foster looked at him, shrugged his shoulders and grimaced. 'Yes. The fact that it was a gas explosion was almost a foregone conclusion. But, even then, I didn't take it for granted. I went in with an open mind. But, almost as soon as I started, I knew: it *was* gas. And, yes, I know what it means, and I don't like it.

'I can't see any other explanation. Somebody, or something, opened the gas supply, poured gas into the inside of the whole bloody plant—where it should quite rightly have been during normal operation. So the leak detectors ignored it. It was in the engines, the ducting, the heat-recovery boiler, the lot. Then something shut off the supply again, without starting-up the plant. And then, after the gas was nicely mixed with oxygen, the same person—or thing—had *then* ignited what was lying there. Lying , waiting to be ignited.'

Cooper stared at him. 'That's bollocks! All the purges would have had to be bypassed,' he said.

Purging was critical to the plant's safety. During start-up of the machinery, automatic safety systems would have started fans that were designed to blow clean air through all the voids and ducts, sweeping them thoroughly to ensure that no gas was present before the supply was carefully opened and the first engines started. If what Foster had said had indeed happened, these safety systems would have had to be rendered inoperative. And *they* were ultra-reliable: with every input, every action, every command triplicated, and then triple-checked to make sure it was safe to proceed.

It was not outside the bounds of possibility that somebody with a suicidal intention may have tampered with the systems, to have altered it to prevent air being blown through before a start was attempted, but if that had been done the fact would have been automatically logged. The computer system was designed so that if somebody wanted to make a fundamental change they would first of all have to identify themselves, and from then on all their actions would be recorded.

The computers could have been fooled if somebody had altered something outside the system, but the rules said that any such action should have been recorded in the 'Interlock defeat log'. Normally, Foster would have carefully read through this, to check whether anybody had accessed the system, changed anything. But the absence of the Log had stopped him investigating the idea.

The absence of that vital record was beginning to look increasingly unfortunate.

But even with that serious gap in his knowledge, Foster knew that if somebody had simply by-passed the safety systems, it was not likely to have been the cause of the blast. Individual checks and interlocks could be bypassed, but only with the operators' knowledge and agreement, and for their own protection these men would have been very careful to personally oversee and control every action that related to the by-passed systems. It was inconceivable that anybody would have allowed all the safety precautions to be by-passed at the same time, as appeared to have happened.

The two men thought about all the implications for a long while. 'Well,' Cooper said eventually. 'That's goin' to be a big puzzle to solve.' Then he added, cheerily, 'But if anyone can do it, it's you, old mate.'

Foster gritted his teeth. 'Thanks, old buddy!' he said, 'Thanks a lot.'

'Well, look at all your experience,' Cooper said. 'Both with power plant *and* out here. You know the business inside out. You know the sort of systems Universal designs.'

'Yes, but remember I've been out of this business for five years now.'

'OK, but once you're back in the saddle I reckon you'll be as good as anybody else I know. And, most of all, you *know* how things work, out here in the Far East. How it's not like at home or the States.'

Foster understood what Cooper meant. The business of building a power plant was a totally different matter out here; right from the beginning, with the haggling over prices, through to the complex commercial and technical processes, and down to the final chaos of construction and commissioning.

'Nothing's changed, has it?' he said.

'Nope!' Cooper replied. 'Not at work, or in the city.'

It was time to move away from the subject of Kung Tau. As ever, when old engineering colleagues got together, reminiscences were in order. 'And, talkin' about Hong Kong,' Cooper continued. 'How d'you like the changes, Dan? We've lost a lot of sea through reclamation, and everywhere's further from the harbour than it was when you were here last time. Even Wanchai's gettin' covered with huge skyscrapers, swish shoppin' malls, office blocks and ornamental gardens. It's not at all what it was once ...' He interrupted himself as a sudden memory came to him. 'Do you remember Wee Willy's?'

Foster grinned. He remembered all right.

Back in the early 60s, amongst the squalid sprawl of Wanchai when it had been the main red-light district—the so-called Suzie Wong area—, there had been a barbershop run by a shrivelled old man called Win Kee, quickly nick-named 'Wee Willy' by the irreverent expatriate community. Wee Willie offered a curious peripheral service in his shop. While he was first spreading the blue cloth over you in preparation for your haircut, he would casually ask if you wanted 'anything extra'. If you nodded, Wee Willie would shout and a girl would emerge from the back of the shop and dive under the sheet. This would bob about on top of her head while Wee Willy calmly continued cutting your hair.

'Never did get there myself,' Foster said. He turned his head and ran his fingertip along the top of his ear. 'Look! Not a mark!'

There was a joke that you could tell the men who frequented Wee Willie's by the little nicks on the tops of their ears...

Just then Cooper tensed and reached for the pager at his belt.

In Hong Kong, any Chinese person, man or woman, who was anybody at all, sported a pager and carried a mobile telephone. Although all these could have been set to silent mode—gently vibrating to inform you of an incoming call—, for the Chinese this would have negated the whole purpose of the thing. Pagers are *status symbols* above all. They told everybody that their owners were important enough to be summoned by some remote Deity. The local shops even sold dummy pagers that were incapable of receiving messages, but could be set to beep at the owner's command; to give the impression that he was an important individual. To be effective, everybody in the vicinity of the wearer would have to know that a message had been sent. So, real or fake, they are never switched to silent mode; all are set to beep, and to do so loudly.

The expatriates, on the other hand, set their pagers to 'silent mode', and it was this gentle vibration that had told Cooper he was wanted.

Foster recognised the situation. The smooth running of a modern city is dependent on the continued operation of its power plants, and this is nowhere more true than in dense, bustling Hong Kong. With this dependence, if something looks like it is about to go wrong it is necessary to be able to instantly summon the key people who will be needed to put it right. If you are one of those people you are paid very well indeed; but it was at the price of your personal freedom.

If the call comes, you go. No matter what you are doing, or where you are; you go.

Such men are always on call, day and night. You can recognise them instantly. If the lights flicker while you are in a restaurant or bar, they're the ones who stop talking and wait, looking anxiously around. If there's no call, and if the lights stay on, they relax, breathe again and carry on as though nothing had happened.

But they are always prepared.

'Shit!' Cooper peered at the pager's display and swore. 'They want me back at the plant. Sorry mate, you know what it's like. Christ knows what's happened now.' He started to get down from his seat and then said, 'But let's get together again, soon. I'll do a bit more nosin' around before then. See what I can find out.'

'Good idea!' Foster stood to see his friend off.

And in doing so his gaze swept over the entrance of the bar.

Even after all these years, he recognised her immediately.

For a while she just stood at the entrance to the bar. She was slender as ever, in an elegant, long green dress, with her fine blonde hair cascading to her bare shoulders. Initially, she had been looking at the crowd in the centre of the room, but then she moved her focus onto the bar itself—and saw him. After a moment's hesitation she realized who he was and gave a little start of surprise.

Cooper followed the direction of his friend's look and smiled. 'Well, well, well! You sly old bastard!' he breathed. 'You still know how to pull 'em, don't you! How did you fix this one up? And when? Christ! You haven't been here for more'n two minutes!' Then he shrugged, raised his eyebrows, grinned conspiratorially, and headed off in the direction of the exit. 'I'll ring you,' he called over his shoulder as he left.

The leer was still on his face as he left the room.

Foster took a deep breath as she headed towards him.

She stopped in front of him and looked at him levelly, a faint smile on her lips. 'Well,' she said. 'This *is* a surprise. Dan! What brings *you* here? After all this time too.'

Now she had come close he could see the changes in her; small lines were apparent at the edges of her eyes and mouth, and there was a slight filling of her cheeks. Her voice hadn't changed though. The softness, the faint Australian accent.

He continued to stare at her in silence, but a foolish grin started to come unbidden to the corners of his mouth.

'Do I get offered a seat?' she asked eventually.

Feeling self-conscious, aware that every eye in the place was on her—the men lusting, the women envious—, he snapped to attention, pivoted in the chair and turned the one next to him around so that she could sit in it. As she perched on it he was aware of her perfume and remembered it instantly: *Femme,* by Rochas.

He had to admire her. She must have been approaching forty now, he guessed, yet she still looked as stunning as she had been when they had first met. Like a fine wine, maturing had improved her.

He had been working for Universal when they met. He was a high-flyer, enjoying his hectic involvement with one of the big power-station contracts in Hong Kong at the time. The colony had seen enormous growth, and demand for electrical power had surged. There'd been plenty of work and he was kept very busy.

Afterwards, he realized how, in one way or another, the time he had spent in Hong Kong had changed the course of his life.

And meeting her had been one of those pivotal events.

Mark, his son had been around fifteen at the time, but already the Fosters' relationship had started to sour. Foster had always tried to maintain a distance between his home life—his family—and what happened when he was away. He had tried to analyse it many times, but had always failed. There had been encounters with many women while he had been travelling, but he had not allowed any of them to threaten his marriage. But his resolve began to weaken when he started to notice his wife losing interest in him.

The drift had been slow but inexorable. Then, one fateful night, it all coalesced. He had been sitting in the Mandarin's coffee shop after a long, wearying day at the plant. The air-conditioning and the calm, well-tempered surroundings of the hotel had been a welcome respite from the strain of working for hours on huge, hot and noisy machinery, all of it baking in the oppressive heat of a humid Hong Kong day. He had been lonely and tired after work, and had come to eat, from habit rather than from hunger, at a table in the bar.

Then he had seen her, sitting across the room, alone at another table. She had looked at him briefly and then looked away. It was a moment that passed fleetingly, one of many such ephemeral brushes in life's swirling dance but somehow, at that instant, the die had been cast. Somehow, they realized much later, at that moment they had both known what would inevitably happen.

She had left the restaurant before him, giving him a small smile as she passed his table. After he had eaten, he wandered into the hotel's shopping gallery, and wasn't too surprised to see her there too. He guessed she had waited for him. When he saw her she was ostensibly looking at a jade statuette in one of the shop windows. He had played his part, walked over and stood beside her, looking at the same statue.

He had expressed admiration for the jade and she in turn had agreed with his judgement and asked him if he was thinking of buying it to take home. When he said he was working in Hong Kong she had asked what he did. The conversation progressed, and eventually he had asked her back to the bar for a drink. It had seemed so easy and smooth, and it was only natural that she would accept. They had sat at this very bar.

Now, all those years afterwards, the barman came over to take her order. 'Is it still Chablis?' Foster asked. She smiled with pleasure that he had remembered, and nodded. Memories had come back to him, crystal clear, as if it were yesterday that they had parted.

'It's good to see you again Alison,' he said as her wine arrived. Already, the condensation had started to form droplets on the chilled glass.

She held it up and he lifted his tumbler and lightly tipped its rim against hers. 'And you,' she said softly. 'Now, I'll ask you again, what are you doing here?'

'Oh, I'm sorry,' he said. Then he told her the bare outlines. She had no knowledge of engineering and had never really understood what he did at all. It hadn't mattered then. It shouldn't have mattered now.

This time, however, she *had* heard about Kung Tau. She told him that it had been very big headlines in the *Hongkong Standard* and the *South China Morning Post*. She was impressed that he had been brought over, from the other side of the world, to become involved with it.

Foster sensed that she showed unusual interest in the incident and in his involvement.

'Will you be here long?' she asked.

'It depends. Three, five days at the most, I'd guess.'

'Your poor wife; managing without you, as always.'

Something about the way she said the words brought back a sudden image. Of her, naked, leaning on one elbow beside him, her breast pressing against his thigh as she delicately removed a hair from the tip of her tongue with her long slender fingers, smiling at him and archly saying, 'Bet your wife doesn't do that!'

She was being light, but he had been angry at the time. Although he was aware that things at home were far from right, his relationship with his wife was something he considered to be intensely personal. It would have wounded his masculine pride to admit to a stranger that anything was wrong with his marriage.

All right, he shouldn't have been in that room with Alison that night—that was another intensely personal thing, this time between the two of them —but it was a separate compartment of his life. She had had no right to pry into the other compartments.

His thoughts came back to the present and he found her smiling at him, looking into his eyes with a wicked smile. As though she had read his mind.

To recover, he took a sip of the Malt. 'We're divorced,' he said quickly.

'Oh.' She looked down at her drink. After a while she asked, 'Is there someone else?'

He thought momentarily about Fiona. She had been the only woman who'd been near him for some time, and although he felt there had been some sort of spark between them, nothing had happened. So he shook his head.

'I don't believe you!' she exclaimed. 'You? Without a woman?'

He gave a wry grin. 'Some drift by,' he admitted finally.

'OK,' she said, smiling. 'Truce! I won't ask any more.'

'Right!' he agreed. 'What about you?'

'Oh, so it's a one-sided truce, is it?' she joked. Then she added, 'Never mind.'

When they had first met, about fifteen years ago, she had been locked into a loveless marriage with Mark Seward, a thrusting, high-flying, highly-paid executive working with Jardine Matthieson. He was rarely home, but he was very rich, and that had suited her adequately.

At that time, she had come down to the Mandarin from her expensive Mid-levels apartment to eat a meal; still by herself, but at least surrounded by other people, even if she didn't know any of them.

She found some companionship among other laughing, talking people.

Mark had been away on one of his many business trips that night, leaving her with only an ageing *amah*—housemaid—for company. The apartment had been poisonously silent; the only sound the slip-slapping of the old woman's sandalled feet on the tiled kitchen floor.

'Mark still around?' Foster now said, breaking her silence.

She nodded.

He became aware that the band had arrived, and was playing *When will I see you again?* It was strangely appropriate.

'I'm working now, though,' she said. 'A part-time job.'

'You?' It didn't fit with what he knew of her, and he was amused at the thought of it.

'No!' she laughed and impulsively put her hand on his arm. 'Don't laugh! It's a job I did before I met Mark. It gets me around. He still spends a lot of time travelling, so the job stops me getting lonely and bored.'

'Or into trouble!' he said. She looked at him sharply, and he added, 'I'm sorry. I didn't mean to laugh. Anyway, what is it? What do you do?'

'I'm a newspaper columnist,' she said simply.

The smile froze on Foster's lips. This was not good news. Now he knew the reason for her interest in this affair. But it wouldn't do if the newspapers got hold of what he was doing.

From that moment, he knew he'd have to be very careful with whatever he told her.

'Freelance,' she continued, seemingly oblivious of his sudden wariness. 'Though the *Post* takes all of my stuff, or most of it at least. I also work with some Australian magazines. Odd columns.'

They sat in silence, thinking their own thoughts. It had been like this before; they were able to be comfortably silent together.

Eventually, as the music came to an end, she brought herself back to reality and looked down at the tiny diamond-studded watch at her wrist. 'Hell!' she said. 'I really can't stay, Dan. We're at a function in the restaurant, Mark and I. One of our clients is having a party. I came down here on an impulse. I'd remembered ...' She looked away, at the dance floor. A few couples had started to dance to the next tune. 'God!' she continued quietly. '*Why* did I come down? It was madness. I'd better go.'

She put down her glass and slipped off the chair. 'Mark,' she said. 'He'll be wondering where I am ...' She had drunk only half of the wine.

She paused and put her hand on his arm again. 'You're staying here?' she asked. He nodded, and she smiled at him. 'I'll call you,' she said softly.

And then she was gone.

Foster caught the barman's eye and his glass was quickly refilled. His mind was a jumble. The thought of her was exciting, but the knowledge of what she did for a living was worrying. He knew he should stay well away from her, but ...

For the moment it was too much. There was no need to make up his mind tonight. For now, he decided, he was going to get drunk.

Very drunk indeed.

Chapter 7

Foster stood at the window of the New Age suite and looked out at the sprawl of buildings surrounding Pacific Place. To his left there was a glimpse of the sea shimmering in the distance between a pair of gleaming metallic towers.

At his wakening, the harbour had still been dark, but the tropical dawn came quickly even at this late stage in the year, almost like a lamp being rapidly turned up, and even as he had watched, pink and yellow streaks of daylight had appeared, streaming from edge of the smoky-violet hills of the mainland, quickly filling the sky with a pale, opalescent light.

Now, almost three hours later, the day had fulfilled its early promise. The weather was beautiful, and from this height the azure sea and sky melded into one in the misty distance. Cocooned in the steel, glass and concrete shell of this building, he was screened from the noise and the smells, so that everything out there looked magical.

He had been pleased to return to the Mandarin. On his second visit to the Kung Tau site he had spent three wearying days picking through the wreckage and correlating the reality of what remained with the drawings of what had once been there. Each evening he had returned to the apartment that Gold Win had provided for him, close to the site, and eaten the supper prepared by an *amah* who had been provided by the company to attend to his feeding, housekeeping and laundry needs.

She had been very old, with grey hair and deeply-veined hands. Her eyes were startlingly bright, glittering and gunmetal-coloured. Foster had guessed that she was well over sixty years old, and he had felt vaguely guilty at having such an aged woman working for him. Since she appeared to speak almost no English he had been largely forced to use sign language to communicate with her.

Silently and mysteriously, she would appear each morning and disappear each evening. Between those times he hardly saw her. He would hear her padding around before she appeared at the table with his meal, and after she had served it she would retreat back to the kitchen. As soon as he had finished she would emerge to collect the dishes. He had the unsettling thought that she had been watching from some hidden vantage-point while he ate.

Still, the apartment was kept neat and tidy, the bed made and turned down before he arrived back in the evening, and his shirts were neatly washed, ironed and on hangers in the wardrobe whenever he needed one. On one occasion, he noticed that she had even replaced a button that had been lost from one of the shirts.

Yes, he had been well looked after by this personal wraith, but it was nice to be back now, amongst the noise and bustle of Hong Kong again.

'Dr Foster!' a voice said from behind him. He turned to greet the small, dark-suited, bespectacled man who had come into the room. 'Good morning,' the man said, 'I am Francis Chung.' Foster recognized the name he had been given in the briefing note. Chung was President of New Age, at least two management tiers above Chau Ki-On. 'I am pleased to meet you,' he continued, his intonation clipped, flat.

Chinese people sometimes have difficulty in coping with the sounds of the English language. In Mandarin, the entire meaning of a word can be altered by the way it is intoned, so when they speak English, it is often with no modulation of tone at all. Possibly it is for safety, in case some inflection should impart an unintended meaning to their words.

'I was sorry to miss you when you visit our offices,' Chung said. 'But I understand from Chau that you have had a good inspection of the site.'

'Yes indeed.' As they formally exchanged business cards, Foster thought that gentle flattery would not go amiss. He said, 'Your company's arrangements over the past few days have been excellent. I thank you for them. And for the facilities you've provided for me here.' He gestured round the room.

They had found him a spacious office, comfortably furnished, with a computer already set up on one side of his imposing desk. On the wall facing the window was a simple Chinese watercolour, almost an abstract, of a lake seen through stylised trees.

'It is nothing,' Chung said, but his faint smile showed that he was pleased by Foster's praise. 'I have heard much about you,' he continued. 'Very interesting, I think: your investigation.'

'It is, Mr Chung: and challenging.'

'Ah yes. I understand you like challenge.'

Chung paused, staring past Foster at the man-made pinnacles of glass and steel outside. Yet it seemed to Foster that he was so deep in thought that he saw nothing. As though his whole concentration was on searching for words.

'Dr Foster,' he said eventually. 'I know you make your own conclusion, but you must understand that I am confident that my company in no way responsible for the accident. We employ only best people, and we take pride in quality of our work.'

Foster believed it. He had spent some time reading through the New Age Quality Manual. This impressive book defined in fine detail the procedures for ensuring that every aspect of engineering major projects was carefully checked and double checked.

In his more cynical moments Foster would have said that a company's performance was inversely proportional to the size of its Quality Manual. He had seen too many organisations that attempted to hide poor control of their business procedures behind weighty Quality Manuals packed full of meaningless padding. When a company's management was out of touch and inept, it was easy for charlatan consultants to compose vast volumes of meaningless drivel and pass it off as a substitute for a good definition of what should have been happening in a properly-managed business.

It was waffle, used to mask incompetence.

But the New Age book was nothing like that; it was concise, comprehensive and thorough, and it left him with little doubt that the company's management team did their work very professionally.

'I will look very carefully at everything, Mr Chung,' Foster said. 'Believe me.'

Chung looked at him seriously for a long time. Then he gave a wintry smile and continued: 'I have complete faith in your reputation, Dr Foster.' He held his hand open in the direction of the small meeting-room table adjoining Foster's desk. 'I like to explain one thing. May we sit?'

Foster nodded and they sat down on opposite sides of the table.

Chung brought the palms of his hands together, fingertips to his lips. After several seconds of silence in this pose he said, 'You have heard of decision to change the control system, the DCS.'

Foster nodded. *So they're worried about that too!* he thought.

'I clarify our part in that,' Chung continued, then paused while he considered his next words. 'At beginning, Universal approach us about idea, but it very late by then. They already discuss the idea with Gold Win. You know Albert Leung, I believe.'

Foster nodded and Chung continued, 'And they... before then ... they discuss it with Greater China Power. So decision already made. We had little choice then but to accept—little choice.'

The last two words were spoken slowly, with resignation and bitterness, making Foster sense Chung's deep regret, and some shame.

'I presume this is all documented?'

'Oh yes, Dr Foster. Definitely.' He took off his glasses and wiped them carefully in his neatly folded handkerchief. 'You will see messages we exchange with Gold Win and with our project manager on the site. We did not even have time to tell our senior engineer, Mr Lee.'

'The man who was killed?'

'Yes. The accident, his death—it was very bad thing.'

Involuntarily, Foster's right eyebrow lifted slightly. He wondered what Pauline Lee would have felt if she had heard her husband's death being described as merely a 'very bad thing'. But he had to remember where he was: Oriental fatalism treated life and death in a different way from the way these things were seen in the West.

'I shall go through all the records, Mr Chung,' Foster said. 'But when somebody introduces such significant change, and at such an advanced stage in a project, and then a serious accident happens, then it must be the first suspect, and it must receive very careful attention.'

'I agree. That is why I mention it.'

Just then, there was a quiet tap at the door and Tony Crabtree walked in. 'Oh, I'm sorry,' he said on seeing Chung with Foster. 'Shall I come back later?' He started to retreat, but Chung waved him back.

'No, Mr Crabtree,' Chung said, rising from his chair. 'We have finish our discussion, I think?' He looked across at Foster, who nodded his assent.

After Chung had left the room, Crabtree sat down at the table.

'They've done you proud, Dan,' he said, looking round the room.

'Yes. And it's quiet here, which is why I suggested you come down here.'

The two men grinned at each other. They both knew that Foster had used his wish for Crabtree to come to the New Age offices as a ruse to get him out of China. The PRC authorities had wriggled at first, unwilling to let the hostage out of the trap, but in the end they'd conceded defeat. The loss of face had been mitigated by the fact that they'd got Foster working on the investigation.

But the need to talk in calm silence had nevertheless been very real.

Although the Kung Tau plant itself had been de-manned, the adjacent administration block was very crowded and constantly busy. Following the destruction of the plant, Gold Win had launched a project to build its replacement in an even shorter time than the record-breaking programme of the original. As a result, the administration building was constantly thronged with a teeming mass of people involved in the work of writing the contract documentation for the extensive repair and refurbishment work. Foster had been provided with an office there but it was continually invaded by people looking for somebody, or trying to find an extra room in which to hold a meeting. He had needed to ask Crabtree more questions, but it had to be done where they could talk quietly for extended periods.

The analysis of the information Foster had collected was a very complex task, requiring careful concentration of many small details and meticulous pursuit of several separate chains of events: whether recorded in the various operational logs, or merely postulated. A single interruption to the chain of thought usually necessitated starting all over again.

Here there was nothing to disturb careful thought. Only the gentle hiss of the air-conditioning system.

'It certainly was a good idea, Dan,' Crabtree agreed. He was also pleased to be in Hong Kong again, and in a quiet office.

'Things still bad up there Tony?'

'It gets worse every day,' Crabtree admitted ruefully.

'Was it like that while you were building Phase I?'

'Of course.' He grimaced at the memory. 'We'd be sitting down, trying to understand some incredibly complex drawings, and all the while the Chinese guys would be walking round, shouting to each other over our heads. And, as you know, for small people they have remarkably good lungs!

'To cap it all, towards the end, they all got issued with walkie-talkies. They'd carry them round with them or bring them into the room, all with the volume-control turned up fully so that in the middle of the confusion, and the already distracting babble of voices in the room, you'd suddenly get some shrill racket blasting across your thoughts.'

On a large construction site it is necessary for people to be able to communicate with each other quickly, even when they were physically separated. A man pressing a button at one point will be told by someone at the remote end of the electronic link that the thing he has commanded to shut or open, or to start or stop, has actually done so. Radios are the only means of dealing with that situation.

'Nothing's changed then?' Foster smiled, remembering his time spent in the chaos of construction in the Far East, desperately trying to make complex systems work, but continually distracted, irritated and interrupted by noise and confusion.

'It's got worse, Dan,' Crabtree rested his elbows on the table and covered his tired eyes with his hands. 'Every new system we get out here: it gets more and more complicated. Or at least, it seems to ..... or am I getting too old for this game?'

Foster shook his head. 'I know how you feel, Tony,' he sympathised. 'It's not just you. I had problems, too, keeping up with technology. It was changing so fast it put me into a tailspin... But then I reminded myself that, behind it all, the basic plant's pretty much the same.'

'Oh yes, I know. But we get things sent to us that the local's just don't understand.'

Foster knew what he meant, but he needed to hear it. 'What d'you mean?' he asked.

'Oh, they're very bright and clever, but they'll never admit when they don't understand something.' Crabtree's exasperation was clear. 'You know something, Dan?' he continued. 'I work with PhDs here who, personally, I wouldn't trust to wire a power plug!'

'Get much help from the suppliers?' Foster asked.

'Pah!' Crabtree snorted in disgust. 'They send out *experts* to help, but I really wonder about some of them. Universal sent us a girl ...' He grinned. 'Don't get me wrong, I've got nothing against female engineers. In fact, your replacement at Universal—Carol Lopez—you met her?' Foster shook his head. 'She's really very, very good,' Crabtree continued. 'Knows her stuff. Quick.' He paused for a moment and then snorted, 'Good looking too!'

'In fact, nothing like me at all!' Foster joked.

Crabtree smiled. 'Different, Dan. Very different. Anyway, she came out here. Spent quite a lot of time on site. While she was here it was all right. Then this engineer, Judith Chang, arrived.'

'Local?'

'No. A Chinese girl all right, but born in England. It was her first trip to Asia, though it was the place her parents came from. She was bright; a real whiz with computers.'

'I've seen lots like that,' Foster said. 'The crucial questions is, did she know power plant?'

'Actually she did. Or at least, she *seemed* to know it. Sometimes I worried about the speed she did things. But then, I put it down to my advancing years.'

'I've seen the type, Tony,' Foster said with a laugh, and then he remembered an analogy. 'You know, I used to have a spaniel once, when I was a kid. Crazy dog! She'd launch herself down the stairs like a rocket. I used to watch her: at the speed she came down, she couldn't possibly have known where each step was. But she just came hurtling down. I was convinced she'd get it all wrong one day and end up in a heap at the bottom of the stairs ... but she never did.'

Crabtree saw the point immediately. 'That's it, Dan. That's exactly it! Judith was just like that. When she was explaining something she'd run through a huge long chain of actions ... so quickly, it was like a blur. I wanted to stop and think it out, but she seemed impatient. And in time I found out that, if I did make the effort to sit down and think it through, I would end up at the same point she had. Only it would've taken me much longer.'

'So you began to take it for granted that she was right.' Foster's statement was more a question.

'Yes.' Then Crabtree corrected himself. He saw where the discussion was heading. 'No! Hold on! It's not that, Dan. I didn't let *anything* go past without checking. I went over everything she did, very carefully. Don't misunderstand me. I'm not saying she was wrong. Since the explosion I've double-checked everything she did, and it was all OK. Absolutely all right.'

'At least, as far as you know,' Foster interjected cautiously. 'But do you really know as much as you should about computers? I mean, how these big systems work. In minute detail?'

At each level, a DCS installation is built up on the understanding that every piece on the level that lies below it works correctly. In a way, the designers are like bricklayers who don't know or care about the details of how a brick is actually made, but who still manage to build an entire house from them. Or accountants who use computer spreadsheets to calculate tables of numbers, trusting the machine completely, not knowing how they work or questioning that they will obey their commands implicitly. They have absolute confidence that the spreadsheet won't make errors in addition or subtraction.

Crabtree was a plant man. He knew the heavy machines of a power station inside out. Like many engineers, he'd picked up a lot of understanding of computer technology, but he understood Foster's point; that he was not expected to fully comprehend the finer nuances of the computers he was using.

''Course not!' he said. 'I'd never claim to be an expert. You know that. I've got to trust that when the system needs something to be done, it gets done. I don't need to know the detail.'

'So, after the explosion, you checked over everything thoroughly?' Foster asked.

'Yes. As I just said. I checked at the beginning, and afterwards. I've been over it all, time and time again. It was all OK.'

Foster wanted to change the emphasis. It had not been his intention to question Crabtree's capability. 'How did the Gold Win people cope with it all?' he asked.

'You know how it is, Dan,' Crabtree shrugged. 'They've got this one guy; a real technical guru. Name of Hsu - *Doctor* Hsu. They all suck up to him. He's very good all right, got a string of letters after his name as long as my arm. But he doesn't always think about what he's doing. And Hsu doesn't want to get bogged down with anything he considers to be trivial. He passes it down to one of his minions to sort out.'

'And the minion doesn't always know what he's doing?'

'Right! But he can't admit it. If he does, Hsu gets all snooty. Shows up the underling. Tells him if he can't do it he should go back to working in the paddy fields. If I talked to anyone like that back home I'd be up with the Race Relations Board in a flash. But it doesn't matter here. Not as long as they say it to each other.'

Foster shook his head.

'So I'd find people fiddling about with things they didn't really understand at all,' Crabtree continued. 'Whenever I found that happening, I'd tell them to stop, then I'd explain it all and get them to start thinking it out. It was all right then, mostly. But, they were really scared to ask me anything. They'd come creeping into my office, looking behind to see that Hsu hadn't seen them.'

'Do you think he understood it himself?'

Crabtree nodded. 'Oh yes. Well, in a funny sort of way, he did. When he was dealing with a piece of equipment, I could almost see the science passing through his head. Complex equations. As long as they balanced out he was happy. But I wouldn't call that *understanding* it; not really.'

Foster smiled. He knew the type. It was not peculiar to China; you met them everywhere. But here the authorities seemed to have perfected the fine art of finding people such as the ones Crabtree had described, and promoting them to high office. The non-technical people were in awe of them.

Crabtree continued, 'And then, if some new piece of equipment came into the plant, it was *his*, all his. Nobody else touched it; at least, not until he got bored with it. The more fancy displays it had, the more he loved it.'

'A true nerd?' Foster commented.

'Absolutely! You know, at times the people in his department would be right in the middle of sorting out some really big problem, when by rights he should have been in there with them, when - all at once - a new gizmo would arrive and then he'd be off! Bang! And his team, who *should* have been sorting out the problem, they couldn't really concentrate on it themselves. They'd seen the gizmo too, and wanted to look over his shoulder.'

A secretary came in and offered them coffee.

When they were sipping at the drinks, Foster asked Crabtree about Galaxy 2000.

'Oh, that was a great concept,' Crabtree said. 'Universal had really dreamt up a fantastic idea. Of course, Hsu loved it with a passion; it was so *advanced!* You could see he thought that, at last, we'd delivered something that came up to his intellectual level. But when it got down to the routine level he got lost, and then Universal didn't help at all. I used to think they'd got so carried away with the grand scheme that when it came down to the nuts and bolts they had just run out of time. Their support was piss-poor.'

'What do you mean?'

'Well, it was everything really. Take the manuals: they were written by people who were computer experts, with absolutely no knowledge of the reality of one of these plants, and no appreciation of the generally minimal level of skill and understanding that's available out here. Or in any of these places. Often there's very little understanding at all.'

'You mean, the only people who could understand them were the ones who were already experts.' Foster nodded.

'Right!' Crabtree agreed. 'It wasn't like that in your days, Dan. Back then, the manuals were good and clear, and they always gave understandable fault-finding hints and tips.'

'It was a simpler world then,' Foster said. But he was flattered. He had always been under pressure to cut the heavy cost of producing the company's instruction books. It was an expensive task to get good, clear manuals written; the designers of the electronic equipment were good at their jobs but they were notoriously bad at communicating the concepts of their work to others who were not deeply familiar with the jargon of modern computer systems. Converting technical jargon to understandable English was never easy. Neither was it cheap.

And when it came to a question of cost, the accountants at Global Associated Industries looked only at the bottom line. Foster guessed that after he had left, Johns had taken the opportunity to make economies in the area of technical support, improved the bottom line in the short term and basked in the resulting glory. The fact that the manuals had previously actually helped to sell the systems—because clients knew they were good—that was a fact that was never understood by the bean-counters.

Neither was the fact that good manuals prevented mistakes.

'Makes you wonder why things don't go wrong more often, doesn't it?' Foster said quietly. 'You can see the recipe for disaster developing here,' He held his thumb up to count and said, 'One: a complex system with poor manuals - difficult to understand.' He raised his forefinger. 'Two: people on site who don't really understand what they're doing, and who're managed by a man who ridicules genuine questions and buries himself in abstract theory.' He continued to count the items with his fingers. 'Three: continual jabbering, distracting people while they try to sort out complex details. Four: a major change - to replace a system that's been tried and tested, and substitute it with one that has never been used before. And all of it done in a hurry.'

'Five,' Crabtree continued for him. 'Fucking horrible standards of construction on site.'

Foster raised his eyebrows in question.

'Oh yes, you should have seen it, Dan. Before the explosion. I went round once and counted the things that were done badly. It *looked* OK, on the surface, but when you got down to the detail ... I found cables that were badly connected; glands that weren't properly tightened; plugs that should have sealed off enclosures, so loose you could easily undo them with your fingers; non-approved equipment in hazardous areas ... I could go on for hours.'

Electrical and electronic equipment that is fitted in the potentially explosive areas adjacent to gas-filled pipes has to be installed very carefully indeed. There must be absolutely no chance of any spark occurring in such a way that the gas can be ignited. It needs extreme vigilance to ensure that this is done for each of the thousands of items that carry electrical current on the plant.

Foster's eyes widened. 'Yes,' he said pensively. 'I did see some examples while I was there. But there was no way of being sure whether that was how they had been beforehand or whether they had been damaged in the explosion. The cables, in particular, were very badly damaged by fire, but I was surprised to see how badly they'd been installed in the first place.'

'Well, now you know. It was bad from the beginning.'

Foster looked at Crabtree. They had both lived with this type of situation for many years and in many different countries. Usually, you corrected whatever you could and lived with the rest.

This time Paul Lee had died because of it.

'And don't forget the other factor, Dan. Number six,' Crabtree continued. He was angry again now. The rage at seeing his colleague die was coming back as he remembered. 'The young jerks who come out here, get given more responsibility than they would ever get at home ... and who go ape.'

Foster nodded. He had seen that too. Young men who found themselves in Hong Kong for the first time and began to lord it over everybody and to live it up. Men who suddenly found themselves being paid expenses by their companies, and who realized that there was very little control over what they spent. They reacted by spending money like water. And when the money attracted women, the lure was irresistible.

Foster had seen men who, at home, would have been meek and timid and would have worn shabby clothes, here sprawled across seats in expensive hotels, dressed in Hong Kong tailored suits, with admiring women at each side. Sexual failures at home, they were suddenly Lotharios here.

There was a long-standing joke out here about these people being nicknamed FILTH, an acronym for 'Failed In London? Try Hongkong'.

In the complex and demanding world of the power station such men were particularly dangerous. Within days of arriving on site they were totally out of control. Convinced that they were invincible, they took decisions that were entirely beyond their real level of training and competence. Their swagger and bluster held the local engineers in thrall and their actions were rarely questioned. Eventually, they began to think they were omnipotent.

On a power plant that could be very dangerous.

Foster looked at his watch and saw that it was almost lunch time. They broke off for a quick meal in the bistro in the basement level of the office complex and afterwards returned to continue their discussions through the rest of the day.

It was a hard day of serious work. Crabtree left at four o'clock to catch the shuttle back to Shantou, leaving Foster to write up his notes before heading back to the Mandarin.

It was a beautiful evening. A steady wind had dispersed much of the usual pollution and it was now pleasantly warm and not oppressively humid. He chose to walk along the new road bordering the reclaimed area of the harbour. The setting sun had turned the sea to burnished metal and already the distant mountains were becoming bulky dark purple shapes around the horizon.

Back in his room he showered and changed and, just as he settled down to belatedly read the morning paper, the telephone rang.

Her voice was exactly as it had been two decades ago; throaty, soft. He had been wondering whether she'd make contact, wondering what he would do about it if she did. But now the moment had come he still had no idea about how to handle it.

'Dan?' she asked.

'Yes. Hello Alison.'

'Can we meet? I'm free tonight. Mark's gone to the States.'

He took a deep breath. He wanted to be with her, but now that he knew of her involvement with the press he had to be careful. 'I'm not sure. I don't think it'd be a good idea.'

He could imagine her pouting. She had never liked to be refused anything. 'Oh, come on, Dan. It was sort of fated... when we met the other night, I mean.'

'I'd like to see you,' he agreed. 'But ...'

'But what?' He felt awkward. How could he explain his wariness?

'Look,' she continued. 'Why not meet me over supper? I'm hungry - and if I have to eat another meal on my own I know I'll go mad. I'll buy, if you let me.'

He weakened. He felt sorry for her; knew only too well what it was like to eat alone. In any case, it would be company for him. 'No,' he relented. 'But I'll buy. Do you want to come down here?'

After he had hung up, he sat down on the settee, put his hands behind his head and looked up at the ceiling. He was still deep in thought when the telephone rang again.

It was Fiona, ringing to tell him that the weather in London was still beautiful, and that her lords and masters were wondering how he was getting on. He replied that he was still baffled, but was following up on some leads.

'And how's it there?' She asked. 'Are you OK? And behaving yourself?'

'Yes on the first count,' he replied. 'And on the second, well ... you know me!' It wasn't a lie, but it avoided the truth.

'Not really!' she said, and laughed.

'What do you mean?'

'Well, I've read all the stuff about you that's on file, and we've shared a drink or two. We've even exchanged some details of our lives. But I don't really know much about you.'

'Do you want to know more?'

There was a long pause before she answered: 'Yes, I think I do.'

He took a deep breath and thought about his options. Then he said, 'I'll be back in a few days. Let's see what happens then.'

'I look forward to it.'

There was little else to say and after a brief good-bye he hung up. He felt a familiar excitement at her words.

He put down the handset and looked at the 'phone thoughtfully. Then he sighed and stood up.

It was time he went down to the lobby. There was old business to settle there.

He didn't have to wait too long there. She came through the door like a whirlwind, stopping people in their tracks, looking exquisite as ever. She swept up to him, stood on tip-toe and kissed him on the cheek. 'Where to?' she asked, linking arms with him.

It was as though they had never parted.

They took the Star Ferry across to Kowloon and strolled along the waterfront promenade to the Shangri La hotel. Foster knew that the French restaurant on the mezzanine floor there was excellent.

During the meal she told him of the continuing wasteland of her empty marriage to Mark, and of his unchanged arrogance and cruelty. When Foster asked whether she'd thought about having children she shook her head and explained that Mark had been cold and clear about that: he didn't want any 'noisy, smelly brats' round *his* home.

'Truth to tell,' she said. 'It probably suits me best too. Though I suppose, like every woman, I'm conscious of the biological clock ticking away.'

When it came to his turn, Foster told her about his departure from Universal and his work afterwards; but he kept well away from the Kung Tau work, and for her part she didn't question him about it.

She was openly curious about the shop. 'I just don't see you behind a counter,' she exclaimed. 'After all that travelling around the world, all the power and influence?'

'It wasn't easy,' he said, the memories flooding back as he spoke. 'You know me. I never liked pretentiousness. But … well, I admit I did miss the power. People snapping to attention when I rang.'

'I can imagine.'

'Losing the travel wasn't really any problem. It had been beginning to get to me anyway. Suddenly I'm not rushing to the airport every week, or commuting to the firm's offices. Instead, I have a nice easy stroll from the boat to the shop. Looking at all the people sitting in their cars, stalled in the traffic, most of them looking tense and angry. No, I didn't miss anything about that.'

'But … Well, it seems such a waste,' she said, pouting slightly. 'All that knowledge and experience.'

'No!' he retorted sharply. 'Nothing's wasted. In the shop I do a valuable job, meet interesting people. Not high-flyers, just ordinary folk. Little old ladies who need help.'

She looked at him and shook her head. She admired him. Something about him reminded her of a passage from Kipling's 'If':

'If you can walk with Kings, yet never lose the common touch …'

It was typical of him.

After the meal, they took the promenade walk back, under the stars, towards the ferry pier. Half way there, they stopped and leaned on the wall to watch the blaze of lights from the island and its dancing reflections in the sea, like a carpet of sparkling metallic confetti flashing brightly as it floated on the constantly moving waters of the harbour. She stood close to him and he was very aware of the constant pressure of her arm against his.

'Dan,' she said quietly, after several minutes of silence. 'Do you ever wonder what would have happened? If we'd met under different circumstances?'

He thought about it for a while. This was getting dangerous.

'You mean if we hadn't both been married?' he said simply. She nodded thoughtfully and he said, 'Who knows? Anyway, we didn't.'

She slipped her arm through his and they stood there in silence for several minutes, each deep in their own thoughts.

Eventually she broke the spell. 'Let's go.'

They walked slowly, arm in arm, through the balmy night with its warm, syrupy air, back to the pier. Then they sat on the slatted seats of the ferry, their shoulders touching as the boat throbbed, bucked and swayed its way across the choppy water to the island.

They hadn't actually discussed any plans, but somehow a contract for the remainder of the night had been sealed between them.

She was as passionate and sensual as ever. Their lovemaking was fierce, abandoned, primitive. At the climax, as he drove deep into her and heard her small gasp of ecstasy, the explosion burst from him and he arched his back, lifting his head skywards with his eyes shut.

And afterwards, as she lay cradled in his arms it felt good again - this impossible dream that he had once dreamed.

And then his mind began to be rational again. It *had* been good. But it was only physical lust. He knew he could never live with her. She was beautiful and passionate; but far, far too shallow.

He lay there in the soft light, feeling her breathing against his cheek as he looked at the ceiling and thought about his life and loves, about the wife he had lost, about his children.

And about Fiona.

Suddenly his life seemed to be confused, with no clear direction. He wondered if, in agreeing to come to Hong Kong, he hadn't made the biggest mistake of his life.

Chapter 8

In the lift, Andy Johns stood in silence beside Carol Lopez. A few days earlier, Brian Ward had contacted him with the news that Dan Foster had requested a meeting at the New Age offices. He had recoiled in shocked surprise when he had heard Foster's name.

Of all the people to be called in! Foster! To judge *his* company!

Obviously, somebody had to be brought in to investigate the incident at Kung Tau—that was predictable—but he hadn't suspected for a moment that it would be his old enemy.

He had snarled in impotent rage when he heard. How could it be?

He'd swept Foster out of his way a long time ago—once and for all, or so he had thought at the time—and he had never expected to see him again. A long time afterwards, he had heard rumours that Foster had set up in a repair shop (*about his level*, he'd thought), that his marriage had broken up and that he was living on a houseboat. But Johns neither knew nor cared about the details. As far as he was concerned, Foster was finished. If he had chosen the life of a drifter, then so be it. He was out of the way.

Then he heard that Foster was to be the Kung Tau investigator and suddenly he realized how wrong he had been.

Foster! When he heard Ward mention the name, he had almost exploded in anger. Desperately, he had done all he could to discredit his old enemy. He had told Ward that he'd fired Foster for gross incompetence, that he obviously bore a grudge against him personally, and against the company. He said that, all in all, Foster was quite the wrong person to carry out the investigation because he was bound to be totally biassed against Universal.

But although Ward had listened politely, he hadn't shifted his position.

Johns had taken a deep breath at that point, and made a deliberate effort to calm himself. As soon as the rage had subsided he had started to think about the most effective way of tackling the situation. He didn't want to alienate Ward; in spite of what had happened, he was absolutely determined that the replacement plant at Kung Tau would have a Galaxy 2000 DCS, and Ward's help would be crucial in the decision-making process.

When his first objections had failed he had shifted his aim, trying reasoned argument rather than an outright attack on Foster's credentials.

He had heaped on the friendly camaraderie. 'Come on Brian,' he had said, warmly. 'I know you have to have an investigation, and you know, of course, we'll co-operate fully with whoever you call in.' Then he added archly, 'Well, *almost* anybody. But what happened at Kung Tau had nothing at all to do with us. And how can we be expected to get a fair hearing with Foster heading the inquiry?'

But it didn't work.

'Andy, I hear what you're saying,' Ward had replied. 'And to some extent I can see your point. But it's not up to me alone. The decision's already been made; and, believe me, where it's come down from it might as well be written on tablets of stone.'

Johns had wondered at that. *Written on tablets of stone?* Was there somebody else behind all this then? And who could it be?

Yet another mystery. He hated mysteries. He'd *have* to find out.

But, in spite of cautious cajoling, Johns had failed to prise any more out of Ward. The man had simply clammed up.

Then Johns had summoned Carol Lopez.

While he had waited for her to arrive, a part of his mind had wondered once again about her. She was a good-looking woman, and he had at one time been tempted to try his luck with her, but he had decided there was too much at stake. In any case, he had received no hints from her that indicated any interest in him at all.

From the day he had hired her, he'd never been able to work her out. She was self-assured, intelligent and very competent at her job. Initially, he had taken her on because he felt that, as a woman, she would be somebody he could manipulate; someone who would be vaguely in awe of him. But he had quickly discovered that in this respect he had seriously underestimated her character.

On the first occasion where she had stood up to him he had been furious but, the more he had thundered and blustered, the more firmly she had stood her ground. He had never made that mistake again.

Now he worked by winning her co-operation, by subtle manoeuvring rather than outright force. And it had worked out.

She had taken the embryonic Galaxy 2000 concept that Foster had started, and turned it into a stunning reality. None of Foster's cold feet; his extreme caution. No, she had been more than willing to press forward with the project and to see the system employed on a prestigious site like Kung Tau. What was more, she had proved to be very able to help Johns in making major presentations to clients. She shared Foster's ability to put ideas over to an audience - even Johns had had to admit that quality of his adversary—but she was better. And, as a good-looking woman, she had a major advantage when it came to capturing the attention of the predominantly male audiences at the sales presentations.

When they had won the Kung Tau project, it had been a complete triumph.

Now it had turned into a total disaster. The explosion had been bad enough, but Johns was confident that he would ride over it. Above all, he firmly believed that no blame could be laid at Universal's door. But then, to have his old enemy brought in to investigate, that was enough to make him shudder.

Lopez had been on holiday in Bermuda at the time of the explosion and he had hauled her back straight away. She had raced to Abingdon straight off the aircraft but he took no pity on her. As soon as she had arrived in his office, tired and angry, he had ripped into her.

The gloves were off, all pretence of respect gone, no allowance made for her tiredness or her gender. But she fought back like a cornered animal. Despite being jet-lagged, she had defended herself and her team very competently. Somewhere deep within, Johns had some grudging admiration for that, but he had no room for weakness. He took no chances; at the end of his inquisition he sent her off to start a detailed investigation immediately.

She reported back to him barely within the 48-hour time limit he had set. *There was no fault with Galaxy 2000*, she said. *The safety systems were faultless; the interlocks were un-defeatable; the error-correction technology worked perfectly*. It simply could *not* have been a system fault. Something else had happened, something quite outside the scope of Universal's supply. But exactly *what* that had been was something she could not say. There were too many factors involved, and the Galaxy system had been only one part of the huge, complex, interlocked array of equipment at Kung Tau.

No, she was sure that, whatever had happened, it was not Universal's fault.

Johns had been relieved to hear this, but by then he'd been called to the preliminary enquiry. In response, within a few hours he had flown out to Hong Kong with Lopez. He was determined to be in the thick of the action, to answer the investigators in person, with Lopez alongside to provide technical backing.

And to take the blame in the unlikely event of Universal being held responsible.

Lopez would be there, but he'd taken care to ensure that she toed the line. It would be *he* that would deal with all questions. *He* would refer them to her if he felt the need. *He* would reply to any and all questions. Her role would be that of a silent assistant, helping him when asked; when, and *only* when, she was asked.

He had sensed her resentment at being put in this secondary, subservient role, but his iron determination had convinced her that this was the only approach that would work and eventually she had agreed, though her reluctance and resentment had been patently obvious.

After they had arrived in Hong Kong and he had tried fruitlessly to prize out of Ward the name of the person who had instigated Foster's appointment, he turned to other sources. Ward's phrase *'Tablets of stone'* pointed to high authority, so he targeted Albert Leung.

Ominously, he had met with some difficulty in getting even a brief audience with Leung. Once he would have had no problem in arranging a meeting, but this time a barrier had descended. It was only through extreme persistence that he had eventually succeeded, and then it was a short, curt affair. Leung had been distant and, for the first time in this horrible affair, Johns had begun to feel a cold dread. In spite of Leung's obvious regard for Lopez's technical ability, it was apparent that he was wondering if it had been a mistake to go along with Johns' proposal of retro-fitting the Galaxy system at Kung Tau.

For the first time, Johns saw that it wouldn't be easy to sell a Galaxy 2000 system on the replacement plant.

That alone was not a problem. He thrived on challenge, and he had every confidence that he would be able to turn the tables in his favour again.

What worried him was Foster.

Even in his brief meeting with Leung, Johns had found out nothing. It may well have been Leung who had handed Ward the *'Tablets of stone'*, but at their meeting it was made quite clear that, in this matter, he was a mere intermediary, a Moses.

That was worrying in itself. *Someone higher than the mighty Albert Leung? Who could it be?* Johns needed to know, but Leung simply wasn't telling.

Johns was forced to delve deeper into his web of contacts and sources of information, but it was useless. Nobody knew anything.

Either that, or nobody was telling him.

He fretted at it. Without the name of the person who had set this up, he had no way of going to them directly, persuading them of Foster's naïvety, his lack of recent experience, his inability to evaluate the matter, either technically or fairly.

There *had* to be some other way of stopping the man; Foster was far too dangerous to be allowed to interfere. But, try as he could, he had failed to find any feasible way of achieving his aim.

Now he and Lopez were about to face Foster. Johns wondered how he would handle it; facing his old enemy. And how Foster would react. He shuddered at the prospect. Then he thought: at least Ward would be present - to see fair play.

The New Age secretary led them to the meeting room and as soon as she opened the door, Johns saw Foster sitting with Ward. The Project Manager stood up and greeted them. He introduced Foster to Johns with the simple words, 'You know each other, of course.'

The two old enemies stood and looked at each other for a long time before Foster broke the silence. Holding out his hand, he said simply, 'Hello, Andy. It's been a long time.'

'Foster.' Johns took the proffered hand coldly, almost shuddering at the touch. He could hardly believe this was happening.

'Carol's our new Technical Director,' he said. Ward had introduced her by name only, not her title, and Johns wanted to belittle Foster by introducing him to his successor. A woman—*woman,* mind you—who was now filling the post he had lost; and doing it so very competently.

Foster smiled and Johns clenched his teeth as he noticed warmth in the woman's returning smile.

'I'm pleased to meet you,' Lopez said. 'I've heard so much about you.'

I bet you have, Johns thought. He knew Foster still had faithful friends in the company. No doubt they had misguidedly praised the man's virtues, whatever they may have been, to their new boss.

Ward took command and gestured to the conference table. 'Let's sit down, shall we?'

Foster sat at the head with Johns and Lopez facing each other at the sides and Ward facing him across the length of the table. A pretty young Chinese stenographer sat near Ward, ready to take shorthand note of everything that was said. She switched on a small voice recorder, a belt-and-braces backup.

Ward asked Foster to outline his findings.

He took a deep breath. 'As you know,' he began. 'I've been called in to investigate what happened at Kung Tau.' Then he looked directly at Johns. 'I must say, right from the outset, that I was unaware that Universal had installed the new system there. And when I heard about it, I was very reluctant to continue with the assignment. In fact, I'm not at all happy about it now. However, I've been persuaded to carry on, and so I shall.

'But I want to reassure you of my impartiality. I know what you must think, but I want you both to know that I *will* be entirely impartial. What happened between Universal and me is finished. Over and done with. I've no regrets and I bear nobody any grudge.' He met Johns' cold stare. 'I promise you that.'

Johns snorted disdainfully and took the opportunity to interject. 'I gave up believing in fairies long ago!' he snarled, almost under his breath.

Foster heard him. 'I said, I *will* be impartial,' he said calmly.

'And I simply don't see how anybody could expect you to be impartial,' Johns growled, more loudly this time. 'You know I'm an open man, Foster, and so I'll tell you right now that I'm taking steps to have you withdrawn from this enquiry.' He leaned forward suddenly and thumped the table. 'I will *not* have the interests of our shareholders put at risk.' Though his voice was quiet, there was steel in his tone. 'I will not allow them to be endangered by the ... the vindictive manipulations of a man who bears me a grudge. More importantly, somebody who resents my taking over the job he secretly coveted.'

Foster shook his head slowly in disbelief. 'You've never understood, Andy, have you? I'm an engineer,' he said. 'It's all I've ever wanted to be. I never wanted your precious MD's job.

'Yes, OK! I've got a personal interest in this project—but, if anything, I should be on your side. As you well know, I was involved with Galaxy from the very beginning. It was my baby, and I hate to think that it might have been responsible for what happened. But, all the same, I have to get to the bottom of it. A lot of men died out there Andy, one of them was somebody I'd worked with; someone I respected.' He paused for a moment, staring at Johns, but he could see that the gulf between them was unbridgeable.

He sighed. 'But,' he said eventually. 'If you do succeed in having me taken off the case it'll be quite a relief to me, I assure you. I really wish I wasn't involved. I could do without all this.'

The atmosphere was angry, electric.

'Look,' Lopez's calm voice broke the angry silence.

Johns glared at her. *Day One, Minute One and she'd broken the agreement with him. She had not been asked to speak.*

'I didn't know you before this, Foster,' she said, ignoring Johns' angry stare. 'So I'm not in any way biassed. If you're taken off the inquiry ... well, that's something to be seen. Meanwhile I'll do all I can to help you. Please accept that.'

'Thanks ...' Foster began, but she held up her hand. She was determined to clear the subject first.

'No! Please hear me out,' she said. 'You see, I've personally looked into all of this. Believe me, I've been through it with a fine-toothed comb. And I must say this: there was nothing wrong with the system; absolutely nothing. Every conceivable failure mode was considered. The engineers were very careful indeed.'

There was a long silence while they looked at each other. Sizing each other up.

'I'm sure they were,' Foster said. 'I'll take that for granted for the moment. But what you've just said does lead me to ask about one person whose name came up during my enquiries: Judith Chang ...'

Johns half rose from his chair, his fists clenched aggressively on the table in front of him, his face reddening. 'Now look here, Foster...!' he exploded. But Foster held up his hand, motioning him back.

'Sit down, Andy!' he commanded. His voice was quiet, but the ice in his tone cut right through Johns' venomous outburst and forced him back into his seat. 'I *will* ask about everything on the project, and I *will* ask about everybody who was involved with the design. That's my brief and I will execute it. Chang's role is vital. She was a key member of the commissioning team. If you stop me I'll have no option but to say that in my formal report. People will draw their own conclusions.' Having silenced Johns with this, he turned to the woman. 'Now, Miss Lopez. Can you please tell me anything about her? About Chang?'

Johns glowered and glanced at Ward, but the project manager was looking down at the notes in front of him. This meeting was not going as Johns had planned. But with Foster putting questions directly to the woman, and apparently with Ward's connivance, how could he take control again?

Lopez nodded in response to Foster's question and opened her briefcase to take out a slim laptop. She switched it on, pressed some keys and after a moment read from the screen: 'Judith Chang. Age 28. Higher National Diploma in Electrical Engineering from Oxford Brooks College. Joined us three years ago after working for four years with Farnborough Technology.' She looked up from the screen and continued from memory. 'Hong-Kong Chinese parents. Mediocre formal qualifications, but a good, solid engineer in spite of that.'

'A late developer?' Foster asked.

'Yes, I'd go along with that. She's put in for sponsorship with us for an Open University degree. She spent a year with our service department, becoming familiar with power plant, and then joined Engineering as a systems designer. She did most of the systems work for Kung Tau. Came out here to commission it earlier this year.'

Foster was glad that the company was continuing to get the designers out into the field. It was something that he'd started. It was always difficult for designers to see that the concepts they'd developed in the calm quiet of their offices, and tested on the factory floor, sometimes came to grief in the harsh environment and hurly-burly of full-scale plant operations. By confronting the facts on site the engineers quickly discovered their own errors, and with any luck they never made the same mistakes again.

Now Foster needed to check how Chang would have reacted to a glamorous overseas assignment. Had she turned into one of the 'jerks' Crabtree had referred to: *jerks going ape*, as he'd said?

He asked Lopez if Chang had worked overseas before. It was a beginning; in time he would assess her attitude from other angles.

'What the hell's that got to do with it?' Johns interjected.

'Easy now, Andy,' Ward said, holding his hand up.

'Perhaps it's got nothing to do with it at all, Andy,' Foster continued calmly. 'I'm just getting all the information.'

Lopez looked at him levelly and answered his question. 'No. This was her first overseas trip,' she said, ignoring Johns' interruption. She smiled. 'I remember that she was quite excited about coming out here; to the home of her parents. Strangely enough, being born in the UK, she herself had never seen Hong Kong. Though she told me that, as a child, her head had been filled with tales of it.

'The fact is, I *wanted* to use her out here,' Lopez answered. 'Apart from being a competent engineer she speaks fluent Cantonese and Mandarin. It was a challenge for her, coming out here. I was concerned that she may have had problems with the local Chinese; you know, perhaps they'd be jealous, or suspicious. But she settled in very well. In fact, I was told by the client—personally—that she was a considerable asset to our company.'

'Good,' Foster smiled. 'I haven't met her yet, and now you've told me about her I'm looking forward to it.'

'She's out at Kung Tau,' Lopez said. 'Waiting for them to release the equipment. She wants to go over it, to see if any of it can be re-used.'

'I'll try not to delay her,' Foster said. 'Actually, I want to go over it myself with somebody who knows it, so it would be handy if she was there.'

'I'll arrange it,' Lopez offered.

'How long before you've finished all the on-site nonsense, Foster?' Johns asked scathingly. 'We need to start working on that equipment.'

'A day or so, I'd say. I'll try not to be longer than necessary.'

He went on to question Lopez about the system itself. The deeper he delved into the detail, the more he was impressed. She knew her subject very well, and in spite of her executive position with the company she had not divorced herself from the front line of the design and commissioning processes. She described how the Kung Tau DCS worked, and detailed the design process, explaining the great care that was taken to ensure that all activities were carried out by trained, competent people whose work was checked at virtually every step.

As much as he crossed and back-tracked over the complex subject, every detail of her story checked out accurately. At the end of it he was convinced that the company had done everything to make sure that the system was safe, and that it was in good hands.

Deep within, he was relieved. After all, the original Galaxy concept had been his. And he had spent too many years with Universal to be able to distance himself from the company. He had too much regard for the many people he had worked with, many of whom were still employed by them. He had always believed that he had picked the best engineers to work for him, and what he was hearing now confirmed that his judgement had been right.

But his relief was tempered with a growing sense of frustration. Because the more he delved into the labyrinth, the more he realized that the truth was still hiding from him. He was still no nearer finding a solution. All he knew now was that the checks and balances had been put properly in place by his successors at Universal, and if the safety precautions had all been working, finding out what had happened would be all the more difficult. Hearing Lopez's words, he understood that any hope of finding a simple, obvious cause for the explosion had gone.

'Satisfied now?' Johns sneered.

Foster looked coldly at him and left a moment or two before replying, enjoying his adversary's discomfort. He had meant what he had said at the beginning of the meeting; that he had come into that room bearing Johns no grudge; but the man's attitude had completely alienated them once again. It was abundantly clear that Johns had not forgotten their feud. Although he'd won the battle with Foster at Universal, surprisingly it was the victor who still harboured the rancour, not the vanquished.

'Yes, Andy,' he sighed. 'I'm satisfied—for the moment.' He turned to Carol Lopez. 'And I must say I'm impressed. You know your business, and you seem to run things very well. I congratulate you.'

There was nothing patronising in the way he said it, and the woman smiled with pleasure.

But Johns' scowl darkened. 'Will there be anything more?' he asked. 'Or can we go now?'

'No, not yet,' Foster said. 'I've not finished. I'd like to ask *you* some questions, Andy.' He took some pleasure in seeing Johns stiffen. 'I want to ask about the decision to change the system for Phase I; *after* it had been commissioned.'

'Now hang on!' Johns said angrily, and turned again to Ward for help. 'I won't have the commercial aspects examined, Brian. I just won't. Foster isn't competent to judge commercial matters, and I won't have him looking into things that are absolutely confidential between New Age, Universal Digital and Gold Win.'

Ward looked uncomfortable. 'I kinda agree, Andy,' he said. 'But I have my instructions. They're pretty clear: anything Foster asks, you answer. *Anything.*'

Johns glared at him. He had expected more support than that.

'Look,' Foster said. 'I'm not interested in any commercial aspects, Andy. Such as what your profit margin was, who your agent was, or what discounts you offered.'

He saw Johns flinch at each item. He knew very well what went on during these contract negotiations, but although they may have raised a few eyebrows if they were known, they had no bearing on the accident.

'But what I do want to know is the background to your decision to retro-fit,' he continued. 'That was as much an engineering decision as a commercial one.'

Johns scowled and there was a further moment's hesitation before he replied: 'All right. But I'll stop this if I feel it's venturing into areas that are too close to being commercially sensitive.'

Foster nodded his agreement. 'OK. But what was it that made you decide to retro-fit?' he repeated slowly.

'Obvious!' Johns replied scathingly. 'We had a new product to launch. You should remember what it's like: nobody wants to be the test-bed for something new; everybody wants a proven system; but at the same time they all want the latest and best. It's always a difficult time, bringing out a brand new system. Kung Tau was ideal: a process we knew very well; a client with whom we had done a lot of business over many years; a key site with a good publicity profile. And a job that was at just the right stage when we brought out the system. Just waiting for it.'

'But it *wasn't* just waiting for it,' Foster said. 'Phase I was finished.'

'Ah yes... but Phase II was waiting. And *that* was the one we really wanted.'

'But then why do Phase I? It must have cost you money to take out all the old equipment and swap it for something new. You could have left it there.'

'And have different generations of equipment on one site?' Lopez interjected.

She was right. By having two entirely different types of equipment at two adjacent plants on the same site, the client would have acquired a real headache with maintenance, training and spare parts.

'OK. Not ideal, I grant you,' Foster answered her. 'But plenty of places have done that. They live with it.'

'It isn't so simple,' Johns said. 'By putting Galaxy 2000 into Phase I, we were offering the client something really advanced, and something that would eventually be totally compatible with Phase II. By putting it in at our own cost, we gave Gold Win a real economic advantage at a good price.'

Foster gave a grim smile. 'And if they installed it on Phase I, it would almost guarantee that they'd buy it for Phase II.'

'Yes,' Johns snapped. 'I've no problem with admitting that. It's good sales tactics.'

'And no doubt you would sell the old equipment—the stuff you took out—to some user somewhere else, somebody who wouldn't mind getting second-hand equipment; if he ever found out.' He regretted the words almost as soon as they were spoken.

Johns reacted angrily to the jibe. 'Hold on...!' he said, but Ward interrupted.

'Now, come on, Dan,' he said, holding up his hand to stop Johns' obviously imminent explosion of rage. 'That really isn't too objective, is it? And it's bordering onto commercial confidences ...'

Foster nodded and smiled. 'Yes, you're right. I'm sorry,' he apologised. He turned to Johns. 'But ... to return to the changeover. I still don't see how you justified it to your Board.'

He knew the strict financial checking and counter-checking that would have had to be undertaken, first by Universal Digital and then at Global Associated Industries. The concept of *giving* something away – especially as something so expensive – would have been anathema to GAI.

'That's a commercial matter again,' Johns said, looking at Ward.

'All right,' Foster backed off before Ward could say anything. He had enough information at present, and that bit of the background could be looked at later.

There was not a lot more he could do at this time, so he moved on. He asked Lopez to arrange an appointment for him to meet with Judith Chang at the Kung Tau site, and then said he had nothing further to ask. Ward wrapped up the meeting with a neat and non-contentious summary of everything that had been agreed. Finally, he thanked the Universal people for coming and said there were a couple of points he wanted to discuss with Foster.

Everybody stood, and the stenographer left the room.

But Johns was not content to let matters rest there. As they reached the door, he grasped the opportunity to slight Foster again. He took Ward's arm conspiratorially; openly snubbing Foster. 'Fancy a spot of lunch, Brian?' he invited. Lopez gave Foster a quick glance and he caught the look. He raised his shoulders in an almost imperceptible shrug, tilted his head and gave her a slow impish wink, inviting her to join the conspiracy against her boss. She coloured slightly and turned away.

Johns' ploy failed. Ward, being wise and wary, declined his invitation.

After the Universal people had left, Ward sat down again, quietly, pensively looking at Foster. 'He certainly doesn't like you, does he?' he said, after a while.

'No,' Foster replied. 'I thought he would have forgotten and forgiven by now, but he hasn't. I can't understand it. He wanted me out and I went. All right, it cost them money but it didn't come out of his own pocket. We never went to court. So why the big grudge?'

'Pass. But, just what *was* it with you two? How did you get to be enemies?'

Foster shook his head slowly. 'Professional rivalry, I guess,' he offered, simply.

'Well, watch it Dan,' Ward said quietly. 'There were times there when it seemed to be getting through to you. You mustn't let it show, or folks'll think you really aren't being completely objective.'

Foster looked at him steadily. He knew it was right, and regretted some of the things he'd said. 'OK, Brian,' he said. 'I'll take care.'

There was no more to be done at the New Age offices, so Foster took his leave of Ward and headed back to the Mandarin.

He was sitting in his room after lunch when the telephone rang. It was Alison. 'I wasn't sure if you'd be finished with work,' she said. 'I'd like to talk.'

'All right,' he said. 'Come on down and have tea here.' He had thought about it carefully, and had decided he was going to tell her that the relationship was over. Bedding a member of the media was not a good idea while he was involved with this mission.

She arrived within half an hour and they went up to the Coffee Lounge. The waiter wheeled up a silver trolley and Alison selected a cream cake. In spite of her slim waist, she enjoyed food that would have put pounds on any other woman.

'You said you wanted to talk,' he said as they sipped their tea.

She shrugged and looked over the balcony beside her into the waiting room of the hotel's entrance lobby below them. 'I don't know, Dan,' she said quietly. 'Nothing special, really. I just wanted to talk.'

'About what?'

'Don't know, really. Anyway, let's talk about you. Tell me about your work. I don't know why you're here really.'

Foster cursed silently. Why was she probing? Was it merely casual interest, or was she asking for a more sinister reason? He should have found out what she was up to before telling her about his work here. True, he hadn't said very much, but it had been unwise to say even as little as he had.

'Why do you wonder?' he asked.

'I don't know. You said you were involved with the Kung Tau thing...' she said.

'Yes. I'm just trying to find out what happened.'

'Who for?' It was asked gently. Naturally. The sort of casual question anyone may have asked.

But, equally, the sort of thing the press would want to know.

'The insurers,' he lied. She was unlikely to know that insurance companies had their own investigators.

'Oh,' she said. 'And what have you discovered?'

'Not much.'

She looked at him and frowned. 'You're being very careful,' she said. 'You don't think I'm snooping into what you're doing, do you?'

''Course not.'

She leaned back and her face broke into a broad smile. 'You do, don't you?' she said teasingly. 'You actually *do* think I'd use what you tell me.'

'No.'

She leaned towards him again. 'Listen!' she said, earnestly. 'I write reports on social things. People visiting here, who's meeting whom, that sort of thing. I wouldn't even know where to begin with the sort of thing you're involved with.'

'Sure.' In spite of his best efforts, he could hear the tone of doubt in his own voice.

'It's true!' She laughed. 'You think I'm bluffing!'

'No,' he protested. 'I haven't said much because there's not much to tell. That's all.'

'OK.'

It was a sort of truce.

'Anyway,' she continued after a brief lull. 'You denied it, but you must have a woman in your life. Do you think you'll get married again?'

He looked at her seriously for a long time. Then he smiled. 'Don't know,' he said. 'Perhaps. But after Jayne ...'

'Your ex!' She swirled the tea before draining the cup. 'She was a bitch. You deserved better. I told you that last time. But still ... you should settle down now.'

She turned her eyes away from him. It was as if she had somehow made up her mind.

'Anyway, I have to go now. It was great seeing you again.' Her eyes were very dark. 'To the next time?'

It was only after she'd left that he realized that he hadn't found out what it was that she had wanted to discuss with him.

Neither had he brought their relationship to an end, as he'd intended.

He chided himself silently: *You stupid bugger!*

Chapter 9

'There's something I don't really understand, Alex,' Foster said. 'Why was Universal so late with the Phase I work? After all, they'd already finished their first pass at it. Well, virtually. Simply replicating the systems with the new Galaxy 2000 kit should have been plain sailing; or at least as simple as these things ever get.'

Cooper had telephoned Foster to say that his investigations had turned up a lot to tell. Foster, still fearful of being overheard, had suggested that they should meet at a place that offered some privacy. So, on the next morning the two men had taken a break from the hustle of the town and indulged themselves with a long hike in the Sai Kung East Country Park in the New Territories, twenty miles to the north of Kowloon.

The choice had been made without much thought. Foster wanted quiet isolation.

It never crossed his mind that Sai Kung might provide him with a vital clue, the one that would finally unlock the mystery of Kung Tau.

As they walked through the park, Cooper revealed his news. By tapping into his extensive network of friends in the industry he had discovered that, at the time of the explosion, the Kung Tau refurbishment project had been running between three and four months late on the planned schedule. Everything was properly in its place on the site, but the systems were just not working correctly. Delivering a working power-plant DCS was an involved process, prone to many errors and delays, often caused by the fact that the plant itself was being designed and built at the same time.

Here the difference between power stations and another hi-tech industry come into play. In the aviation industry, a prototype aircraft is built first and everything is then flight-tested on it before the succeeding aircraft all absolutely identical to the prototype—are put into commercial service.

With big power stations, each one is more or less unique. There *is* no prototype; the control systems are designed on a basic understanding of how the finished system will work and where everything will be located, although on the huge mechanical plant things were always being changed. The control-system designer was very much 'Tail-end Charlie' in this process; largely forgotten when, for example, somebody realized that a pump had been accidentally omitted from the design. In the panic to make sure the missing item was specified, bought and installed correctly, the facilities to start and stop it were often left to the end, sometimes until *after* the control system had been designed, built, shipped to site and installed.

But these problems shouldn't have arisen on a plant where an identical precursor had already been built; and built very recently. Here, there would have been little time to allow things to be changed, or for information to have become forgotten or lost. The plant side of it would have been fixed, cut and dried, and every aspect of it would have been thoroughly familiar to everybody involved with it. So what had delayed commissioning of the control system?

'That was *very* interesting,' Cooper said. 'See, they'd been having problems... with the kit itself.'

'What kind of problems?' Foster felt himself tense. Was this the answer he so desperately needed to solve the problem? Was it the oddity that Tony Crabtree and Paul Lee had set out to identify on that fateful day? ''Fraid that's the bit I *don't* know,' Cooper said, deflating Foster's hopes. 'But it was big. They sent a team of boffins out from the UK to look at it. They arrived with shed-loads of test equipment.'

'Oh? And did they find anything?'

'Nobody knows, mate. Apparently they changed a few bits and pieces, and then they buggered off home ... so I suppose they cracked it.'

Foster thought about it. The equipment that made up the Galaxy installation would have been checked over very thoroughly at the factory before it was shipped to Kung Tau. For something to go wrong later, or to be discovered later, something that warranted the expense of shipping engineers and test equipment to a site many thousands of miles away ... It must have been something very elusive, not the usual slip-up caused by pressure to ship equipment out of the factory before the end of the month. *That* sort of cock-up was commonplace, a problem simply left to the people on site to fix as best they could. No, this was a big one; something that had slipped unnoticed through the factory tests, something that those tests had not simulated.

That meant it had to be something in the particular installation, perhaps in the way it had been put together on site ... or even something in the environment.

In his time Foster had known of equipment that had worked well in the cool, calm and quiet surroundings of a factory floor in England, but which stubbornly failed to work properly in the heat, noise and humidity of a power station in the tropics. For that reason, most systems were thoroughly tested under conditions of high temperature, artificially applied on the shop floor. But even this couldn't cover all the factors. Say it was humidity?

He remembered Crabtree saying the incident had happened during a tropical storm. Could that have had a bearing on it?

'What was the weather doing at the time?' he asked Cooper, almost absent-mindedly, and then realized what he'd asked. He grimaced. 'I'm sorry, I was deep in thought. How could you know a thing like that?'

Cooper laughed. 'Christ! I know you think I know everything, old mate,' he said. 'But that *would* be a bit of a tall order! All I know is that it was summer.'

'Hot and humid,' Foster said quietly. 'Typhoon season.'

Was that it? He looked pensively across the lush countryside towards a small golden beach far below.

The silent, vast expanse of the park's hills was a temporary respite, a remedy for the noise-sickness most outsiders felt after spending any length of time in Hong Kong. Here, in the New Territories, they were still in Hong Kong, but here it was quiet, unlike the business areas of Kowloon and Central with their incessant bustle of traffic and noisy crowds.

The Park covered thousands of hectares of a ragged-edged peninsula pointing Northeast in a line running roughly along the edge of mainland China. From the air it looked like a loosely crumpled ball of green-and-brown paper that had been tossed carelessly into the sea. The area was what geologists call a *ria*, a series of coastal valleys submerged by rising seas at the end of the Ice Age and comprising a complex, rumpled mass of land, with fingers reaching seawards, separated by deep-cut creeks and inlets. It was a true haven of silence, punctuated only by the cries of birds.

The only man-made sound there was the occasional hooting of the *kai-do* ferry that called twice a day at simple jetties in the area's little inlets. The boat would arrive at a jetty and tie up while the echoes of its siren died away and silence returned to the surroundings. Then, in their ones and twos, figures would emerge from the hills; people summoned by the siren and coming to board the ferry, making their way towards it along narrow paths leading down to the pier. When they were aboard, the vessel would fuss away from the jetty to enter the channel, moving on to the next calling-place and the next few straggling passengers. And after it was out of sight, silence would once again return to the bay.

With the promise of a fine sunny day ahead of them, Foster had arranged for the Mandarin to provide a picnic. He and Cooper had then ridden the railway to the bustling town of Sha Tin, from there taking a double-decker bus to a fishing village, Sai Kung. From the bus terminal there they had taken yet another bus to the park. On alighting there, they had walked for two hours, firstly along a winding concrete path and, after that, along a narrow track running through empty grassland.

Now they sat on the edge of an escarpment, looking down across a broad hollow covered with shrubs and low trees. This silent sweep of land led to the coast and a beach of yellow sand.

Foster had once heard that if you sailed due east from this spot your first landfall would be Peru. To their left, a serrated, dragons'-teeth line of jagged hills edged the horizon, the nearer ones green-brown, the farthest pale violet, veiled with haze. The highest mountain in that range, *Nam She Tsim*—Sharp Peak—looked as if a gigantic finger had pressed skyward from beneath the earth's mantle, stretching the skin into a spectacularly pointed nipple of rock. Its steep and dangerous slopes provided, for anybody fit enough to climb it, a spectacular view across the shimmering waters of Mirs Bay, to the Chinese mainland.

Foster had scrambled up Sharp Peak once, his boots slipping and sliding on the narrow path with its frequent man-traps of decomposed granite; glass-like beads that had several times threatened to roller-blade him down the steep slopes to the rocks hundreds of metres below. But it had been worth the effort. As he had stood beside the stubby white surveying pillar at the mountain's summit he had felt as though he had conquered Everest!

But that had been many years ago. *Now I might think twice before trying it again*, he thought.

And as he looked at the peak he remembered the unpleasant shock he had experienced then; of finding a mess of cans, plastic bottles and discarded garbage at its summit. He wondered if that had been cleared up now, in anticipation of the Peoples' Republic imprinting its sterner disciplines on the territory.

He turned his eyes from the rock and handed his companion a chilled can of beer from the insulated lunch-bag.

'They treat you all right,' Cooper said against the sudden pop and hiss of the can as he tugged the ring-pull. 'The Mandarin, I mean.'

Foster grinned and nodded his agreement. The lunch was cold chicken-legs, smoked salmon sandwiches, crusty rolls, salad, fresh fruit, beers and a half-bottle of white wine in a chilled insulated container. He had ordered lunch for two, although from past experience he knew that one would have been almost enough for both of them, hungry as they were after their strenuous hike.

They ate and drank almost in silence. The only sounds here were the cries of the gulls and the incessant, gentle soughing of the wind sweeping up from the sea and skimming through the narrow vee-shaped valley beside them.

After the meal they packed away and began the gentle descent along the path to the beach. When they reached the shoreline and were walking along the water's edge, Foster decided to ask if Cooper had heard anything about any other contracts where the Galaxy system had been used. If there were it would partly explain the urgent need to solve the mystery; to prevent the same fault from causing yet more damage.

If there was such a project, he was sure the news would have leaked out among the tightly-knit engineering community in this part of the world.

Cooper laughed at the question. 'Yes,' he said. 'There's rumours of another Galaxy system. But it's *numero uno* big secret,' he said. 'It's one everybody asks about. But no! Nobody knows anything about it; except that it's a big'un.'

'No clues?' Foster asked. 'Nothing at all?'

Cooper shook his head.

They walked on in silence along the golden bay, with the Pacific rollers crashing to the sand to their right. Eventually, reaching another footpath at the far side, they took it and headed up towards the hills.

Cooper broke away from the dry discussion of power stations. 'I don't mean to pry, Mate, but that bird in the Mandarin the other night,' he asked. 'Who was she?'

Foster grinned. There were few secrets between them. 'Just an old flame, Alex,' he said thoughtfully. 'Someone from way back.'

'Well, she was a cracker. Like I said at the time: you know how to pull them. You always had a way with the birds.'

In a moment of sombre introspection one evening—aided by considerable quantities of alcohol—Cooper had confided to Foster that his wife, with all her severe pretensions, was frigid. After her smiling wet-lipped enticement of him at the beginning, after he had swallowed the bait and was firmly hooked, *then* she had become metallically cold. Their nuptial bed had become a barren, cold reminder of battles long since fought and lost. Without actually putting it into words, she had convinced Cooper that it was his fault, that he was a clumsy lover, incapable of understanding a woman's needs. As a result he had retreated from any further involvement with women and seemed to survive vicariously on tales of other men's exploits. He never showed jealousy or malice when listening to the stories, but his expression sometimes showed an empty sadness.

Even as Foster now spoke of the women in his life, there was no resentment in Cooper's expression.

'She was from a long time ago,' Foster said. 'Oh, it's good for the ego to know you're not too old. But this one ... well, she's a complication ... one I really don't need at present.'

'Looked fun though.'

Foster nodded and smiled. *Fun?* He thought. It depended on your point of view. If you could blinker yourself to the implications and risks, a fling with her might well have been very enjoyable. But in his present situation that was a luxury he simply could not afford.

The two men's path now veered away from the water and, after an hour's strenuous climbing, followed by a gentle descent along a winding tree-covered path, they reached a narrow inlet. The beach was invisible from this low trough, but they could hear the surf quite loudly ahead of them. Tucked into the trees ahead was a small group of dilapidated buildings.

Foster and Cooper walked through a narrow alley between whitewashed walls and reached a tiny shelter; no more than four low brick walls topped with a sheet of rusty corrugated iron supported on poles. At the front, the entrance was merely a gap in the wall, beside a crude window of slatted wood.

'Ah! It's still there,' Cooper said, peering through the slats into the gloom within. 'The bush bottle-shop.'

Cooper had told his friend about this strange little enterprise that he had once discovered here, a café in the middle of nowhere, and he'd given it the name normally used for small bars found in the African veldt.

Suddenly, as they entered, a premonition came to Foster.

He didn't know where it came from, but it was almost shouting at him: *Here! The answer will be here!*

It was ridiculous. He shook aside the stupid idea and entered the dark interior of the café.

A few plastic-topped tables and rickety chairs were scattered under the sun-baked metal roof. In the far corner, a scrawny Chinese man of indeterminate age sat hunched over an open can of beer at his table. He looked up and grinned briefly in an alcoholic haze at the Westerners as they entered. Then his sombre attention returned to the drink in front of him.

Two women had been sitting at one of the tables, and at the arrival of the Westerners one of them stood up and hobbled slowly towards them, using a stick to support her slight weight. Foster judged her to be at least eighty years old.

She looked incredibly frail, almost skeletal, and her blue-grey skull shone through sparse grey hair. Her skin was a mass of creases and folds, like scraps of dried grey canvas stretched across the bony frame of her skull. She cackled something unintelligible at the Westerners and gestured towards one of the tables.

The two men sat down and Cooper said 'Beer!' which drew another burst of unintelligible noise from her. '*Tsing Tao!*' he added and this evidently resonated with her because the flow of words stopped and she repeated his phrase slowly, all the while staring hard at him. He nodded and she turned to wobble towards a drinks-cooler near the back wall of the place. The machine was emblazoned with the Coca Cola logo.

'It's a wonder it doesn't overload the circuits!' Foster said, indicating the cooler. Engineers as always, they had noticed the power cable dangling untidily outside the building. The lines were strung carelessly from hovel to hovel, the fuses and meters dangling precariously from the walls. Foster wondered if anybody ever ventured out here to read the meters.

The crone arrived back and put two straight-sided glasses and ice-cold bottles of unlabelled Chinese beer down on the table, then she dragged her way back painfully to her own chair and slumped down.

Throughout this performance, the other woman had sat totally still, glaring at the men intensely. The look in her face was hard to interpret, but it was near hateful malevolence. She was younger than the one who had brought the beers, but only by a few years. She wore a neatly ironed grey shift whose surface was almost undisturbed by the tiny frame within it. She was painfully thin, and her short black hair cropped close to her skull accentuated her high, prominent cheekbones and the unblinking, glittering eyes beside the hooked nose that gave her face the look of a hunting raptor.

Foster leant forward as he poured beer into his glass. 'Do they want customers,' he asked quietly. 'Or are we intruding on something?'

Cooper smiled. 'Neither!' he replied. 'They're Hakka.'

Hakka in Cantonese means 'Guest People'. The Hakka were a semi-nomadic folk who had once worked the fields of southern China. Now they were drifters, a strange community; isolated by dress, language and customs from the others around them. Their women were to be found everywhere, in isolated fields, on construction sites and at roadworks. While working, they wore round, conical wide-brimmed straw hats with long black fringes that almost covered their faces. Without those fringes the hats, with their hemispherical black centres, would have looked like small flying saucers that had settled on their owners' heads.

'Once they would've worked in the paddy-fields round 'ere,' Cooper continued. 'But their trade's been killed. By a combination of collectivization to the North, commercial development to the South. Plus, this place being zoned as a Country Park. This is survival for them. The few bucks they make on our beers'll probably feed 'em for a week. Any'ow…' he fingered the droplets of condensation running down the bare glass of the bottle. 'The beer's probably been smuggled or pirated!' He paused for a moment and looked thoughtfully around at the primitive structure. 'Shame really,' he said finally. 'They'll die or leave soon, and this place'll be abandoned. You can find old villages like this all over this area, all of 'em deserted.

'I found one once, y'know. It looked like the *'Marie Celeste'*; everyone'd walked out. It was weird. There were cups on the tables, even a pair of spectacles standin' on the bottom edges of their lenses. As though the owner'd just taken them off for a bit.'

'Why?' Foster asked. 'What happens?'

'The youngsters don't work on the farms any more. They go off to the bright lights, so there's no continuity. In fact, some of the people who used to live in places like that were the first to emigrate; you'll find them or their descendants running fish-and-chip shops or Chinese restaurants all over Blighty! Or Canada for that matter; lots of the buggers have drifted out there now. Anyhow, for whatever reason, the villages gradually fall empty; all that's left in the end are the old folk. And when they eventually die ... then there's nothing left.

'Y'know, I sometimes think about what happens when the kids have gone and one of the parents eventually dies. The poor bugger that's left, coping alone and dealing with the body...'

It was a sombre thought, and the two men contemplated it for a while before Cooper continued, 'They've restored one of the old walled villages in Tsuen Wan, y'know. It's just like the ones I saw, but they've turned it into a museum, a tourist attraction. It's pretty good. Though they've filled it with classier furniture than the original owners would've owned, I'm sure.'

Throughout this time, the lone man at the other table had studied the westerners with considerable interest between pulls at his beer. At last he spoke to them cheerily.

'You lorra trawwel!' he called noisily.

Foster looked at Cooper who smiled back. *The local lush*, his eyes said. He addressed the man. 'That's right mate! We've travelled a long way.'

The man's grin widened in delight that he had been understood.

'Wha' you caw?' he asked, nodding at Cooper.

'I'm called Alex.'

'Ah! Vewwy good! Ar-ex! Ar-ex!' He seemed to be rolling the words in his mouth, tasting them. Then he turned to Foster. 'An' you?' he asked, pointing at him.

'Dan.'

The man was hugely delighted. The word evidently amused him for some unknown reason. 'Ho!' he cried. 'Good! Ho! Ho! Vewwy good! Dan!' Then he asked, 'Where you come?'

When he heard that Foster was from England he beamed. 'I been Yingran',' he said proudly. 'Riwwerpoo'. Sairor on Wee Air See-See.'

Foster slowly deciphered this in his mind, until he understood it; the man had been a seaman on a supertanker. He would have been one of the many Chinese who crew who worked on these vessels, the 'Very Large Crude Carriers', or VLCCs as they were known in the industry. In his many voyages, Foster had met these people working as deckhands or galley-staff of the massive vessels as they ploughed their way through the world's oceans. He knew that many of them had settled in ports around the globe. In this man's case, it had evidently been Liverpool.

'But you've come back home now,' Foster said. 'To Hong Kong.'

The man's mood turned instantly from beery *bonhomie* to lugubrious sadness. He nodded, but evidently whatever had taken him half way round the globe to a strange and alien place, and then returned him here, would remain a private mystery, because he abruptly changed the subject. 'You go Kai-do?' he asked. The last syllable was almost spat out, yet softened by being pronounced with the tongue between his teeth.

'No,' Cooper said. 'We walk.'

'You no lai' Kai-do?' the lush asked, scowling. Foster wondered if this was now the man's trade, running a ferry between these islands. Such a vessel would have been a huge contrast with the gigantic slabs of steel and roaring machinery that he had once worked on across the oceans.

'Kai-do fine,' Cooper reassured him. He grinned and patted his belly. 'We walk. Otherwise we get too old and fat. Need exercise.'

The man nearly fell off his chair in delight. 'No! You no fat! You vewwy strong men.' He pointed at Foster. 'Spesharry you, Ar-ex.'

'I'm Dan,' Foster said and pointed to Cooper. 'He's Alex.'

The man ignored this and returned to finishing his beer. Suddenly he lurched to his feet and wobbled his way towards the door. The conversation was evidently over. 'I go now,' he called, at nobody in particular. 'Kai-do!'

As he reached the door he turned. 'Come, Ar-ex! Look!' he beckoned.

Cooper started to stand but the man scowled disapproval. 'No you,' he waved Cooper back. 'No, you!' He pointed to Foster. 'You! Ar-ex!'

Seeing that the error was probably past correction, Foster winked at Cooper and stood up.

At the door the man reached up to put an arm round Foster's shoulders and pointed down a steep slope beside the shack. There, tied up in a narrow creek was a small boat with a huge Mercury outboard motor at its stern. 'Warra-warra!' the man said, breathing beer over Foster's face. 'Tay' you Kai-do?'

Walla-wallas were tiny ferries, named after the recognized method of hailing them with an upraised arm and a shout. Here the walla-walla would be used to carry passengers to the jetties where the larger Kai-do ferries arrived.

'Thanks, pal, but no. I don't want to get to the ferry,' Foster insisted. 'No Kai-do!'

The man looked crestfallen, released his clasp sadly and shambled away down the path in silence. Foster stood at the door sipping his cold beer and watched as the man boarded his boat. Very soon the engine started and, with a mighty roar and a cloud of light blue smoke from the exhaust, the craft set off towards the shimmering sea and the incoming Kai-do.

Foster now understood. This was probably only the man's day job. Foster had few doubts that the huge outboard was there for other compelling reasons; perhaps such as evading the PRC patrols as he smuggled goods or people across the sea after dark. He was probably related to the two women at the bar and was the provider of their supplies of smuggled beer and *Coca Cola*.

Foster turned round ...

And then he stopped in his tracks.

Suddenly something in the man's words had registered in his brain, and all at once realization hit him.

Cooper frowned as he saw his friend, standing stock still, staring at him without seeing him. For a moment Cooper wondered uneasily if a larg cockroach or spider had crawled up the back of his chair and appeared on his shoulder.

'What's up, Mate?' he asked.

Foster shook himself back to the present reality. 'Jesus Christ, Alex!' he breathed. 'How could I have been so blind! Why didn't I see it before? It's so bloody obvious: Dan, Ar-ex! Ar-ex, Dan!'

Cooper sighed with relief and chuckled. 'OK. He was a mite confused. That's all.'

'No!' Foster said, sitting down heavily and looking out of the window. 'No! It's not that. It's something else. Something relating to Kung Tau.'

'Pardon?'

Foster shook his head again. 'Sorry Alex. This must sound like gibberish. But, what that guy said; it's just given me an idea. I can't be certain, but I wonder ...'

He paused and Cooper looked at him quizzically.

Eventually Foster said, 'I wonder... I wonder if I've just stumbled onto what happened at the plant. The day it blew up.'

Cooper stared at him, his eyes widening.

Chapter 10

Relaxing on a settee in the British Airways' VIP lounge at Heathrow, Foster mused at the events of the past few days, which had so transformed his life, catapulting him from obscure penury back into the jet-setters' high life that had once been so familiar to him. He wondered wryly whether he'd be able to settle back into running the shop when all of this was over.

The *shop?* The very idea of it seemed weirdly out of place now. With the fee he was being paid he'd certainly be able to write off his debts, with a generous amount left over, so from the financial point of view he would be a free agent.

The question was: what did he really want to do with his life after this was over? Having mused over the options for a while he had come to no firm conclusion, so he then returned to considering the present.

As soon as he had returned to his hotel from Sai Kung, he had called Fiona Wilson in London and told her that he believed he now knew what had happened. He stressed that, before he could confirm his suspicions, he needed to go to Universal Digital's complex in Abingdon.

After a brief consultation with her superiors, Fiona had called him back and told him it was all agreed. The following day, a first-class reservation had been confirmed for him to fly to Heathrow.

It amused him to think that he had left Andy Johns in Hong Kong. At first, Carol Lopez—who had already returned to England—had tried to avoid letting Foster come to Abingdon while Johns was still in Hong Kong, because she was sure her boss would not want the meeting to proceed in his absence. But Foster had applied pressure via Arnold Coward and Partners, and after much frantic argument and many calls to an increasing angry and impotent Johns, it had all been agreed. As Foster turned these thoughts over in his mind, the door opened and the suave BA Special Services agent who had escorted him off the plane came into the lounge with Fiona Wilson. She was smiling as she approached and, to his great surprise, she stood on tiptoe as they met, and kissed him. It was quite unexpected; it was a soft, warm and inviting kiss, lips to lips. Suddenly Foster was confused.

What did she want from him?

She gave him no time to think, but instead took his arm and led him to her car, which was parked in the VIP area. It was a Honda convertible, and from the confident way she gunned it onto the link road, Foster guessed she was very fond of it, and he soon discovered that she was a competent driver to boot.

As they swung onto the M4, she asked him what he had discovered.

'It's quite complicated ...' he started.

'You mean, for a budding lawyer to understand!' she laughed.

'Well, for anybody really. Unless you're in the know.'

'Try me.'

'OK.' He thought briefly about how best to explain it, and then decided to lay it out in simple terms. He started by telling her about the incident at Sai Kung. Seeing that she was puzzled at the connection, he went on to describe how the Kung Tau computers had operated.

'Systems like the one that was controlling the plant are made up of lots of separate computers, all talking to each other. Each one does a defined job, and messages from each one are broadcast, each with an address of the intended recipient.'

'Like letters in the mail?' she commented.

'Well, yes and no. It's more like circulars, where everybody gets to see a message, and if it's for them they take action. If not, they pass it on to the next person.'

'Who also looks to see if it's for them?'

'Exactly. In the Galaxy system, each computer is identified by a unique number, known as its 'address'.'

'Go on,' she said as she switched the Honda into the M25 approach lane.

'Well, the systems on a big, hazardous plant like Kung Tau are very carefully designed, with all sorts of checks and balances to make sure that very little can go wrong, and even if it does, the problem is detected and rectified before any harm can be done.'

'But something *did* go wrong,' she said. 'After all, it was the computers that blew up plant!'

'But I didn't know that at first,' Foster said. 'In fact, I was sure that it simply could *not* have been the computer system. But now I'm sure of it.'

'But something changed your mind.'

'Yes. When I looked through the logs ...'

'Logs?'

'Yes, the computer-generated records that keep track of events. It was then that I discovered that, in the brief seconds before the explosion, it seemed as though the plant was deliberately being directed towards a catastrophe.'

'What do you mean?'

'Well, as I trawled through the evidence, I became increasingly convinced that it was the computers that had somehow created the right conditions for a disaster. But I just couldn't see how they did it.

'And then, I met that guy who confused my name with Alex's.'

'Confusion?' Fiona asked, throwing him a puzzled look. 'You think the same thing happened at Kung Tau?'

'Exactly!'

'But what about all the checks and balances that you mentioned?'

'That's what threw me at first,' Foster replied. 'You see, there are several levels of checking. At one level, when the system asks for a valve to open, it looks for an acknowledgement that the valve's responded. If it doesn't, an alarm is raised. The system certainly won't move on to the next step until it receives an assurance that it's safe to do so.'

'OK,' Fiona answered, concentrating on the road ahead. 'So much I understand.'

'That's not all,' Foster continued. 'There's something else. If a message somehow gets sent to the wrong valve, which acts on it, the system will get a signal saying the valve has moved, although it wasn't asked to.'

'So how could it go wrong?'

'That's what fooled me,' he said. 'And then that mix-up happened in Hong Kong. When the guy spoke to me, but used Alex's name, it was only when Alex and I both decided to ignore the mistake, and effectively swapped identities; it was *then* that the real confusion started.'

'Are you saying that it wasn't just one computer that got confused, but two?'

'Yes!' he said. 'Perhaps—well, almost certainly—even more than two.'

Seeing her looking puzzled he went on, 'You see, when one computer picks up a message intended for another, and reacts because its addressing has been scrambled, the alarms will be raised when it answers.'

'Because it's answering a question that wasn't addressed to it?'

'No! Because the device that the message was intended for will also answer.'

'So the sender gets two answers!'

'Right! And that would raise the alarm. But say the other computer also has a scrambled address…'

'Is that possible?' she asked. Then, after a long pause she continued, 'Surely two faults like that are very unlikely.'

'They are! Statistically, the likelihood of one fault is tiny; the chances of another occurring at the same time are infinitesimal. It's impossible, really.'

'So how …'

'Don't know, Fiona,' he said. 'That's why I need to talk to them at Abingdon.'

By then they had joined the M25. In half an hour or so, he guessed, they'd be there.

In Universal's glass-walled headquarters, the Technical Director's office looked out over a broad sweep of the Thames. A thin wind was snatching at the last few leaves that clung stubbornly to the trees. The branches whipped against the flat grey sky, and Foster couldn't help but compare the scene with the lush green vegetation in the sunlit tropical land he had left just a few days before.

'A bit different from Hong Kong!' Fiona said quietly as they waited, having checked in at reception.

'You said it!'

Just then Carol Lopez came in behind them, and they turned from the window.

'Dr Foster!' she said, offering her elegant hand. 'I'm so pleased to see you. And you, Miss Wilson.'

He grinned as he took her hand. 'My pleasure! I'm not sure about Andy though.'

'Andy?' Her voice was sharp.

'I know how hard he worked to stop me coming here.'

'Oh.'

'Never mind. There's something I want to discuss with you.'

'Come through to my office,' she invited, and led the way.

They all sat down, Foster and Fiona facing Lopez across her massive desk. Foster noted that the desk was devoid of paper. There was just a speaker-phone on it, alongside an elegant tooled blotter-pad. He was impressed; he was very familiar with the huge volume of paper her job attracted, and the clean expanse of desk indicated that she was very well-organised.

'This is just a possibility,' Foster said, cutting to the chase right away. 'But I wonder: have you ever had—or suspected—an addressing problem with Galaxy?'

'Addressing?' Lopez exclaimed.

She looked baffled. What Foster was querying was very basic, a fundamental tenet of many computer systems. 'You can't be serious!' she exclaimed, shaking her head slowly in disbelief. 'You can't really be suggesting that the explosion was caused by something that basic!'

'I know!' Foster agreed. 'It seems incredible, I know.

'But just imagine what would happen if the device addresses could somehow get mixed up. A command would be acted on by an unauthorised device…'

'That's ridiculous!' Lopez interjected. 'We have software checks to guard against such a thing happening. Lots of checks. Hardware as well.'

'Anyway, a single fault would be picked up immediately.'

'I'm sure,' Foster said. 'And at first I thought the same thing. But say—just say—that you had a whole batch of decoders that were faulty.'

A decoder was a type of computer chip that received commands and compared them with addresses in their memory. If a correspondence was detected, the message was forwarded for action.

Lopez stared at him. He could see from her expression that she could see that what he had described was a real possibility. It *could* have happened. It was not impossible.

Eventually she sighed. 'All right,' she continued, trying to keep her voice calm. 'But let's be rational about this. I have to admit that what you've said is a possibility. But there's no more than a *chance* of something happening, and a pretty minute one at that. Have you any evidence that it *did* actually happen?'

'Well, no,' Foster replied, doubtfully. 'Not actually. I can't hold up a faulty chip and say "*This* is what did it!" But it *has* to be the answer. Once you follow it through, you can see what happened... It explains everything.'

Suddenly she paused, and breathed, 'Oh my God!' There was a catch in her voice when she said it.

'What?' Foster asked.

'I've just remembered,' Lopez said, her voice very quiet. 'Our Resident Engineer at Kung Tau reported a series of chip failures to me. Weeks before the explosion. But I didn't think it was serious. I was sure that the system would check and alarm the fault. But now I think I can see implications.'

'This is terrible!' Foster said. 'Even as I came here I was still hoping you'd say that the faults couldn't occur. Now you're telling me you have a *multiple-fault* situation?'

She nodded. Her expression was bleak.

Suddenly Lopez straightened her back and took a deep breath. 'We don't know,' she said. 'Let's not jump to conclusions. We have to be certain. Let's go to the shop floor.'

She stood up and led the way out of her office towards the factory. Her two guests followed on, Foster sniffing at the prospect that the puzzle was at last going to be resolved, one way or another.

The factory floor was a vast, cavernous area. Its clinically-clean plastic-tiled floor, bathed in the harsh white glare of the overhead lights, was covered with a mass of steel cubicles linked to each other and to overhead power-distribution channels by a jungle of cables trailing liana-wise upwards and sideways into the dark void above the striplights.

In one area, a suite of ten cubicles was being heat-soaked; subjected to an artificially-high temperature to check its operation under extreme conditions. The cabinets were for a power-station contract in the tropics, where the sensitive electronic equipment would be required to operate faultlessly even if the power-plant's air-conditioning systems broke down.

The system was enclosed in a frame of scaffolding covered with plastic sheeting that formed an all-enveloping tent, inside of which hot-air blowers raised the temperature to a stifling 50° Celsius.

As they approached, they could make out through the milky plastic screen a pale shape moving inside, like a sea horse swimming upright inside the clouded glass walls of a dirty fish-tank.

Lopez signalled to them to wait. 'It'll be a tad uncomfortable in there,' she said.

Foster knew it well, but he decided to wait outside, to keep Fiona company.

Lopez raised the entrance flap of the tent—and the breath of hell licked out at them. Apart from the stifling heat there was an incessant deep hum from the fans that were mercilessly blasting their hot breath into the enclosure.

The man working in this Hades was writing on a clip-board. He was wearing a white boiler-suit over nothing more than his pants because, although most of his work would in fact be done outside the tent, it was at times necessary for him to enter it to check something or other. Although he wouldn't remain there long, even a short exposure to that temperature would saturate his clothes with sweat.

Now he looked up as the draught of cool air announced the arrival of a visitor.

'Got a minute, Bill?' Lopez said, raising her voice to be heard above the din, and pointing over her shoulder. What she had to ask would be better done in the cool and quiet air outside the tent.

Bill Reid was head of the company's Quality-Assurance team. He nodded, hung the clip-board up on a bolt protruding from one of the panels and followed her out.

As Reid saw Foster, he gave a broad grin and the two men shook hands warmly. Their friendship went back a long way.

Lopez introduced him to Fiona and they too shook hands.

'What's up, Carol?' Reid asked. He was a large-framed man, almost completely bald, and now he mopped at the vast expanse of his sweat-beaded forehead with a large handkerchief. Reid had a lot of respect for his Technical Director, as she had for him. They each understood the other's viewpoint, even when they came into conflict.

And come into conflict they occasionally did, because at times Engineering made demands that were difficult to implement, and QA had to steer a tricky course between what was demanded, what Manufacturing preferred and the constant financial pressures of the contract. Reid answered directly to Andy Johns, theoretically to satisfy clients that Quality Assurance had a direct line to the Managing Director, but practically to ensure that Johns had *total* control of everything that happened—and of everything else that was reported to the clients' own QA teams.

Manufacture of one of these large systems was an intricate process involving immensely long, tightly interwoven chains of instructions and decisions. To satisfy the accountants, as much as to meet clients' deadlines, a quantity of systems valued at a certain amount, had to be shipped out of the factory door each month. Theoretically, QA could hold back a shipment if a serious fault were to be discovered in it, but in practice this would have brought red-hot coals down onto Reid's head.

Staff and suppliers had to be paid each month, and if a major shipment was delayed the company could not issue the necessary invoices to the client. No income that month to support the inevitable outgoings meant a serious dip in the cash-flow.

The accountants would not like that. At times, corners had to be cut. QA would look for a waiver: Engineering would fight against it. In these circumstances Andy Johns would inevitably overrule Lopez and the company service department would eventually have to sort out the errors after the equipment had been delivered to site, often tens of thousands of miles from the availability of informed technical assistance. To make things worse, the remedies would have to be performed under the critical eyes of the client and against a rapidly approaching deadline.

And by then the deadline would be totally irrevocable; for all its complexity and cost, a plant's DCS was only a minor part of the whole, and contracts worth many tens or hundreds of millions would depend on the system being commissioned on time.

A fault that could have been resolved in Abingdon in the matter of a few days—cheaply—with expert help around, and all the necessary parts and test equipment within easy access, would have to be corrected on site, with all the attendant costs and difficulties.

And this happened simply because a few days' delay would have carried the shipment out of one month's financial output figures and into the next.

The concept of the Managing Director being personally responsible for the quality of the company's operations was a fine one. But Johns was always careful to obtain written evidence that he had acted on his executives' advice, so that if anything went wrong he would always have someone to blame. A scapegoat.

'Dan's raised a question, Bill,' Lopez said. 'Have you ever heard of an addressing problem in the Galaxy system?'

Reid thought for a while, then shook his head. 'No,' he said. 'What sort of problem?'

She didn't want to prompt him; if possible; she wanted him to point to the problem independently. Most of all, she didn't want to cause any unnecessary panic or to start any hares running without good reason.

'Any problem,' she said. 'Anything at all.'

Reid scratched his head. 'No, I don't think we have,' he replied. 'We did at one time wonder if an addressing problem was the source of the 'Ghost', but we checked. You remember; we found nothing.'

''Ghost'?' Fiona asked.

'Yes,' Reid said. 'We had a problem with the systems at Kung Tau. Because the problems came and went mysteriously, somebody nicknamed the phenomenon the 'Ghost'.'

Fiona nodded.

'What do the statistical failure analyses show?' Lopez continued. 'Any pattern?'

A DCS consisted of tens of thousands of individual electronic components. Nothing is ever faultless; even a batch of brand-new components will sometimes contain a few bad ones among the good, but the company maintained careful records of all failures. These records were regularly analysed to determine if any pattern was observable in the types of failure. If one type of component, for example, showed a rising curve of failures, the manufacturer would be asked to tackle the problem before it became troublesome.

Components arriving in a faulty state at the factory could be easily detected and rejected. But components sometimes suffered 'infant mortality'; they worked correctly on arrival, only to fail shortly afterwards. By then they had been incorporated into complex sub-assemblies, and removing them was difficult, if not impossible; and it was certainly expensive.

If the components survived long enough to be built into complete systems and *then* went wrong, the problems were compounded.

Reid went over to a nearby computer terminal and tapped at the keyboard. He studied the screen and tapped again. After doing this several times he shrugged and shook his head again. 'No pattern that I can see,' he said. 'Nothing.'

Lopez frowned. Then she had an inspiration. 'Any rise in purchases that doesn't match production?' she asked.

Normally, purchases of components would match what the factory was producing. Everything arriving at the Goods Inwards department would eventually leave the factory again, either in a completed assembly or in the scrap bin. Correlation from one set of figures to the other wasn't easy—varying production timescales, usage of spares and so on made it a complicated matter—but, over a long time, trends could be detected.

Reid frowned at her briefly before returning to his computer. This enquiry was not in the normal pattern and he needed to make a few more entries. He tapped furiously at the keys. 'Nope!' he said, as he finished. 'Everything seems to track ...'

Suddenly he stopped in mid-flow and bent to squint at the screen. 'No, hang on!' he said, a puzzled tone in his voice. 'That's odd! There *is* something funny going on. It's with the 9000 series chips.'

'Funny?' Lopez asked. 'What way?' The beginnings of a dreadful fear were gripping at her stomach.

Reid tapped at the keyboard. But evidently the same answer came back. He frowned and clicked his tongue. 'I don't believe this!' he said. 'We bought twenty thousand of the 9000s last year.'

'*Twenty thousand!*' It was Foster's turn to exclaim in surprise.

'That can't be,' Lopez said. 'We shipped, what...? Twelve-odd systems during the year...'

'And each system has a couple of hundred of them?' Foster said.

'Well, the biggest system we've built so far had two hundred decoders. The average is around a hundred to a hundred and fifty.'

'On that average of a hundred and fifty that's eighteen hundred in a year,' Lopez gasped. 'Yet we bought *twenty thousand*! What's going on, Bill? How come we used more than ten times as many as we should have?'

Reid looked helpless and held his hands out sideways, palms upward in a puzzled gesture. 'Pass!' he said.

'Hasn't this been reported back to the manufacturer?' Foster asked.

'No, Dan,' Reid replied. 'Because we haven't got them recorded as defects.'

'What?' It was Lopez's turn to be shocked. The discrepancy between the numbers implied that the number of faulty chips they'd received was huge. 'So where are they?' she asked. 'Over *eighteen thousand* dud chips? Surely not in the scrap bin?'

Reid frowned at her. 'Well, with the pressure we're under, it's possible. You know what happens. The guys are pressurized to get systems shipped. If they find a fault, they're supposed to record it; but, practically, there's never enough time. So they remove the component and scrap it. Maybe they mean to log it, but for whatever reason they never get down to it. Anyway, they sometimes blow up chips themselves, during manufacture.'

Foster knew it was true. During the long stages of test, manufacture and re-test of a system it was possible to inadvertently damage components by subjecting them to conditions they had not been designed to meet, and which they'd probably never meet again, once they had left the factory.

In this respect, a complex electronic system is little different from the human animal. A man may run, jump or swim; he may be fired from a cannon or launched into space; he may travel through the heat and dust of a desert. In each case he is subjecting his body to enormous stresses, all of which he survives. But if he is taken seriously ill, and is operated on, his internal organs become very vulnerable, fragile things while they are exposed in a hospital's operating theatre. The surgeon has to deal with them in clinically clean conditions, and with great care and precision. A minor infection when the patient is so vulnerable could be fatal.

In the same way, while completed electronic systems can be immensely robust and designed to tolerate extreme conditions, at the time of their manufacture great caution has to be exercised in handling their individual parts.

Nevertheless, in spite of all the precautions that were taken, sometimes things went wrong at that stage and a component would be damaged.

'Do you mean somebody could be scrapping these chips in big numbers, and never reporting it?' Lopez asked, staring at Reid in open amazement.

He shrugged. 'They cost pennies, Carol; twenty-three pence each, if I remember correctly. And, if you remember, Development originally chose the 29000 series, but they were twenty-nine pence each. When Andy set up one of his cost-cutting exercises, they looked around and found these. They had almost the same performance …'

'But?' Foster interjected.

Reid looked bleak. 'The 9000s have a smaller current rating,' he said quietly. He could see the inferences of what they had discovered.

Lopez shook her head slowly. 'I suppose somebody checked,' she asked. 'Made sure that the current rating was high enough?'

If the tiny devices were connected to a circuit that drew too much current from them, they would be overloaded. They would overheat and some would fail, and there was a possibility that the failure could be such that they acted as though they had been switched on.

In the world of computers, everything is either 'On' or 'Off'; a 1 or a 0. A typical address would be made up of sixteen of these binary—two-state— digits. A device that was stuck on 1 instead of 0 would make the same address different by just one digit—a small difference, but one with colossal consequences.

'You'll have to ask Development about that,' Reid said. 'I assume they checked.'

Foster was amazed. 'You *assume*?' he said, very quietly. 'Bill, don't your people think about the job these things do?'

Reid shrugged and defended his department's actions. 'Come on, Dan!' he said. 'They're address decoders! Why should we know more? Or care? They go wrong; we find them; we fix them; the system gets shipped; the depleted component stock gets replenished. It's all automatic. And it all works.'

'Maybe,' Lopez interjected. 'The procedures work if the components go wrong here. But what if they go wrong later? On site?'

Reid stared at her for a moment. Then he shrugged his shoulders again. 'The DCS will know, Carol,' he said. 'The self-checks and monitors that the systems people build in. They'll pick it up.'

'Will they, Bill?' Foster asked. It was a rhetorical question really. His mind was speeding after the quarry. 'And what if they don't?'

After her visitors had left, Lopez telephoned Andy Johns in Hong Kong.

When he answered, his voice was sleepy and she suddenly wondered what time it was over there. *Never mind, this was critical.*

When she told him what her discussion with Reid had uncovered she could tell he was instantly wide awake.

As the realization of what she was saying hit him, his voice became angry.

'You fucking idiots,' he barked and she winced at the expletive. Even over a long-distance 'phone line, his fury was palpable. 'You fucking ... you academics,' he continued. He wasn't slowed, his language wasn't tempered, by any consideration of her gender; if she wanted to be in a man's world she'd bloody well have to take what a man would take.

'You professors, with all your degrees; you're all the same. One minute it's 'No sir, it's not possible, sir'. The next minute it's...' he mimicked a high-pitched, pleading tone: '...sorry sir, we ballsed it up, sir'.

'How could you have been so bloody wrong?' he continued. 'How could you let it go so far?'

She was taken aback. She had expected him to be concerned, even angry, but there was something else here. It was almost personal. 'Hold on, Andy,' she said. 'You have to remember how complex this system is ...'

'You bet your fucking life I know it!' he interrupted. 'You don't have to remind me that I've poured millions into it! Shareholders' money! And then watched your people spending it like water. All of you believing you were being clever and responsible. Now, after all this time, when you've been *forced* to go over it all again ... *Now*, you come and tell me you've made a fatal mistake.

'Why didn't you see it before?'

Lopez saw red. It was her turn to be furious now. 'Listen to me!' she yelled. 'We're dealing with things that are incredibly complex,' she said, articulating each word slowly and separately. 'So complex that nobody can understand every small part of what's happening. At each level, the engineers have to take *something* for granted. Bill Reid's people discard a component because it goes wrong and it's so cheap that it isn't worth carrying out an expensive analysis of what's causing it; or worrying about what the consequences are. They're under constant pressure—from YOU, remember—pressure to get systems out of the door, at any cost. They're not paid to be investigative sleuths.'

There was silence from his end, so she continued, 'Even the systems people don't notice. The chip works fine while they're running the checkout. They ship the system, confident that it's all right. Even when it gets to site it works OK. It goes through acceptance tests and passes them all.

'My people design the systems to try and catch all the problems they can possibly imagine. But then, in all the millions of possibilities, there's one they miss, just one. A single chip. One we were led to believe was reliable. Only, now, we know it wasn't. And so, all along, it's sitting there, like the detonator of a time-bomb. Armed. Waiting to go wrong.'

'Exactly!' Johns was calmer now ... but there was something sinister about his icy calmness, something even more threatening than his overt rage earlier. 'So what can we do?'

Lopez snorted angrily. 'Simple!' she said. 'Go back to the more expensive decoder.'

'And what does that involve?' he asked.

'Buying the decoders is easy. We can have them here in a couple of days. But we can't just send them to site and ask them to un-plug the old and plug in the new. They're soldered into the circuit boards.'

'So?'

'It means new boards.'

The 'boards' were the small printed-circuit boards that held all the components.

'Do we need a new design?'

If the layout of the replacement decoders turned out to be different from the old ones—say, a different number or arrangement of connecting pins—then a new circuit board would have to be designed. That would take time.

'No,' she replied. She had taken the opportunity to check before calling him. 'Fortunately the pin layouts are the same, so we can use the old ones.'

'Thank God for that, at least,' Johns said. 'So how long before we get replacements?'

'Two hundred boards?' she said, looking out of the window while she thought. 'I'd need to check. But if I had to guess I'd say a couple of weeks.'

Manufacture of the circuit boards was a highly automated process, so rapid production was easy. However, even two weeks was too long.

Johns said bitterly, 'Well! So there it is.' There was flat resolution in his tone. Acceptance. 'We haven't any time.'

'No,' she agreed. 'We haven't.'

'So, what's important now is damage limitation ...'

'What!' Lopez almost laughed. '*Damage limitation*? After a plant costing hundreds of millions of pounds has been wiped out, people injured; *men killed*, for God's sake? And now an even bigger risk because of our mistake?' Suddenly she was seeing him for what he was and realized that his prime interest now was in protecting his own hide.

'And all you can talk about is damage limitation?' she ended.

The calm evaporated. 'You stupid fucking bitch!' he shouted at her. 'You still don't realize what you've done, do you?'

'What *I've* done?' she shouted back. She wasn't going to forget he'd called her a stupid fucking bitch, not ever. But she'd get that settled later. 'It's what we've all done,' she said. 'Everybody here ... led by you. And I'll remind you it was *you* who told us to use the 9000 series. We wanted to use the 29000s but you said they were too expensive. They had plenty of capacity to feed the circuit. The 9000 series can feed them too, but it's right on the margin. But the 29000 series cost six pence more! Six *pence*, Andy! That's what cost those men their lives.'

He was suddenly very calm again. Terribly calm. 'For Christ's sake!' he said. 'Listen to me. You're still missing the point. You're just looking at the fault and its effects. I'm doing that as well, but I'm looking at the bigger picture too. That's something *you're* paid to do, I'll remind you; but you're not doing it, so I have to.'

She stiffened at the insult.

'Let me put it to you as simply as possible,' he continued. 'Foster knows what's wrong. He'll blow the whole thing wide open. He'll get us taken to the cleaners over Kung Tau. That bastard hates me. He hates Universal; he'll make sure we suffer. He'll claim it was *his* discovery and trumpet it so loudly the whole world will know about it. You can bet on that.'

Lopez marvelled at the way he could ignore the obvious. It *was* Dan Foster who had found the problem, yet Andy couldn't bring himself to admit it even now.

There was a long silence before the voice from 6,000 miles away slowly and deliberately continued: 'He's got to be stopped.'

'Oh come on Andy!' Lopez interjected. 'He's left here! Gone! His report will probably be with the authorities tomorrow morning.'

During the long pause that followed, she could hear only the crackle of the line.

When he spoke again, his tone was very quiet. 'Does he know about Far Point?' he asked.

'I don't know, Andy. But it's academic. His client will know.'

The response was short and conclusive. 'Oh my God.'

Chapter 11

Leaving Abingdon, Fiona and Foster talked about what had happened, but while they sped along the motorway the conversation slowly died. In silence they both began to contemplate the next steps they would have take in their own relationship.

'I'll drop you off at the boat,' Fiona said eventually.

'Thanks.'

They lapsed into silence and a long time passed before she said, 'Dan, I don't know what to do.'

'About what?'

She glanced at him momentarily, and then looked back at the road. 'About us.'

'What's there to think about?'

'I'm not sure,' she said. 'But… there's something between us, isn't there? I'm not imagining, am I?'

'No,' he said. 'Look, if it's any comfort, I'm not sure about what's going on either. I'd hoped to be able to handle things like this, but … '

'But what?'

'You must know that I'm attracted to you.'

'And I'm attracted to you,' she returned.

'But it's different,' he protested. 'You're young, beautiful, vibrant. Everything about you is so full of youth and vitality.'

'And?'

He gave a short laugh. 'I'm half spent! Approaching old age. In my day, old men who got involved with young women were called 'poodle fakers'. Am I turning into one?'

She laughed. 'Hardly!'

'Thanks, but all the same, what right do I have to have someone like you in my life?'

'Every right,' she said. 'As long as it's what *I* want too.'

And with those words, silence descended once again. Soon the lights of London brightened the darkness ahead and they swung off the motorway and threaded through the lamp-lit streets towards his boat.

As they entered the boat he swung her round, pressing her to the bulkhead. Her lips were soft and yielding, but the passion behind her kiss was stunning.

He grasped her buttocks and lifted her, staggering towards the bedroom as her tongue continued to explore his.

Their actions were feverish as they undressed each other; fingers frantically fumbling with buttons, clips and zips.

He looked down at her perfect, slender body and marvelled at it. Her breasts were small and firm, her belly flat. He felt the urge to hurry competing with the desire to wonder at her youth, vitality and beauty; and to savour every second of the delicious moments ahead.

'*Slow down!*' he said to himself. '*Take it easy!*'

He kissed her neck, and then her back arched as his lips moved to her breast. He stared for a second at the already erect nipple and then bent to lick at it. He sensed her shudder as his teeth closed on it, gently biting at the pink flesh.

He rolled onto her and somehow her hands felt for him and guided him in. A moment's hesitation and then he thrust home, exulting as he felt her shudder with ecstasy.

They twisted and writhed together as he drove even farther into her, and then—suddenly—it was all over. He felt the explosion and had the satisfaction of hearing her cry out in sudden delicious pleasure as she climaxed.

When he woke, dawn was filtering through the autumn haze, across the river into the porthole. For a while, he looked at her lying peacefully beside him, then he kissed her neck and she smiled sleepily.

'Coffee?' he asked, and she nodded.

He got out of the bed, pulled on a robe and headed for the galley.

As he brewed the coffee he looked out of the window as a pair of early-morning joggers trotted past. A lone grey heron, startled by their approach, lifted off from the bank and dipped over the water, giving a harsh *quarrannk!* of protest as it flapped to the safety of a small jetty on the opposite side of the river. The noise disturbed the peace of the Thames. The river, unrippled by the slightest breeze, reflected an almost unblemished mirror-image of the dawn sky as it flowed placidly between its bright hem of ragwort and willowherb, past wooded banks on one side and the silhouetted silent pubs, cafes and restaurants opposite, the buildings crumpled-looking, seemingly exhausted, sleeping off the noisy exertions of the night before.

It was too early in the morning for most people to be up and about. The world was a tranquil place; a secret, silent place for early risers to enjoy.

Having set the percolator, Foster went off to the shower, and was feeling refreshed and relaxed when he returned to the galley.

She was standing at the cooker, wearing one of his shirts.

'Hey!' he protested. 'I was going to bring you coffee in bed!'

'This is fine.' She smiled at him. 'Anyway, I'm hungry. After a night like last night a girl needs more than toast to re-build her strength!'

He grinned at the compliment. The smell of grilling bacon and freshly-ground coffee was drifting through the boat. It was a wonderful blend of smells. It was a wonderful day. Life was wonderful; a peaceful, satisfying existence that nothing could spoil.

He took the spatula from her and said, 'Off you go!' and patted her lightly on her buttock with it. As she left for her own shower, he set to work to finish the cooking.

Breakfast was waiting in the saloon by the time she had returned. She was tying up the cord of a white bathrobe that she'd found in the bathroom, but Foster pulled her towards him and started to undo the cord again. She laughed and pushed him away. 'Uh, uh!' she said, pulling the robe across her nakedness. 'Some of us around here have to go to work. Remember?'

'Spoilsport!'

As they sat down to eat, she said, 'You know, I don't really understand why you run that shop of yours.'

He frowned at her, his knife poised over the toast on his plate. 'Why not?'

'Well, when we were at Abingdon you seemed so... at home, I suppose. You obviously know your stuff very well. I watched Carol Lopez, and she seemed to respect what you said. It seems wrong to be running a little shop by yourself, when you've clearly had positions of great power.'

He sniffed and looked out of the window again. It was a long time before the words came. 'I'd had enough,' he said. 'OK, I loved the job I used to do. I enjoyed solving problems, dealing with things as they happened. But I always had trouble dealing with things if they went seriously wrong. Things where people...'

She waited for him to finish, but he just exhaled, looked down at his plate and jabbed a piece of toast into the yolk of his egg.

'It was bad luck, I guess,' he said.

Again she waited.

'Never happens to most people,' he said, very quietly. 'But I was unlucky enough to get involved with something that ended up with well...' He took a long breath before continuing, 'Some people died.'

'I know.'

'No, not Kung Tau,' he said. 'Something else. Earlier on. And there were some who blamed me.'

'Your old enemy, Andy Johns, I suppose?'

He nodded.

'But it wasn't your fault?' she asked.

'I don't think so. Oh, there were things I could have done better. But nobody ever found out the truth behind what happened.'

'Was it like that power station in China?' she asked, wondering just how risky his work had been.

'No. It was a ship.' Then he shook his head. 'Look,' he said. 'I don't want to talk about it right now. It's too nice a day.'

She looked into his face for a long while, saddened to have lost the brief moment when he'd begun to open up something of his past to her. Then she smiled. It would come. Eventually.

'And I ought to be getting off to London,' she said. 'They'll be wondering what's happened to me if I don't arrive on time.'

She went off to change and in a few minutes was back. She bent to kiss him and asked, 'My bosses will want to know; when will your report be ready?'

'Shouldn't be too difficult now. I think I'll be able to e-mail it to you this afternoon.'

'That fast?' She was surprised.

'It'll only be a summary,' he replied. 'The detail can come later.'

'OK!' She started for the door, then hesitated and turned. 'Shall I come back here tonight?'

He grinned. 'Don't think of anything else,' he said. 'I'll be waiting for you.'

True to his word, the summary went off early in the afternoon and within an hour she was on the 'phone, telling him that her masters wanted to meet with him in London the next morning.

'Why?' he queried, holding the phone to his ear with his shoulder as he frowned across the river. 'I told you. They'll have a full report within a few days. If they want to discuss it then, I'll certainly come up. But tomorrow? No, it's much too soon.'

There was an extended silence before she spoke and when she did, he sensed tension in her tone. 'There's something going on,' she almost whispered. 'I don't know what it is … but when they read your report, well, the place just erupted.'

'That's crazy! I've told them what happened. All they need to do now is come clean. Get the fault fixed, so when they re-build the plant it will be OK.'

'Apparently it's not so easy,' she said. 'There's something else. And, by the sounds of the commotion going on here, it's big.'

He thought about it. He'd done what they'd asked. Against the odds he'd solved the mystery. And in the process he'd made enough money to get him off the hook with the bank, *and* been left with a comfortable margin. In the process, he'd revived many memories that he'd thought had been lost in the past. He'd even met an old lover—and come close to re-kindling the passion they had once shared. But he was home now, surrounded by all the things he'd built around himself. And he had a new lover; a beautiful young woman who in one night had managed to bring back a passion and vigour he had once thought was gone.

That was enough for him, and it should have been enough for Arnold Coward and Partners. Why should he return to his past?

Once had been uncomfortable enough.

'Dan?' The voice at the earpiece interrupted his thoughts. 'Will you do it? Come here, I mean?'

'I'm not keen,' he replied. 'But, well, my curiosity's going to get the better of me. Yes, I'll be there.'

'Oh, thanks Dan! Is 10 o'clock all right?'

'Yes. Who'll be there?'

'It's a chap called Ian Forsyth. One of our senior partners.'

'You'll be there?'

'I doubt it. Though I hate to be kept out of it.' Then her voice softened. 'I'll see you tonight anyway,' she said. 'Tell you more then.'

But there was nothing more to tell him that night—and precious little time for talk. He took her out for a light dinner and when they returned to the boat they had made love in the galley and, a couple of hours later, again in the saloon. In the morning, breakfast was followed by an ecstatic twenty minutes together in the shower.

He made the journey up to London in a daze.

When he arrived at her offices she greeted him coyly, and he sensed she did not want anybody to guess at their new relationship. After a brief chat in her small office she took him in the lift to the top floor of the building to meet the senior partner.

'I'll see you later,' she said as they stood at the door.

'You're not coming in?'

She smiled and looked towards the door across the corridor. 'That's the entrance to the inner sanctum,' she whispered. 'A minor mouse like me doesn't go past here. I told you the time would come when they'd take this from me and hand it to a partner. Well, it's happened.'

Foster stared at her. It must have been tough on her but, if she was frustrated by the glass ceiling that had inevitably stopped her progress, she betrayed no rancour. If she was simply putting a brave face on it, her underlying disappointment wasn't showing.

She pressed a button and the lift door closed.

Foster sighed and tapped at the door.

'Come in!' a voice called, and he opened the door.

Ian Forsyth was a portly little man with half-moon spectacles and a thinning thatch of red hair. His appearance was un-prepossessing but, judging from the size of his office, he was a power to be reckoned with here.

He peered at his visitor over the tops of his spectacles as he stood to shake Foster's hand.

'Ah, Dr Foster,' he said. He had a strong Scottish accent, probably Glaswegian, Foster guessed. 'It's nice to meet you. I feel we have worked together but never met.'

'I've read your summary report,' he continued. 'And although I can'na say I understand it all, it does make it clear that this Galaxy system has a serious problem.'

They sat down, facing each other across the desk.

'Yes.'

'Y're sure about that now?'

'Absolutely! I've been through the data-logger information; or at least what's still available. What it shows is that there was no operator input recorded, so the men in the control room didn't initiate any action; but the unit that was on standby was made to explode.'

At the time of the incident, one of the Kung Tau generators had been shut down. Idle, waiting to be started. Foster's examination of the wreckage had confirmed that this was this machine that had exploded.

Forsyth blinked. 'You said '*made* to explode'. Precisely what do you mean by that?' He held up his hand. 'But, please be easy on a puir old, non-technical ignoramus. My puir brain can'na handle too much of this!'

Foster grinned and reached for his briefcase to extract the photographs he'd taken at the site. 'All right!' he agreed, laying the most important pictures out—one by one—on the desk between them, as he proceeded to explain what he had seen. He showed how his analysis of the wreckage, and of how various objects had been thrown by the series of explosions, had pointed to the idle machine as the source of the damage.

'But how could that be, man?' Forsyth queried. 'If it was not running?'

'Good question!' Foster said. 'But if you look at this picture you'll see signs of severe scorching *inside* the ducting, here,' he pointed. 'And here. Burning, where there should never have been any significant amount of heat at all. And look how these cables have been burned. Where they were laid, under no circumstances would they have been exposed to anything like the temperatures that would have caused this damage. At least, not during normal operation.'

'But how ...?'

'By the whole thing being filled with gas,' Foster cut in. 'Filled with gas ... which was then ignited.'

'A leak, d'ye mean?'

'No. Definitely not a leak; that would have been accidental. There were valves there for the express purpose of preventing any gas from leaking to the inlet. And, as for any stray leakage from any other source, the normal monitors would have picked it up straight away.'

'So, how did it happen, then?' Forsyth asked. 'D'ye know, now?'

'Yes,' Foster said simply. 'I do know. Definitely. I now know they'd been having problems with some of the computers' components, and I think I can see how that would have made the system operate very strangely. That would explain what happened. I still don't understand everything, but I do know that, although nobody had asked it to do so, the DCS had gone through the full start-up sequence for the machine; and then, for some reason, it didn't complete it. It didn't light off the gas. But– again unasked–it then shut everything down. And then it waited a while ...'

'Leaving the gas it had already allowed to pass, inside the machine?'

'Yes.' Foster looked at him in a new light. For a non-technical man— one who, in his own words, was 'no longer in his prime', —he had managed to grasp the gist of it very quickly.

'But that by itself wasn't fatal,' Foster continued. 'What happened next was the incredible part. You see, the computer then skipped the entire pre-start purge; the automatic process that blows air through the machine before trying to start it, to make sure there's no gas left around. It skipped the purge and then lit off the burners. What happened after that was inevitable.'

'Mmm.' Forsyth looked thoughtful. 'How can you be sure that that was what happened?'

'By analysis of the damage, for one thing,' Foster replied. 'And I found enough information to confirm it, recorded on the logger. It kept a pretty complete record of everything that happened. The data-logger was a separate Galaxy system, so it wasn't affected by whatever made the control system go berserk.

'And what it says is weird. It says that the machine—the generator—*was given the start command*, though that's something that all the operators deny having done. But in any case, the command to start should have been followed by an instruction to purge the system. But that purge was never executed. In spite of that, something signalled that it had been purged, *and* for long enough. *And* then something said that there was no gas in the machine—though there very obviously was.

'All in all, it's almost as if the Galaxy system deliberately set out to destroy the plant. By itself.'

'Dear God!' Forsyth said. 'You make it sound like the computer system was almost a living thing, a sort of electronic saboteur.'

'I suppose it *was* a bit like that.'

'But what were the men running the plant, the operators, doing at the time?' Forsyth queried. 'Surely they saw something happening?'

'You bet they did! I've talked to them. They were going frantic, watching it all happen but completely unable to stop it. It was very scary for them. They all say the same thing. It must have been like watching a piano being played by a ghost; the keys being pressed by invisible fingers.'

Forsyth walked over to the window and looked out. 'It's verra bad, mon,' he said quietly. 'Verra bad indeed.'

'Bad for Universal,' Foster said.

'Aye, but… I'm afraid it's worse than that.'

Foster sensed he was about to find out about what had been worrying everybody so much.

Forsyth seemed to be thinking long and hard as he stared out of the window. Then he made up his mind.

'You asked once, at the beginning of all this, who had commissioned us to hire you,' he said.

'Yes. And, as a matter of fact, I was going to ask you that question again. Fiona wouldn't say, but I do really need to know now.'

Forsyth waited again. 'Weel, I'll tell you now.' There was another pause before he spoke again. Then he continued very quietly: 'It's the Department of Trade and Industry,' he said finally. 'The Government.'

Foster rocked back in his chair in absolute shock. He had suspected a big wheel behind all this, but … *Her Majesty's Government*?

'Y'see,' Forsyth continued. 'Although the Government was not directly involved in Kung Tau, it did use the project as ... well, as a sort of reference ... to promote British Industry. For another project.'

All at once, Foster was tense. It confirmed his suspicion that it was not Kung Tau alone that was the real problem. But what was it?

'There's another one?' he asked, his tone urgent, demanding: 'What is it?' he barked. 'And where?'

Forsyth saw his expression and forestalled the question. 'You have to understand, Foster,' Forsyth pleaded. 'I'm only the agent in this. I can'na pretend to know all the details, or the issues, let alone understand them.'

And at last Foster knew.

From his discussion with Alex Cooper, he knew every large project running in the Far East. And he sensed now that his worst fears were about to be confirmed. Nothing else would have caused this furious activity. It had to be.

But of all the fucking stupid things for them to have done ...

'All right,' he said, the fury in him boiling over. 'I accept you weren't involved,' he barked. 'But if it's what I think, then this whole thing is more bloody serious than anything else on this planet. And I've got to know everything. I'm not going to be pissed about with any more. I need to know everything about this mess ... and I need to know right now!'

Forsyth recoiled at Foster's anger. 'Aye, Dr Foster,' he said, rubbing nervously at his cheek. It was so deathly quiet in the room that Foster could hear the rasp of the fingertips on his skin. 'Of course. I'm only sorry you weren't told more at the beginning, but the matter was out of my hands. Anyway, now you'll be told the whole sorry tale. Not by me, but by somebody much more *au fait* with all the facts than myself. You'll have the opportunity very soon. Right away in fact.'

After the rush to apologize, he paused, as if for dramatic effect. 'The Secretary of State's here,' he continued. 'In fact, he's just down the corridor. You'll meet him in a few moments.' Then he added an afterthought: 'Dr Foster, your meeting with him must be kept very confidential, of course.'

Foster reeled again. The Secretary of State for Trade and Industry! The very head honcho! His mind skipped to Alison's interest as a journalist. He knew he had to be careful. But this whole thing was getting out of hand. Who else was going to appear on the scene before this saga had run its messy course? The PM himself?

Still, he had to go along with it now. 'Of course!' he agreed.

'Ye'll understand the unholy row there'd be if the press were to get hold of this...' Forsyth said bleakly. 'They would quickly put two and two together. At present, we believe they're not aware of your visit to Kung Tau.' Foster scowled, wondering why Forsyth was so concerned about the press. He wondered if in their spying they had discovered his liaison with Alison.

'Right now,' Forsyth continued. 'Things are at a difficult stage. With the approaching handover of Hong Kong to the Chinese, the Government can't show its hand over this.' He stressed his next words: '*It is absolutely vital that the government is extricated from this mess with as little publicity as possible.*'

Foster nodded. He could indeed see the difficulty. Nerves were taut anyway. It would be bad enough if the Kung Tau disaster were to be shown as having been caused by a fault in a British-designed, British-manufactured computer system, installed at the British Government's behest. It would be far worse if what he suspected were true.

'I'm sorry,' Forsyth said, looking at his watch. 'But we must go now,' he said. 'We're expected.'

They left the office and walked along the deeply-carpeted corridor to another office. Forsyth tapped at the door and after a minimal delay they were admitted by a secretary who slipped out of the room as they entered.

Foster guessed that this was a sort of inner sanctum, more hallowed even than Forsyth's office, that was out of bounds to the likes of Fiona. It was where Cowards entertained their most important clients.

Roger Jeffreys, MP, Her Majesty's Secretary of State for Trade and Industry, was a tall, urbane man, with dark slicked-back hair greying at the temples. He came forward as the two men entered, and offered a firm hand. 'Dr Foster, I'm pleased to meet you at last,' he said. The words were warm, but Foster sensed an icy edge to his tone; as though he wished the situation had never come to this pass.

'I've heard so much about you.'

They shook hands.

'Let's sit down, shall we,' Jeffreys said, pointing to a large and comfortable settee and they sat down beside each other. Like conspirators, Foster thought.

'Can I offer you a drink?' Jeffreys indicated a large cocktail cabinet in the corner of the room. 'A Malt, perhaps?'

Foster nodded. He marvelled at how much at home Jeffreys seemed to be here; clearly he spent a lot of time here, and Coward's facilities were very much at his disposal. Forsyth had immediately slipped into the role of a lackey and was fussing over the cabinet and pouring the drink. Unlike a true lackey, however, he poured another for himself.

Jeffreys' glass, standing on a table beside the settee, was already full. Foster sipped at his drink and recognized the Balvenie. He smiled inwardly. Was it Coward's good taste, or their legendary research again, which had told of his favourite drink?

Forsyth gave Jeffreys a brief but thorough run-down of what Foster had told him. When he had finished, Jeffreys turned to look at the engineer. 'Please,' he said. 'Would you explain the implications? But ...' he held up a finger. 'Don't forget my abysmal level of technical naïveté!'

Foster smiled. 'OK,' he said. 'Here it is.' He paused, remembering the incident with the drunken ferryman at Sai Kung, where the man had confused him with Alex Cooper; the confusion so total that Foster had little choice but to play along with it. He needed an analogy again, to explain it to Jeffreys.

'The whole point of the computer system at Kung Tau,' he continued. 'Galaxy 2000 that is, is its use of micro-controllers at every large piece of the plant: pumps, fans, valves and so on. The whole computer system is broken up into dozens of tiny processors…'

He saw a frown cross Jeffreys' face and added, 'They were small computers. They process the many tasks.' Jeffreys nodded to indicate that he understood.

'Well, each of the processors continually exchanges information with the others.'

'I understand.'

'To do that, every computer has to be given an 'address', to identify it uniquely.' On his journey to town that morning, he had sought for an analogy, something to clarify it to the uninitiated. Then he had found it and had spent the rest of the journey honing it in his mind.

'Imagine a playground,' he said. 'In a school, in a busy town. A playground with lots of swings, slides and carousels, plus the usual playing area. With gates leading to the street and into the school buildings.

'Now, imagine that the staff has arranged for some of the older kids to stand beside everything that can move, including the main gate that links the play area to the busy street outside. They're there to make sure everything is safe before the smaller kids are allowed out.'

'They're like the… the micro-controller that you described just now?' Jeffreys said.

'Exactly! Then, imagine a teacher standing in the middle of the playground and calling out, 'Jimmy! Is your gate shut?' Jimmy's gate is the main one leading onto the street.' The teacher needs to know that it is shut, and that the kids can be let into the playground. Seeing that Jeffreys had followed so far, he continued, 'When the kid replies that it's shut, the teacher knows she can let the kids out of the buildings to play. So then she calls out to the pupil beside the door linking the school to the playground, 'Jane, open the doors!' OK so far?'

'Yes. Go on.'

'Then, as the kids come out, the teacher listens for any alarm calls, things like 'Sally's fallen over!' or, 'The carousel's overcrowded!' and so on. Still clear?'

'Yes.'

'All right. But now imagine it goes all wrong. Remember that, when the teacher called out to ask Jimmy whether the gate he's watching is shut, she meant the gate leading to the road. But say that, for some reason, another kid, Sam say, responded to her call by accident. Perhaps it is noisy and he mis-hears her call. Anyway, the gate that he's in charge of is a small one, say, keeping the smaller kids away from the big slide.'

'All right.'

'Now, Sam's gate is closed, but Jimmy's is wide open; open to the busy street. When Sam hears the teacher ask about the gate, he looks at his and sees that it is shut. He gives the answer 'It's shut!' But the teacher had actually intended the message to go to Jimmy, so she thinks it's he who answered. And she lets the kids out.'

'Into a playground that's open to the busy street!' Jeffreys exclaimed. Understanding lit his face.

'Well, it's not quite so easy in fact,' Foster said. 'You see, in a system like Galaxy, every command is followed by a response, and if one device goes wrong and starts responding to the wrong messages the system will get two responses, one from the correct node, and one from the wrong one.'

'Node?' Jeffreys asked.

'Sorry! A point in the system where the information is processed.'

'Ah!'

'OK. In the analogy of the amazingly complicated playground, when Sam answers, the teacher would actually get two responses, one from Jimmy, the other from Sam.'

'I see that.'

'That's what happens in the Galaxy system. If two nodes reply to a message that's addressed to just one of them, the system raises an alarm. It's expecting one reply and gets two. It would know something's wrong from that.'

'Then how would the problem have passed unnoticed?'

Foster grinned. 'That's what foxed me at first. But then something happened, and I suddenly saw a possibility.

'Say *two* addresses were faulty at the same time. It would be as if the two children *exchanged* names; Jimmy pretended to be Sam, and Sam pretended to be Jimmy, because they were deliberately messing around, playing a game of their own ...'

Jeffreys' eyes widened. 'Now I see!' he said, beginning to understand. 'You can tell if one of them responds wrongly... but if they *swap* names, then, confusion reigns!'

'Exactly.' Foster confirmed. 'The two faults mask each other.'

The possibility had dawned on him when he and Cooper had played along with the drunk's confusion at Sai Kung. When he called 'Arex', Foster had responded and Cooper had stayed in his chair. The deception had been complete.

'I'm certain now that that's what caused the explosion,' Foster said. 'Though at first it seemed impossible. The chance of two faults like that existing concurrently should have been a billion to one chance. But after I checked with Abingdon—Universal's HQ—I now know they had an addressing problem. It meant that, far from being a one-off fluke, the fault was actually very common. It happened, and it was the resulting mix-up that led to the blast.'

Forsyth and Jeffreys stared at him. 'But surely there are checks ...' Jeffreys began.

'Of course!' Foster replied. 'The Galaxy system includes lots of checks and balances to prevent that sort of thing happening. But things do go wrong, and if the system *did* get screwed up somehow, if the mistake was a transient thing, something that came and went ...'

'You'd have chaos!' Forsyth exclaimed. 'Good God! Was that it?'

Foster nodded. 'I'm certain of it,' he said. 'My theory's still got some holes in it. But I feel sure it could explain it. What I needed to do was to work it all out. And, most of all, I needed to be able to pinpoint the exact thing that went wrong. The actual culprit. That's why I went to Abingdon.'

'And you found the answer there?' Jeffreys asked.

'Yes. It turns out that Universal has experienced multiple failures of a key component. One that sets and reads addresses. Because of a basic design fault, that component is stressed, and because of that, it fails. And, by the laws of physics, that fault is more likely to occur at higher temperatures.

'By distributing those components through the plant, where they would be exposed to heat, rather than being in a nice cool, air-conditioned room, everything was made worse. And it's not just one component; the whole system was riddled with decoders that, sooner or later, *would* go wrong.'

'Christ!' Jeffreys said quietly. He thought for a while, then continued, 'But there's still one thing I don't see, one aspect that's puzzled me from the beginning.'

'What's that?'

'Wasn't the system tested?'

Foster laughed. 'Sure it was tested,' he said. 'But tests can never cover everything. And they surely missed this one. And, remember, the component is stressed. It works for a while, and fails much later. *After the equipment's left the factory.*'

Jeffreys looked gloomy. 'How can all this have happened,' he said quietly. 'Is there no legislation, are there no safety rules?'

Foster laughed. 'Rules!' he exclaimed. 'You're joking.'

'Oh come! There must be!'

'Correct. There are safety rules all right. But they're about pressure vessels and pipes, mechanical bits and pieces; things most people can understand. But there are none for computer control systems. Well, not too many.'

'I find that hard to believe...'

Foster shrugged. 'It's history,' he said. 'And the steady acceleration in the progress of technology.

'You see, at the end of the nineteenth century there were a number of serious accidents in industrial plants - exploding pressure vessels and so on. As a result, there was real public concern about it all, and laws were framed to protect against it happening again.'

'There *are* laws then.'

'As I said ... Yes, but only relating to the incidents that had happened at the time. So they all relate to how strong the pipes and vessels should be. And they're very effective laws. Even now, over a century later, plants like Kung Tau still have be fitted with certain types of devices whose origins date back to the 1890s.'

'So they're safe!' Jeffreys observed.

Foster grimaced. 'In some ways,' he said. 'Oh, the rules legislate in some areas. But what's happened is that the parts of the plant that were the most dangerous ones—or at least, were at one time the most dangerous—, nowadays represent only a tiny part of the risk.'

'And there are *no* rules to govern those areas?'

'Not really. For example, around the whole world, the design of the furnaces that are at the heart of power stations are expected to meet rules defined by an organization, an American one mind you, that sprang from

US insurance companies trying to cut their losses after there'd been a string of explosions.'

Jeffreys picked up on a clue. 'You said *'Expected'* to meet rules,' he commented.

'Yes,' Foster said grimly. 'If you want to go ahead and build a plant that doesn't meet those rules, then there's actually nothing to stop you.

'The insurers won't cover the plant, but they have to be made aware of what's happening. And when technology runs ahead of everything, the insurers may never be aware ...'

'Come, come! I find that incredible!'

'Far from it, that's the way it is. And as for computer systems ...'

'Nothing?' Jeffreys' expression was stricken as he asked the question. He was beginning to anticipate the answers.

'Right! And that's largely because computers have advanced so quickly that the law hasn't had time to catch up. Various Governments have tried. In the UK for instance, there are rules defined some time ago by the Health and Safety Executive ... but those rules are really out of date already.'

'But surely designers have to comply.'

Foster shrugged. 'Nope!' he said. 'Mind you, you'd be in trouble if the plant was in the UK and there was an accident, and if they discovered afterwards that you hadn't complied. But that's *after* the event. And the rules don't cover plant exported to the Third World.'

'No?'

'Nope,' Foster confirmed. 'You're expected to comply with the laws in the destination country. And if the US and UK don't have rules they certainly won't exist elsewhere...'

'Jesus!' Jeffreys said. 'That's irresponsible.'

Foster looked at him in a new light. Somehow he'd been expecting a politician's glib shrugging of the shoulders. But here was a spark of honesty. He hadn't expected that.

'Perhaps,' he said. 'But that's the way it is.'

Jeffreys stared at him. 'But why haven't there been more accidents then?' he asked.

'More?' Foster asked. 'How many more do you want?'

'We've had accidents? Before?'

'Oh sure! Well, it depends on your perception of things. But most people agree about some disasters that, if they weren't actually *caused* by computer systems, were actively *assisted* by them.'

'I've not heard of them.'

'Oh no?' Foster queried. 'What about Three Mile Island?' When Jeffreys' eyes widened he added, 'And Chernobyl. And Bhopal ...'

In the tense silence that followed, Jeffreys could only stare at him with horrified understanding. Eventually the politician sighed and said, 'I think I've heard enough.'

He stood up and walked over to the window. There was a long silence before he eventually turned and looked at Foster. 'Well!' he said. 'I must say you've lived up to your reputation.' He stretched his back and thought for a moment. Then he returned to his seat and took a deep breath.

'But now,' he said. 'I must apologize to you; for the fact that we had to be so secretive at the outset; about HMG's involvement that is.' He pronounced the initials carefully, slowly, as if wanting there to be no doubt.

'You had your reasons, I suppose,' Foster said, sipping his Malt. 'But now... Now I *do really need to know the other plant involved*. Mr Forsyth has told me a little bit about it.' The title 'Mister' seemed to be normal around here. It had always been a permanent attachment for Forsyth; it didn't seem right to use the man's Christian name. Indeed, he suddenly realized, he didn't even know it. In these circles, such formality seemed *de rigeur*.

'I've begun to get an idea of what it is,' Foster said. 'But now I need to know; though, as I said, I do have my suspicions.'

'Ah!' Jeffreys picked up his glass, took a long sip and looked at the drink steadily, as though preparing his thoughts.

When it came, the answer was exactly what Foster had feared.

'It's Far Point,' Jeffreys said.

Foster let out a long-held breath and sat very still, staring at Jeffreys. The nightmare he'd feared was suddenly a horrific reality.

Far Point was a power station being built on an island off the east coast of China, near a place called Tangshan, a couple of hundred kilometres from Beijing. It had been the talk of the industry when the contract was placed.

Because Far Point was nuclear.

The contract for building the plant had been hard fought over, but in the end it had been awarded to a British consortium in a spirit of warm friendship, aided by generous British grants, much to the dismay and loud protests of the rest of Europe.

The massive project had been trumpeted abroad as a triumph for British engineering expertise.

Very strangely, however, nobody had seemed to know much about its control systems.

Or perhaps it was not so surprising. On the scale of things, the control system represented only a tiny part of the overall contract value. It was therefore often omitted from the argument over nuclear power, in spite of its ability to cause havoc.

For example, even when a major public enquiry was assured that England's massive Sizewell 'B' nuclear power plant would be 'identical to plants operating safely for years on end in the USA and France', the vital fact was missed that the control system that was finally used there was very different from the ones that were defined at the time of the Public Enquiry.

Consideration of the control systems had simply been discounted, although they were identical in function, if not in form, to those that had played such a crucial role in the events at Three Mile Island, and at Chernobyl.

But if that was history, the present was little different. People in the select inner ring of computer *cognoscenti*, especially those in the control-systems business, were interested in the Far Point DCS, of course, but they were alone in asking questions. And not too many people were interested enough to ask where the answers could be found.

Now, in that lofty meeting room in Arnold Coward's offices, after a long silence while the two men simply stared at each other, Foster put his head in his hands and murmured, 'I don't believe it! How could anybody install a control system this new—totally unproven! —on a project like that?' He looked up, straight into Jeffreys' eyes. 'On a nuclear power station,' he said. 'Goddamit! And one in China!'

'It was nothing to do with me,' Jeffreys said, unabashed at Foster's criticism of the Government's actions, but still defensive of them. 'I wasn't party to the original decisions, and I'm still not sure about the reasons behind them.

'Actually... privately, I would probably admit to sharing some of your misgivings. But I can only surmise that the Departments involved were given very strong assurances at the time that the decision was taken. And that they were told that the engineers had checked it all, very carefully.'

He shrugged. 'But, be that as it may, the decision *was* made. And now you've confirmed that it carries a risk...' He broke off, then added, 'You *would* say the same fault could happen at Far Point, wouldn't you?'

'Oh yes! It's a generic fault, all right. If it was at Kung Tau it'll be at Far Point as well. Definitely!'

'So we have a far greater risk than anybody could have imagined.'

'Well no,' Foster said. 'You see, a DCS like Galaxy would only be controlling the heat-exchangers of a nuclear plant. The parts that aren't so critical. The really safety-critical systems—those for the nuclear reactor, that is—are under the control of a much simpler, proven and absolutely safe system.'

But when he saw Jeffreys begin to shake his head he knew the worst.

Foster stared at him and shook his head slowly in disbelief. 'You're not telling me ...?'

'I'm afraid so,' Jeffreys said. 'For the first time ever, the controls for the nuclear reactor were entrusted to a Galaxy system.'

'Christ all-bloody Mighty!' Foster exploded. How could they be sitting here so calmly, talking about a possibility so horrible that it didn't really bear thinking about? And why hadn't it been nipped in the bud? Right at the beginning, as soon as Kung Tau had blown up?

Jeffreys bit his lip, an absurdly childish gesture from somebody in his exalted position. 'I know what you're thinking,' he said. 'But the decision was masked by subterfuge. By somebody playing for time, perhaps.

'You see, because of concern amongst our European partners, and because of the considerable pressures exerted by the Green lobby at home, we had to try and minimize the reaction that there'd have been to the use of new, unproven technology on a nuclear plant in China. Because of this, it was arranged that Universal Digital would handle the work under the guise of another project. We even arranged some background, to convince anybody who might have been interested, that the work was being executed for a client in the Middle East; for a refinery, not a nuclear power station.'

But Foster wasn't convinced. It still seemed too strange, too convoluted. 'I don't understand,' he asked. 'Why not resolve it in a simple, straightforward way? You must have suspected the Galaxy system immediately after the Kung Tau incident.' He shrugged. 'So why take any chances? Why not just get Universal to go back to their old system. There are plenty of those around after all. And they've been used on nuclear plants before now; very successfully.' As the man who had been instrumental in those contracts, Foster knew the ground and was confident of it. 'But it's not too late, even now. If the madness wasn't stopped then, you can still do it now!' he added. 'But it'll have to be soon. There's no time to waste.'

'I wish it were so simple,' Jeffreys said. 'But the Government is very embarrassed. You see... it was they who—under the guidance of others, you understand—promoted the use of such advanced technology at Far Point. *And they used the Kung Tau project as evidence of its safety.*'

Foster stared at him in disbelief. 'Christ!' he said bitterly. 'The explosion must have given you plenty of food for thought, then.'

'It did.'

'But I still don't understand. Why not just get Universal to fix it?'

Jeffreys looked gloomily into his drink and sighed deeply. 'I fear it simply isn't possible,' he said. 'You see, Universal's parent company, Global Associated Industries, has called in their lawyers. And those good gentlemen make a very strong and telling point. That is: if any change is made to the equipment at Far Point—where, I need hardly remind you, absolutely nothing untoward has so far occurred—it will be as good as admitting that the Galaxy 2000 system carries an inherent fault. The clear implication would be that it was this fault that was responsible for the incident at Kung Tau. In other words, it would be an admission that the explosion was indeed the fault of their client.'

'As it was.'

'So we may argue. But there are others who would dispute it. And in the meantime there's no doubt that it would leave Universal open to a very large claim for damages, direct and consequential. A very large sum indeed.'

'Absolutely! They'll have to cough up; or their insurers will...' Foster said.

But Jeffreys held up his hand to stop him, and continued, 'That's another aspect of the problem,' he said. There was a long silence before he spoke again. 'You see,' he said finally. 'In order to obtain the contract—or perhaps it was simply an oversight—Universal accepted unlimited liability.'

Foster was aghast. Horrified. It was usual in the industry for some form of penalty clause to be included in contracts, to cover things ranging from late delivery or to major accidents, but the scale of the penalties was always limited to a small percentage of the overall contract value. It was still a large amount, but it *was* limited, and therefore bearable.

What Jeffreys had just told him was that no such limits had been agreed for the Kung Tau project.

The liability for Kung Tau was unlimited.

It was sheer madness to accept unlimited liability for the enormous losses that could arise: the compensation for the victims of the accident, the cost of rebuilding the plant, the lost profits on all the electricity that should have been generated and sold while it was out of action. The amount of money at risk was immense.

'Oh, come off it,' Foster said. 'GAI would never have sanctioned unlimited liability.'

'Ordinarily not,' Jeffreys said. 'But in this case the contract was deemed exceptional. The Government was determined to undo the damage that had been done to industry by earlier administrations. It was bent on winning the contract, and you must remember that it had been persuaded that the risk was minimal.'

'So it underwrote the risks itself.'

'That was enough for GAI to waive its own rules.'

Foster stared at him. 'And what happened afterwards was Sod's Law,' he said, very quietly. 'If you bank on something *not* happening, as sure as night follows day, it *will* happen.'

'With hindsight,' Jeffreys continued, 'It was a poor decision.'

Foster couldn't help himself. He laughed out loud.

'But the decision *was* made!' Jeffreys said, ignoring Foster's amusement. 'And that, of course, makes the matter very significant. And even though HMG covered the risk—and that in itself is a political embarrassment that would be hard to swallow, you understand—even so, GAI are still very exposed, and both parties' lawyers are quite adamant they will not agree to anything that may prejudice the outcome of the argument.'

Foster stared at him. The words burst out: 'I don't believe it! You're saying that they're prepared to endanger another plant—a nuclear one at that —one costing hundreds of times more, and in the process put the lives of millions of people at risk? They'd risk all that, rather than admit liability for one fatal accident that's already happened?'

'Dr Foster,' Jeffreys said smoothly. 'You don't understand these people.'

'You bet I don't!'

'For them, it's a matter of simple statistics,' Jeffries continued. 'They see the world in terms of cold numbers, a balance of probabilities. On one hand you have something that's happened already, but the blame for which, from the lawyer's point of view, cannot be laid at their clients' door—at least, not without definite proof. On the other hand, they balance that against something that has *not* yet happened, and which in fact may never happen at all. At present, in spite of your work, there is still no absolute *proof* that the Galaxy system *was* responsible for the explosion, and in that situation the lawyers will fight to deny that there was any such fault.

'To do otherwise would be asking them to roll over on their backs and admit defeat; to give up without a fight, merely to counter the faint possibility that another incident *might* happen. Yes, might—*might just possibly*—happen.'

Foster shook his head and was silent for several moments. 'You're right on one thing,' he said finally. 'I don't understand these people.'

Jeffreys gave a wintry smile. 'To be frank, and within the privacy of these four walls, I'll admit that I don't understand them either. But they are powerful people, Dr Foster, and not without their own influence in the Government.'

'Is that why they weren't simply overruled? Forced to jump to the Government's tune and to forget the normal rules of commerce?'

Jeffreys smiled. 'Partly,' he agreed. 'But it's also something else. Something called Democracy.'

Foster stared at him, trying to see if he could detect a slight indication that it was a joke. But there was nothing.

Foster sighed. 'So what happens?' he asked eventually.

The Secretary of State looked down at his drink again. 'Ah!' he said, and Foster had a foreboding of trouble. 'This is where I would like to enlist your continued help,' Jeffreys said. Then he looked up to look Foster in the eye, very steadily.

The atmosphere in the room almost crackled with tension.

When Jeffreys eventually continued, his tone was very firm and precise. 'Dr Foster, I want you to go to Far Point…' He held up his hand to silence Foster's imminent protest.

'No! Hear me out. Please,' he continued. 'I want you to modify the electronic systems there. In that exercise, you'll have all the assistance you could possibly need. I have every confidence that you'll rectify the problem. And, above all, it will *not* be referred back to the Kung Tau incident.'

Foster thought about it for a few moments, and quickly saw the weaknesses. 'Oh, come on!' he said. 'What excuse will I have? To go there, I mean? Elderly British shopkeepers don't just pop over to China so easily, to start fiddling about with one of their nuclear power stations. And the People's Republic of China is hardly likely to invite me to visit, on the spur of the moment.

'Anyway, after the Kung Tau they'll be suspicious as Hell. And don't think that they won't be very aware of that disaster. But even if they did invite me in, if they then found out that I was modifying the equipment it would still be a huge embarrassment. A London shop-owner messing around with a nuclear contract in the PRC? Any row about it and Albert Leung's own lawyers would be bound to hear. And it wouldn't be long before they found out that the problem was inherent in the Galaxy system. After that, GAI's argument that their system was not at fault would be blown clean out of the water anyway.'

'But don't you see?' Jeffreys said smoothly. 'That's exactly why I need the services of a man of your abilities. You know exactly what to do, and you've got what it takes to do it. Oh, we could use some lesser technicians—and less expensive ones, I must say! —to resolve the matter.

And we could then leave it to Universal Digital to put it right. But, as you have rightly said, that would expose both ourselves—HMG I mean—and Universal, to enormous financial and political risks. The company and the Government would be forced into a very expensive legal settlement. And it would leave the Government open to serious criticism. And after that, to national ridicule and international condemnation.

'Any chance of winning further orders of this type from China would vaporise. And with Britain shown to be incompetent–even devious–would cause serious damage to our export opportunities across the globe.'

Foster sat back and looked at the Minister in amazement. Then he shook his head in disbelief and took another sip of his drink. He needed something to calm him.

'Dr Foster,' Jeffreys continued, his voice pleading. 'We need *you* to go to Far Point; and don't worry, we will make all the necessary arrangements with the PRC. But, when you've got there, you must resolve the problem: without the PRC, or anybody else for that matter, knowing about it.'

'Jesus!'

'Oh, I agree it will be difficult. But I have absolute faith that you can correct it quietly and effectively. On the plant. And without anybody noticing what you've done.' He held up his hand again as he saw Foster's growing expression of incredulity at each phrase. 'Yes, I know. But I have every confidence in you. And I've already set the wheels in motion to help you. The government has twisted Universal Digital's arm and persuaded them to send somebody to help you, somebody who is very familiar with the details of their equipment. We didn't know the details when we asked, of course, but we did know you'd be needing some help.

'But even with that help, it'll be difficult, I know. I'm not an engineer, and I can't pretend to understand the details, but I do see that it's an almost superhuman task we're asking of you. Since your summary report came in we've been working frantically to find a solution. My scientific advisers have informed me, in detail, of all the barriers you'll have to overcome, the protection systems—the interlocks, I think they are called—before you can institute the change. A change that will be undetectable to the engineers at the plant.'

He looked seriously at Foster and continued, 'The engineers say it's a comparatively simple change, and something that can be done on site. I've been told that, in a way, making the change would be a form of sabotage ... but it would be *benevolent* sabotage.'

Foster could feel himself breathing very deeply. 'You're damned right!' he said, shaking his head again. 'I don't know if it would even be possible. But if it is, it'll still be a nightmare.'

'And, it's desperately urgent,' Jeffreys continues. 'As you know, Far Point is at an advanced state of completion. What you don't know is just how far things have progressed.

'You see... Well, the fact is this.' He stared hard at Foster as he concluded: 'The nuclear reactor is due to be put on line within the next two weeks.'

There was an icy silence while Foster stared back at Jeffreys. Then he exploded. 'Jesus Christ!' He leaned back and rested his head on the back of the chair, looking heavenward for help.

'I know.' Jeffreys said quietly. 'But I think you'll see now, Dr Foster; there's just nobody else we can turn to. Nobody who could tackle such a challenge. Nobody else has the depth of knowledge of the particular system. Nobody else has the necessary experience and the international standing. And you... you're familiar with the Galaxy system. It was conceived while you were still with Universal Digital. To some extent the system was your own brain-child.

'But, most importantly, you know exactly what happened at Kung Tau ... And nobody else has been made privy to as much of the background as you have.

'No, it *must* be you.'

Foster turned his head and looked at Forsyth. The Scotsman was standing at the window, looking out over towards the bustling streets far below. It was as though he was not really involved any more, as though being uninvolved was what he preferred.

Suddenly, Foster saw what he had been drawn into. The sheer, dizzying depth of it. It was sickening, frightening.

The countdown to the commissioning of the Far Point control system was inexorably ticking onward. The moment was fast approaching when the button would be pressed to start up the nuclear reactor; but it was one with a dangerously flawed and unpredictable electronic system that was in absolute command of it.

Foster saw that he was trapped like an insect caught in a spider's web.

There was no escape from the ordeal ahead.

But he had to plan for it.

'OK,' he said. 'I'll do it. I don't have much choice. But I can't do it alone.'

'I understand that,' Jeffreys said, His tone displayed his evident relief. 'I've already said that we'd make sure you have help ...'

'No! I need very special help. Help from people that I know and trust, and trust absolutely.

'And the best guy is in Australia, so it'll mean a delay of a few days before I can start.'

Jeffreys slammed his fist onto the table in frustration.

'Australia!' he spat out. 'Absolutely not. We can't have any outsiders involved.' There was real anger in his voice.

'Then I can't go.'

The two men stared at each other, but Jeffreys could see that Foster had the upper hand.

Finally Jeffreys' shoulders slumped and he sighed. 'All right,' he asked. 'Who do you want?'

Foster named his man.

But what he couldn't know was whether that man would agree to go to the doors of Hell with him.

Chapter 12

Foster rang the bell at the door and stepped back to admire the scenery while waiting for a response. This was the Mornington Peninsula, to the South of Melbourne. Sleepy, gentle, relaxed. Vacation and retirement territory, and the house was typical for the area; a white-painted bungalow sitting peacefully on the side of a hill overlooking Port Phillip Bay. Far below, the wide arms of sand encircling the cobalt sea were visible as a thin platinum crescent whose tips blurred into the hazy distance.

It was spring in the Southern Hemisphere and the day was bright, clear and not too hot, and Foster had enjoyed the pleasure of driving from the airport without having to have the car's air conditioning running.

The bungalow was screened from the lane by one of the tall, well-kept hedges of Bougainvillaea that flanked the drive connecting it to the road. There were few properties here and those that were there were widely separated.

It was a placid scene, if a little lonely.

Over the quiet ticking of the car's engine as it cooled, Foster heard footsteps from within and the door was opened by a tall, angular, red-haired man with a tanned, deeply-creased face. He tilted his head forward to peer at Foster for several seconds over half-moon spectacles. 'Well! I'll be buggered!' he exclaimed eventually. 'You old bastard!'

'Pleased to see me then, Alan!' Foster smiled.

Alan Turner was an old colleague and friend who, for over four decades before his retirement, had worked in Universal Digital's world-wide commissioning department. After the Kung Tau incident he had suddenly retired, and after all those years of faithful service, his departure from the company had come as a shock to many people. He had been a very popular and well-respected engineer who had travelled the world extensively, commissioning and trouble-shooting the company's systems.

There were many who saw in his departure a symbol of the new direction of the company; the old, battle-hardened hands fading away, their mantles being assumed by young, computer-wise professionals, all full of management-speak: mission statements, task forces, risk assessments, empowerment and paradigms.

To the world he presented a wary shell, but anyone who penetrated his tough defences found that Turner was a kindly person. He gave the impression of a crusty old man in whose eyes civilization was deeply flawed, with humanity graded merely into different degrees of badness.

His friends—merely referred to by him as 'bastards'—were at one end of the scale. At the other end were his enemies, and any fools he met. In his exacting standards the latter (and there were many) were either 'wankers' or 'dickheads', depending on the degree of danger they represented. These definitions were crude, even cruel, but Foster had always found them to be uncannily accurate. Wankers were time-wasting idiots who rarely did enough real work to create any significant hazard. Dickheads were dangerous: impulsive, thrusting incompetents who could create serious hazards for themselves and anybody else unfortunate enough to be working with them.

The dickheads were particularly dangerous when, as their type often did, they acquired, in spite of their incompetence, rank and authority. Such men needed to be watched warily. Continually. Treated with extreme caution.

Turner ignored Foster's response. 'Well, now you're here, you might as well come in,' he said, and waved his old friend in over the threshold. It was a welcome of sorts.

The house was tidy and cosy, and smelled slightly of furniture polish. On one side of the hallway, framed photographs hung on the walls. Turner had always been a keen photographer and, apart from having an artist's eye for composition, he had an engineer's attention for detail. He eschewed modern digital cameras, and relied on processing most of his own photographs. This gave him the opportunity to maximize the impact of his work.

As Foster stepped into the house, his attention was immediately caught by one of the photographs: a dramatic black-and-white study of a power-station site, which Foster guessed was Kung Tau. The photograph had evidently been taken quite early in the plant's construction stage, because much of the structure was vacant, a skeletal steelwork festooned with scaffolding.

What made the picture so stunning was the composition. Turner had captured the construction from some distance away, with a glittering jet-black sea heaving metallically in the foreground and a heavy bank of dark cloud looming behind, accentuating the ominous, brooding presence of the cliffs below them. Through a break in the clouds, a single shaft of sunlight had fallen onto the plant and, like an actor caught by a blinding shaft of a spotlight on a darkened stage, the glistening metal of the structure was dramatically enhanced, the sharp-edged steel shining like a razor's edge, the scaffolding an enormous spider's web that had trapped the massive machines and appeared, impossibly, to support its entire gigantic mass in free space.

'That's a fantastic shot!' Foster said in open admiration.

Turner nodded and grinned. 'Yup!' he agreed modestly. 'You should have seen me taking it! Everybody thought I was crazy. A typhoon was brewing that day, and I suddenly saw this break in the cloud out near the horizon. The wind was blowing it towards us and I guessed the sun would spotlight the site, so I took one of the company launches out to sea. It was a bit hairy, because it turned out to be rougher than I'd expected, but it was worth it because I was right; the break in the clouds arrived just on cue.'

Foster shook his head in admiration. 'Was anybody with you?' he asked.

'No,' Turner growled, shaking his head. 'No other wanker would come, so I had to take the boat out on my Jack and turn it around at the right spot and try and steer it with my arse on the wheel, while I took the picture.'

Foster was amused by the impression of this wiry man making a colossal effort, risking his life against dangerous elements, to create something artistic out of what many people would have considered to be a dull, prosaic and somewhat frightening artefact. Perhaps it was a demonstration of a core of sensitivity that lay deep beneath the gnarled and hardened skin; of a soul that saw grandeur and beauty in the stark steel and heard a sort of music in the mind-numbing racket of a power-station construction site.

Turner led the way to the living room and gestured to one of the two deeply-padded armchairs. 'Sit down, Dan,' he said. 'Malt still your poison?' At Foster's nod he opened the connecting door and disappeared into a small dining room.

As Foster eased himself into the comfort of the chair he sensed the calmness of the house, and he suddenly realized the completeness of the curtain Turner had drawn between himself, and the pace, noise and danger of his previous occupation. Turner's home formed a stunning contrast with the roaring bellow of the huge machines that had surrounded him for most of his working life.

Through the wide picture window, a shaft of bright sunlight bathed the floor and part of one wall in silver, the brightness reflecting from the carpet onto the grandfather clock that stood in one corner, its slow deep ticking hypnotically restful, the only sound against the silence of the place.

There were mementoes of the past everywhere. The room was lined with glass-fronted cases displaying the memorabilia of a lifetime of travelling to the remotest parts of the world, very far from the tourist trails. The cases contained delicate and intricately-carved jade ornaments from

China, embroidered silk scrolls from Japan, Indian teak elephants, carved African masks, Australian Aborigine ornaments; there were some reminders from every continent and almost every country in the world.

Turner returned with a bottle of Glenmorangie and two cut-glass tumblers. He poured out a generous measure into each glass and handed one to Foster. 'Cheers!' he said. 'Personally, I'd say that it's a bit early in the day for me now..., but then, I always was easily led. Anyway, *Sláinte Mhath!*'

Foster smiled, and returned the Gaelic toast. 'Nice place,' he said, as he sipped the Malt.

'Thanks.'

Foster grinned. 'I heard you'd got entangled.'

'Entangled!' It was a growl. 'You always did like making stupid statements.' But he looked hard at Foster, as though searching for words. Then his manner softened. 'But it's right; I've got married. Catherine's her name. Still, you're going to be disappointed; she's not here today.'

Foster was indeed sad at not meeting the woman who had managed to tie down this world-weary, set-in-his ways, bachelor. Earlier, he had glimpsed a photograph on a nearby table, and had been surprised and puzzled. The woman in the picture was, at least in comparison with the grizzled Turner, hardly more than a girl, seemingly in her late twenties or early thirties—slender, dark-haired, dark-eyed and with an almost ethereal beauty. He wondered if she was the one Turner was talking about.

In the past he had often wondered about Turner's lonely existence, constantly jetting around the world with little or no foreknowledge of where he would be at any time. He had never settled down. He had bought this house only late on in his career, just before he retired. Even then, there had been a lot of surprise when he made the move. Australia was scarcely close to China, so his visits to his new home had been few and far between.

But they had evidently been enough, and his life's savings had been sufficient to buy this beautiful place, and to fit it out to provide a good standard of living when he did eventually retire.

He had always been good company, full of jokes and tall stories, ever-willing to stand his turn and buy a round in a pub.

Then, quite suddenly, out of the blue, Turner had married. Now he was keen to tell Foster how it had happened. Foster listened, fascinated.

After he retired, Turner had been called in to deal with a problem in the complex computer-controlled air conditioning system at the Sydney Opera House. Even in retirement, he still liked to keep his hand in, and people knew of his abilities. They were well known and there was a steady trickle of freelance work to keep him amused.

The convoluted make-up of this man included a deep love of music, and the chance of working at the Opera House had been too good to turn down, especially as the Australian National Ballet was performing there at the time. He had quickly identified the technical problem, and then he had started to 'nose round', as he put it. On discovering that the Ballet Company had a supporter's club and that they were holding a reception, he had brazenly joined in... and it was there that he met Catherine, one of the company's *corps de ballet*.

Somehow the attraction of opposites had worked its magic and she and Turner had married after a six-week courtship.

Foster shook his head slowly and smiled. 'You always were an old rogue. I'm not surprised at her falling for your tales.' He stared at Turner carefully. He wasn't one to intrude in anybody else's life, but he was curious about the abrupt and unexpected change to the course of this man's life. 'But why the change now?' he asked. 'You've been single forever. Don't tell me she was the first candidate; I won't believe it!'

Turner smiled. 'Nah!' he said with an easy, sly grin. 'There were others before her. But what kind of life did I have to offer? I was always travelling. You know what that did to the married ones.'

It was true. The rate of failed marriages in Universal's commissioning department was renowned. Attractive young wives, left alone at home for long periods, eventually became bored and found other, more constant companions. Suddenly-cancelled evenings-out, disappointed children missing Dad at a party, friends upset at having to hurriedly rearrange dinner-dates, all these were things that didn't make for stable marriages.

It was a little easier for those who had been travelling all their lives, preferably long before they married; in their cases, the partners knew very well what they were getting into. But it was much harder for those who started travelling after they became married.

'It's more practical, now that I've left Universal and got this place,' Turner said. 'I really do believe I've settled down. Fact is, Catherine travels more than I do.'

'Well, your getting hitched was a hell of a surprise, Alan,' Foster said. 'But, as I said, I wish you both the best of luck. Knowing you, I'm sure it'll work out very well.'

'Thanks,' Turner said gruffly. His old colleague's approval of his decision apparently pleased him considerably.

'Anyway,' he continued. 'Don't tell me you came by to hear about my love-life.'

Foster laughed. 'No,' he said. 'Actually, I need your help.'

Turner was suddenly serious. He sipped at his drink and said, 'Oh?'

Foster thought about it. Turner had just told him how he had settled down to a quiet married life, and now he was going to try and winkle him out of it. The odds were stacked against him.

But he had to try.

'You left Kung Tau half way through commissioning, didn't you?'

'Yes. I resigned ... Well,' Turner growled. '"Took early retirement' is the euphemism. But it comes to the same thing. I'd seen it coming, months before, and got together the money to buy this place as a bolt-hole.'

'You did well. But can I ask why you left?'

'Sure!' The response was angry, bitter. 'Because I was fed up of the stupidity of it all. The arguments, the cover-ups, the unwillingness to admit things weren't right. There've always been small balls-ups in the job but they got put right. Then, suddenly, when there was a huge almighty fuck-up, nobody wanted to know.'

'In what way?' Foster asked.

Turner stood up and re-filled their glasses before replying. 'It was the new system,' he said eventually. 'Galaxy 2000. Oh, it was very clever all right, and generally it worked just fine.'

Then he shook his head. 'But there was something wrong with it.'

Seeing Foster's frown, he elaborated. 'You know me, Dan. I'm a practical bastard. I may not know all the advanced theory and I'm the first to admit that I'm not up to speed with the latest computer technology. But somehow, in spite of that, I'm the one who always makes it work in the end—on site, where it all comes to a head.

'Or at least... I was.'

'Yes I know.'

'Well, it all *seemed* to be OK at first. But then some weird things started happening. It was hard to pin down. The operators filed Defect Reports, but I couldn't find anything—as hard as I tried ...'

'I've heard that before,' Foster interrupted. 'I've talked to Tony Crabtree. He was looking into the problem—I'm assuming it was the same one—when the explosion happened.'

He paused for a moment and watched Turner's face as he continued.

'And, by the way, the Chinese were holding him.'

'Tony?' Turner asked, frowning.

'Yes. They used him as a sort of hostage, or bargaining counter. But he's out now. They let him go home to Hong Kong as soon as I arrived and started getting involved.'

He didn't mention that it was through his machinations that Crabtree had been released.

'Poor sod!' Turner said.

'Yes. Anyway, we have to move on. The explosion at Kung Tau was just the start.'

'Yes. The explosion.' Turner scowled. 'That was a hell of a thing, Dan.' He was suddenly reflective. 'That poor bastard, Lee,' he said finally. 'It could have been me, you know. I could have been there when it went up...' He was thoughtful for a moment. Then he took a deep breath and continued, 'But... well, never mind. The point is this: I'm sure that whatever caused the explosion was tied up with the problem we'd found. We'd sorted out everything else, but this ... it was a real odd-ball.'

'What was?' Foster was tense.

'Well, it's hard to define. It wasn't anything consistent. Everything would be OK for days on end, and then it would screw up.'

'What would?'

Turner shrugged. 'Any part of it,' he said. 'Sometimes it would be one bit of the system, then another. We'd go crazy trying to track it down. Then it would seem that we'd cracked it; the system would settle down and be all right. For days, weeks sometimes.'

'You reported it back?'

''Course I did. And that's when I started to get really pissed off. Abingdon acted as though I was imagining it all. Would you believe it? They accused me of 'siding with the client'. In the end it all flared up into a bloody great row ... It was the last straw. Anyway, I'd been getting more and more frustrated with the Company for a long time. It had been coming to the boil for years.'

He tilted his head back and looked at the ceiling. 'You know,' he said reflectively. 'After you left, things went steadily downhill. And when the system started all this messing about, it was the end. It was just dangerous. Fucking dangerous.'

'But you're convinced that the fault caused the explosion?' Foster asked sharply.

'I'm bloody sure of it. I couldn't prove it, though, or I'd have done something about it.'

'What do you think happened?' Foster asked.

'That's just it,' Turner shrugged again. 'I simply don't know. But anything that makes a big system like that do weird things just has to be put under the microscope. I tried to get Universal to see that. I even rang Andy to tell him.'

'What?'

'Yes, I rang Abingdon but it was early in the morning. I'd forgotten the time difference. The only person there was Andy. He picked up the 'phone, so I told him.'

'What did he say?'

'He said he'd get QA or Development to look into it.'

Foster stared at him in disbelief. 'He didn't do that,' he said quietly. 'He must have decided to ignore it.'

'That's why I'm glad you're involved, Dan,' Turner said, then he paused and stared hard at Foster. 'But you still haven't said what's brought you into this thing.'

Foster sipped at his drink while he thought about it.

'You're absolutely right,' he said. 'About Galaxy. It's got a design fault. It's in the address decoders.'

'I fucking knew it!' Turner exclaimed, thumping the table in front of him. His eyes were shining in triumph. 'I'd been telling them for months.'

'Well, apparently it fell on deaf ears,' Foster said. 'At least until Kung Tau blew up.'

Turner just looked at him and shook his head. 'The idiots!' he said finally. He shook his head. 'And look how much damage it caused. How many people died.'

'Too many, I know. But there it is. The mess Tony Crabtree was in ... that's what made me decide to get involved without knowing the whole background. Someone had to help him out of the hole he was in.'

'But you did it,' Turner said. But from his expression, Foster knew that he was suspicious. That he sensed some other motive behind this visit.

'Yes,' Foster said. 'And I thought that was that.'

'But it wasn't.'

'No.' He took a deep breath. Now was the time. 'There's a problem, Alan. The decoder fault is generic. It's in every Galaxy system. Any one of them could go berserk. At any moment.'

And then he saw from Turner's bleak expression that he knew what was coming.

'That's right, Alan. *Far Point* too.'

'Oh fuck!'

'Exactly!'

'They're going to tell the Chinese, aren't they?'

But Turner's tone indicated that, once again, he knew the answer already.

'No.'

'Then what the fuck's going to happen?'

'They want me to go and fix it,' Foster said. 'And to do it without the Chinese knowing.'

Turner stared at him. Then he shook his head very slowly, like somebody who finds their eyes drawn to a scene of a terrible accident. 'Oh no!' he said. 'I know why you've come here ...'

Foster gave a wry smile. 'Exactly! You know I could never do it on my own. They're fuelling at any moment. I need help, Alan.'

'And you thought that I'd be prepared to get involved?'

'I hoped so.'

Turner stared at him and then snorted. 'Bollocks!' he said. 'Nobody in their right mind would give up an easy life to stick their heads into a nuclear plant with a known design fault. One that's so crucial to its operation that it could blow up.

'Forget it, mate! Sorry!'

Foster felt bleak. He really needed Turner's help.

'I know how you feel, Alan,' he said. 'Believe me. I felt the same. Life was ticking over quietly for me. Then this thing came along ...'

'Yes,' Turner said. 'And you did your bit. You don't have to do any more. And you certainly don't have to pull me into the mess if you do.'

'I know, Alan. But I can't do it alone. I need the best team I can put together to help me, and you have to be in it. Otherwise there's no hope.'

Turner looked at him steadily. And said nothing.

'Alan, if we don't do this thing a lot of people are going to be exposed to risk.'

'I know that!' Turner barked. 'But it's up to Universal to sort it out.'

'They can't,' Foster said.

And as he told him about the Government's involvement and the dilemma into which they had fallen, Turner's face showed increasing shock and incredulity.

At the end, Turner looked devastated. 'Holy shit!' he murmured. 'And now you want me to help get them out of the mess.'

'Yes. The job will need a small team...'

'A team? Who else have you got?'

'You're the first—if you agree to come. Then there's George Perring.'

'That bastard!' Turner exclaimed. But there was little rancour in his tone.

Perring was Universal Digital's most senior commissioning engineer and like Turner he had spent decades travelling the world, living for months on end in hotels or bachelor apartments in remote towns and villages in a wide variety of countries.

'I know what you think,' Foster said. 'But he knows his stuff. And he's been on the Far Point site right from the start; he knows the equipment there —and the people.'

'OK,' Turner admitted grudgingly. 'But I never trusted him. He was always, well ... an Andy Johns man—likely to run to him with tales out of school.'

'I know,' Foster replied. 'But the fact remains; technically he's good, he knows the plant and he knows the Galaxy system. There aren't too many who I can get to help, and in spite of his faults I know he'd be a good man to have alongside us.'

There was a moment's thoughtful silence.

Turner took a sip of his drink and said, 'OK. You, me and Perring—that's three. Who else have you lined up?'

'That's where it gets difficult,' Foster said. 'I reckon the job will need at least five people …'

'At least!' Turner agreed. 'So who are the rest?'

'Well, I'm planning to bring in the systems engineer who was working on Kung Tau.'

'Judith Chang?'

'Yes.'

'God! You're scraping the barrel, aren't you? She's OK, but she's very young.'

'I know,' Foster admitted. 'But I need somebody who's really up with the technology. I've never met her, but from all I've heard she's very bright.'

'She is.' Turner looked at him seriously. 'But she's got her life in front of her. How do you feel about putting her at risk like that?'

Foster's expression was bleak. He shrugged. 'What choice do I have?' he asked bitterly.

Turner looked up at him. 'OK, so who's the fifth team member?' he asked.

Foster took a deep breath before replying, 'Andy Johns.'

Turner spluttered, and almost spat out his drink in surprise. '*What?*'

Foster laughed. 'Not my choice, Alan. But the Government wants him to go with us. I'm not sure why—probably to show the importance Universal attaches to Far Point.'

'Oh yes,' Turner said coldly. 'The Chinese are going to buy that, are they? The MD of a big company like Universal getting his hands dirty?'

'No, of course not. But he can be the administrator.'

'Someone's barking mad!' Turner said. 'And I hope it's not you. Why not send Carol Lopez? She'd be better than Andy.'

'No chance,' Foster said. 'I tried that. But the Government won't budge. It has to be Andy.'

Turner sipped thoughtfully at his drink before continuing, 'So that's the five of us.'

Foster brightened at the expression 'five of *us*'. Turner was beginning to think of himself as part of the team!

'Yes, Alan. Though I think Andy will be useful. After all, he was a qualified engineer once.'

'Once!'

Foster looked at his watch and clicked his tongue. He had stayed too long. He had to get back to the airport now.

He stood up and said, 'I've got to go now, Alan. I wish I could stay, to meet the lady in your life. But I do need to know—definitely. You are coming, aren't you?'

Turner went over to the window and stared out over the bay for a long while before answering. Foster found himself holding his breath as he waited for the reply. Turner could still back off—and Foster wouldn't have blamed him if he did.

When the answer came, it started as a question, 'You realize what you're asking, old mate?' Turner asked. 'I've waited all my life for someone like Catherine to come along. And the chance to put down roots.'

Foster nodded. 'Of course, Alan,' he said. 'But I really need as much help as I can get. And you're the best one to help me.'

Turner was pensive. A long moment passed before he replied. Then he gave a deep sigh and said, 'OK pal, count me in. Though I'm shit-scared at the thought, I'll do it.'

Foster almost let out a whoop of delight.

'Fantastic!' he said. 'And, as for being scared, don't you think I lie awake at night, thinking about it?'

'I'm sure you do. But, you could have backed out too, you know.'

Foster stared at him sadly. 'I wish I could have,' he said. 'But somehow I feel responsible for what's happened. If an accident happened at Far Point, I'd feel that it was due to the decisions I'd taken all those years ago, when I launched the Galaxy concept.'

'But you can't take the blame for that, Dan. Yes, the problem came about because of the concept. But if you'd stayed with Universal—if you'd got to control things rather than that bastard Johns; you'd never have cut corners like he did. You'd never have built up the atmosphere of fear, so people were too scared to speak up when they saw that something was wrong.'

'Perhaps not,' Foster said grimly. 'But that only makes it worse. I should have fought harder to stay.'

'Anyway,' he added. 'I'm really pleased that you're on board.'

Turner stood, smiled grimly and held out his hand. 'I wish I was pleased too. But I'm glad you asked me, Dan, and I'm happy to help you.'

They shook hands and Foster said, 'I'll get tickets and money to you right away.'

He smiled as he thought that Turner had made the commitment without even asking about remuneration.

The look of absolute amazement was still pasted on Turner's face as they parted.

As Foster walked back down the long drive to the car he mused at his situation. It was a major boost that he had managed to persuade Turner to join his team.

As he opened the car he looked back towards the bungalow. The shock on Turner's face had been replaced by one of wonder.

Chapter 13

Unlike power stations that burn fossil fuels such as coal, oil or gas, a nuclear plant has no chimneys to discharge smoke and exhaust gases to the atmosphere. However, just like its fossil-fuelled counterparts, it uses steam; though, this time it is generated, directly or indirectly, from the heat produced by radioactivity within the reactors.

The reactors are housed within a 'containment vessel': a massive steel and concrete structure that isolates it from the atmosphere and guards against any accidental discharge of nuclear contamination. Within this structure is another one, containing the nuclear reactor itself. The reactor is thus doubly shielded but, even so, great care is taken to monitor and protect anybody entering any of the areas within the outer shell that could be flooded with invisible, silent and lethal radiation if anything went wrong. The entrances and exits are protected by strong steel turnstiles, like giant vertical combs with interlocking teeth that allow passage in only one direction, and which do so only when the barrier's electronic systems confirm that the person is authorized to pass.

Foster was wearing the electronic badge issued to him at the power station's health-physics laboratory. The badge contained an electronic transponder that enabled the surveillance systems to keep track of his position wherever he went in the plant. It was also a film badge; it contained a single sheet of photographic paper wrapped in protective layers of foil. At the end of the day he would hand the badge to the security guard at the gate and the film would be developed overnight. If he had encountered any radiation during his work it would have penetrated the foil and left tell-tale signs on the film, resulting in his being called in quickly for a detailed health check.

As he neared the gate, the transponder in his film badge signalled his presence to a detector. The lamp above the gate turned from red to green, confirming that he was authorized to proceed.

He grasped one of the steel rods of the turnstile and pushed his way through. Once inside the protected area, he started to walk round the corridor that circled the inner containment.

It was an unearthly place here. With no windows to let in natural light, the off-white walls and bare concrete floor were permanently bathed in the ghastly yellow wash of light from high-intensity sodium lamps mounted high on the ceiling above. Soon, when the plant was running, there would be a dull roar of machinery here too, though there would be less of the heat and vibration that you would encounter in a conventional power station—at least, not here.

But for now the place was eerily silent.

Foster found a small office and knocked before opening the door. The young Chinese woman working there looked up and smiled. She was petite, with sleek black hair tied back in a simple pony-tail. She was Judith Chang. She was wearing a regulation white boiler-suit that all the engineers wore while working on the plant.

'Hi!' she called. 'You're just in time! I'm going over the systems diagrams. I could do with a bit of help.'

In response to the 'arm-twisting' Jeffreys had mentioned to Foster during their meeting in London, Chang had been recalled from the Kung Tau site by a deeply unhappy and resentful Andy Johns, and sent to Far Point. Her assignment was to help Foster with his work.

On his first meeting with her, Foster had explained the problem and what they were going to try and do. At first she had been shocked, but then she began to come round. Eventually she had agreed to assist, although it was plain that she did not approve of the scheme and was in fact more than a little frightened of its implications, and what it would demand of her.

This fear had not affected her work however; she was clever and thoroughly familiar with the Galaxy system and had been immensely useful to him.

Since his arrival on site Foster had worked closely with Chang and they had developed a mutual respect for each other's skills; her quick, sharp brain with its knowledge of the detail of computer systems, acting as a foil to his years of experience in the power industry and his vast knowledge of all the complex machinery of a power plant. All the same, he several times found her skipping over details to reach conclusions; a worrying trait of hers that Turner had described to him earlier.

Now she smoothed out one of the drawings on the desk and asked him to run through the system with her. She was trying to relate the neat lines and symbols on the diagrams to the apparent mess of equipment and cables woven through the fabric of the buildings. Soon, with Foster's help, she was able to locate some key items she had missed and which had been confusing her. Together, they pored over the drawings for hours, occasionally walking out to different areas of the plant to clarify some detail or other.

As a result of Jeffreys' machinations, Foster had been invited by the PRC to act as an 'adviser' on the project, with the girl acting as his assistant. As far as the Chinese were concerned, in this role his experience would be available to help with any particularly tricky questions, while not detracting from their own engineers' efforts. From Foster's point of view, he felt he was actively contributing to the progress of the job, while working surreptitiously to deal with the underlying task that Jeffreys had set him to tackle.

The initial plan had been short on detail. Foster quickly realized that he had many problems to face. For a start, he had to identify all the places where the faulty equipment was located. Then, he had to work out ways of making the change without causing a further risk or alerting the Chinese.

The work had proved to be more difficult than they had anticipated, for political reasons as well as technical ones. Foster had detected a degree of suspicion among the Chinese over his presence at the site but, nevertheless, they were pleased to have a respected expert working with them, and they had produced a schedule that had proved to be more than enough to keep him busy. The problem was that this left scant time to work on Jeffreys' hidden agenda.

In the end, Foster had insisted that he and Chang would need to spend time familiarising themselves with the plant and its electronic systems before they could begin their work. He also insisted that this process would be best done by themselves, with no assistance from the Chinese. All this was true, but it also provided him with short periods when he could quietly delve into the areas that he wanted to inspect in detail.

Chang's role was a double one. Her fluency in Mandarin and English enabled her to act as an unofficial interpreter, for although most of the Chinese engineers spoke reasonable English, their command of the language was far from perfect. Without Chang's help this could often have led to difficulties, since the Chinese engineers never wanted to lose face by admitting when they had failed to understand something. Chang's understanding of the Chinese mentality was also a help in these situations: she could anticipate problems and head them off before they became significant.

At around noon Foster stood up and stretched his back. He had been hunched over the table for too long. 'I'm bushed,' he admitted. 'Let's go for lunch.'

They went through the long rigmarole of checking their bodies and clothes for radiation and then went to the locker room to change out of their boiler suits.

Surprisingly, the egalitarian PRC had agreed to the power station's designers providing separate locker rooms for senior and junior staff.

Perhaps they understood that it would be hard to persuade professionals from overseas to accept some of the habits of the less-Westernised of the Chinese staff.

On the occasions when his changing-room key was not handy, Foster would use the junior staff room; it was clean and adequate, but he had once been shaken to find dusty boot-prints on the toilet seats, indicating the local habit of defecating while squatting with boots planted on either side of the pan.

But, in spite of all their forethought, what the designers had not provided for were separate facilities for men and women. In consequence, Foster and Chang had worked out an arrangement whereby he would first check that the washroom was clear of people before she went in. Then he would wait outside, guarding the door until she re-emerged and he could go in. This was a little complex but it worked well enough. Any Chinese who came by while he was standing at the door would continue past, no doubt wondering at the strange antics of the *round-eyes*. Foster had wondered what he would do if any of them looked as if they were about to go in; fortunately it never occurred, because on seeing him there the Chinese would usually change their minds about where they had wanted to go.

Once this complicated toiletries procedure was over, Foster and Chang emerged into the bright winter sunshine. It was cold outside and they hurried to the administration block.

Meals were served in an excellent dining facility built by the owners of the power plant for the many foreign staff employed on the site. The food was generally Western-style, though the Chinese kitchen staff somehow managed to give most dishes a slightly oriental touch. *Steak-and-kidney pie with sweet-and-sour sauce* was how Foster had described it once.

Foster and Chang served themselves to salad and took their plates to a table in the corner of the room to join Alan Turner, who was already sitting there, alongside George Perring, Universal Digital's resident engineer, or R.E.

Perring was a tall well-built man with massive and elaborately-tattooed forearms. He had a pronounced scathing disdain of most of the local engineering staff in the countries he visited. Like a bad penny, he had a habit of appearing on the various sites that Foster had visited over the years, during his time with the company and afterwards. The last time they had met had been in Bolivia, and Foster had then once again wondered at these engineers' nomadic existence.

Perring's life, like Turner's, had for several decades consisted of travelling the world, living for months on end in hotels or bachelor apartments in remote towns and villages in a wide variety of countries. Rumour had it that Perring had travelled to every country in the world, though he had once told Foster that, to him, every country was made up of the same interminable combination of airport, hotel room and power station.

Now, Perring looked up from his food and nodded a greeting as the pair arrived.

'All well?' Foster asked as they sat down.

'As well as we can expect!' Turner muttered.

Perring raised his eyebrows. 'That's right,' he said. 'We're going to carry on with the dry-run tests today. They said they were going to tell you. Did they?'

Foster shook his head. It wasn't unusual for communications to break down; the plant was big, with many hidden rooms and twisting corridors, and efficient communications were not the Chinese strong-point. Although they could have paged him—his pager was always at his belt—they rarely did so, and he had become used to finding out at the last minute about meetings he had been meant to attend, or tests he was expected to witness.

The plant had not yet been fuelled—the reactors were not yet active—and this was the time for testing the various control systems *in situ*, with simulated conditions of operation. This 'dry testing' process had started several days ago, but a minor fault in the power-supply system had interrupted the programme.

'They found the problem then?' Chang asked.

'Yes, it was a faulty relay,' Perring replied. He studiously avoided eye contact wit her. From his point of view she was a dangerous anachronism, a woman first, but also an engineer. The fact that she was Chinese, but not really Chinese, complicated things further. Whenever possible, he preferred to act as though she wasn't there at all, and now he addressed his reply to Foster. 'Don't ask me why it took two days for them to find it. But I did warn you, didn't I? Anyway, can you two be ready to re-start the tests this afternoon?'

Foster had long ago recognized Perring's technique. On arriving at a site he would spend a short time identifying somebody on the client's side who was in a reasonably responsible position—the higher the better—but who was weak-charactered or technically unsure of himself. Then he would do everything in his power to humiliate the man in front of his colleagues.

It was an easy thing to do during the early days on site, when Perring was the one with most experience of the new equipment. If it was left too late, the edge would be lost, because the target could have learned enough to be able to defend himself.

Before long, even if the victim was technically competent, he would become nervous and harried into making mistakes—and every one of these would be highlighted and maximized by Perring. It was all very public, and soon everybody would be afraid of becoming the next target. Then he would be free to force his way through any difficulties.

It was a cruel technique, but Foster had to admit that it usually worked.

Perring was experienced, and he had the ability to deal with a wide variety of problems, but Foster knew that his knowledge was superficial. He would often bluff his way through a point during technical discussions. At first Foster had been fooled by his confident manner, but on one occasion he had been given cause to check on something that the man had done and he had found a serious error. After that, Foster had treated him with extreme caution.

There was a double edge to Foster's caution: Perring was known to be an Andy Johns man.

Universal's MD had long ago recognized Perring's ruthlessness, and he relied on his shrewdness to get the company out of any difficulty. No doubt he wished now that Perring had been at Kung Tau, but he had been involved on a plant in Argentina at the time, and the Chinese project had been allocated to Turner.

'I wish we had more people of Perring's calibre,' Johns had once said to Foster. 'With one like him at every site we'd be in clover.'

True to form, Johns had rewarded Perring well. In a situation where there was little possibility of 'fiddling' expenses, Perring had been able to get away with murder.

Once, while Foster had still been at the company, and when Johns had been away on an extended trip, Foster had been asked to authorize Perring's expense claims, and he had then become aware of the pattern that had been allowed to develop. At a time when Foster's own people were subject to rigorous control over their living expenses, Perring was submitting claims for expenditures that were rarely supported by proper receipts. Foster had raised this with Johns at the earliest possible opportunity but had been fobbed off.

'I know,' Johns had said, unabashed and with a conspiratorial wink—he had the ability to briefly forget animosities when it suited his purposes—and said, 'He's a rogue. But he's a good man. We can't possibly pay him enough, and anyway, if we did, the Revenue would take their cut of it. This way he stays tied to the company. And he's worth every penny of what he gets, by fair means or foul.'

As R.E., Perring had total responsibility for the technical and commercial aspects of the work on site, and he was adept at ensuring that the best possible face was put on the company's activities at all times. He would generally offer to produce the minutes of any meetings—an offer that was usually accepted gratefully, since engineers were not too keen on minute-taking. This gave him the opportunity create records that suited Universal's purposes, or his own. Even if the client insisted on producing the minutes Perring would ensure that they passed through his hands before being formally issued. Either way, they would be carefully honed, always showing Universal in a good light; he had a magical way of ensuring that any delays or errors were laid at the Client's door, or attributed to other contractors, even if the fault was patently Universal's.

Now he was harassing his own people. As far as Perring was concerned, the fact that the programme was delayed and that this was due to somebody else's incompetence would be made abundantly clear to the client, but he would not allow his own people to reduce the furious pace of their work. This much was always made plain, and they were all aware of it now: the resumption of the dry testing would be paramount.

'It's all right,' Judith Chang said in response to Perring's question about the resumption of the tests, pointedly ignoring his slight to her. 'We can break off what we're doing. I need to think a bit anyway.'

'Are you sure?' Foster asked. 'I can ask for a hold.' He sensed Perring's glare, but the woman's reply saved him from having to fight for a delay.

'No trouble,' she said. 'We can get back to it afterwards.' Then she looked at Perring and asked, 'How long for the tests?'

'Two days,' Perring growled. 'I'd guess. But with these slit-eyed jokers running things it could just as well take two weeks.'

Foster looked disapprovingly at him. Apart from the obvious insult to Chang, in the crowded dining room their words would be easily overheard, denigrating the Chinese so loudly and openly was a stupid and dangerous occupation, but Perring seemed not to care.

They continued eating in silence, thinking about what they would have to do during the afternoon.

At the point where the tests had stopped, the Galaxy system was being subjected to a series of simulated inputs and operator commands, to see that it responded correctly. The tests were as good an approach to reality as was possible, though they could never replicate all the combinations of things that could occur in reality.

One of the most arduous tasks for a big DCS is for it to respond to a sudden event which triggers off an avalanche of others—hundreds of things, all happening more or less at the same time. In such situations the system has to receive, recognize, interpret and deal with the events in a carefully structured way, and it has to do it quickly.

For all its power, and in spite of its designers' claims that it is an 'intelligent' system, a DCS is incapable of true deductive reasoning. Its response must always be one that has been thought out carefully by the designers. Give it something the designer hadn't anticipated, and it could either fail to react or, worse still, it could react in an unexpected way.

Following a serious incident, the hundreds of messages flooding into the DCS can threaten to overload it with information and decisions. The objective of the tests being carried out now at Far Point was to simulate as nearly as possible the conditions of such an incident. The weakness of the tests was that they subjected the system only to those circumstances that the designers had already anticipated. The situations were therefore not unexpected; the designers knew how to tackle them, and would have programmed the necessary actions into the DCS.

The tests could simply never simulate the totally unexpected. Nothing could.

For their separate reasons, the quartet sitting or standing round the table were thinking about their respective parts in the coming test programme. Perring would have to cover for any deficiencies or errors, Chang and Turner would have to deal with them. Foster would be looking for a link to Kung Tau, though he did not expect to find one quickly or easily.

'Who's going to call the shots this time?' Foster asked quietly. 'The last time was really chaotic.'

'Don't I know it,' Perring replied sourly, without any attempt to lower his voice. 'That's another problem; they haven't the faintest idea.'

Perring's scathing disdain for the Chinese engineers surfaced at the slightest opportunity. During the tests, the Chinese project manager, Da Shengju, had been indecisive and confused, leading to everybody arguing about what should or should not have been happening.

It was not unexpected. It had been Da Shengju whom Perring had targeted as his victim. He had been quick to spot that the man was weak-willed, and he had gleefully set about undermining his self-confidence and destroying any shred of credibility he may have had with his own staff. The fact that Da Shengju was the client's project manager was a bonus; the higher-ranking the patsy, the more effective the bullying technique.

Da Shengju had crumbled under the attack. Desperate to preserve his self-esteem he had become increasingly panicky, issuing streams of contradictory instructions to his bewildered staff, and nervously looking to Perring at each and every turn, waiting for the ridicule and abuse that he knew would inevitably descend on him in spite of his best efforts. In a culture where 'losing face' was the worst fate that could befall anybody, the fact that he was continually being made to look foolish in front of his own underlings was even more terrible.

Remaining superficially cowed, deep within he harboured bitter resentment and the burning desire for vengeance.

'Well,' Foster said. 'We'll be ready for the tests this time. Perhaps things will speed up now.'

Perring smirked as if to say, *Some hopes!*

After they had finished eating they headed for the control room. It was a vast room; a dramatic space. The control consoles were pale cream desks with computer screens showing the operation of various parts of the plant on their displays. To allow the screens to be easily read, the lighting in the room was subdued, with tiny spotlights directing concentrated beams of light onto the operator's keyboards and the nearby writing desks.

Lining the whole of one wall of the room, a huge panel of mosaic tiles showed the network of power lines, switches and transformers that took electricity from the plant to the cities and villages of China. Tiny red, yellow and green lamps showed the status of every component in the vast network of cables and pylons fed by the transmission lines that radiated away from the plant.

On the other wall, a massive window of armoured glass provided a direct view onto the top of the top of the reactor, the pile-cap, and the huge machines that were used to load and unload the reactor's radioactive fuel.

The three engineers in white boiler-suits who were clustered around one of the consoles looked up as the Westerners entered the room. Da Shengju smiled nervously at Foster. 'We ready to start again,' he said.

'About time!' Perring snapped, and Da Shengju tried not to show his disappointment at this casual dismissal of the truly praiseworthy progress that his staff had made. Perring jabbed his finger to point at the console.

'Come on,' he said. 'Let's do it.' His tone was irritated.

At his signal, a command would be fed into the system, simulating a reactor-trip incident— a sudden shut-down. Hundreds of electronic inputs would be suddenly triggered into the DCS and the observers would look for any signs of incorrect or slow operation.

'Everybody ready?' Perring asked, looking round the room. Everybody nodded agreement.

'OK. I'll start the countdown,' he said.

'Three!'

Involuntarily, Foster found himself holding his breath. Although this was a simulation of what would happen in reality and although he had been through several similar tests during his career, he still found it a tense experience. This time he was only an observer; the people who would be most involved were Turner, Chang and Perring, and he looked at them to see how they were reacting.

They were all looking intently at the screens, the girl sitting down, Turner looking over her shoulder, Perring standing beside them, scanning the screens. The heel of Chang's hand rested on the edge of the console, her index finger hovering over a red button. She had lifted the clear plastic guard that normally covered the button to prevent inadvertent operation. She seemed very calm, almost as if she was a dispassionate observer.

But as Foster looked at her he detected a barely-visible tremble in the finger poised over the button.

'Two!'

Perring's voice was quiet. His attention was concentrated on the displays. What happened when the red button was pressed would provide a good indication of the system's response to an emergency. If all went well it would be a good omen for the actual operation of the system after the nuclear fuel was loaded into the reactors.

'One!'

Foster turned his attention to the Chinese engineers. Da Shengju was standing at Perring's side, his face a study in intense concentration. Once again Foster felt pity for him. In spite of Perring's continual scathing criticism, the Chinese engineer was a very clever man with a deep and thorough understanding of the reactors and their control systems. His frequent mistakes were due more to Perring's goading than to any actual incompetence.

'Zero!'

At that word Chang's finger jabbed down on the button.

Instantly, an urgent chime sounded and a stream of information began to spill onto the computer screens. A printer beside the console began chattering excitedly and spooling paper into a box on the floor. Beside the console, a bank of lamps that had been shining green immediately turned to bright red. These were essential alarms, backing up the computer displays.

Foster noticed that the girl had let out a slow breath.

The insistent chime was silenced as one of the operators pressed a button to tell the system he had received the alarm and was dealing with it. The lines of information cascaded rapidly over the computer screens for several seconds, then gradually began to slow.

When the screen displays were steady again, Chang looked up at Perring. 'Seems OK,' she said quietly, and he nodded.

'Yeah!' he grunted. 'We'll go through the print-outs, but it looked all right. I'd have spotted anything out of place. Right away.'

Foster decided to test the water very gently, to see if Perring had detected even a small hint of what he suspected. Jeffreys had said that the number of people who knew about Foster's mission should be restricted, and Perring was not one of the privileged few who were 'in the know'.

'George, have you ever come across problems with the addressing?' he asked casually. 'In Galaxy 2000, I mean?'

Perring scowled at him. 'Nope!' he said. 'Why?'

Foster shrugged his shoulders. 'Oh nothing! I was just wondering... But what would happen if a fault did come and then went away again—an intermittent one.'

Perring's tone was sour, even dismissive, as he replied. 'I'd have seen it.'

Foster looked at him. It was true; a commissioning engineer of his experience would have been able to detect an oddity very quickly.

He had been studying Perring's face very carefully during the exchange, looking for a hint that he was covering up something. But there was nothing; perhaps Perring was a good poker player, but Foster felt instinctively that the man was genuinely ignorant of any such fault in the Galaxy system.

Turner smiled at Foster, fully aware of the irony that Universal's senior engineer was unaware of the company's machinations.

Foster smiled in return.

He contemplated his small band of engineers.

His most trusted confidant was Turner; grizzled and experienced, drawn reluctantly into the plot when all his instincts must have been to stay in his hard-won, comfortable Australian retreat with his new bride.

And then there was Perring, oblivious of what was really happening, but arrogantly convinced that he was fully in charge of it all.

Then Chang, a hard-working and intelligent foot-soldier, there to implement Foster's commands.

But his trump card—the fifth member of his team—was Andy Johns himself.

He remembered the rage in Johns' voice as he had cursed Foster roundly for putting the screws on him via the Government.

And for forcing *him* to fly out to China at an instant's notice!

'I don't care, Andy,' Foster had said. 'I've got a job to do, and I'm going to do it. I'm going to fix the problem and you're going to be right beside us, while we do it. It'll give me the greatest pleasure to watch you sweat. And if you make as much as one single attempt to get in my way you'll get screwed, my friend. First by the Government, and then by me—personally—and in the most painful way. You can't even begin to imagine the damage I'll do. But if the DTI hasn't destroyed you first, I'll personally blow you right out of the water. I'll make sure the world knows all about your attempt to cover up the almighty balls-up your company made, and how it's all of your making.'

'You wouldn't dare ...' Johns had begun.

'Wouldn't I?' Foster had interrupted. 'Just try me! I promise you that every newspaper and TV station will be at your door, asking if you'd really been about to risk the safety of a nuclear power station, just for the sake of protecting your own putrid skin.'

Even over the telephone link, he had been able to sense Johns' rage and impotence, his frustration at knowing that what he wanted to do most of all—to slam down the 'phone and sever the link—would only speed his own destruction.

Foster had absolutely no doubt that Johns was still convinced that the Galaxy system was not at fault, and in the end it was that conviction that had forced him to comply with the DTI's command. If nobody else would champion the system—*his* system—then *he* would.

Foster knew that Johns was a coward at heart, and that he would have found some way of escaping if he suspected the slightest element of risk, but his actions were indicative of more than a simple expression of faith in his company; it was proof of his absolute self-confidence.

But in the end—whatever his motivation—he had agreed to come; and that, in itself, had been a show of bravado, to demonstrate to the Government that, apart from being fully confident of the system's innocence, he was prepared to lay his own life on the line to prove it.

As Foster thought about his small, disparate band, he wondered if it was enough.

But it was all he had.

Chapter 14

Resting in Judith Chang's small hand, the tiny black device looked like a multi-legged beetle; dead, with its metal legs pointing to the sky in final supplication. It was the memory chip that she had programmed with the new instructions.

'It doesn't look like it could save tens of thousands of lives, does it?' she asked.

Foster looked at it, and then at her. He caught the light of triumph behind her shy expression, smiled broadly and understood.

'You've done it!' he exclaimed.

Foster had realised that simply changing to higher-quality decoders would not provide an absolute guarantee of safety. He wanted to be sure, and had asked Chang if she could devise a way of getting each device to check that, once set, its address never changed.

It had taken her two days; two long days of intense work, during which she had hardly paused to eat or sleep.

A grin shone through her fatigue. 'Yes. And I've tested it on the simulator. It works! The problem's gone away.'

'Completely? No side-effects?'

'None! At least, none that I can find ... and I've been pretty thorough. I've tried sending duplicate commands, I've disconnected one of the highways... In fact, I've done everything I can think of to make it go wrong, and it just doesn't. It's good, Dan! Really good!'

Foster reached out and pulled her towards him until he was embracing her tightly. She was embarrassed.

'Easy on,' she laughed. 'You could crush mankind's saviour to death!'

But she returned his embrace.

'OK. What now?' he asked as he released her.

'I replicate it. Copy it to all the PROMs we've got.' She referred to the programmable read-only memory devices as PROMs. 'Then we shut down the nodes, one at a time, and swap the PROMs over. Just like we planned.'

'That won't be too easy,' he said. 'I've counted them. We're going to need two hundred of the little blighters, Judith. Have you got enough?'

'God no!' she gasped. '*Two hundred?* That many?' The question was rhetorical; in reality she probably could have worked out how many they'd need, but she hadn't stopped to think about it.

He nodded. The device she had programmed was a simple memory. To copy the instructions that she had loaded into it, they would need blank chips, one for each node.

She sighed deeply and considered it. 'Well, it's just about possible, I think,' she said. 'Though it'll be tight. But at least we have enough hardware. I sent off for a batch of PROMs—five hundred—as soon as we'd decided what to do. Said it was urgent. They DHL'd them while I was working out the program. They arrived last night.'

'Great!'

'But programming two hundred?' The enormity of the task had returned to her. 'And how do we get them past George?' she asked.

'Ah! That's where I've been doing my bit. I rang Abingdon, and a few other friends of mine.'

He smiled as he remembered his conversation with Arnold Coward and the DTI, and Forsyth's solemn promise to pull all the strings that needed to be pulled. 'We needn't worry about keeping George away; in fact, he'll help us.'

'He will?' she asked, amazed. 'You got Andy Johns to agree to that?'

'I did better than that,' he said. 'Andy's going to be here himself.'

'Mr Johns is actually coming here?' Chang asked, shocked amazement clearly audible in her voice. 'To Far Point?'

Foster nodded.

'But what about George Perring?' she asked. 'I feel we can't trust him, and yet ... I don't see how we can manage to do the work without him.'

Foster had thought about it and she was right; the logistics were inescapable.

'I know,' he said. 'I don't trust him either. Which is why I don't want him to be in on the details of what you've done. But with two hundred nodes to change before they start fuelling the reactor, we need all the help we can get. With five pairs of hands ...'

'Five pairs?' she exclaimed. She started to count on her fingers. 'You, me, Alan, George ...'

'And your M.D.' Foster grinned at her. 'He's the fifth one that I promised you.'

'Mr Johns?' She looked amazed. She had assumed Johns would adopt some sort of management role. 'Would he know what to do?'

'You mean, can he screw the lid off a terminal box?' Foster laughed; but behind the banter there was a serious point. The task that lay ahead of them was going to be more than a simple exercise of opening a metal box and looking inside; it would be a tense, ball-aching grind, a repetitive chore that had to be done very carefully, with meticulous accuracy, and without alerting the Chinese to what was happening. And it had to be done against a remorselessly ticking clock.

Fuelling of the reactor would be starting in four days.

And the risk of the Galaxy system causing a serious accident would begin as soon as fuel began to be loaded.

Foster had estimated it would take around twenty minutes to make each change to the Galaxy nodes; counting the time taken to disable the relevant part of the system, turn off the power to the node, walk over to each one, perhaps climb a ladder to reach it, unscrew the cover, remove the original component and substitute the new one. Three an hour; and if only three engineers were available they could change only one device at a time, since one of them would have to distract the Chinese engineers while the other made the switch. Taking it in turns to sleep and eat, it would require a full week to complete the job, with each of them working flat out for twelve hours at a time.

It was too long; much too long.

But with an extra pair of hands—two *extra* pairs if they involved Andy Johns himself—then they could do it in the four days available. Four or five people to beat the clock; if they worked as a tightly-knit team. And that required everybody's total commitment.

'You've got a point there, Judith,' Foster concluded. Then he smiled. 'Andy's only the MD,' he said. 'But I think I can show him what to do.'

And the more he considered the prospect, the more he relished it.

Andy Johns stared at the telephone in a white-hot rage. It had been a long time since somebody had *instructed* him to do something; *commanded* him to do it, or else. And it was all Foster's fault. Foster, the incompetent engineer who had been dispensed with so long ago; but who doggedly refused to lie down and admit defeat.

What could he do? The instructions from the Department of Trade and Industry were clear. He was to go to China, and to do so right now! He was to go there and follow Foster's instructions.

There had been no disguising the threat. He would do as instructed, or else.

He wondered what they would do. Discredit him? Have him sacked from the Board of UDS? Charge him with some trumped-up crime?

He gritted his teeth and slowly shook his head. It really didn't matter; he'd still be finished.

It was all wrong! So unfair! Quite unnecessary!

There was nothing wrong with Galaxy.

Oh, all right, there was the problem with the address decoders, but that was a simple foul-up. His software engineers were good. They simply wouldn't have designed a system that lacked the checks to flag up this type of error. To make it safe.

Ergo, whatever had happened at Kung Tau had nothing to do with the Galaxy system. It had to be something else. Something that was totally unconnected with Universal Digital.

But Foster just *had* to interfere. To fiddle with it. It was crazy; simply crazy.

Suddenly he smiled. That was it! He couldn't let Foster do it. The risks were too appalling to contemplate. He would have him stopped. And in such a way that the fool would be publicly humiliated. And finally discredited. Better still, since they were dealing with the Peoples' Republic of China it was even possible that Foster would be arrested and imprisoned.

That thought pleased him. Now *that* would really fix him!

He swung his chair round to face the desk and tapped at the keyboard of his computer. A diary page flashed up and he scrolled down until he reached the **W** section. He peered at the numbers. That was it!

Wei. Su-ko Wei. Head of Engineering, Ministry of International Trade Development, Beijing.

He tapped out the numbers on his telephone keypad and listened to the dialling tone.

Perring listened in sullen silence. He knew better than to argue; for a start, Foster out-classed him technically, but also he'd had a call from Andy Johns, and the instructions had been curt, clear and absolute. He was to co-operate with Foster, and to do so fully.

That didn't mean that Perring was happy. He had never been able to relax in his dealings with Foster, because he had never been able to slide anything past him. But he didn't understand what was going on now. He knew of the phantom fault that had bedevilled the Galaxy 2000 system from the Kung Tau days, and he was also aware of the wild speculation in informed circles that the system had been responsible for the disaster. But he was totally confident that the rumours were unfounded.

Or at least he had been, until Andy Johns' telephone call had sown the first seeds of doubt.

And now Foster was saying it as well. Now he was *really* becoming unnerved.

'Change the PROMs?' he exclaimed. 'But why, man? It all works fine, doesn't it? And what about Abingdon... have you sent the proposal back for them to approve?'

The engineers at Universal Digital's head office were meant to be responsible for the system, and in theory they should have been informed of any proposal by site-based people to introduce any changes.

That was the principle. In practice, however, the pressures of commissioning often forced the engineers on site to introduce small changes to overcome some point that the designers had missed. But in these cases there was a cast-iron rule that such changes had to be made known to Abingdon and endorsed by them before being implemented.

There were good reasons for this rigid procedure. If there was any possibility of a system being altered on site without the designers' approval it would be very difficult to find out the cause of any resulting incident. Tracing the cause wasn't a witch-hunt; it was a vital step in the process of ensuring that mistakes were corrected, and that they were never repeated.

'No,' Foster said. 'Abingdon doesn't know about it yet, at least in general—officially. But Andy Johns does... and he's approved it. I'll explain later.'

That was a lie. He had no intention of ever explaining it to Perring. He needed his help now, but the man could do what was needed without being aware of the full reasons for it.

'Christ man!' The words exploded from Perring. 'But there're hundreds of the bastards here. And you want them *all* changed before fuelling starts?'

'Exactly!' Foster nodded. 'That's why we need to work every minute of every day.'

After Foster had explained the plan to distract the Chinese, Perring stared at him in open disbelief. 'You're serious!' he exclaimed. 'You're fucking serious.'

'You bet your sweet life.'

Suddenly Perring felt terrified. Though he couldn't work out the details, he saw a connection with the ferocity that had been responsible for the unbelievable wreckage at Kung Tau. He realized that he was standing beside a nuclear power plant that was just as vulnerable; and as the awareness grew he began to feel the hairs at the back of his neck rising in fear.

He stared at Foster. 'For fuck's sake man,' he said, desperation in his voice. 'If there's something here that could do the same as what happened to Kung Tau...' A pleading tone came into his voice as he asked, 'Christ! You'd tell me, wouldn't you?'

Foster didn't know what to say. He didn't want to frighten Perring to the point that he could make stupid mistakes, but he had to see the true stakes in the enormous gamble they were about to take. He had to let out a little of the truth. He had to win the man's trust and co-operation. 'There is a risk,' he said, and then added a lie, 'but it isn't a significant one. I shouldn't worry about it too much.'

Perring reached forward and gripped his shoulder, and suddenly Foster wondered if he had made a mistake in trusting him with even this little piece of the truth. 'Jesus!' Perring whispered in fear. 'How can you say that? "Don't worry too much?" This is a nuclear plant, for Christ's sake. We should run, Dan. Leave them to it. Put as much distance as possible between us and this almighty fuck-up.'

'No!' Foster barked, praying that he could somehow inject some strength into Perring. 'It really is a tiny risk. But that isn't the point. What matters is this: we *know* how to eliminate the risk entirely. And, we *must* do it.'

Perring stared at him for a while. Then his lip curled in a sneer. 'Oh no!' There was a wild glitter in his eyes as he looked at Foster. 'No,' he continued. 'You may be a bloody hero, man. But *I'm* not about to be one.'

At that, Foster lost his composure. He swept his hand up, grabbed Perring's wrist and twisted it outwards and upwards, slamming it against the wall, enjoying seeing the expression of pain in his face, the look of shock and indignation in his eyes.

'You listen to me, Perring,' he shouted. 'You've no choice. Believe me. I've covered the risk that you may decide to make a run for it. And in case you don't believe me, just you try to get a plane out of here. Try it! The Chinese will be frog-marching you back here so fast you'll meet yourself going out. Trust me!'

It was a bluff, of course. He couldn't have set that trap without the Chinese wondering what was happening. But he was banking on Perring being too scared to test it.

'Then I'll drive out of here!' Perring snarled. 'You can't stop me doing *that*.'

Foster laughed. 'Oh yes? And how far do you think you'll get?'

'What do you mean?' Perring's eyes glittered in desperation. 'In four days I'll have put...' he thought about it and shrugged. 'A thousand miles between me and this death-trap; perhaps more. That's far enough.'

Foster's mind raced, searching frantically for an answer. He decided to play for time. 'Oh yes?' he said. 'And how much gas have you got in your tank?'

'I dunno. Half full, I guess, but I'll get more.'

Foster grinned. He had the answer at last. 'And how'll you pay for it?' he asked jubilantly.

'I dunno! RMB, credit card. Anything.'

Foster laughed. 'And how much cash will you need? For a thousand miles' driving?'

'OK. Amex, then.'

Foster stared at him. 'Just try it!' he challenged.

Perring stared back, and then he shook his head. 'You haven't...'

'Try me,' Foster said quietly. 'Your credit cards are all in the company's name. They've all been stopped. Already.'

It was another lie. But, just in time, he had remembered signing Perring's expenses once, many years ago. He had noticed that all the cards were on Universal Digital's account. Now he was bluffing, banking on Perring believing him and not trying to fill up his car's tank straight away.

For a long moment, Perring stared at him. Then he spat, 'You bastard! You fucking bastard.'

Foster gave a grim smile. 'Say what you like, Perring. But I've stitched you up, well and truly. So, let's get down to work, shall we?'

He saw from Perring's expression that he had won this battle. But he knew that the war was far from over.

Da Shengju was nervous. He had received a call from the Head of Engineering at the Ministry—a call that had deeply disturbed him. For reasons that were impossible to understand, Foster was suspected of trying to sabotage the Galaxy system. It seemed incredible, and even the Ministry was doubtful, but apparently they had been warned, and they were taking the warning seriously. Seriously enough to tell the Project Manager to watch Foster very carefully.

The instructions were clear. No change would be introduced to the Galaxy system. It had been fully approved and accepted by their experts. If Foster tried to change anything he was to be stopped immediately.

The sudden, unexplained arrival of Universal Digital's Managing Director added to the mystery.

But, whatever was happening behind the scenes, Da Shengju found himself suddenly free of Perring's continual humiliating harassment. His shock at the experience didn't hold him for long, however. Within minutes he began to flex his muscles, revelling in his new-found freedom from open criticism.

He reacted to the change with a vengeance, questioning everything the foreigners did or said.

Judith Chang, as a woman, and—moreover a Chinese who wasn't truly Chinese—became his preferred target. 'Why you do that?' he asked now, as she tapped a command into the engineers' console. Although he knew well enough that she spoke and understood Mandarin, he spoke to her in English, to show that he did not really consider her to be truly Chinese.

He was suspicious of her. Was she somehow involved? Was she helping Foster? Or was Foster using her as a decoy to distract them while he tampered with the system?

Chang frowned and pretended to concentrate on the screen in front of her. With Da Shengju devoting more and more time to probing into what she was doing, it was becoming increasingly difficult to conceal the truth.

Three days had passed since they had started modifying the system, and they were still less than half way through. It was worrying, but not altogether unexpected; they had been trail-blazing with the first nodes, and progress had initially been painfully slow.

Now the pace of their work was speeding up, but the need to respond to Da Shengju's continual, interfering requests had delayed them more than she or Foster had anticipated. From the Chinese project manager's point of view, the Westerners were in China to advise on the commissioning of the reactor control systems, and he was both mystified and annoyed by their frequent secretive diversions to areas of the plant that were of no apparent concern at this time. He lost no opportunity to bring them back to what he felt were more important matters, and the remedial work was suffering in consequence.

Now, Da Shengju decided to repeat the question. 'What you do?' he asked.

Chang was forced to answer. 'I'm checking the response time from the feed-pump remote,' she replied. It wasn't really untrue; Alan Turner had just made the alteration to the node, and she needed to check that it was working correctly. Ignoring Da Shengju, she picked up the walkie-talkie and pressed the 'Transmit' button.

'Alan,' she said into the microphone. 'Come in, Alan. It's Little Judith.'

Earlier on, they had agreed to use code words to warn each other if one of the Chinese was listening. Otherwise there would be a risk of an unguarded comment giving the game away. The diminutive 'Little' was attached to her name only when such a warning was needed.

The receiver crackled in response. 'Yes, Little Judith. Big Alan here.'

So somebody was near him as well! They would have to be very careful.

'I'll call for more speed,' she said. 'Are you ready?'
'Yes!'
'OK. I'm doing it ... NOW!'

As she spoke she touched the screen in front of her and a tiny rectangle changed colour from green to yellow, indicating that the system was responding to her command.

'It's moving!' Turner's voice confirmed that the lever he was watching, far away in the basement, had begun to move. The response had been virtually instantaneous, so all was well.

'Is good?' Da Shengju asked from beside her, almost spitting with his sibilant accentuation. He was leaning forward to squint at the screen, but she was sure he didn't know what to expect from it.

'Yes, fine!'
'Come in, Little Judith!' Turner called.
'Yes, Alan.'
'I'm going over to the gas circulators now. I'm going to give George a hand there.'
'OK. Tell me when you're ready.'

She rubbed at the tip of her nose and thought for a moment. She had had enough of Da Shengju. It was time to send him away.

Deliberately and languidly, she leant back in her chair and clasped her hands behind her head. She knew the movement would unsettle Da Shengju; he would stare at her raised breasts for a moment and then quickly scuttle away. He always did.

She smiled as he reacted on cue. *I wonder what's with the little guy,* she thought. *Doesn't he get enough from his wife?*

She marvelled at her own impudence. In spite of many decades of living in Britain, her parents were still very Chinese. They would have been shocked at her behaviour. But Da Shengju was right; she was not really Chinese; she even thought like a foreign devil.

Just then, Foster came into the control room, accompanied by a tight-lipped Andy Johns. They had been modifying some of the other nodes. It was the time of cross-over between shifts, when all five were briefly working at the same time.

To everybody's surprise, Andy Johns had proved to be an able helper. From the moment he had arrived on the site he had shown little sign of resentment, and he had quickly and quietly settled into the unfamiliar role of being a mere assistant. He was resigned to it; there had been no option.

Foster had taken no pleasure in the situation. The job needed to be done and Johns was there to help. Very quickly, the two men had developed an efficient routine. Now, having checked that the latest nodes were working correctly, they had returned to the control room.

'All OK?' Foster asked.

'Yes,' Chang replied. 'I had Da Shengju here, but I sent him off.' She smiled at her private joke.

But Foster was oblivious to the nuances. 'What's George doing?' he asked.

She explained that Perring was at the circulators and Turner was on his way to help him.

The circulators were giant enclosed fans that would push gas through the reactor, to cool it and transport the heat to the steam driving the turbines.

Foster looked around to make sure that the other people in the room were far enough away before whispering, 'Has anything odd happened yet? The system's gone live now and we haven't fixed all the nodes. So for a time there's a risk of the problem coming up again.'

'I know,' she replied quietly. 'But, so far at least, everything's been OK.'

Turner arrived as Perring looked up at the hydraulic actuator that controlled the circulator. The actuator was a steel cylinder containing a ram that would move in or out as oil was pumped to one side or the other of it. As the ram moved, it re-positioned the massive stainless-steel vanes controlling the gas flowing through the fan.

When the reactor was fuelled it would be necessary to wear ear defenders here; the roar of the nearby fans would be intolerable otherwise. But at present everything was still and quiet.

Deathly quiet.

Perring pointed at the shining steel rod extending from the cylinder high above him. 'I'll get to that one next,' he said.

'Want a hand?' Turner asked.

'I'll manage,' Perring growled.

Cursing at the need to exert himself, he unlocked the barrier protecting the vertical ladder against unauthorized access and began to climb to a small platform beside the ram. On his instruction, the Chinese engineer who had been assigned to help him stayed behind, watching.

When Perring reached the ram, he took the radio out of his overall pocket and called up the control room.

His receiver hissed briefly and then Chang's voice broke through the static. 'Yes, George?' Her response indicated that the coast was clear. 'Over!'

'I'm at the circulators,' Perring said. He looked down to ensure that the Chinese engineer was out of ear-shot. 'I'm going to switch over the chips now,' he said quietly into the radio. 'But this one will be tough; the node's on the other side of the ram. Over!'

'OK.' She understood. They had looked at this one earlier and realized it would be difficult. The box of electronics had been positioned by somebody who had given little thought to the need for maintenance. To reach it, it would be necessary to climb onto the cylinder and sit astride it while reaching up to the box. 'I'm ready,' she said. 'The ram's isolated.' This meant that no commands could be transmitted to the ram, so that it would not move.

'Over!' she concluded.

Perring took a deep breath and cursed again. He could do without this.

He scrambled up until he was on top of the cylinder. Then he steadied himself as he reached into his overall pocket for a screwdriver.

Then, as the first screw came loose, he heard an unexpected click and whirr, and for a brief moment he felt he could detect a tiny motion under him, as though something within the the ram had come alive... But then it stopped. He stiffened and looked down, but the ram was static. Puzzled, he put down the screwdriver and brought out the radio.

'Come in Judith,' he said.

'Yes George?' The voice from the radio echoed in the silent void. 'Over!'

'Did you do something just then?' Perring said, looking around him to see if he could see anything else that could have caused the sound and the movement. 'Over!'

There was a moment's delay and then the radio hissed briefly and came to life. 'Not on the circulators,' she said. 'They're out on Permit. I've isolated them. Over!'

The strict safety rules always employed on large power stations dictated that before anybody was allowed to work on a piece of the plant they had to be granted a 'Permit to Work'. This was issued by the engineer in charge at the time, and only when he had satisfied himself that there was no likelihood of injury or damage being caused. Usually, this involved locking the relevant control switches to a safe position.

Before replying, Chang had double-checked that the circulators were indeed locked to a safe condition because, even though the fans themselves were not running, any inadvertent command sent to the powerful hydraulic cylinder could cause it to move and perhaps injure Perring. But her check had shown that the system was safe.

'OK,' Perring said and reached out to undo the second screw from the cover of the terminal box.

Christ! he thought grimly. *I hope she's right. I wouldn't want this thing to move while I'm astride it. The old wedding tackle's in just the wrong place. It'd be Curtains, George!*

'Alan?' Chang's voice broke from Turner's radio. 'George called me just now... he thought something moved. Can you give him a hand? Over.'

Turner froze. He felt his heartbeat pick up in sudden fear.

'Sure, Judith,' he said, and began to climb to join Perring.

At his arrival, Perring frowned.

'I've come to help,' Turner explained. 'Judith said you reported a problem.'

'I'm not sure,' Perring said. 'But thanks anyway.'

Back in the control room, Chang gave a worried look at Foster and whispered a question to him. 'Could it be the 'Ghost'?' she asked. 'I'd just sent a command to the feed pumps, and George said he heard something happen at the circulator that he's working on. Could the addressing have gone wrong? The Permit works through the second Galaxy system. They're the two systems we haven't yet modified.'

Foster stared at her. 'Christ!' he said, 'Then it *is* possible. Be careful—very careful.'

But it was already too late.

The 'Ghost' had indeed returned.

It entered the 'brain' controlling the actuator and changed it. The circulator now reacted to a different set of commands pouring through the plant-wide information highway—commands intended for another part of the plant. In its turn an actuator there also adopted a new *persona*—it stopped working and froze. Convinced that it was the one on which Perring was working, it locked itself out of service.

Under Perring's legs the quiet click and whirr recurred. At first it happened too quickly for Perring to comprehend as he saw the shining rod begin to slide out of the cylinder under him. He watched in disbelief, but then his look turned to one of horror as he realized what was happening.

Turner saw it too. But, unlike Perring, he knew what was happening. He scrambled onto the ram and roughly pushed the Resident Engineer aside. But in doing so, he placed himself in danger.

Perring tumbled onto a nearby strut and fought for a handhold. 'For Christ's sake, Turner!' he yelled. 'What are you doing?'

But, before Turner could answer, the actuator started to swivel. Slowly, inexorably, its ram extruded itself from the cylinder. Perring started to scramble back off his perch to push Turner clear of the scissor action... but it was too late.

With irresistible force the glistening metal caught Turner and trapped him, mercilessly crushing him against the steel ducting.

He fought for breath as the enormous pressure built up. He thrust frantically and uselessly at the unyielding metal. His fingers slipped on the smooth surface as he made a desperate attempt to gain some purchase; to let him push himself away. Finally, a bubbling scream of agony burst from his bloodied mouth.

The Chinese engineer at the ground level started to scramble up the ladder, but there was nothing he could do. He stopped and stared in horror as with a sound of splintering bones Turner's chest cavity collapsed under the inhuman pressure.

Perring tried to move out of the way, but he was too late. He shuddered in horror and disgust as a stream of hot blood cascaded into his face.

Chapter 15

Anger erupted from Da Shengju. 'It is im-possible,' he spluttered angrily, dividing the last word and barking out the final syllable with a visible spray of spittle. 'Not one of our engineer gave command. None!'

'How can you say that?' Foster shouted. 'The bloody thing *moved*. It killed a man, for Christ's sake. *Somebody* must have initiated the action.'

Since Turner's death, Foster's manner had changed. Before, he had been coolly bent on a mission to deal with an engineering problem. Admittedly it was as serious a problem as he could have ever imagined but, until that terrible moment, his motives had been coldly professional. Now he raged at it all.

Alan Turner had been a good friend; a man he had known and admired for many years. More than that, Foster had taken him from a cusp in his life, when he was changing direction from constant work and travel to a more relaxed time; a time to settle down and share with his new-found, late love. In doing so he had projected him into danger. Turner had not hesitated to help. And when he saw Perring's predicament he didn't hold back.

And that selfless heroism had cost him his life.

Yes, Foster thought bitterly, now this was personal: *very* personal.

He looked over to where Andy Johns sat in a chair, his face ashen. The accident had finally broken Johns' defences. He was as shaken as anybody by Turner's death, but for him the horror had been increased by the sudden, inescapable realization that the Galaxy system really was flawed. It wasn't just the existence of the fault that concerned him, it was the knowledge that in it lay the seeds of his inevitable personal destruction and vilification.

After the accident, he had slumped immobile in a chair that somebody had brought when they had seen him begin to sway. There he had stayed and they had virtually been forced to prize him out of it at the end of the working day, and on the next morning he had returned to it as though it was a safe haven, he held to it as a small child clings to a security blanket.

He had played no part in the impromptu investigation that had been carried out following the incident.

In deference to Turner's death the commissioning programme had been delayed for a day, but now—with fuelling of the reactor only a day off—they needed to have some idea of what had gone wrong. A full, formal enquiry would be held in due course, but immediate answers were needed. Now. Before somebody else could be injured, or perhaps killed.

Getting the answers was proving to be more difficult than it should have been. Soon after starting to probe into the event, they had discovered that, in line with the one totally infallible rule of engineering— Murphy's Law or Sod's Law—the plant's data-logger had been switched off at the time of the accident. If it had been operating, the logger would have pinpointed exactly the instant when the command had been given, and the console from which it had come.

To Foster, its absence was a godsend. He was sure it wasn't human error that had caused the fatal accident; he knew that it was the lethal addressing fault that had killed Turner. The thought was unpleasant, because it raised the point that he had known that something like this could happen.

This was an unforgiving world. Turner had known that any of the actuators could move without warning, and when he realized that Perring was at risk he had bravely tried to save the RE. In doing so he had put himself in a position where the unwanted movement had killed him. That had been his decision, his choice.

But that didn't stop Foster from feeling that he was, at least in part, responsible for the tragedy.

At last, ruthlessly, he put that feeling of guilt behind him. But he swore that, when this was all over, he would visit Turner's wife and tell her of her husband's heroism.

For the moment, the fact was that the data-logger's evidence would have been damning. Now, without any possibility of having evidence to the contrary flung in his face, he had a chance of retrieving something from the catastrophe.

If only the Chinese would let him alone. For some unaccountable reason they had been watching his actions very closely for the past few days, and he had been forced to deploy Chang to deflect their attention at every opportunity.

Desperate to avert them from any possibility of discovering the truth, Foster had resorted to bluff and bluster. Like now claiming loudly that the only reason why the actuator could have moved was because one of the operators had inadvertently commanded it to move.

Da Shengju had denied the possibility. 'Perhaps somebody else make mistake. Maybe one of you,' he added desperately. 'You! And Chang! You were both at console.'

'We were working on the *pump* systems,' Foster interrupted. That much, at least, was true. 'But your own guys were at the other consoles,' he continued. 'Any one of them could have done it.'

'They say no. They not touch circulator controls.'

'Perhaps they didn't realize.'

'They trained operators.' Da Shengju bristled in defence of his staff.

Foster shook his head apologetically. Perhaps it was time to extend a friendly hand. 'I didn't mean to imply anything,' he said quietly. 'Anyone could have done it. Without noticing. After all, the plant wasn't running, so it shouldn't have mattered.'

'The Permit system...'

'I *know* about the Permit system,' Foster insisted firmly. 'But that's for an operating plant.'

This part wasn't at all true. The Permit-to-Work system was designed to prevent just this sort of incident, which could happen at any time; and on this occasion it *had* happened. But he was hoping he could hold off any further questions. He needed every second that he could gain. The bluff was worth trying.

Even as they argued, Judith Chang and George Perring were working in a remote part of the plant, frantically changing chips. Badly shaken by Turner's death, they had at first been reluctant to carry on. For Chang's part, it wasn't fear that held her back, but her latent honesty that had come to the surface, and it had taken all Foster's skill and diplomacy to persuade her to return to the job in hand.

Because, tragic as the accident may have been, a bigger tragedy needed to be averted.

In the end he convinced her, and once she had started she threw herself into the work with furious enthusiasm.

Cots had been installed in a small annexe nearby, to enable people working long hours to take a break, but she had laboured well into the night before collapsing into one of these in a sleep of utter exhaustion.

But before falling asleep she had found Foster and told him the news; by their valiant efforts they had brought the programme well up to schedule. They had only thirty nodes left to tackle in the twenty-four hours that remained before fuelling started.

Now, as he confronted Da Shengju, Foster thought about her achievement. If only he could disentangle himself from the man and return to work, he would be able to start helping with those thirty remaining nodes.

'Look,' he said. 'This isn't getting us anywhere. We've got no record from the datalogger... so what happened is anybody's guess. Let's get on with it, shall we? Otherwise we'll have to put a hold on the programme.'

He saw the shudder go through Da Shengju's body. A delay? That was unthinkable! It would bring his masters down on him like a pack of jackals.

'All right Dr Foster, we proceed.'

The admission was grudging, but it represented victory for Foster, and he had difficulty in preventing his face from breaking into a huge grin of relief.

Da Shengju turned on his heel and walked stiffly away, and Foster almost ran out of the room in his haste to start work.

Foster closed his eyes in horror. 'You WHAT?' he shouted at Johns, unwilling to believe what he had just heard. He wondered if Johns' actions had been taken from spite, or out of sheer stupidity.

Johns stared sullenly at the floor. 'I told them you were meddling. Sabotaging the system,' he repeated quietly. He looked up, pleading in his eyes. 'I'm sorry,' he said. 'I... I didn't believe you. I thought... I *really* thought that you were out for revenge.'

'Revenge?'

'Yes. For what happened. For the past. I don't know. What you said sounded so absurd, man. I just couldn't bring myself to believe it. But then... what happened to Turner. It convinced me.'

Foster stared at him. 'Christ, man,' he said bleakly. 'What've you done?'

'They didn't want to believe me when I said it. Couldn't believe somebody with your reputation would do anything like that. So, if I say it was a mistake they'll accept it. They're half prepared for it anyway.'

Foster thought about it. *No wonder they had been overseeing him so carefully!* They had been tipped off. They were watching him. To see if he was sabotaging the system. It was lucky that they hadn't simply elected to blame him for the incident that had killed Turner, and expelled him from the site. It would have been so simple.

He wondered what had saved him. Was it his reputation or was it because they couldn't find any proof? Nobody had spotted his team changing the components and they had no evidence that the instruction-set of the nodes had been modified.

But if Johns admitted his mistake now he would also have to admit the truth, and there was no telling what they would do then.

If they were to find out that the instruction-set had been changed it was almost certain that they would insist on the original version being restored. After all, the original concept had been carefully vetted and accepted by the Chinese experts, and for them to sanction any change now would be an admission that they had been wrong.

To the Chinese, the resulting loss of face would be unthinkable.

Foster realized that there could be only one outcome to such a disastrous scenario: restoration of the original devices and, in consequence, the inevitable resumption of the danger. The system would be re-commissioned with its original fault.

This time, though, he had all the proof he needed. He *knew* what the result would be. This time there could not be a shadow of doubt. Far Point would be destroyed.

'No, Andy,' he said, finally. 'Don't tell them. It would only delay things.'

He saw the look of relief on Johns' face and realized how painful it would have been for him to admit that he had made a mistake.

'All right, Dan,' Johns said. 'But what now?'

'We carry on. It won't be easy. They were watching me very closely before. Now, I guess they'll be virtually sitting on my shoulder for every step I take. And if they catch me—or any of us—changing the PROMs... that'll be the end of it. We'll have to revert to the original ones. And nothing we could say or do will change their minds.

'Not unless we come clean and admit that a seriously flawed design had been sold to them.'

Johns looked horrified at that prospect. It would certainly bring the authorities down on his head and destroy Universal's reputation forever. It would almost certainly end up with him facing a Chinese court and then decades working in a forced-labour camp. He thought about it and nodded slowly as he let out a deep breath.

'I'm so sorry, Dan,' he repeated. 'So bloody sorry.' And there was genuine contrition in his voice.

Foster shrugged. 'Nothing we can do,' he said, more calmly than he felt. 'I'll just need your help in distracting them.'

'Judith?' She felt her shoulder being shaken gently. 'Judith. Wake up!'

She rolled over and forced her red-rimmed eyes open to stare at Foster. Her mouth felt dry and stale.

'I was dreaming,' she said sleepily. 'I was on a beach, lying under a straw umbrella.' The words came slowly. 'It was warm. I could hear the surf breaking. I smelt the ozone.' She sighed. 'It felt good.'

Foster grinned at her. 'I let you sleep on,' he said.

She snapped wide awake. 'No! You shouldn't have.'

'It's OK Judith. We've cracked it.'

She stared at him for a moment, uncomprehendingly. 'You don't mean ...?'

'No, I haven't finished the whole job,' he laughed. 'Not quite. I've left some for you. But... there're only ten PROMs left to switch.'

'You've converted twenty nodes?' Her tone was incredulous.

He nodded.

'How on earth?' she asked. Her drowsy brain fumbled at the arithmetic and suddenly she was wide awake. 'Oh no!' she said. 'How long have I been asleep?'

'Don't worry,' he said, holding her arm to restrain her as she struggled to sit up. 'Only four hours. We found that the work got easier as we got on with it. We had it down to five minutes per node at the end.'

She stared at him in disbelief. 'That's not possible! It takes longer than that just to walk from one to the other.'

'Yes. But if you take five of them out at a time... if you take them down to the work-bench ...'

'Five?'

'Yes. Remember? They shut the system down after the accident.'

Her eyes widened even further.

Then, quite suddenly, she realized that Alan Turner's sacrifice had unwittingly bought them an opportunity ... though it was one he had paid for with his life.

Da Shengju crept slowly and carefully along the corridor. He braced himself against the wall, almost as if to save himself from falling. He could not yet see Foster and Chang, but he knew they were just around the next corner. He could make out their whispers, though he couldn't quite decipher what they were saying.

Just a few more paces; then he'd have them.

Judith's hands shook as she lifted the chip. She looked at Foster, holding the device above the electronics enclosure that would be its home.

'Amen?' she said quietly.

'Amen,' he agreed. It was the last one.

She bent forward, and gently started to offer the device up to its socket. To Foster the action seemed to take minutes. It was as though he was watching her in slow-motion. At last she had it positioned correctly.

Gently and firmly she pressed it home. Then she straightened her back and gave a sigh.

Foster let out his own breath and looked at his watch. 'We're twenty minutes early,' he said with a grin of relief. 'The fuelling starts at ten.'

'Time for me to shower and change into something pretty for the party!'

He held out his hand. 'Congratulations!' he said.

She took his hand and gave it a small shake. 'Thank you, Dan Foster. And thanks for everything.'

'I only helped,' he said. 'You found how to do it.'

They were still holding hands as Da Shengju suddenly appeared around the corner, a light of triumph in his eyes.

He'd caught them!

'What you do?' he barked.

Foster spun round. 'What?' he asked. The PROM they had just removed from the node was burning a hole in his left hand.

'What you do?' Da Shengju repeated. 'Why you work here? It not on programme.'

'Neither's going to the toilet,' Foster said sarcastically. 'But we all do it.'

A puzzled look crossed Da Shengju's face. His literal mind wondered what toilets had got to do with it.

'The programme doesn't show up all the checks we have to do,' Chang explained. 'Everybody knows that.'

'Of course, of course!' Da Shengju nodded wildly, anxious to make it seem that he was not unaware of the basic operational procedures. 'But why you work here? What you check here? Why now?'

As the Chinaman turned his attention to Chang, Foster seized his opportunity. Praying that his action would not be noticed, he slowly and carefully began to slide his left hand upwards, towards the pocket of his overalls.

Judith Chang saw the slow movement out of the corner of her eye and tensed. She mustn't inadvertently betray him now. She stared at Da Shengju, almost hypnotizing him into looking back into her eyes. *Don't turn away*, she willed at him. *Don't you dare turn away.*

Da Shengju's eyes bored into hers. It was a challenge he was determined to accept; staring her out. He was oblivious to anything else.

Foster's fingers found the pocket. Slowly and casually, they slipped into it. Repeating his fervent prayer, he released his grasp and felt the PROM fall silently into the material. Only when it was done did he allow himself to breathe again.

'We have to check each node before we start the system,' Chang said, hurriedly. She had seen Foster's action and now she too let out a pent-up breath. 'Make sure the covers are on. No loose wires. That sort of thing. We've been doing it all along. You didn't need to be bothered with such small details.'

Da Shengju's eyes glittered. It was an admission of his exalted status. They were right: such trivialities *were* below him, after all. 'No,' he agreed. 'Is right.'

'Anyway,' Foster said. 'It was the last one to be checked. That's why we were shaking hands.'

'I see.'

'We're about to go back to the control room now,' Foster continued. 'You coming?'

'I go now. I see you later.'

He turned on his heel and walked away.

Chang smiled at Foster. There was clear relief on both their faces.

'Jesus!' Foster said quietly.

'That was close.'

'Too damn close.'

They started to walk down the corridor to the lift that would take them back to the control room.

'You know, Dan,' Chang said quietly. 'We all owe you. We owe you a lot.'

'It's all a team effort Judith,' Foster said. 'Like everything on these plants,' he gestured to indicate the massive structure around them, the huge machines it contained. 'It needs a team to design it, another one to build it. And a team to track down a problem when it happens.'

'I suppose so.' Then she added sadly, 'Yes. And our team… we lost one of them.'

Turner had been a stranger to her, really.

An unwelcome thought came to her. *It should have been Perring* Somebody cold and disdainful. She remembered how he had despised her Chinese ancestry, and that he doubted her ability. But… She shook her mind free of the thought.

Turner had been nice; a good and trustworthy colleague.

'Yes,' Foster agreed. It was a short acknowledgement of Turner's loss. He had died trying to help a man that neither he nor Foster had trusted.

And there was still the nagging thought in Foster's mind that he could have prevented his colleague's death…

They walked the rest of the way in silence.

When they reached the control room, Da Shengju was waiting impatiently. He glared at them as they came in. 'What you do now?' he asked, again suspicious.

'We're ready to start,' Foster replied innocently. 'Is everybody else ready?'

'Of course! Of course!'

'OK,' Foster said. 'Then let's go for it.'

Da Shengju signalled to one of his operators and, in response, the man reached forward to touch the screen in front of him. A chime rang from hidden loudspeakers, followed by an urgent phrase in Mandarin...

And the long slow job started.

The first few steps were to prepare for fuelling. Foster watched the screens like a hawk as the process unrolled, his eyes darting from one to another to look at each aspect of the work, stopping to examine a line of text here, a trend there, ready to pick up the slightest hint of a malfunction. Something about his interest heightened the natural tension in the room, and the atmosphere became electric.

Judith Chang felt it keenly. Of all the people in the room only she, Foster and Johns knew what was really at stake. *What if we're wrong?* she asked herself. *What if we haven't really fixed it after all?*

Her mind refused to contemplate the possibility. It was too terrifying.

After a while, Da Shengju's voice broke into her thoughts. 'We put system on auto now,' he said. Control of the plant was about to be transferred to 'automatic'; finally taken away from human control and entrusted to the Galaxy system.

From that instant, their safety would become totally dependent on the control system.

Chang glanced at Foster and saw him looking back at her, his face expressionless. Then he turned his gaze to Da Shengju and nodded. 'OK,' he said.

Da Shengju turned to the console and lifted his hand to touch the screen...

But he never made it. His action was stopped by a shout.

'No!' The interruption came from Andy Johns, and all eyes turned to him. His face was grey, his expression strained. His eyes shifted from one of them to the other. 'No!' he repeated 'We should wait.'

Foster looked at Johns and was appalled by what he saw. The brash bravado of the man had completely disintegrated. His red-rimmed eyes seemed sunken and dark against the pallor of his skin. He was standing now, gripping a corner of one of the control consoles for support. His hands were visibly trembling.

Jesus! Foster thought. *The guy's cracking. And if we're not careful he'll pull us all down with him. He'll blow the story—and if he does, all our efforts will have been wasted.*

Da Shengju looked at Foster for advice.

'It's all right,' Foster said. 'Go ahead.'

'But Mr Johns say...' the Chinese man said, looking from Johns to Foster and back again.

After his outburst, Johns had relapsed into silence. He had once again slumped in his chair, his hands on his knees. He stared, wide-eyed, at his hands as though for the first time noticing their trembling.

'It's not important,' Foster said. His mind scrambled for an idea to explain away Johns' outburst. *We can't lose. Not now. Not after everything we've been through.* He glared at Universal's MD.

Then an inspired thought came to him. 'Mr Johns was just... he was referring to a superstition,' he said suddenly.

'Super... stition?' Da Shengju asked. His knowledge of English was excellent. But this was a reference to something his lords and masters denied.

Foster saw him hesitating. 'Well, more of a tradition really,' he volunteered calmly. 'An old custom in the Company.' Foster stared at Johns, willing him into silence. 'Before we go onto automatic we have to ... Er...' He thought desperately and then the inspiration was complete.

'Ah yes!' he cried. 'I nearly forgot! We have to shake hands with each other. Yes! That's it! Shake hands!'

He grasped Da Shengju's hand and pumped at it, and smiled as he saw Judith Chang catch the idea and start shaking the hand of one of the Chinese engineers.

'It brings good luck!' he said to the bemused Da Shengju.

The project manager's face slowly broke into a smile. A tradition! Like having a *Feng Shui* man check over your house before you moved in. Not superstition. No rational, high-ranking comrade of the New Republic held any superstitions, of course!

Before long, everybody was smiling and joining in the suddenly-invented ritual.

Foster went over to Johns and grasped his hand tightly, glaring a silent threat at him. He applied intense pressure to reinforce the message: *Just you dare! I'll kill you if you say anything.*

Da Shengju was still grinning at the Westerners' old-fashioned rituals as he looked at Foster once again. 'We start now?' he asked.

Foster nodded.

Da Shengju touched the screen and a group of small squares changed colour from green to red.

This is it! Foster looked across the room at Judith Chang. He saw that she too was holding her breath, and as he watched he saw her make an effort to release it.

Easy on, lass! He willed the thought across the room. *Don't panic. We're committed. Even if we started running now we'd never make it.* She looked up and met his eyes, and his smile strengthened her. She straightened her back, hunched too long over the glowing screens, and smiled back. It was a bleak smile.

At Da Shengju's command, gigantic machines swung into action far below them. Unseen and unheard from the control room, they lifted the containers holding the nuclear fuel and started to swing them from their storage positions to the fuelling machine. Foster clenched his teeth and stared at the screen in front of him. A bitter thought had occurred to him: if something were to go wrong now, after all their efforts... if the unthinkable happened... he had no idea how he would even begin to stop it. It only needed one tiny slip. And now no human being would be able to act quickly enough to counteract the consequences.

The tension in the room was palpable as, one after another, the complex sequences unfolded. The symbols on the screens changed colour. They tracked the complex steps being made by the machines outside, everything moving in an intricate dance, choreographed long ago by the plant's designers.

The people in the control room watched as the computer began to execute the long chain of actions programmed into it long ago by the engineers. The Westerners were praying that all would be well. The Chinese, unaware of what had so nearly happened, had picked up some of the tension through a sort of telepathic osmosis.

The process ran for almost two hours until, eventually, a quiet chime announced that it was complete.

Foster let out a sigh of relief, looked at Judith Chang and smiled. *It's all right,* he signalled with his eyes.

She came across to him. 'That's it,' she whispered. 'For now, at least.'

'No!' he said quietly, sharply. 'For ever. It's all right, Judith. It's working all right,' he stressed. 'It's all OK. If we hadn't fixed it, the system would have already gone wrong. And I don't somehow think the Almighty would have replicated all this in Paradise. We're still in China.'

She looked at him, and slowly her expression began to change from grim resolution to outright relief. Then her face broke into a smile. At last she believed it. The threat had finally gone away. She was finally free of the enormous burden she had carried since she had proposed the solution; finally, she knew that it had indeed worked.

And now, at long last, Foster had time to turn his attention to Johns.

There was unfinished business to deal with. Now that they had solved the puzzle, he had to deal with Johns and make sure that his kind would never again be able to unleash on humanity a terror such as they had just averted.

Johns was a powerful man, and the systems his company made were vital to the safety of complex processes right across the world. His actions had destroyed Kung Tau. Then they had threatened Far Point, and in the process killed kindly old Alan Turner. Where would the danger arise tomorrow? What would be the risk then?

As he looked at the broken and quivering man lolling in his chair Foster realized that, for him, it was already all over. It wouldn't take much to finally close him out of the scene, but it was still important to make sure that no one else would ever be able to create the risks they had faced—and that nobody else would die as a result. He had to make sure that no dangerously flawed design could be pushed through into a critical role by the unbridled ambitions of people who didn't understand what they were doing, and whose sole objective was short-term financial gain.

And he was determined to avenge Alan Turner's death. The white heat of anger he had felt after his initial grief at his friend's death had moderated, but it was still burning.

He knew what he had to do. He would tell Alison. It would be his gift to her, the biggest scoop of her life. She would be certain to make the most of it. Now that the risk was over, the whole truth could come out. The Chinese would be furious, and sensitivities would be hurt, but the tangled mess would at last be exposed to public scrutiny.

Yes, it would be a sensational headline in the *South China Morning Post*.

Chapter 16

As the Clerk to the Inspector called out his name, Foster's memories blew away like so many fallen leaves being scattered by a sudden gust of autumn wind. He scooped up his precious notebook from the shelf on the back of the seat in front of his. Then he stood up and worked his way along to the raised platform adjacent to the Inspector and facing the body of the room.

Meanwhile, Sir Peter Mallett, the Inspector, looked steadily down at the papers in front of him. There was a long, tense silence in the room, and Foster felt uneasy. He wished he were ten thousand miles away from this place. It was *not* his scene.

The breaking of the news in the *South China Morning Post* some six months earlier had triggered an avalanche of media interest. Within a few hours TV stations in China, England and the USA were featuring harried-looking government officials caught on the hop, desperately trying to extricate their masters from the mess. But it was too late; under intense diplomatic and political pressure, an embarrassed British Government had been forced to call a Public Inquiry into the débacle.

The first of many inquiries to come, this was intended to be a somewhat informal affair, with the Inspector asking questions of the various parties directly. The responses would be recorded and fed forward to the next stage, which would be a full-scale hearing. The original idea had been that lawyers would not be involved at this time, but Universal, GAI and the other big players had insisted on having professional representation.

After Foster had taken his place on the stand, the Inspector asked him to tell the Inquiry his name and qualifications, and to explain the nature of his work, his involvement with the Kung Tau investigation and his conclusions.

This Foster did, with the help of occasional references to his notes, concluding with his conviction that the Galaxy system had been the cause of the explosion at Kung Tau. He explained how it was only after he had reported his findings that he had discovered that it was the UK Government that had requested his involvement.

'And what happened next?' Sir Peter asked.

'At that point I was informed that the same design of equipment had been supplied to a nuclear power plant in China; at a plant called Far Point.'

'And it was this that was reported in the Press?'

'When it was all over. Yes.'

'I see.'

For a moment Sir Peter gazed thoughtfully at Foster.

'In the light of your knowledge that there was a dangerous fault in the system, you must have been very concerned that the same type of incident may have been imminent at the second plant.'

'Yes. Very definitely.'

'And if the fault arose, it could have caused a nuclear explosion?'

Foster hesitated, thinking about it.

'No,' he said. 'I don't think so. It depended on the exact form of the fault, of course. But, to be absolutely clear, a full *nuclear* explosion would have been very unlikely. More possibly, the plant would have been damaged, perhaps severely.

'But the point at issue is that you just *don't* take risks like that with a nuclear plant; it's likely to become very expensive, and it could lead to real trouble.'

'Such as?'

Foster shrugged. 'Difficult to say,' he said. 'But the fact is that if something untoward happens suddenly and the human operators are startled—caught off guard—then they can be panicked into doing the wrong things.'

'So you were concerned?'

'Yes. After all, it was something very similar that happened in the States, at Three Mile Island. The operators there were misled by the readings of their instruments, and by the huge number of alarm signals that flooded in after a single incident—the system raised over a hundred alarms in the first two minutes. The operators couldn't handle it. They panicked... and then made some bad decisions.'

'And this could have happened at Far Point?'

'Yes, I feared so. Or something like it.'

'I see. So what did you do then?'

'Well, at that point I was asked to go to Far Point.'

'Was that not very odd?' the Inspector asked. 'Surely, once you had identified the nature of the fault to the Government–the fault that had caused the explosion at Kung Tau–the simplest thing would have been for them to tell the Chinese about it, and about the risk to Far Point, and to force the Company to advise them of the remedy?'

'Of course.' Foster looked across the room at Jeffreys. The Minister was staring straight ahead, avoiding eye contact with him His face was impassive. 'I suggested that. But...' He took a deep breath before concluding, 'The people involved said it wasn't possible.'

'Why was that?'

Foster had thought about it carefully. He had little option but to tell the truth. But he knew that what he was about to say would be a devastating blow to Global Associated Industries. 'I was told that the company wouldn't agree to it,' he said finally.

The Inspector's eyebrows rose. 'Why not?' he asked.

Foster took a deep breath. 'Because an agreement would have been an implicit admission that their system was to blame for the explosion at Kung Tau,' he said. 'And for the deaths that occurred there.'

Against a sudden outbreak of sibilant whispering, he saw the huddle of legal men at the table put their heads together and whisper unhappily. One of them, evidently the more senior, shook his head slowly at the others.

'But surely your study had reached that conclusion anyway?' the Inspector asked. 'You had already convinced yourself that the electronic control system *was* the cause.'

'Yes. *I* felt I'd established that without reasonable doubt. But my full findings hadn't been presented to the company at that time.'

'And in the meantime they were arguing?'

'Yes.'

'But would it not have been better to enter that debate? To give the company the opportunity to present its own case.'

'There wasn't any time for debate. Far Point was at an advanced stage of commissioning. It was getting very near the time when the fault—*when* it occurred—would have been likely to cause an accident.'

Sir Peter nodded slowly and again looked down at the papers in front of him before continuing. 'So, Universal Digital Systems put up a strong defence, arguing that their system was not at fault...'

'Not Universal,' Foster said.

Sir Peter looked at him, frowning. '*Not* them?' he asked. 'I thought you said they had designed and supplied the system.'

'That's right. But they weren't the ones who were arguing. They weren't in a strong negotiating position and though they're a fairly big company, they're not big enough to exert enough influence on the government.'

'Then who was in a position to do so?'

'The parent company, Global Associated Industries.'

At this, the leader of the group in front of him jumped to his feet.

'Objection!' he interjected. Then he stalled, bowed his head to the Inspector and added, 'I'm sorry, Sir. I'm Keith Maddison. Representing Global Associated Industries.'

'Thank you, Mr Maddison,' Sir Peter said. 'But I will remind you that this is not a Court of Law. You will have an opportunity to present your own arguments in due course.'

'I apologize, Sir. But I feel it should be made clear that the witness is in no position to judge whether that company had applied pressure of any sort on the Government.'

The Inspector consulted his notes. 'I believe Dr Foster merely said they were in a *position* to apply pressure,' he said. 'Not that they had actually done so.'

'There was an inference ...'

'I believe the inference was yours, Mr Maddison,' the Inspector interrupted, coldly. 'As I have said, this is not a law court, but I will deal with the matter by saying that your objection is overruled. But I would ask that you kindly do not interrupt again.'

Maddison bowed his head again and sat down. He was looking very unhappy.

'Please continue, Dr Foster,' said Sir Peter.

'As I was saying, G.A.I. were in the position to apply pressure. I don't know whether they actually did or didn't. But I *do* know—because the gentleman involved told me at the time—that any change to the Far Point system would be tantamount to admitting that the Galaxy system had been responsible for the earlier Kung Tau incident. It was a legal impasse...'

'You said 'the gentleman involved' ...'

'Yes.' Foster looked across at Jeffreys, who was continuing to stare impassively straight ahead. 'The gentleman was Roger Jeffreys, Secretary of State for Trade and Industry.'

The whispering became a hubbub of quiet voices. Foster could see the reporters busily writing in their notebooks.

'This was the member of the Government, the one to whom you had presented your findings?'

'That's right. I was called to meet him in London. I gave him my verbal report there. He'd already seen the preliminary summary.'

The Inspector leaned forward. 'Dr Foster,' he asked. 'Would you please be very clear about what the Secretary of State did at that time?'

'I remember it very clearly,' Foster replied, and then proceeded to outline his discussion with Jeffreys in Arnold Coward's offices.

'You're saying that you were asked to introduce a change to the vital control systems of a nuclear reactor?' the Inspector exclaimed. '*And to do so without telling the owners about it?*' There was an incredulous edge to his voice.

'Correct!'

The Inspector stared at him. 'But was that not very dangerous?' he asked. 'It seems to me that this could not be considered a safe operation to undertake.'

Foster looked down as he thought about the effects of his next words.

Then he replied, 'At that stage I had no idea of exactly *what* I was going to do. The solution hadn't been found. I was instructed to devise a fix on site ...'

'A *fix*?'

'Yes,' Foster allowed himself a slight smile. 'A solution. And then to install it.'

'Was that normal?'

'No! Not at all. In normal circumstances, such a change would have had to go through a process of careful vetting, approval by all parties, and testing before it was applied to a real plant. Also, the design would have been undertaken by software engineers and then carefully evaluated. I'm not a software engineer.'

'But these were *not* normal circumstances, were they?'

'No, they were not.'

After a long pause while he consulted his notes, the Inspector said, 'So you believed that what you were being asked to do was dangerous. Would you say, *very* dangerous?'

'I didn't like it,' Foster admitted against a rising background of noise in the room. 'But I would call it risky rather than dangerous, because I knew what I was doing, and I had good, competent engineers helping me.'

'But it *was* risky,' Sir Peter said quietly.

'Yes.

'But what option was there? There were only two other choices. They were to tell the Chinese, or to do nothing. The first would have led to the total collapse of any pretence that the Galaxy system was safe, and I had been told that this could not—*would* not—be done. The lawyers would not allow it, because it would mean admitting that the Government had promoted the use of new and unproven technology on a nuclear power plant.'

The hubbub in the room rose to exploding point. Foster could see the reporters' pencils scribbling madly.

'Silence please!' the Clerk called. 'Silence!' Eventually the room quietened.

'You must remember,' Foster continued. 'The project had been actively concealed from the public in the UK; even to the extent of creating a false identity for the contract, and a false destination. Exposure would have damaged the Government's credibility and impacted on Britain's relationship with China.'

'And the other choice?' Sir Peter asked. 'The option to do nothing at all?'

'That would have run a different type of risk: one of a serious incident occurring at Far Point. The lawyers may have argued differently, but I was sure—and I think Mr Jeffreys and his advisers were by then also convinced—that the Galaxy system was seriously flawed.'

'So,' Sir Peter said pensively. 'Taking a chance on correcting the problem was the safest choice.'

From the barely-subdued racket in the room, the frantic scribbling in the reporters' notebooks and the worried exchanges of whispers among the G.A.I. representatives, Foster could guess at the devastating impact of his words.

Once again the Clerk was forced to call for order.

'Please continue, Dr Foster,' the Inspector said as the noise subsided.

'I was reasonably sure I could find a solution,' Foster continued.

'But what if you didn't find one?'

Foster looked at him. 'Then I would have told the Chinese myself,' he said, very firmly. 'Before the plant began fuelling. Before any risk could arise.'

Sir Peter returned his look for a long moment.

'All right,' he said eventually. 'And it appears that your confidence was not misplaced. A solution was found.'

'Yes.'

Foster omitted mentioning how Andy Johns' actions had brought them to the brink of disaster, when he had warned the Chinese about the plan to tamper with the system.

'And the remedy was successful?' the Inspector asked.

'Absolutely! Far Point has been on full power for several weeks now, and there has been no recurrence of any similar problem, though they did have a bunch of spurious alarms at the beginning. That's something that has been resolved since then, by Universal shipping out new components. The problems have now been completely eliminated.'

'I'm pleased to hear it,' the Inspector said archly. 'Although, this does sound to me like a very unorthodox and risky type of engineering. At least, I *hope* it is unorthodox.'

'No. It certainly isn't the usual way of doing things,' Foster said, smiling grimly.

'Thank you, Dr Foster,' Sir Peter concluded. 'This has been very illuminating.'

To escape the tension, Foster took Fiona to a bistro on the South Bank after the day's proceedings had come to an end. The meal had been pleasant and, away from the Inquiry, nobody had taken the slightest interest in his presence; there were no reporters, no inquisitive onlookers to intrude.

As they sipped their coffees, Foster looked at the other people around him and wondered what it would be like to work in London and commute daily between the office and a nice home in the suburbs; nine to five, five days a week. Two or three weeks on vacation with the wife and children each year, then back to the routine. Had he been heading there once, so long ago? It was hard to imagine, but when he remembered Jayne and the children it seemed that it may have been possible. Once.

In fact, Jayne had wanted him to make the break, to settle down and to stop his incessant travelling. 'The kids hardly know you,' she had said on several occasions, and he had known that it was true. OK, the children ran to greet him when he came home, but he had often wondered if it was more to see what goodies he had brought them, rather than pleasure in being hugged by him again.

He had watched them as they grew. He was more conscious than Jayne of the changes in them, because she was with them all the time, never noticing the subtle daily changes in them; the changes that were so apparent to him whenever he came home.

And he had realized that they were closer to her than to him. When they became teenagers he had often found himself at odds with them and their mother. She seemed to accept what he couldn't. He had put it down to her better judgement being blunted by constant exposure to their behaviour, but each time he came home some minor rebellion would inevitably happen and he'd flare up in anger. He sometimes felt she took their side in the arguments, and this had widened the gulf between them.

Now I hardly know them, he thought sadly. *What a fine father I've become!*

He sniffed angrily at the thought and Fiona gave him a puzzled look.

'Sorry!' he said. 'I was just thinking.'

'The Inquiry?'

No. About life …. my life. Where it went wrong.'

'Wrong?' Her expression mixed alarm and sadness.

'With Jayne,' he said quickly. 'And the kids.'

Fiona sensed a further breaking down of the barrier between them.

'I don't know what happened, Dan,' she said, pensive. 'But I do know this: I know you and I can't believe that you were anything but a good husband and father. And there's something else …'

She was looking down at her hands, avoiding his eyes.

'What?' he asked.

It was a while before she replied, and when the words came she still avoided his eyes. 'It's been happening for a while now,' she said. 'I've been afraid to admit it ... But I'm falling in love with you.'

He stared at her. 'You don't know me!' he said quietly. 'Not really.'

His thoughts flashed briefly back to Alison. She had relieved the tensions within himself, but they were merely physical. There was another need, much more deep-rooted, that sex alone couldn't alter.

Suddenly he saw Fiona in another light. Suddenly, she had become the one good and constant factor in his life, and he saw that the recent brief fling with Alison had been a brush with the past. They had been very close once, and the memories could not be easily dismissed. But he knew that sex was all that there was between them.

Fiona was still looking at him. 'I do know you, Dan!' she said. 'I know you and I love you, and ...'

'And?'

She gazed at him earnestly for a few moments, then dropped her eyes as she finished, 'You're a good man. Strong. Jayne should have been proud of being your partner. She must have been proud to bear your children.'

He stared at her in amazement.

'I mean it, Dan,' she said. She hadn't said the actual words, but her meaning had been clear.

'I... I don't know what to say,' he sputtered. 'You mean we should get married?'

She nodded demurely.

'It puts things in a different perspective,' he concluded.

'Yes it does. But I've been looking at things differently recently. And I think it's time.'

'But it didn't work out before, Fiona,' he said. 'I was married and I fathered kids... and I wasn't able to hold onto my wife or to them. And now I'm a stranger to them really—well, more than a stranger perhaps; more a friend of the family; someone who drops by occasionally. It's a hell of a thing to realize that I won't be there if they need advice as they grow up.'

'They'll ask,' she volunteered. 'If they really need your help. Surely.'

'I hope so. Sometimes I think it's better this way. I seem to get on better with them now that I'm not there so often.'

She smiled. 'Distance lends enchantment?'

'Sort of! But the fact is, my marriage broke up. That's not a good track record for trying again.'

'Millions do. Anyway, the problem wasn't just your fault. It was … oh, so many things as well; Jayne herself, your work at the time, with Universal…'

'So what's different now? Yes, you're different from Jayne. She was hard as nails …'

'What's different?' she exclaimed. 'It's me. I'm here. I'm not like her. I think we can make it work. It's already working. My firm's impressed, so I'm sure you can get more work like this. Where you'd be your own boss. There'd be plenty of work, I'm sure. But you could pick and choose the jobs you take on. That'll give you the time to be with me.'

He stared at her.

'You do want that, don't you?' she asked.

'I suppose so. All of this has shown me that I've been missing the excitement of my old work, I guess. For some time now I've been beginning to think that I can't go on forever as I have. The shop wasn't enough.'

'Right! And perhaps this is the time to make the break!'

'Perhaps. But I'll be travelling again. And if I do, what then? Will I wreck your life too?'

'I don't think so, but I'm prepared to take the chance.'

He leaned forward and took her hand. All at once he realized how beautiful she was. He reached over to slip his fingers behind her neck, feeling the softness of her hair behind his hand. He drew her face gently to his.

'In any case,' she continued afterwards, as though nothing had interrupted the flow of words. She was smiling archly at him. 'I know you'll never give up engineering. I'd never expect that, and I certainly wouldn't want you moping about the place. But if you can pick and choose, then you can have the best of both worlds.'

'Something I could never do at Universal? Because I wasn't in charge of my own destiny?'

'Exactly! Here you can do just as much as we need to keep the wheels oiled.'

'That's assuming we get the opportunity,' he said finally. 'This Inquiry … I don't know where it's going, Fiona. If it goes wrong there's a chance I'll be finished. I could still end up carrying the can. What happens then? I'm sure they'll hang me out to dry. What could I offer you then?'

'It'll be all right,' she said. 'I'm sure about it. I agree with what you say, but we can't tell yet. Let's just see it through.'

He grinned and said, 'I'll drink to that!'

The next day, it was Universal Digital's turn to come under the microscope. Keith Maddison, Global's barrister who had interjected earlier, stood up and said that he would be representing the company.

'Very well,' the Inspector said. 'It is acceptable for the Company to be formally represented, although I may require individuals to appear in due course. To answer my questions.'

Maddison bowed his head in acceptance, and the Inspector nodded. 'You have heard Dr Foster's evidence,' he asked. 'And his contention that there was a serious problem with the electronic control system?'

'I have,' Maddison said. 'Although I wish to point out that my clients strongly dispute the validity of Dr Foster's findings, or his ability to be fully objective.'

He sounded bored. As though Foster was an irrelevance.

'Dr Foster is a professional engineer,' the Inspector said. 'As such, he carried out a very detailed and thorough investigation of what happened to the Kung Tau plant. Do you dispute that?'

'No,' Maddison said. 'What I question is the *objectiveness* of that study, and therefore the validity of its findings.' There was a hard tone in his words. Not sarcasm, but a cold edge. 'They may have been distorted, or not complete.'

'What basis do you have for saying that?'

'The fact that Dr Foster had been, at one time, Universal Digital Systems' Engineering Director.'

'He told us about that,' Sir Peter said. 'To my mind, that makes him uniquely qualified to comment on these very complex technical issues.'

'Perhaps, but I should point out that at the opening of this Inquiry he failed to explain the reasons for his departure from the company.'

'Perhaps he felt it wasn't relevant.'

'Perhaps,' Maddison said. 'But when the facts are known you may decide that it *is* extremely relevant that Dr Foster's investigation gave him the jdeal opportunity—if he so desired—to blacken the standing of the company that had previously been forced to dismiss him from its employment.'

The room was filled with whisperings again.

'It is a matter of record,' Maddison said. 'That after Dr Foster's departure from the Company, he consulted a solicitor with a view to entering a claim of 'Repudiatory Breach of Contract' against them.'

'Is this relevant to the present proceedings?' Sir Peter asked, looking quizzically at Maddison.

'It is, Sir,' Maddison replied. 'You will appreciate that the inference of that claim was that the company had forced Dr Foster's resignation.'

'Yes. But that was a dispute in the past ...' Sir Peter started.

'Yes,' Maddison interjected. 'But the company's point of view was quite different, as it so often is in these circumstances. Their view was that Foster was not competent to maintain his position.

'Also, I suggest that Dr Foster's previous occupation with the company had coloured his judgement. Because of an incident that occurred while he was manager of Universal Digital's systems engineering division.'

'An incident?' Sir Peter asked.

'That's right,' Maddison said. 'One that occurred after the company supplied a major electronic system to a large ship. An oil tanker.'

Foster tensed and clenched his teeth. The spectre that had stirred him at the beginning of this episode had come back.

'The vessel was called the *Boston Venturer*,' Maddison consulted his notes. 'A three hundred thousand tonne ship,' he read out. 'A major contract for the company. The name may seem familiar to you, Sir.'

'Yes,' the Inspector said, frowning. 'But I am struggling to remember why.'

Facing him from the body of the room, Foster had no such difficulty.

'It was a major achievement for the company. And for Dr Foster, personally.' Maddison's voice was pleasant. Praising. 'Because at that time he was in charge of the team of engineers that designed the systems,' the voice continued. 'The vital control systems of a huge vessel. Sailing the world's oceans.'

'Yes, yes,' the Inspector said impatiently. 'Go on.'

'The ship sailed for several months after it was commissioned,' Maddison said. 'Between Japan and the Gulf.' He looked at Foster. 'And elsewhere. But then, in January 1986, whilst off the Philippines, something went wrong. Very seriously wrong.'

'Ah, yes!' Sir Peter said contemplatively. 'I remember it now.'

'The name was very well known at the time.' Maddison's next phrases came suddenly. One after another like bullets from a machine-gun, 'Because she became a total loss. Lost with all hands. A crew of forty. Gone.'

Now the memories were fully exposed, and Foster had little choice but to hear the tale recounted. He listened with pain and distaste. Maddison pressed on relentlessly; bent on destroying the last vestiges of his quarry's credibility. 'As the evidence emerged,' he said. 'It became clear that the cause of the ship's loss was a sudden and complete failure of its vital electronic control systems...'

'No!' Foster interrupted, standing up in anger. 'That's not right.'

'Dr Foster!' the Inspector said. 'Please! You'll be given the opportunity to comment on all of this later on.'

Foster sat down, and Maddison smiled. 'The reports I have here provide a full explanation,' he said.

Foster scowled. He knew what the reports would say. But their conclusion represented just one possibility.

Yes, the control systems had been suspected as being the cause of the loss. But in such cases *everything* came under the microscope and it had never been established for sure that the control systems had, in fact, failed. The ship had been in the region of a typhoon, so anything was possible.

But, whatever had happened, disaster had certainly struck so suddenly that there hadn't been time even to send off an emergency call. It seemed the ship rolled over, or broke her back. Nobody ever found out what happened. No wreckage was ever found. No survivors.

One theory had been that the very sophisticated electronic control systems fitted to her propulsion machinery could have simply instructed it to shut down. At the worst possible time. In a tropical storm, when the ability to manoeuvre was crucial.

And Universal had supplied those systems.

'I fail to see the relevance to the present inquiry,' Sir Peter said.

'It is very relevant,' Maddison said. 'Because it shows that Foster was in charge of a team that had been involved with the design of a system that came under suspicion of causing the loss of forty lives. And the total loss of a ship worth millions of dollars, together with its valuable cargo of crude oil...'

'No!' Foster interrupted again. 'She was in ballast when she was lost.'

'Dr Foster!' the Inspector said angrily, and Foster sat down again.

'Actually, that's right,' Maddison admitted. 'The ship had delivered her cargo of crude oil. She was on her way back to the Gulf. Carrying sea water in her tanks, to keep her low in the water. In other words, in ballast.'

'So there was no pollution as a result of her sinking?' Sir Peter asked.

'Very little,' Maddison said. 'I apologise for the error. But yet... All the same, the incident was a serious loss, and it did cause considerable distress.'

Foster gave a deep sigh. Too right! It had caused *him* distress, let alone the relatives of the victims. He remembered the agonies of waiting, the detailed, unfeeling cross-examinations later on, by the representatives of the various interested parties. The sleepless nights. The nightmares that had come unbidden, infallibly, whenever sleep finally overcame him.

The regular nightmares had now faded, but even after all this time, he would sometime wake from a dream about the incident and find himself sitting bolt upright in the bed, sweating profusely. It always took a long time for him to fall asleep again.

'Nevertheless,' Sir Peter said, as he again consulted his notes. 'It seems that the company cannot have thought that any blame could be attributed to Dr Foster. Because it was not long afterwards that they appointed him to the Board.'

'Yes,' Maddison said, smiling. 'It was a triumph. No doubt he was even flattered. However, there were some members of the Board, notably Andrew Johns, the company's current Managing Director, who remained suspicious.'

Foster grimaced. So that was it! Somehow they had got onto the fact that Johns had always remembered. Kept the accident up his sleeve. Never saying anything directly, but missing no opportunity to drop hints.

At the time of the *Boston Venturer* loss Andy Johns had been Sales Manager. His rise through the rank of Marketing Director to Managing Director had come years afterwards. After then, he had used the incident at every opportunity. Used it to throw doubt on Foster's abilities.

'Mr Maddison,' the Inspector said. 'I hope this will somehow be relevant to the role played by the company in the events before me now. Because that is about those events that I am questioning you, as the representative of the company.'

'I fully understand, Sir,' Maddison said smoothly. 'The relevance is that Foster, who claims to have been unbiassed in his investigation, was in fact very prejudiced. He bore a deep and bitter grudge against the company, and personally against Andrew Johns. Because he had been forced to leave, and because the person who had forced him to leave knew the truth about the *Boston Venturer*.'

Foster growled to himself angrily. So many lies! The only truth about the tragic sinking had been that nobody ever found out the cause. But here he was, being blamed for it all, with scant opportunity to defend himself.

'So,' Maddison continued. 'When Dr Foster was asked to look into the Kung Tau incident he must have realized that if his report blamed Universal Digital Systems, it would be a very serious blow to Mr Johns. And to the company from which Foster had departed in some acrimony.'

Foster shut his eyes. It was all so wrong.

'I see,' the Inspector said. 'And there were similarities between what happened to that vessel and the subsequent events in the Far East?'

'Yes. For example, although there was a suspicion in both cases that the systems were at fault, there was no real evidence one way or the other. And yet, in the incident with which Dr Foster had been *personally* involved, the *Boston Venturer*, he somehow made up his mind that his designs had not failed. Yet in this, a broadly similar case, later on—at Kung Tau—he came to a very different conclusion. That the company's designs *were* indeed to blame for the tragic accident.'

Maddison's tone was smooth. The blow had been struck. He folded his papers very slowly and carefully.

'The basis of my argument,' he concluded. 'Was that when Dr Foster was asked to investigate the incident he saw it as an opportunity to exact revenge. And, seen in that light, it becomes apparent that none of his supposed 'findings' can be substantiated.'

Foster could only stare at him in silence. It must have seemed so clear.

By the time that it was Carol Lopez's turn to be questioned, Maddison was looking very smug, clearly confident that he had blackened Foster and put his findings in doubt. He smiled confidently across the room at Universal's new MD as she stood on the stand to answer the Inspector's questions.

'Mz Lopez,' Maddison asked, after he had obtained from her the details of her present appointment, and her background and experience. 'I understand that your company has tested the changes that Dr Foster developed at Far Point, and that they have operated quite satisfactorily.'

'Yes,' Lopez said. 'We did a full-scale simulation, and the modifications passed with flying colours.'

'Good!' Maddison paused and looked round the room. Then he returned to the questions. 'You mentioned a simulation. Such simulations,' he asked. 'Were they carried out as a matter of course on *all* your systems.'

'No. Not all. Just the bigger ones. We factory-test every system, but that's a simple matter of proving that if you do certain things, the system reacts correctly.'

'I see. So these ... simulations ... they are something more elaborate.'

'Yes. Considerably so.'

'And the Kung Tau systems?' he asked.

'They weren't as complex,' she said.

'But nevertheless, the system there *was* quite extensive. A truly large-scale installation.'

'Yes.'

'And it was built in something of a hurry. Because it was being supplied at a somewhat later stage than usual.'

'That's correct.'

'Was it, too, tested on a simulation?'

'Yes.'

'And was there evidence of this phantom 'addressing' problem of which we have been told?'

Lopez shook her head. 'No,' she said. 'Nothing significant happened then.'

'The problems appeared *after* the system was shipped?'

'Yes. We had to send a crew out to look at it on site.'

'That was unusual?'

'Certainly.'

'And expensive.'

She smiled. 'Sending men and machines to China? Of course it was expensive!'

'Not something one would undertake willingly.'

'It was a serious response to an apparently serious problem. We...'

'You mean Universal Digital Systems.'

'Yes. We—the Company—we always took great care to make sure that the systems we designed were quite safe.'

'That shows that the company, even while it was under the command of Mr Johns, was extremely diligent about safety.'

Maddison looked around the room again. This time, his eyes locked on Foster while he asked Lopez his next question. 'But your engineers found no evidence of an addressing problem?'

'We weren't looking for it at that time. We did encounter some odd effects, mostly during the first tests on site, at Kung Tau. And now, with hindsight, we realize that they could have been caused by the address decoders.'

'Could have?'

She frowned. 'Yes,' she said simply.

'But there may have been other reasons...' the lawyer continued.

She thought about it for a moment before replying. 'I suppose so. Possibly. But we don't know what they could be...'

Maddison interrupted her. 'There could have been other reasons,' he said. 'Some mysterious fault... a 'bug', I believe they are called. Something that lay hidden.'

'Yes. Like the address decoders,' she insisted.

'And possibly other faults.'

She glared at him.

'Mz Lopez,' Maddison continued before she could respond. 'Were you aware of what Dr Foster's report said about the Galaxy system?'

'Not at the time he submitted it to the DTI. No.'

'So you were not given the opportunity to counter his claims?'

'No.'

'So the report was a one-sided evaluation of the possible cause of an accident.'

'In a way. But ...'

Maddison cut across her. 'It was the opinion of one man,' he said. 'And no opportunity had been given for anybody else to advance any alternative explanation.'

'Well ... I suppose not.'

'So it was one-sided.'

She shook her head slowly in exasperation. But still the admission was wrung from her. 'Perhaps,' she said softly. 'In those terms it could... appear to be... one-sided.'

'And it was compiled by a man who we have just learned had no love for the company, or of Mr Johns ...'

'Maybe,' she said. 'But that's hardly fair!'

'Perhaps,' Maddison continued. 'But the author of the report had left the company under a cloud.'

'Well, sort of. But...'

Maddison held up his hand. 'No, Mz Lopez,' he said. 'We are not looking into the rights or wrongs of what happened then. But the fact remains, does it not, that Dr Foster did not *choose* to leave.'

She was quiet for a while. 'No,' she said eventually. 'I suppose he didn't.'

'And there was no love lost between him and Mr Johns.'

'No.'

Sitting in his narrow seat, Foster felt even more bleak. From the beginning it had seemed to him that the Inspector was a fair and dispassionate man. But after Lopez's words had been extracted by Maddison he could see how the Inspector was being presented with a very different picture.

'Now let us turn to the technicalities,' Maddison said. 'When the possibility of a fault in the device... the address decoder... was brought to your attention, did you feel it could have caused the accident at Kung Tau?'

'Oh, yes! Definitely!'

'And did you carry out any tests? To prove it, one way or the other?'

'Yes. And we were convinced that it was the cause of what had happened.'

'But you said just now there may have been other reasons...'

'Yes,' she replied. 'Of course. We should never shut our minds to alternative possibilities. It's rarely completely so cut and dried. But we were very confident that this was the one. The decoders. All the evidence stacked up.'

'But you did nothing about it?' Maddison asked.

'No,' she replied. 'At first I thought it was a very remote possibility. One that the normal checks would have trapped. And then there would have been no risk to the plant.'

'You said "At first"?'

'Yes. Then I looked at our Quality records, and discovered an anomaly. The device failures were high. Very high.'

'The devices being the... the decoders that you mentioned earlier.'

'Yes.'

'And that changed your opinion?'

'Yes. What had seemed a small possibility suddenly became a definite probability.'

Maddison shook his head.

At this point, the Inspector interrupted. 'I have a question, Mz Lopez,' he asked, and Maddison sat down. 'What did you do then? After you found out about the high failure rate?'

She turned to him and replied, 'I reported it to Andy Johns.'

Foster looked at Maddison and was pleased to see him looking clearly discomfited.

'And what happened then?' the Inspector asked.

Lopez took a deep breath and looked up at the ornate ceiling for a moment. Then she turned her attention to the Inspector and replied, 'He told me that we would have to cover it up.'

'Cover it up? With the safety of a nuclear plant in the balance?'

Maddison jumped to his feet, clearly concerned at the direction the proceedings were taking. 'Sir Peter, I would like to continue...'

But the Inspector was not about to let go. 'Mr Maddison,' he said sharply. 'You will have the opportunity in a while. For now, I want to clear up some matters. Go on Mz Lopez.'

'There were risks,' she continued. 'But it wasn't so clear then, of course. We didn't know then what we know now.'

'But you knew there was a risk.'

She nodded. 'Andy persuaded me that it would be all right.'

'You believed him?'

'No. Well... perhaps he addled my thinking.' She shook her head as if confused. 'I don't know.'

'But you did nothing.'

'I suppose that's correct.'

There was a long pause while the Inspector wrote in his notebook, then he flicked through the pages to refer to earlier notes. The tension in the room was almost unbearable while he searched for something.

'Mz Lopez,' he said finally. 'What you just told me... It doesn't sound quite right.'

'It's what happened,' she replied.

The Inspector stared at her intently. 'As far as it goes,' he said. 'But I think it didn't end there, did it?'

She returned his look. For a long few seconds, the room was silent. Tense. Expectant.

Her voice was very quiet when she replied. 'I suppose not,' she said.

Foster suddenly looked at Sir Peter with new admiration. The Inspector had somehow seen through her words, realized there was something lying hidden behind them, and now he was about to expose the truth.

'There was something else, wasn't there?' he asked. 'Or someone.'

She stared at the Inspector resolutely, then took a deep breath and nodded.

'Yes,' she said quietly.

'Tell us.'

'Andy said there was another dimension,' she said. 'Something I hadn't considered.'

'Which was?'

'The DTI,' she responded. 'The Department of Trade and Industry.'

'You mean, their advocacy of the Galaxy system for the nuclear plant?' Sir Peter asked.

'Yes... and no. It was much more than that.'

'Would you please explain?'

She was silent for a moment, and when at last she replied her voice was very quiet. She was about to destroy a very special relationship.

'They'd *funded* the whole thing,' she said.

Sir Peter frowned. '*The whole thing*?' he asked. 'What "whole thing"?'

'The Galaxy system. The Government had underwritten the entire development.'

Foster sensed the ripple of excitement. At the front of the room, the Inspector sensed it too, but he didn't want to release his grip on Lopez.

'They financed it?' he asked. 'All of it? The entire development of the system?'

'Yes, and more. Much more.'

'More than funding the development? That must have involved a lot of money. Yet you say it went further than that?'

'They backed it's use at Kung Tau; and later on at Far Point.'

'So all the work of installing the systems there; and the process of putting it into operation–commissioning it, I think is the expression–all of that was backed by the Government?'

Her voice was almost a whisper: 'Yes.

'Oh, the client paid for the routine work of course, but doing what we did there.. that was far from routine. And it was very expensive. Very expensive indeed.'

'And the Government picked up the bill?'

She gave a nod and whispered, 'Yes.'

The room had fallen silent once more as everybody strained to hear her words. Sir Peter looked genuinely amazed.

'But isn't that against European Union rules?' he asked.

'Yes. It's highly improper. Basically, the EU rules are designed to maintain a 'level playing field' between member states. Individual Governments are not meant to independently subsidize the sort of commercial development we were doing.'

'But they did?'

'Yes. Only a few of us knew. We were told to keep it quiet. The money was channelled in under the disguise of payment for "consultancy services".'

Sir Peter stared at her. 'On the basis of that statement,' he said. 'I could well understand that there would be alarm—considerable alarm—at the prospect of the Government's actions being exposed. And a public admission of the problem at Far Point would have thrown a powerful spotlight of attention onto the company.'

'Yes. If there *had* been a serious incident it would have opened up the whole business to public scrutiny and made it difficult to suppress the Government's involvement.'

'I'm sure,' the Inspector said quietly. 'I'm sure it would have been very difficult indeed.'

'Yes,' she said. 'We all knew it. And so did the DTI. Although I suspected that it was the Secretary of State's personal baby and the Government's awareness of the full facts was quite limited...'

'Roger Jeffreys?'

The Inspector glanced briefly at the Secretary of State as he interrupted her.

'Yes.'

'You're saying that an individual could carry through a thing of this scale?'

'At the beginning, yes. It was Mr Jeffreys' personal drive and ruthlessness that made it happen. He had a huge reputation and could force his departments to do whatever he wanted.

'But then everything started to snowball.'

'So you believe he was worried!'

'Desperately!' she said quietly. 'Andy was called to London. He saw the Secretary of State... The Minister said that, at all costs, his Government's involvement in the original development, or the financial support during commissioning, must not be allowed to become exposed. I now see that what he wanted was for *his* part in the fiasco to remain hidden.'

Foster looked across the room at Roger Jeffreys and remembered their conversation in the Arnold Coward offices. How the Minister had claimed that he had not been involved in the original Government decisions. How he had feigned ignorance of the reasons behind them, shared Foster's misgivings.

Jeffreys had lied! He had stood there and calmly lied! He had known about it from the beginning. He had probably even been active in the decision-making process.

Foster shook his head slowly in incomprehension.

But now in that room the Secretary of State was hanging his head, staring at his knees. His crumpled bearing told of defeat—total defeat.

And across the room, Maddison was staring at him in amazement. Seeing his expression, Foster suspected that what was now emerging was as unexpected to GAI's lawyer as it was to almost everybody else in the room. It was plain that his clients had not told him everything. Not by a long chalk.

'So what you are saying,' Sir Peter continued, 'is that the Secretary of State for Trade and Industry wanted Mr Johns to do something,'. 'To help cover up what had happened.'

'Yes.'

'But what could he do?'

'Simple! He could go to China and supervise what Dr Foster was doing.'

'But wasn't that exactly what Dr Foster wanted, anyway? We've heard it from him during his statement to this Inquiry.'

'Yes. But remember, Andy still believed there was nothing wrong with the Galaxy system. He would never have gone to Far Point of his own accord. So it came as a complete shock to be told that, on the contrary, he *had* to go.'

'But why? Why was it so important for Mr Johns to go.'

Lopez then turned to look straight at Jeffreys as she spoke.

'I didn't know at first, but Andy told me when he got back,' she said. 'He said that Roger Jeffreys had told him that if the problem couldn't be resolved before the replacement equipment arrived on site, he was to make sure that commissioning was stopped, and that Dan Foster was to be blamed for the delay.'

There was a collective gasp from the audience.

Sir Peter waited for silence to return before asking, 'How would that have been possible? And even if it was, how would it have helped?'

'Foster was a loner—an outsider. He had been called in by the DTI but there was no written proof of that, only a vague contract via an intermediary—an intermediary who could be trusted to deny any direct instructions. If blame could be laid at his door it would clear Universal, and the Government. The truth would not become known. And since Foster was small fry there would be no risk of him mustering enough firepower to fight the allegations. Nobody would believe any protestations of innocence from him; he was just one small player in a big field.

'So if things became difficult, a few words to the Chinese would have stopped commissioning while they looked into what was going on.'

'And in the confusion the original problem would be forgotten?' Sir Peter summarized.

'No, not completely,' Lopez said. 'But, in the meantime, Universal would have been given enough time to install the new equipment.'

'Ah!'

'And there was another back-stop,' Lopez said. 'Andy told me.'

'A back-stop? What was that?'

'He also told somebody very high up in the PRC administration about Foster's mission.'

In the silence that fell on the room, the Inspector's next question rang like a bell: 'Why?'

'It was the beginning of the process to blame him for anything that happened.'

Sir Peter stared at her, plainly thinking furiously.

'But… wasn't there a considerable risk in that?' he asked. 'A risk that, once the Chinese became aware of his work, they would discover the details of what he was doing. And that they would then restore the Galaxy system to its original state?'

'I suppose there was such a risk.'

'But the original system had a defect. One that had already caused a fatal explosion!'

'Yes—though at that time Andy wouldn't acknowledge that it *had* caused the Kung Tau incident. In fact, he denied that there was a defect at all. Believe me, he'd never have agreed to go to Far Point if there was any element of danger. But I feel sure that Jeffreys was very well aware of what might happen if the Chinese restored the original system.'

'And that didn't worry him?'

'You'll have to ask him that!'

She brushed her hair away from her face, took a deep breath and said, 'But I suspect it was a risk he was prepared to take. Because he would win either way.'

'How so?'

'Well, if Foster had been wrong in what he suspected, and that there was no fault with Galaxy, nothing would happen when the system was restored; the plant would work quite safely.'

'But if Foster was right?'

'Then it wouldn't matter anyway. With the original, faulty, system in control, Far Point would be damaged; perhaps even destroyed. And in that event, Foster was there and he'd be blamed. If the worst came to the worst, the plant would be destroyed and all the evidence would go up with it. And afterwards they'd make sure that Foster would be blamed for it.'

At those words uproar exploded in the room.

'Mz Lopez,' the Inspector asked when his clerk had restored order. 'Are you saying that you believe a Government Minister was willing to gamble with the safety of a nuclear power plant, with the sole purpose of concealing his own actions?'

'Not really,' she said. 'I'm sure he never seriously believed it would come to that.'

She looked across the room at the ashen-faced Jeffreys.

'Remember, the first preference was that Foster would succeed in finding a solution while he was on site. It was only if he failed that the second plan would be brought into action. But then, before he could actually do anything, the whistle would be blown and he would have been blamed for interfering. They wouldn't know how far he had gone, so the commissioning process would be interrupted, in case he had sabotaged anything. That would have given us time to get the replacement nodes out to China and quietly install them. The possibility of the Chinese deciding to restore the system and proceeding with commissioning was remote. Very remote.'

'Remote!' Maddison interrupted. 'But not impossible. I find it incredible to think that the Minister would take even such a small risk. Why should he want to walk such an irresponsible path?'

It was a rhetorical question really, but she answered anyway. 'I don't know, of course, but I suspect that it was because he was up to his neck in it. He needed to cover every possibility. And this did it.'

In the bedlam that followed, a couple of the journalists slipped out of the room. Mobile telephones were not allowed in there but, in the corridor outside, the communications channels would be very busy indeed.

'And meanwhile,' Maddison continued when the noise had quietened. His voice was weak, as though he did not want to turn over any more stones but was too fascinated to stop probing. 'Mr Johns had agreed to go to China?' he asked.

'Yes. By then I don't think he was rational at all. He was still marching to his own drum-beat. He was still convinced that Foster was wrong. He was determined that he should be stopped from interfering with the system. If Andy told the Chinese, they could set a trap and catch him red-handed.'

'And by this means Dr Foster would be finally dealt with. Permanently.'

'Yes. Andy said he was sure the Chinese would jail him and throw away the key.'

'But things turned out differently.'

'Yes.'

Carol Lopez looked straight across the room at Foster. 'In spite of everything. With Judith Chang's help Foster worked out a solution, and they applied it on the site. They were working against the clock. By the time Andy told the Chinese, it was already almost too late, though Foster had to try and finish the work without them intervening.'

Sir Peter shook his head and looked at Foster.

'And in the course of what followed, an engineer was killed,' he said.

'Yes. Turner. He was killed by a fault that occurred during preliminary testing.'

'And after that was Mr Johns finally convinced that the fault really did exist?'

'Yes. It shook him to the core.'

As it shook all of us, Foster thought bitterly.

Foster looked across at Maddison and saw obvious relief in his face. The barrister had been fighting to retrieve something from it all; to extricate his clients from the mess into which they had got themselves. If he had intended to discredit Foster at the beginning he had failed. But blame was now falling on a completely unexpected third party. Foster wondered how the Government would get out of the hole they were in, though he had little doubt they would wriggle out of it somehow. Politicians were good at that.

'So,' the Inspector continued. 'In the event, when it came to Far Point, Dr Foster actually protected the company's interests.'

'Yes. He solved the problem, and he did it without anybody knowing.'

She looked across the room at Foster.

'But there was more,' she continued, very quietly. 'You see, Andy Johns knew that—now that it was all over—Foster wasn't going to let any of them off the hook. He was so proud of his profession... and so angry at the politicians for corrupting all he stood for. Now he really *was* out for vengeance.'

She looked at Foster and smiled.

'It was strange,' she said. 'They were rivals, but if only they could have worked together while they were both at Universal—who knows what would have happened? In the end they left it very late in their careers before they co-operated with each other. If they had worked together earlier as they did at Far Point, none of the tragedies would have happened.'

'But they were both too set in their ways?'

'Yes. And when Foster told the press about how near they'd come to having a serious incident at Far Point, Andy's future was determined. He was finished anyway. I found out later that he had already made plans; bought a small hotel in Portugal. But he was determined that he would take Jeffreys down with him. That was quite all right with him. It was his own vengeance.'

It was a simple answer but it put the seal on the proceedings. Foster let out a deep breath.

To all intents and purposes, it was all over. The final technicalities would take their course; the Inspector's report would be published, but the outcome was now obvious. Jeffreys' actions had finally been exposed and he would pay the penalty.

Foster felt a strange pang of sympathy for the Minister. But he was also relieved that his own actions had been vindicated.

What he'd suspected about the fault in the Galaxy system had been confirmed. His actions at Far Point had been opened to painfully intense scrutiny; and somehow they had received a strange form of endorsement.

But there was something much more. He had taken revenge for Alan Turner's death. Nothing would bring him back. Nothing could erase the thought that he had invited him onto the road that led to his death. But he had done what he could to put things right, and hopefully this Inquiry would lead to new legislation to protect others.

And he had at last wiped bitter misgivings from his own past. He realized at last that, for too long, he had been suppressing his own self-doubt over the *Boston Venturer* incident. But now, having had the events refreshed and examined, the ghosts had been exorcized. Now — after all those years—he *knew* he had been right all along.

And somehow the knowledge had shattered another barrier within himself. He knew that he could now face the many realities of his personal life; of his past, his family and children, and of his present and future life… with Fiona. She had stood firmly beside him through the whole episode, believing in him and trusting him. It was a new experience for him, to have somebody trust him so completely.

He looked up at the public gallery and saw her smiling down at him. Even at that distance he could see the tears of joy on her cheeks. He grinned at her and held out his fist with the thumb upright in a triumphant gesture.

We've won, Fiona! We've won! And I've got something to say to you. Something very important.

For both of us…

THE END

Printed in Great Britain
by Amazon